PAGE PUBLISHING, INC.
Conneaut Lake, PA

First originally published by Page Publishing 2021

ISBN 978-1-6624-4598-9 (hc)
ISBN 978-1-6624-4599-6 (digital)

Printed in the United States of America

FALL *of a* SPARROW

MITCHELL RYAN

There's a special providence in the fall of a sparrow. If it be now, tis not to come.

   If it be not to come, it will be now. If it be not now, yet it will come.

William Shakespeare Hamlet Act 5-2

So we beat on, boats against the current, borne back ceaselessly into the past.

Scott Fitzgerald. The great Gatsby

FOR BARBARA

Beautifully written by this remarkable actor, this book reveals, with insight and passion, the astonishment of living.

Richard Benjamin
Actor and writer

A accurate, honest and compelling narrative that took immense courage to write, and is a joy to read.

Jamie Cromwell.
Actor Director

"This book is a gift, it's an unsparing, eagle's-eye exploration of the journey of a lost youth who finds a life in acting and in acting finds a life. In these pages Mitch Ryan explores with urgent, incisive, often bitter honesty the realization that the comedy and tragedy of life seduce and enthrall exactly as they do in the theater. The power of his writing is staggering and the pain is almost unendurable."

Mike Farrell,
Actor, Director and Writer.

Mitchell Ryans sweeping and profound new work, Fall of a Sparrow, brings to beating life, a family and a country. This soul searching generational journey vaults Mr. Ryan to the very first rank of modern American writers

Donald Freed
International writers seminar

This book is a gift to anyone who is interested in the American theater over the last half century, arguably it's golden age This book is at times emotionally overwhelming but always a surprising journey of an actor, practicing his craft, deeply personal, illuminating, and engaging.

Salome Jens
Actor and teacher

For his great help. To my comrade and great friend Donald Freed for all his help in writing this book.

For getting me started. Claudette Sutherland

For all her great help and insight into the process.

Marsha Frank Berke
Writer

PREFACE

I'M BLESSED. I'm blessed that, 30 years a drunk, I've managed to live a working actor's life to be envied. And I've lived a great deal of real life while I was at it. Sober for the next 30 years, I'm told I've come out of it all a good and a useful human being. And when asked I'm happy to say that I'm a happy man.

So why read my book? Why, in this cynical world of ours, read the work of a man who begins by shouting out his happiness. Because this happiness I speak of isn't a bright sunshiny yellow. It's been hard-fought and hard-won. It's made up of all the colors on the palette, not only the true blues and reds and yellows, but also the muddy browns and the dreary greys. The muddy browns that come from trying to mix together all the primary colors at once. We must learn balance. Or the dreary greys that come from mixing black and white, while refusing to understand that life isn't ever only black and white.

This book is my story. My story and also the story of my son Tim who, wretched, ended his life without ever really having one.

This isn't a typical actor's autobiography. "And then I made this film." "And then I did that play." It's the story of an actor becoming. Today a man becomes an actor by going to university and studying his craft. I came up in a different time. I found my way in the school of hard knocks and the university that is the theater itself. It was a different time. A young man became an actor because someone thought he had the right look for a part. A pleasing voice. And he wasn't doing something else just then. Or anything else, really, ever. And he stayed an actor because, remarkably, he was good at it.

Another actor might say, The book's as good as my credits. Credits, yes, but this is an honest book. Oh, don't get me wrong. I'm happy to tell you I've worked for the likes of… I've worked with and mostly count among my friends…

But more than all, this is the story of a man becoming. I was lucky enough to survive my mistakes.

—Mitchell Ryan, Los Angeles,
California, 2021

CHAPTER 1

The War Is Over
1945

"Where did it go, the three dollars I gave you yesterday? Gen, calm down. All I want to know is what did you spend it on?"

The skillet landed somewhere near the door. Leroy, the iceman, who had entered at the wrong moment, skipped out of the way almost in time so that the skillet hit him on the shin, but most of the grease landed on the floor. Leroy dropped the block of ice and slid free. At the same time, Charles moved to the living room door, but before he could begin another sentence, Genevieve threw a nearly full bag of flour at him. He was not as quick as the iceman and flour snowed down the front of his good gabardine suit and stuck to the now-congealing grease on the floor.

The children, Mitch and Maggie, cowered in the corner, their eyes big. They all stood in stony silence, then Genevieve went down the hall into her room and slammed the door. Mitch looked at Maggie and tried to keep back a giggle, and Maggie laughed out loud.

"Stop that, clean up this mess, and throw that ice block out in the yard," their father ordered over his shoulder on the way to the phone in the hall.

Genevieve lay down on her bed and threw all the pillows at the window. "Goddamn bed, goddamn bastard won't buy a new mattress, asking me about money!" She jerked the drawer completely out of the little night table and watched as loose papers, hard candies, and matches flew to the floor along with the cigarettes she wanted. "Oh, fuck!" She picked up the Chesterfields, lit one, stepped over the contents of the drawer, went to the bathroom, and splashed cold water on her face, then sat down at her desk just under the one small window and sucked on the cigarette. *What did I just do? I threw a skillet at Charles.* Elated and humiliated at the same time, *Jesus, what's the matter with me?* There was a knock. Two big steps to the door and locked it.

"Gen, are you all right?" Charles rattled the door. "Please open. I'm sorry, I didn't mean to upset you."

She stood guard rigid at the door until she heard him leave. "Thank God. Never any goddamn money, what a way to live." She began to shake and sweat, chest tight and nausea creeping up from her belly. Moving to the bed, she curled up in a ball, breathing as deeply as she could to stop the cramps, pulling her legs up to her chin. She stayed in this position for several minutes and then rolled over on her back in an orgy of violent rubbing, rubbed her breasts, and moved down to her belly, then up to her face and then her scalp, her red hair flying in all directions as she rubbed and rubbed. Feeling alive, feeling… *When was the last time I had sex?* Nothing.

Another knock. "Genevieve, let me in."

With effort, she stood and moved to the desk, peered down at the pages she had written about a trip to Yale when she'd lived in New York so many years ago when she was young. How beautiful that spring day to be out of Manhattan. That was the day she first realized how she loved to be alone. She remembered the vow she'd made to herself that day sitting on a bench in the Yale yard: *I will live alone and write and never let any kind of foolish attachment take me away from a dedication to self-reliance and the study of writing.*

"You're acting childish, Gen, open the door."

"Childish! Childish!" She spun and threw a china figurine at the door. Charles's impotent reply, "Stop doing that," made her laugh. She advanced on the typewriter and picked it up with a violent movement; but before she could throw it out the window, she sank down, her whole Being bereft, tore the pages out of the machine and methodically ripped them to small pieces. In one more violent movement, she sent the books on the desk flying across the room.

Charles at the door: "Gen, what is it? What are you doing, are you all right?"

"Go away!" She moved to the scattered books and papers lying across the bare wooden floor and kneeled to pick up the beautiful beloved early edition of *The Pickwick Papers* she had found at an auction in New York. All the anger dissolved into hopeless weeping. Keening, holding the book to her breast, she reached out to gather in the other books scattered and abandoned—*Bleak House*, Mrs. Gaskell, the copy of *Persuasion* Charles had given her for some birthday. "My husband used to give me presents and take me to the country on Sundays. Nothing now. No more. I want to go to the country!" she shouted at the door, her energy vanished, and she said in a whisper that was almost a plea, putting the books back on the desk, "I want to go to my mother's farm and see the hills and walk in the woods and…" Then she shouted at the door again, "No fucking gas. Rationed. This fucking war has gone on forever!" Clutching the *Pickwick Papers* in one hand, she lit another cigarette and pace madly up and down the little room.

"The doctor's here. Will you talk to him?" Charles again.

"No! I want to see Sarah. Get Sarah. Give the doctor a drink and have a couple yourself." She picked up a cloth-bound copy of Shakespeare's sonnets. She sat on the side of the bed leafing through the little book until she came to the eighteenth, remembering in an instant the god-awful suit Charles had worn when they had first met and read to her at the library. Who was that man? Where had he gone? So silly but sweet and romantic. *"Shall I compare thee to a summer's day thou art more lovely and more temperate…"*

Genevieve let the book drop and studied the painting on the wall opposite the bed. A copy of a Delacroix. A large woman with bare breasts holding a flag leading a crowd of ragged people. Charles had painted it for her before they were married, saying it was a picture of her "leading the fight for art." She leaned back on the bed. *What is life? What is art? What is conciseness? Has it come to this after all these years, I know nothing?* She felt the lump in the goddamn

13

mattress, smiled, and went to sleep. She dreamed she was at some large assembly getting ready to make a speech about the powerful effect her new book was having on the public, but when she reached the podium, the whole audience started to stamp their feet. The stamping went on and on, and someone in the hall kept shouting her name, "Genevieve, it's Sarah. Open the door." More knocking. "Gen, it's me, Sarah, open up, please."

Genevieve awoke with a jerk. For a moment, she was lost, then it all came back. She unlocked the door. Sarah held her for a long moment. "I'm glad you're here." Genevieve rested her head on her friend's shoulder. "What did I do, Sarah?"

"Well, you threw a skillet at Charles and hit the iceman on the leg, and then you flung a full bag of flour that went everywhere."

Genevieve laughed. "The iceman?"

"Yeah, you did, and it was pretty spectacular, got everyone's attention. Mitch and Maggie are still cleaning up."

Sarah had been Genevieve's only friend for almost thirty years, had been with her in New York back when. Sarah was a beautiful dark woman who wore discreet makeup and spent all her money on expensive clothes. People whispered she was homosexual. Genevieve knew she wasn't but liked the idea that the neighbors thought they were lovers. They sat on the bed, smoking. Genevieve loved smoking. It made her think of being single and living in a garret, writing great towering books, and having many lovers. She knew that to indulge these fantasies was foolish and only fed her unhappiness, but she called it her addiction. Lighting another cigarette with the one she was smoking, she began to move around the room aimlessly. "I'm cold!" She hugged herself.

Sarah moved to her. "Why don't you get under the comforter, I'll make you some hot tea, and you should see the doctor. He's right outside."

"No! I don't want to see him." Then, hearing how childish she sounded, she said, "Oh God, this is awful."

"He'll give you some pills to make you calm."

At the window, Genevieve turned and looked at Sarah. "I'm so unhappy, what can I do?" She was shaking again. "I don't know where to turn. Nothing is leading anywhere. I need to know where my life is taking me, don't I? I'm just floating. It's sickening." She held her face in her hands. "Pills?" She fell on the bed. "Yes, I can take a pill."

The doctor came in with a small paper cup of sleeping pills. She took them. "That's it, Doc, putting us all to sleep is your solution for everything." He left without a word. "Fucking world." Sarah held her hand, and she slowly closed her eyes and drifted off.

Genevieve stayed in her room for two days after the incident. On the third day, she woke to church bells ringing and people shouting. Charles came smiling to the door and announced, "The war is over, Gen!" She allowed him to help her up, and then she put on her robe and went with him to the front porch. In spite of her weakened state, Charles guided her down to the gate, shouting at friends in the street.

The war was over! She saw her son Mitch and all the people in the street laughing and shouting, husbands swinging their wives around, children chasing each other, yelping with delight. Mitch's heart turned over at the sight of his mother, coming out of the house, stepping down to the gate with his father. Charles laughed and kissed her. She pulled away. "Oh, Charles!" Then she waved to Mitch. The boy leaped into the air and raced toward her. He dodged between people crowding the street, but before he could get across, she had gone back inside.

He leaped up the porch steps after her, but his father called out, "Don't bother Mother just now." This stopped him flat.

He did a military about-face, then off his father's stern look, he was immediately sorry and stammered, "It's great she came out...She must be better."

"Yes, she does seem better." His father turned and walked away, closed the gate, and crossed the street to talk to Mr. Miller, who owned the drugstore. Mitch moved to the porch steps and sat. Watching his father's back, he couldn't stop comparing him with the other fathers who would hug their sons and be happy to talk and play. His father did none of these things, but what did it matter. Mom's okay. This was the way things were. He sat on the steps taking in the wild scene before him. The war was over. The middle of the day, yet everyone in the neighborhood was outside. Something rose up inside, an irrepressible feeling of happiness that made him giddy. He moved back out into the street to join in. Mr. Shanebackler, of all people, grabbed him in a bear hug and passed him to Mrs. Shanebackler. Mr. Ewing shook his hand, so did Mr. Johnson. Mr. Griffin, who was always jolly, even while his wife was sick and dying of cancer, danced Mitch down the street into his yard and gave him a beer.

"Good Lord, what am I doing?" He snatched it back. Mitch heard his father's laugh. The boy broke away and ran over to be near him but stood a little apart. "Isn't it great, Dad, the war is over?"

"Don't interrupt, son, can't you see I'm talking to Mr. Miller?" Mitch turned to walk away. "Son, stay and listen. Don't mean to chase you away."

Before Mitch could say anything, Mr. Miller called to him, "Can you remember when it started, boy? It's over four years now. You must've been what? How old are you?"

"Twelve," his father answered for him.

"I remember," Mitch protested. He would never forget the scene. "Dad came in with the paper, told me to turn on the radio, and said the Japanese were bombing Hawaii. And Mom started to cry."

All the other families except his were together, laughing and horsing around. He waited in case his father might take his hand. He looked toward the house where his mother always retired to her bed in the middle of the day and thought of going to see if she would let him into her room. From time to time, she did call for Mitch and his sister Maggie to sit at the foot of the bed, and she would read to them, mostly Dickens or Mark Twain's *Life on the Mississippi*, and almost always she read Shakespeare. From time to time, his father would come in, too, and join them. At those times, Mitch would watch his father and wonder who this man could be. *Does he love me?* He longed for some sign that never came, but at those rare moments, they were almost like a family.

His father continued talking to Mr. Miller, so Mitch drifted away and walked to Miller's Drugstore at the corner. It was cool inside, and he could hear the voices in the street.

Mrs. Miller gave him a free ice cream cone in honor of the war being over. "Thank God the boys can come home." She had no children of her own, but because she sold ice cream, she was every kid's favorite. She asked if Mitch had seen her husband.

"He's talking to my dad in front of our house."

"How's your mother, poor thing?"

"She's doing much better," Mitch mumbled, then ran out, humiliated that everyone knew about the "incident," the talk of the neighborhood. His mother had what the doctor called a "nervous condition," but to Mitch, the nervous condition was just plain bad temper, and it made him sad to have to think that way.

He walked home, enjoying his ice cream, and sat down on the front porch again. This porch was maybe the best thing about their small four-room wood-frame house. The hot afternoon was moving toward a gentler early evening, and the crowd was beginning to thin out, though people still walked up and down talking loudly. How different life would be if they could just stay this way. He licked a long leisurely swipe almost completely around the cone, and there was his father coming down the walk and slowly up the steps.

His father sat in his rocker that looked out over the hedge to the street and declared, "I love this chair," just as he did every evening, all spring and summer. "Fudge royal?"

"Yes."

"Well, that's one good thing you've inherited from me, your love of fudge royal ice cream." There was only the creak of the boards on the porch from the rocking chair and the low rustling of the birds settling down for the night. Now and then, they heard a shout from up the street.

"Mother seems better." His father said nothing. "I hear it's going to be a national holiday tomorrow."

"Where's your sister?"

"She went over to Rosalie's."

His father rocked. "What does she see in that girl?"

Mitch stood up. "They're always together. She must like her."

"Go get her, will you, and get something for dinner, hamburger meat and some corn on the cob. Corn's real good now." He gave Mitch a dollar, but before Mitch could tuck it away, his father took it back. "Ask Ropple to put it on the bill."

Mitch went down the stairs to the tree-lined street and turned toward Rosalie's. Although Mr. Ropple never said anything, "the bill" always made Mitch uncomfortable. His father, who owed money everywhere, constantly berated Mitch's mother about money, at which she would scream, cry, and fling herself into the bedroom. Mitch and Maggie would hear it all, lying in bed and hugging pillows over their heads.

On the way to Rosalie's, he saw his best friend speeding toward him on his Schwinn bike. Bobby had one of the deluxe models with a solid compartment between the top crossbar and the lower one, plus a chrome horn. The shiny black-and-silver Schwinn was the envy of the entire neighborhood. Bobby's father, Mr. Gutterman, owned several hardware stores, so Bobby had the newest of everything. Friends since first grade, Mitch trusted Bobby and told him almost all his secrets. Almost all.

"French and Piss Head are over at the Dairy Queen trying to get Skippy to eat mud," Bobby yelled in delight. "Come on, I'll tote you." Mitch's old bike had two flat tires and was just about done, and he was dreaming of a new one as he jumped up on the handlebars, and they wobbled off.

Donald French and Jack Parsons, whom they called Piss Head (but never to his face), were ninth-grade bullies. In the vacant lot next to the Dairy Queen, Don French had his arm around Skippy's neck. Skippy, who wasn't even in junior high yet, wore glasses and was slightly girlish. Piss Head stood in front of him, holding what looked like a hamburger. Mitch jumped off the bike and walked toward them.

"Where you going?"

"Just to watch." When he came close, he could see that Piss Head was holding a flat mess of mud shaped like a hamburger patty.

"Well, here comes the cavalry," Piss Head laughed. "You think they can save you before you have your dinner, you little shit?"

"Why don't you let him go, Jack? You'll make him sick." Mitch's voice was more forceful than he meant it to be.

Skippy looked more terrified at this intrusion. "It's okay, Mitch, we're just playing around."

"Does this look like playing around, asshole?" French pushed Skippy right up to the mud burger in Piss Head's hand. "Eat that—I know you're hungry. Come on, Jack, feed him." Piss Head grabbed Skippy by the neck and started to push the mud in his face.

"Jesus, Piss Head, stop doing that, leave him alone," Mitch shouted on purpose this time.

Jack stopped and looked at Mitch for a minute. "What did you call me?"

"I didn't call you anything. I just think you should stop doing what you're doing."

"You called me Piss Head. Is that what I heard? Is that what you heard, Don?"

"Yeah, I heard Piss Head, he called you Piss Head."

Mitch backed a few steps toward Bobby and the bike for a quick getaway.

"Well, I think maybe *you* should eat this hamburger, you fucking worm." Jack grinned, starting toward Mitch. French dropped Skippy and followed Jack.

Mitch's fear made him charge Jack, driving the mud into Jack's chest. They both fell to the ground. with Mitch landing on top. Piss Head tried to push him off as Mitch punched him right in the nose. Blood spurted down the bully's face as Mitch leaped up and started to run. French grabbed him, but he struggled free just in time to see Bobby pedaling off down the street. Skippy, meanwhile, had run away the minute French let him go, and now Mr. Griffin, Skippy's father, came shouting up the street in his undershirt and slippers. Piss Head and French took off. Mitch's father came up fast behind Mr. Griffin.

"What the hell is going on?" His father was out of breath. "Is that blood on your shirt?" Mitch looked down, and there it was, a big blotch of red blood and dirt. When he touched the gooey mass on his shirtfront, he felt something strange and unfamiliar—a burst of pride as he looked at his red hand. "It's not mine," he told his father, watching the man's face for a sign.

"What is this? You're not a fighter. Have you turned into a neighborhood bully-thug?"

"It was Jack, he was the one—"

But before he could finish, Mr. Griffin said, "Skippy is scared to death and won't tell me a thing."

"Come on home, we'll finish this later," his father said, turning away.

Murray Brooks, one of Mitch's friends, came out of the Dairy Queen with Mr. Brooks, his father. "What happened, Mitch?" he asked, his eyes wide.

"Nothing, it's nothing, Murray," Mitch's father said. "Come on, son." His father was walking down the street toward the house.

Mitch tried to catch up. "Dad, wait—"

"Not now, damn it, come on." His father walked back and grabbed Mitch's arm.

"Dad, listen! It wasn't me—"

"Not now!" His father pulled him along. Mitch wanted to speak, but it was too late. He jerked free and ran down the street across the railroad tracks into Finley Woods, tears burning in his throat. He ran and ran until he was deep in the woods, then stopped and fell down on the dry leaves under one of the large oaks, breathing hard, heart pounding, considering how he could hurt his father in some way. He told himself he'd leave home forever and join the navy.

Finally, lying flat on his back, he calmed down and put his hand across the blood on his shirt. Still damp. Then he noticed the silence. The tall oaks were still as night, not even a leaf moving. The stillness washed over him, breaking the schoolboy obsession for revenge. He stood and began walking toward the river road on the other side of the woods. What he had done started to sink in. As he came to the dry creek bed where he and Bobby always acted out war stories, his fear and sadness began to transform into a sense of freedom. His handling of Piss Head made him feel strong and proud. I'll never be able to go back to school. They'll be waiting for me at every turn.

He found the huge grapevine they used to swing out over the creek. As he began to untangle it, he heard a rough voice: "It's all lies. The war is not over. The Japs are at this moment in California and headed this way."

Somehow not afraid, the boy looked to see where the strange but formal voice had come from. A man wearing a filthy white suit stumbled out of the underbrush. "Yes, they are coming this way and will destroy our way of life!" Turning to Mitch, he held out a dirty bottle. "Here, Tom, have a drink. You've had a rough time, I can tell, but you managed to escape. Good. You're safe here. They will never look in these woods. They're all afraid to venture in here."

Mitch fell back. "No, thank you."

The old man pushed the bottle closer. He had no teeth, and dirt was ground into the creases of his face. "Come on, it'll do you good, and for God's sake, wash that blood out of your uniform—the captain's in the area, and you know what a stickler he is about 'personal deportment.'" He paused and studied Mitch, his face fierce, and then his look softened and resolved into worry as he stepped closer. "I heard what a rough time you boys had at Iwo. You're one of the lucky ones." He let out a low moan. "Have you heard any news of my brother? He was there in the first wave, poor fucker." His ripe smell forced Mitch a little farther away.

The old man sat down on the ground, hung his head, and cried over and over, "All lost, all lost..." This seemed to wear him out. Mitch thought he must be drunk. He had sometimes seen bums in the woods. They rode the rails and would stop here to camp. He stood waiting near the edge of the dry creek bed, then took hold of the grapevine, pulled on it, and swung out over the creek and back again, and any fear he felt was gone. The light filtered down through the canopy in bright shafts as he threw his head back and took it all in. He heard birds fussing up in a tree as he landed back near the stranger, who now seemed to be asleep. What a funny feeling, standing there in the woods with a sleeping old bum who wanted to play his favorite game, war.

He walked away deeper into the trees with the idea of heading to the river road and then down below Crescent Heights, where he and Bobby had a hideout—a nice small hidden beach across from Six-Mile Island. He and Bobby went there after school every day and in the summer to swim and lie around and smoke, but he had gone only a few yards when he heard his new friend calling, "Where you going? You can't leave the post. You'll have a court-martial for sure. Besides, we need you. Every man is expected to do his job." Then the voice became soft and direct. "Are you planning to run away from home?" Said so calmly that Mitch turned to look closer, wondering if he had heard right. The man had a sweet smile on his weary face.

"Thought I might."

"Where's your stash? Do you have money? Do you have a plan?" The old man pulled out a knife and an apple.

"Don't need one," Mitch said, inching away.

"You can't leave home without a plan, and it's plain you have no stash or provisions, and I'd be willing to bet you have very little money."

"I'll be fine." Mitch started off toward the river road.

"Well, go if you must. Good luck. Do you want some apple before you head out?" He started cutting up the apple.

"No, thanks."

As Mitch walked along, he thought about what the man had said and of the dollar and twenty cents he had in his pocket. That would get him a meatloaf dinner at the Blue Boar Family Restaurant, or Errol Flynn at the Vogue Theater and five White Tower hamburgers, or six packs of cigarettes. He felt the tiredness in his legs, and he was hungry. Seven or eight o'clock in the woods, which even now blocked out most of the light. It would soon be completely dark. He'd get to the river road, and then what? Maybe it would be better to head back toward the house, or maybe go into town and see Errol Flynn.

Eleven, when the last showing of *Captain Blood* finished, and Errol Flynn had leaped from one ship to another, winning every swordfight and every girl. Oh boy! He had stayed through two showings. Even better the second time. Standing at the entrance in the gentle rain, watching the lights of the marquee make a rainbow on the sidewalk, he decided to go down the street to the White Tower and spend twelve cents on a hamburger. He began to run through the rain. At the White Tower doorway, he stopped when he saw a familiar car pulling up to the curb.

"Mitchell, it's Sarah. You want to talk?" Miss Stevens, his mother's friend, was one of the few grown-ups who actually talked to him. She had a prewar 1940 Ford with leather seats. He slid in and tried not to look at her naked legs or where her loose skirt had crept up her thigh. He turned to the window, always excited around Sarah, who was exotic and Jewish and wore lots of jangling bracelets and vibrant scarves.

"Your mom and dad are very worried. Do you want to go home?"

"Is Dad mad at me?"

"No, he's worried is all."

"He was so unfair about the fight. Wouldn't listen, wasn't my fault, they were picking on Skippy."

"I'm sure it's all forgotten by now." She patted him on his shoulder. "They just want you home."

"Okay."

Miss Stevens pulled up in front of the house. Mitch sat feeling an extraordinary mix of sensations. When she leaned over and gave him an awkward hug, he felt her closeness.

"Please don't come in with me," he opened the car door.

"No, dear, I won't." She touched his arm.

The porch light was on. Sarah waited at the curb until he reached the porch and looked back at her, and then she drove away. Impossible. Could he be in love? This amazing day, the fight, the man in the woods, and now his exhaustion and Sarah in the car.

Coming through the door, he found his mother sitting in her usual chair, her sweater pulled around her shoulders, her expression unreadable. His father stood by the kitchen door in a shadow. "You bad boy," his mother blurted out, "we were worried sick. What were you thinking?"

"I'm sorry," he looked at his father, "I was just mad." His father didn't move to him.

"Is that all you have to say?" His mother pulled at her face.

His father walked into the light. "Go to bed, son, we'll talk in the morning." Then he went into his room and closed the door behind him.

Mitch looked back at his mother, hoping to see forgiveness or be told it was okay. She didn't look at him. "He was so upset and worried. You should be more thoughtful, Mitchell." Speaking his name, she became more animated. She looked at him. "Your actions have consequences. You might have thought of me and what I might feel, you know I've been sick."

He stood pulling on his jacket fringe. She reached to turn off the table lamp, stopped, then pushed herself to her feet and straightened her back in the familiar move he had seen so many times, and put out the light. "Well, go along to bed. Wait...give your mother a kiss good night." She reached out to him, and he stepped into her arms—a stranger who smelled like medicine. So different from the hug Sarah had given him.

He went to the closed-in back-porch bedroom where he and Maggie slept. He never liked this room, cold in winter and the opposite in summer. He thought of Captain Blood and what he would do if he were here, then he thought of Sarah again and her touch and her legs and her breath.

He heard his sister waking up as he slipped out of his pants and into the single bed next to hers. He could see her face in the bit of moonlight from outside the unshuttered window. She lay with her head propped on her arm. A breathless whisper, "Where have you been?"

"I walked mostly and had a very interesting talk with a war hero just back from the Pacific. Then I went to the movies."

Maggie let out a breath. "Oh boy, Dad called the cops! I could tell he was really worried."

He turned toward her. "Wow! What do you know? The cops, you say. I'll be damned." He rolled onto his back and put his arms behind his head. "Well, they never found me!"

CHAPTER 2

Back Home
1951

MITCH HAD FORGOTTEN a lot of simple things, and his eyes and ears were hungry for everything. All he had seen for a year was a concrete cell and the bare compound of a Marine brig. So he jumped off the bus at the top of a hill. The huge bay of San Francisco spread out before him, with little wispy clouds off to the west over the ocean. It was a clear evening, and he saw none of the rain and fog he had heard so much about. Sidewalks were miracles of construction, and along the walks, old-fashioned glass-and-lead streetlamps stood like museum pieces. Green leaves burst out of large fat trees. Bluebirds nesting on a branch in a maple behind a tall iron fence chattered away. From high on this hill, the streets reached like fingers to the bay, and the city below swarmed with life. He could hear the faint noises of horns and streetcars and an occasional siren, and he was at the center of it all, nature and culture and he himself at the center!

Sitting down on what looked like steps into a garden, he had to laugh as he lit a cigarette and grinned at how simple it had been to leave. He'd spent the last month at Treasure Island, the huge naval base in the middle of San Francisco Bay, after serving almost a year in a marine brig in Japan. He had been sent to the Treasure Island base to await his discharge. He'd been waiting day after day for his ticket to freedom to come through, checking the provost office every morning and evening, constantly being put off, invisible to the clerks. So on this morning, Mitch had just walked out of the Bay Bridge gate, continued down to the bus stop, and boarded the first bus to come along. When the guard didn't ask for ID or a shore leave pass, a wild adrenaline rush came into him and animated the image he'd harbored of the escaped fugitive. He loved these games where everything became a film set, everyone an actor, and him the star.

When he finally left his perch at the top of the hill to ramble down the steep streets that led toward the city below, he passed a young mother with a fussy kid and two old men in proud hats speaking what sounded like Italian. As he slowly walked down and down to the harbor, a chilling disquiet settled in him like a shadow. Still, the spell of peace and beauty followed. When he came to a small lush park, he sat on a bench and smoked another cigarette before deciding what was next.

He thought of a drink, ducked into a liquor store, and picked up a pint of rum. Coming out to the street, he became aware that the harbor's covered docks were just ahead, massive, frightening dark empty dens. In the first warehouse was a small party of men sitting around an empty cable spool. One old man, holding their attention, was telling his tale of whatever.

Moving closer Mitch, his pint of rum, his calling card, went to the table. "What are we discussing today, gentlemen?"

The withered face of the storyteller looked up. He smiled, eyes blotchy but twinkling as if he had a secret. The old wreck of humanity eyed the new bottle. "We're having a serious talk on what the fuck is the point, or for the more esoteric members, what is the meaning of life."

Mitch sat down on a cement block, took a drink, listened for the meaning of life.

The storyteller's voice was smooth, in command, a red scarf around his neck and a large black overcoat over his shoulder, which seemed strange for the heat of California. Mitch could see only the one hand that the storyteller used to punctuate his story. "As I was hinting… Oh, may I have a taste of your 'cough medicine,' young fellow?" Without waiting for an answer, he picked up the pint and took a slug. Then Mitch saw that the old man had only one hand. The other was a metal stump. There was an eerie silence as the old man drank. Everything was still for a moment as Mitch became aware of mingled cavern smells—diesel fuel, brackish water, piss.

"What if Plato was wrong?" The teller gathered himself. "How many of you have read Plato?" No one responded. "How many of you have heard of Plato?" Nothing. He winked at Mitch and went on. "We only have Plato's word that Socrates gave us the revelation that human beings have a soul and life has a meaning but, after all, Socrates never wrote anything down, so how do we know? Are we to believe Plato? Does man have a soul?" He started to cough. A hideous cough. His whole body shook like terror. A trembling, shaking, ripping cough, inarticulate noises along with copious amounts of phlegm rattled out of his throat. The hags started and stirred around. The old man, through his fit, said, "You secret, black, and midnight hags." Still he coughed. Howling through his fit, he added, "Hags. Hags."

Mitch escaped to the sea opening at the end of the warehouse. Steel railing. Bleak shoreline opposite. Sun flashes on oily water—red, green, mauve. A man stood looking out. A surfer? An angel? Shoulder-length hair, head down. Praying?

"Do you believe life has a meaning?"

The man slowly raised his head, turned, and gave the younger man a look through intelligent eyes. "Sure. Have you got a drink?"

"No." He remembered he'd left his bottle back at the lecture.

"Have you got a cigarette?"

Mitch gave him one.

The man lit it, walked away, then turned. "If life has no meaning, how can I be a failure?"

Faint echo. Failure.

Mitch leaned at the side of the opening. *Life has no meaning, and I am a failure.* He felt the tide under him, looked down to the black water. He was suddenly lonely and needed something. What, he did not know.

"You hold your life in the most fragile disregard."

Mitch looked up. The old man with the red scarf was beside him. "Disregard?" Mitch mouthed.

"Disregard! Disregard! Funny word, 'disregard'! We all disregard the most important things." He took almost a year to slide down the ship anchor post and sit. "No one really cares about anything that can maintain a life that is uncluttered."

The man talked to Mitch as if they were the oldest of friends. "That's why we drink. Drinking is uncluttered, and its great virtue is you have to give up your meaningless life, give up everything, be a monk to drink. Also drink, if you believe in it too much, will consume you, it is a killer." He stopped and looked back at the sad congregation. "Look at them, no one can see what is needed." His hand shook. Troubled breathing, hampering his voice. Another coughing fit. He spat a gob of blood into the water.

"You all right?"

The old man cleaned his mouth with a handkerchief from his deep pocket. "Yes, I'm fine. I don't have much time. But I'm fine. Do you have a cigarette?"

"Should you smoke?"

"The little pleasures are all I have left, smoking and my stories. You're the one who shouldn't smoke." He looked into the young man's eyes, weighing him, judging what to do with this boy. "How old are you, son?"

"Don't call me son." Mitch handed him a smoke. "Is it hard with one hand?"

"Doesn't bother me telling stories, and I keep kitchen matches for the smokes." He lit the cigarette and took a long drag. Cough again ripped through him. "What's better than a cigarette and a good story," he laughed. "Let me tell you a story. I won't charge you a thing."

"Go ahead."

"Once upon a time, there was a young prince who had everything and ruled over a small island. He wandered up and down his kingdom, looking for the answer to why he was so unhappy, why he was always searching for how to live and enjoy his beautiful island."

"Wait, wait, wait a second. I'm not in the mood for morality tales."

The old man paused, his look kind, patient, irritated. "It's tragic to stop a man in the middle of his story."

"Sorry. I have problems."

"Problems are what the world is made of, son, and they need to be attended to."

"Stop calling me son. What do you know about me? I've heard all that crap."

The storyteller laughed. "This story is not about you. Not everything comes back to you. The world is not about you. This story is about me." He stopped, and his head dropped to his chest as if he had died. Mitch sat on the damp floor and watched the motionless man.

Screeching seagulls.

Lapping water against the dock.

Shore bleak across the inlet.

After what seemed like a long time, the storyteller raised his head. "What's your name?"

Mitch said nothing.

The old man's smile turned into a chuckle. "What's in a name? A rose...would smell as sweet...will you give me a hand getting up?"

Mitch took his one hand and stood him up. Both teetered, then looked at each other for a moment.

"Take care of yourself, son." He shuffled off.

Mitch turned and looked out. The oily water of many colors looked alive. "Don't call me son," he whispered as if to the gods.

Later he found himself in the honky-tonk part of the city. The streets were so crowded with people it became impossible to walk, and the whole district had the air of a carnival. Open shops sold anything you wanted. Sexy whores strutted back and forth with gaudy makeup and skimpy dresses, so different from the Jap whores he had known who waited for you in bed and never dressed up. These American women were beautiful and brazen, making him blush whenever they came close. Sailors and marines were everywhere, in twos and threes, laughing and raucous. He felt part of the world again. He'd heard all about San Francisco from the sailors in Japan. Now here he was, amazed with this feeling of acceptance.

Still, eighty-four bucks was his worldly estate. He began to have a vague notion it would be dangerous to hang around San Francisco. Military police were evident all around the downtown area. He moved into the throng, letting himself be pulled by the crowd into a bar. He ordered a beer. His body tensed as through the mass of people, he saw two MPs appear, survey the premises, and leave. He hesitated a moment, realized he'd better vacate this part of town. He finished his beer. His honeymoon with San Francisco and her Golden Gate was over before it'd started.

He thought of Louisville and his mother. A stab of gloom pene-trated his heart. He had joined the navy to get away from his family, and now they were the only ones who would or could welcome him back.

Back out on the street, a chill city wind caused him to shudder and pull his arms tight around his chest. His navy dress whites were made for the tropics, and in his hasty exit, he'd brought nothing more with him. Who was this lonely boy not knowing where to go or what to do? Where to spend the night? The Greyhound bus station. There was no cash for a hotel. "San Francisco, welcome me home again." Forget it.

At the bus station, he picked up a paper and claimed a dark bench to curl up, smoke a cigarette, and read the sports page. The big clock above the ticket window said 9:20 p.m. Through the window, he saw two more MPs and pulled the paper up to cover his face, then laughed at the old movie cliché. Should he turn himself in? This was crazy, going AWOL while waiting for his discharge.

A heavyset red-faced man in a rumpled suit lumbered along and sat down next to him. He mopped his face with a handkerchief and turned to Mitch with a fawning smile. "Where you headed, sailor?" The man had a face that was so large and red it looked like he would explode.

For a second, he thought the man might be queer, but a sailor on the run gets desperate for any kind of human contact: had his short life brought him to this moment? Start a tale that would lift him into a feeling of self-regard. "Discharged and done with the rolling sea, and I'm going home, thank God."

"Where you from?" The man put down half a dozen small packages. Mitch paused to think of his myth. "Montana." Where Montana came from, he had no idea. "Folks got a ranch up near Billings. Been gone almost two years, can't wait to get there." He took out a cigarette, offered one to the man.

"No thanks, don't smoke. Never did."

Mitch lit up and took a deep drag. "Hell yes, I was raised on a ranch and been doing a man's work since I was ten. Love to ride, course haven't done too much lately, miss it something awful." Mitch stood and stretched the way he had seen a cowboy stretch in the movies. Then with his best Western twang, he said, "My dad taught me. He's a great horseman. My grandfather built the place, came over from Ireland. Then my dad got it. Now it's my turn." Caught up in his story, captivated by the thought of having come from such a family, he barreled on. "He's not ready to retire by a long shot, but he wrote me he wants me to take my place."

"Sounds okay, serve your country and back home to reap the rewards."

The loudspeaker banged, "Santa Rosa, Eureka…"

"Oh, there's m' bus," the fat man said, gathering his packages. "Good luck, sailor."

Mitch watched the man move away, sorry to cut off his story so fast, just when he was warming up. "Oh well, what the fuck." Then he saw the MPs standing at the entrance under the huge stone arch. He carefully creased his paper and slow-walked toward the ticket window. The loudspeaker announced, "Sacramento, last call." Eyes away from the police, he picked up his pace till he reached the ticket window and then the bus dock and climbed aboard.

He pushed to the back of the bus, stood a moment, worried if this was smart, looked out the window, no sign of the police! A new rush of energy—savoring the drama, his body falling into the attitude and gesture of a fugitive suddenly safe. In his new character, he spotted a seat next to a tough-looking cowboy type who had his Stetson pulled down over his eyes, boots out in the aisle. Yes, sir, this cowboy fit right into Mitch's movie, so he stepped over him and took the window seat.

"I was a marine," the man sat up, tipping his hat back. "You done?"

"Yep."

"Where's your gear?"

Mitch coughed. "Threw it all away."

The cowboy let out a hearty laugh. "No shit, that beats all. Where's home?"

"Born in Fargo, raised in Montana." He was back in the story, back home.

"Goddamned cold up there."

"Sure is." Mitch relaxed into the seat with a groan of relief. He admired the way this cowboy seemed to know what he was about as he slipped his hat back down over his eyes and leaned back. Mitch turned and looked out the window, wanting to keep in contact in some way. He pulled the peanut butter crackers out of his pocket. Chewing and eating, he brooded over this B-movie he was starring in and allowed a lonely homesick fear lurking just under his skin to surface. The bus veered out of town, past the huge inner bay heading toward Sacramento and the Sierras. The cowboy stretched, sat up, and turned in his seat.

The film started up again. Mitch took the first line. "Where're you from?"

"Fresno."

He started to ask something, but the cowboy cut him off. "I'm going to sleep now."

Mitch turned back to the window and thought going to sleep might be a good idea. He watched the moon on the big bay as the bus climbed. He shut his eyes. Jesus, he wanted to talk, but he knew better than to bother the cowboy. Too bad, they could have been friends. He dozed for a while. When he came to, they were in the country. So dark that he could just make out some large barns in a sea of blackness. He thought of his father. What would he say about his discharge? He smoked a cigarette and climbed over the cowboy. The bus driver told him he had to stay seated. He tried to sleep again and finally dozed. When he woke, the bus was pulling into Sacramento.

The cowboy said goodbye, and Mitch climbed down, not knowing what his next move should be. Too late to go to the movies. He walked out of the bus station into a warm spring night and looked up and down the dark, nearly deserted streets. He decided to wait in the bus station, then find the road east in the morning and try his hand at hitchhiking.

The state police picked him up in Colorado, outside Steamboat Springs. The frigid weather made him almost grateful. The warmth of California had yielded to a bitter cold in the mountains. The older officer laughed. He had a sunburned weather-beaten face and a bushy mustache. Mitch started to sweat despite the cold.

The younger one said, "What's so funny, Ed?'

"Don't you notice anything strange?"

"No, he looks like shit is all."

"Get in the car before you freeze to death," the older man told Mitch, then to his partner: "He's wearing a white summer uniform, and it's forty degrees outside." Turning to Mitch, he said, "You got ID, son?"

"I got my navy card, going home on leave."

"You got any leave papers?"

"No, they never gave me anything like that."

"Get in the car, son." Mitch squared his shoulders and put on an easy air. They drove him to the jail more out of pity than anything else. "Where you headed, son?"

"Kentucky." Better not continue this film after being on the road for three days now. Somewhere inside, maybe because he had been stopped, he felt his armpits sweating despite the cold and had a need to get to Louisville, to home.

"Looks a little strange that you don't have any papers, son."

He was barely holding on to his act of calm. The patrol car pulled up in front of a small building with "Sheriff Station" and "Jail" carved in wood over the door.

A flicker of hope as he took in the simplicity of the single main street with its inviting shops and large evergreen trees. He was walked inside the friendly-looking brick jailhouse and was put in one of the two cells. Through the glass partition, he could see the sheriff and the state police talking.

The wife of the local sheriff brought him a delicious hot meal of pork chops, roasted potatoes, and green beans. He realized he hadn't had a home-cooked meal for two years. She sat on a low bench by the door while he ate. "My, you were hungry. Want more?"

"No, ma'am."

She was handsome and large-boned with an open face, generous mouth, and blue eyes. This was as close as he had been to a woman in a long time, not counting the Japanese whores. He had a strong urge to have her hold him. She smelled like flowers or bread. "What's your name?" He had to take the chance.

"Sara, no 'H.'"

"Could I have some water, Sara no 'H'?"

"You surely may." He couldn't remember his mother ever holding him. Mitch looked around at the small barred window, the toilet, and narrow bed: cells, all alike—he sat on the bunk. He envisioned his mother's red hair but couldn't remember her face. Sara brought back a glass of water and opened the cell door. When he realized it wasn't locked, he stood up "We never lock down nice sailor boys." She smiled. "What's your name?"

"Mitch."

She stood close as he drank, almost as tall as he was.

He remembered another Sarah, his mother's friend who'd brought him home that night he ran away so many years ago. Funny, he couldn't recall her face either, but he remembered her scent, her legs, and her breasts.

Just then, the sheriff came shouting into the cellblock, "Sara, get the hell out of there!" She stepped out, and the sheriff slammed the door shut and locked it. "This boy is wanted. We just got the report from California. He's also dangerous."

"Oh, George! Does he look dangerous?"

"He escaped from the navy prison in California." George's voice was almost gleeful. They both turned and looked at him. "You're such a young boy to be in so much trouble," Sara said softly, "What in the world have you done?" Mitch didn't know what to say. He turned red and looked down at his chapped hands.

Then to her husband: "George, could Public Enemy Number One have a piece of pie?"

The MPs came three days later. While he waited those three days, Mitch felt his world closing in on him. Back to prison for God knows how long. Only the sheriff's wife was a comfort. They talked of simple things. She gave him a Bible and told him about Jesus and his miracles. She said that if you loved Jesus, he would see you through all your trials. He tried to listen, but an irresistible urge would fill him, and he kept sneaking looks at her breasts. When she stood up, the movement of her legs sent a shiver through him. At one point, she was reading close to the bars when he reached through and touched her hand. She didn't pull away, just looked at him and smiled, then removed his hand. He turned red. "I'm sorry."

After that, he thought she paid attention to him in a different way. She brought him cookies and milk or a slice of pie she had baked, like she wanted to be his friend. She asked about his home and family, and he felt a small twinge of shame at making things up, but he quickly got over it. When he was alone, he thought of home and wondered when he would ever get there and what his father and mother would say about his navy brig experiences. His father would doubtless consider it another failure, and indeed bad conduct discharge can't be called anything but a failure. Home seemed far away, in the life of another person.

The two MPs who arrived to get him were young men not much older than Mitch. The older one wore a stoic expression and ribbons all down the front of his jacket; the younger one had a soft face and a friendly smile. They came from Great Lakes Naval Base. Sara made them a good meal, which they ate outside the cell, and finished with a tasty piece of pie. "The train leaves at five. Let's get a move on, Jeff. It's an hour to Denver."

His name was Sergeant Poe. They escorted Mitch out to the van underarms. "Get the irons, Jeff." And out came the leg chains and handcuffs.

Sara and George followed. When she saw the irons, Sara let out a little cry, "Oh, you don't need those, do you?"

"Regulation, ma'am."

When Mitch felt the weight of the irons on his legs, he couldn't meet her gaze. She turned away and walked back inside. They put him in the car. The day was gray and overcast. For a moment sitting there alone, looking at the bleak mountains that ringed the town, he wished he were dead. She had turned her back and gone inside. Had to, she had to. He knew he would always remember the shape of her back.

They took the train from Denver. Chicago was fifteen hours farther. He slept most of the way. The MPs took turns. He asked them to take off the irons. Jeff would have, but Sergeant Poe refused.

For some reason, at the Great Lakes Naval Base, he decided not to speak. But he couldn't have said why. When the marine officer on duty asked for an explanation, Mitch withdrew and wouldn't say a word. "What's the matter with you, sailor? Are you being smart with me? You're in deep fucking shit, and this won't help." Several other officers came and shouted at him. Finally, the one in charge came right up in Mitch's face: "I hate punks like you. Faggot sailor." Then with disgust, he said, "Put him in the isolation cell, and when he shits on the floor, he'll talk."

The cell was padded. He sat on the floor and wondered why he wouldn't talk. He'd only done it on a whim, mainly hoping they would leave him alone. Later that day, he asked if he could go to the bathroom. There was a lot of laughter and excitement. "He talks, the swab jockey talks!" They finally put him in a regular cell and left him alone.

The fear of going back to the brig wouldn't let him sleep, so he walked up and down until he was exhausted. Then he sat, head down, counting the cracks in the floor. Sorrow. Fear. Why? It was just a game. Never wondering about this game of life. Never for a moment thinking why he was this way. Never, until after many years of suffering, would he begin to see what it was that drove him and shaped him. Only after long years of life would it dawn on him to question. In this lonely lack of communication with anyone, all he could do was smother himself in self-pity. His meals were put through a small opening at the bottom of the door. Every hour on his cellblock, the marine guard would stop outside the door: "Hey, scumbag, they'll throw the book at you—you'll get two more years at least." Some days the guard would cut loose with his idea of justice: "I hate cocksuckers like you who can't even do easy navy time while I was over in Korea getting my ass shot off." Mitch never knew what he looked like, but he had a picture in his mind and found himself looking forward to this daily abuse. At least it was some human connection.

At last, his discharge came through. For some reason, there was no court-martial. He wondered why, but it would be stupid to ask. He was given, along with the bad conduct discharge, a train ticket to Louisville, where he had enlisted, a suit of clothes with a shirt, tie, shoes, and socks, and twenty-five dollars. Sitting in the train station bar drinking a beer, a great flood of relief brought on a giggling fit. In the coach car, he made friends with everyone and had a great time telling stories all the way from Chicago to Louisville.

As he left the train in Louisville, the humid early spring night felt like a warm blanket. He smelled the night-blooming jasmine and followed his shadow from the overhead streetlights as he walked up Market Street toward Central Park. He loved this park. Small and fed by several wide tree-lined streets, it had always seemed an especially romantic place. He'd come here with Susan Otto, to walk through the dark St. James Court down the island that split the street, and he remembered with sweetness that he and Susan had held hands and kissed.

Boarding the bus at Fourth Street, he noted that things were looking increasingly familiar. From Fourth, the bus turned left at Franklin Boulevard, then turned into Lexington Road, then right at Ballard's Mill, where he had worked one whole summer. He left the bus two blocks from where his folks lived on Ingle Avenue so he could walk through the neighborhood and recall the jubilation of this street on the day the war ended. He smiled as he went past the plain little houses of his boyhood. The Mueller house all neat and trim but painted a strange green. The rambling old Shanebackler place set back from the street with a long brick walk. He sat down on the bottom step at the end of it, hoping someone would come along, but it was late, and everyone was asleep. Only the crickets and a single car passing.

Down past Miller's Drugstore, he walked like a schoolboy with a bad report card, wondering about his sister, the sweet little girl who had followed him everywhere. Was she still living at home? He shivered when he remembered he'd taken her to see *Wuthering Heights* when they were maybe fourteen and twelve. They had talked that night for the first time about the movie and about him going to college. Talking and walking home with her in the lush spring, like tonight, dark and warm, the black trees making a canopy over the street.

He stopped across from his family's house, smaller than he remembered. The paint was peeling and the screen, door hanging crooked. The hedge needed trimming, and the front gate still leaned on the sidewalk. Suddenly his mother opened the front door. He couldn't see clearly, yet he knew it was her. Her way of standing and the angle of her head brought every detail rushing back. After a moment, she waved. He was washed up to the porch on a flood of tenderness.

"I saw you through the window." A pause and then she put out her arms. He could not remember the last time they had held each other. They were shy and awkward. Over her shoulder, he saw his father come out of his study-office and stop in the doorway. Mitch walked up to him, amazed to find his own face wet with tears. His father held him in that tight grip he would use when he didn't know what to say or how to feel. Mitch, the son, surrendered to the feeling—the recognition of being home. Nothing had changed so much after all.

CHAPTER 3

The Theater
1952

THEY HAD GONE to high school together. Mitch saw her coming out of the Loews Theater. He thought of walking away but heard some calling: "Mitch, how great to see you!"

Pretty, a lot prettier than he remembered. Cigarettes behind the gym. "Joan, what a surprise."

"Let's have some coffee. You remember the Space Station?"

"Oh my god, still there?"

They sat in a booth at the Space Station Coffee Shop. The name was a clock from the past. The decor was still futuristic, with large primary colors in big slabs on the walls and ceiling, pre- or postmodern depending on your point of view. The waitresses still wore spacesuits. Mitch remembered that in high school, he had thought this high concept the height of cool. High school, what a disaster. This was the last place he wanted to be. He kept fidgeting in the booth, trapped in the past. Was he ashamed of what'd happened in the navy?

"Mitch, what's wrong, you're nervous as a cat. Come on, tell me what you did in the navy."

The spacesuit asked, "What'll it be?"

"Just coffee. Mitch, were you in the action? I didn't pay much attention during the war, but I know there were naval battles." She leaned into the table. Thrown back to high school, he remembered he'd sat behind her in science. He wanted to run away, or she would see right through him.

He tried to talk. "Where is everyone these days?" As she gave him a rundown on old classmates, he could feel his face starting to tic.

"Mitch, would you like to go see a play with me tonight?"

"No, I don't think so. I should get home." He'd never seen a play and didn't think he could ever be tempted to see one. He moved to get up.

"Don't go. Look, I've been working in the theater since I went to U of L. I'm going to be an actress. It's wonderful. I love it so much. You don't have anything else to do tonight, right? You'll like it, you will." She took his hand. She had cream-colored skin and smelled good. Her hand felt small in his. "Tell me about the navy," she urged him again. "I really want to know."

So he made up a bunch of lies about the war in Korea and fabricated a story of adventure and heroism in the North China Sea when his ship had been hit by enemy fire. He could see she was caught up in the story, and that gave him confidence. Warming to it, he went on to tell her about Japanese Kabuki Theater, although he had only seen a film of it. They stayed and talked for more than an hour, and he left with, "I don't know, Joan, maybe I'll be there tonight."

At home that afternoon thinking about Joan, he was torn, but as evening approached, for some reason, he put on his best shirt, combed his hair, and went out the door.

Joan saw him crossing the parking lot to the theater and caught up to him. "We're almost late. Come on." He stopped and surveyed the large, impressive building, a wood-frame structure with tall pillars every ten feet or so holding up the portico that spanned the front. A sense of what he would later call awe settled in him. He was sure he had never seen this building before, despite having come to this campus many times to see basketball games. "It's a replica of the famous Booth Theater in New York City." Joan pulled open the huge double doors, then had to come back to take his arm again and lead him into the crowded lobby. A threadbare carpet covered the floor. Circling the walls were photos of people in costume. Across from the door was a large painting of a man wearing tights and a black cape and holding a skull. Underneath in large bold lettering was the name "Edwin Booth."

Several people greeted Joan, and she in turn introduced Mitch, but he couldn't keep track. Across the lobby were three doors hung with drapes. Joan pulled him through the crowd past the ticket taker and into the theater. An aisle sloped down from each opening to a red curtain across the stage. When they sat, Joan put her hand on his arm and began to chat. He had no idea what to expect. Something was coming to meet him; he had known that as soon as he'd taken in the outside of the building—something coming, strange and familiar at the same time. After what seemed like a long time, the audience quieted down.

The lights faded and finally went out. In the dark, out of the silence, low pulsing music played for some moments, followed by a single light on a woman wearing a revealing black dress. The red curtain had disappeared. Slowly the uncovered figure started to move to the music. From nowhere, a woman in white and a bare-chested man joined the woman onstage. Joan put her arm through his and touched his hand. Then suddenly, there was a blackout, and a flood of light came upon a great number of people milling around a town square. Mitch relaxed, forgot where he was, and laughed, and everyone else was laughing too. Never had he heard so much laughing. The shared enjoyment of the people in the audience, the grace and power of the actors, this was something he had never imagined. Yet it was something he had always known.

After the play, Joan led him backstage. Following her, he gradually made his usual adjustment, this time from the nervous boy who had never seen a play to one of the many personas he assumed on occasion. Joan continued holding on to his arm, and that made it easier for him to contain his excitement. Being backstage with all the actors was magical. He tried not to stare at a woman in a bra and panties pulling on a skirt while a man came up behind her and gave her a big hug. Everyone was hugging, clapping each other on the back, talking loudly, and laughing. It was like an extended family celebration.

The play *Dark of the Moon* was Southern, so he fell into his impression of a naive country boy with a touch of mystery, very much like the leading man in the play. He added the walk, the slightly accented speech, the deferential attitude, and everyone seemed to accept him! The role fit him so naturally that when he spotted a tub of beers on a large table, he grabbed one.

"Come on, I want you to meet Doug Ramey, the director." She pointed to a man standing smoking at the door to the parking lot, talking to a dark exotic-looking woman, who watched their approach with bright, curious eyes.

Doug Ramey was slightly built with a pockmarked face and an air of amused detachment that suggested he didn't miss much. The woman with him wore a coat draped over her shoulders and ropes of gold at her neck and bangles on her wrists. Mitch had never seen anyone like her outside of the movies. She reminded him of Sarah, his mother's friend, who had captured his heart. Now just like with Sarah, his made-up character started to fall apart. This woman was not in the play. He would have remembered. He froze, and his mouth dried up.

Joan threw herself at Doug, going on about how wonderful the play was. "The way you handled the witches, *so* sexy. This is my friend, Mitch Ryan." Joan took his hand, and the other woman, whom he now noticed was older than he'd first assumed and had been studying him, took the other hand. She was tall and held his gaze. He flushed, tried to free his hand, then turned to Joan, who tucked her arm under his and moved her body against him. "This is Jill, Mitch."

The beautiful older woman kept looking at him. "Put him in a play, Doug, he's delicious." She touched his cheek then floated out through the clusters of actors and their guests without looking back.

Mitch watched Doug Ramey. He had a commanding style and a rich baritone voice. He also wore a bad hairpiece. "How about Sally. Did you ever see her so good?" The director spoke to Joan like family. "What did you think of the girl who played the lead, Mr. Ryan?" Before Mitch could answer, Doug continued, "Are you an actor, Mr. Ryan? I surely hope so because we need men." He paused and took a deep drag on his cigarette. "The theater needs men. Young men who can speak."

Joan laughed.

"I've never—" Mitch began.

"Before you answer, consider this. You must think of it as an experiment. All art is an experiment." Doug gestured widely, taking in the whole room. "Oh hell, life is a great improvisation. Don't you think so? Besides, what else are you doing that's so important? Do you have a job?" Before he could answer, Doug ran after several people who were leaving, calling over his shoulder as he went, "Don't go anywhere. Joan, take Mr. Ryan to the party."

At the party, the only person he recognized was the leading actor, who fairly danced through the room and threw kisses to everyone. His face was flushed as he stopped by an elegant older man and, to Mitch's great surprise, kissed him on the mouth. There was something electric about this, but no one else seemed to notice or care. Mitch realized he wasn't shocked. This kiss only added to the otherworldly way this night seemed to be headed. As Joan drifted off to get drinks, he studied the dark wooden chairs and deep leather couches, the elegantly carved tables with gold or silver boxes sitting like museum pieces on them, the marble bar at one end of the room. Many people, none of whom he knew or recognized, glided about talking loudly. Mitch felt suddenly seized with an overpowering awkwardness that prompted him to look for the door and start edging toward the nearest exit.

A loud yell and applause came from the hall. The leading actress, looking scrubbed and radiant, strode into the room along with Doug and other members of the cast, including the two witches. A great cheer went up, followed by much affectionate hugging and kissing, which only underscored Mitch's feelings of estrangement. He plunged his hands into his pockets, then took them out and turned to go.

"Mitch, isn't it?" It was Doug. "There you are!" And before Mitch could demur, Doug was guiding him down the hall. "I'm starving," he confided, "let's eat something." Despite having just met this man, Mitch was being treated like an old friend. The kitchen, almost as large as his father's entire house, was all shining copper and rough stone.

As Mitch ran his hand over the stone countertop that continued all around the room, he finally confessed, "I enjoyed the play very much, Mr. Ramey."

"Of course you did, the play's been great fun. A wonderful play, great cast, but now it's over and on to the next one." He balanced a huge sandwich, piling meat and cheese on rye bread. Oversized platters of food were laid out on large tables in the center of the room and on the counter stood bottles of wine, whiskey, and silver buckets of ice.

"I think I'll have a drink." Mitch surprised himself. "Is that okay?"

"Of course." Doug was slapping gobs of mayonnaise on his sandwich. "Have you thought about what I asked, and are you available to have lunch with me tomorrow?"

"I guess so." Mitch's voice sounded neutral as he poured a few fingers of whiskey and gulped some of it with a shiver.

"Good. Do you know where Cunningham's restaurant is?"

"I'll find out."

"I'll meet you there at twelve sharp. In the theater, we are never late. How do you stand, my boy, are you an actor or not?"

A panic startled Mitch. "No, I don't think so. I don't know, you know, anything about any of it." What would people think? His parents? What if he made a fool of himself?

"None of these people here tonight have ever studied acting. Well, maybe Jason, the fellow who played the lead, and Warren, but the rest started just like you. They jumped in." His confidence and enthusiasm made it all seem possible.

Joan came bouncing up with the dark witch, who had a habit of touching everyone. "Here we are, Mitch. This is Gretchen. She played the dark witch."

He recognized her. "Yes, I know."

Gretchen took him by the arm. "Are you going to be in the next play?" She reached out and began straightening Mitch's tie. "What's it to be, Doug—come on, you can tell me," Gretchen cajoled, released Mitch to hang on to Doug.

"More will be revealed, Gretchen, I promise, darling, but for now, you must excuse me. I have something to tell Joan. Come!" he commanded her, and off they went.

Joan looked back at Mitch. "I'll be right back."

Gretchen read Mitch's mind. "He's always doing something mysterious like that. Don't pay it any mind." She slowly pulled him by the arm toward the kitchen door. "It's beautiful out back. Let's go." He downed the rest of his drink, felt the effect, and looked off longingly at all the food. Out back was warm and smelled of honeysuckle. Chinese lanterns hung all the way to a high fence. Gretchen clung to his arm and nestled into him. "You're very good-looking, do you know that?" She wore her long black hair coiled into a low bun. Her nose was large and wouldn't have fit her face except for her enormous searching black eyes. She had lovely half-bare breasts.

"I never thought much about it." The pressure of her breasts on his arm made him nervous. "I mean, there are other things, like feelings, and all the stuff that's inside a person." He knew it sounded silly, but he was distracted by the way she looked at him. Her breath floated across his cheek, he started to tremble as he became aware of her fragrance, then she kissed him and held her body up to his, thighs to lips.

"Will you walk me home? It's not far. I have to get up early." She was leading him past the gardenia bushes and into the darkness at the back. Laughter floated from the house.

"I don't know."

A delicious sexy laugh rolled out of her. "Why? Are you with Joan?"

"No, I'm not. She just brought—"

"Joan won't mind," she cut in with a warm laugh. "You can come right back if you want."

The smell of the flowers, the warm night, her hand on his arm, and the memory of her soft lips eliminated any hesitation. "All right, sure, don't think I'll be missed."

The throaty laugh bubbled up again as she led them out of the gate. She held on to him as they walked down a tree-lined street to an elegant Victorian house now reconfigured into apartments. She led him down a dark mahogany hall into her rooms and once inside turned to him with a powerful kiss that took his breath away. She started to unbutton his shirt. "Get undressed if you want." Then she fell onto a round bed such as Mitch had never seen, and it made him laugh. She held out her arms. He had never been with a woman who wasn't a whore.

"My name is Gretchen," she purred, sitting up and running her fingers down his thigh. In the play, she'd kept touching the leading man, and now she was touching him, her hands creeping up under his shirt. She was definitely different from the whores in Japan.

Getting dressed the next morning, he remembered Doug Ramey and looked over at Gretchen. She opened her eyes and held out her arms. "Don't go. It's early."

"Do you know where a place called Cunningham's is?"

"Fifth and Walnut." She took his hand and put it on her breast. "Going to meet Doug, are you? You'll be in a play for sure." She let go of the hand, rolled over in the sheets, and stretched her legs. "Thanks, honey. It was great last night. Be sure to come back," and laughed. Everything she said came out as a delicious laugh. He liked her. She reached for his hand again, pulled him down on the bed, and started to undress him.

He walked down Fourth Street, turned into the park, and sat on a bench. The air was soft and warm. The three-note song of a bird filtered through the trees. A slight breeze flickered the sunlight over the moving leaves, resolving them into a pattern of light and dark. Gretchen's scent, mingled with the beautiful summer day, brought forth from Mitch's sated body and relaxed vocal cords a throaty, "What a night! This acting business is okay with me." He watched the old men playing cards on the stone tables along the walk, so easy and friendly together. He couldn't remember ever seeing his father play cards.

Cunningham's had a run-down elegance about it—dark wood paneling and faded burgundy drapes. As Mitch looked around thinking he was early, an older man in tails appeared out of a dark hall. "Looking for Mr. Ramey, are you?" Then the waiter whisked him down a hall with small rooms along one side opposite a picture gallery and left Mitch at the door of the last room. Doug was inside with two women and the man who had played the town bully in last night's play, all sitting at a large round table covered with a checkered tablecloth and littered with the remains of salads, old fries, and half-empty coffee mugs and glasses of beer.

"Never be early. It shows an eagerness and smacks of ambition," Doug Ramey pronounced with a laugh, standing to make room at the table.

"Oh, for Christ's sake. Don't scare him before he gets in the room." The beautiful older woman he had seen backstage last night held out her hand.

"Sit down, Mitchell." Doug gestured. "You hungry?" Again, he didn't wait for an answer. "This is Jill Anderson, our leading lady, Ann Marie, our stunning ingénue, and Warren," pointing to a tall thin dissipated-looking young man. "And this is Mitchell Ryan. He says he's an actor."

Jill took his hand and pulled him down beside her.

"Wait, I never said—"

"Oh, never mind." Doug turned to the rest of the party, resuming their conversation. Jill kept holding his hand. He felt he had been taken into a secret coven of artists. A beer and a hamburger appeared. Doug talked excitedly about a play called *Bus* something and joked about Warren moving to New York. Then back to Mitch. "Where did you disappear to last night? Joan and I looked around, but you were gone."

They all stared at him, and as the silence grew, they fell into gales of laughter. Mitch flushed and stood up, knocking over the beer, and stumbled back out the door, but before he could get two feet down the hall, they were after him. "Mitchell, no harm," Jill cooed, "we didn't mean a thing. It was just the look on your face. Please come back, come!" She pulled him gently by the arm back into the room and sat him down again next to her. "It's certainly none of our business when you left or where you went."

"Well, I was tired and…ah, the…ah, the dark witch, Gretchen, asked me to, ah, walk her home so…"

Warren raised his beer in a toast. "Gretchen is a lovely girl and a wonderful witch." At which they all burst into laughter again.

Doug Ramey held up his hand. "That's enough. Let's get back to work. Tomorrow we have a reading of our next play." Again, there was a pause as they all looked at Mitch.

He didn't know whether to laugh or curse. "What's going on?"

"Okay, Mitch, do you know a play called *Bus Stop*? No, of course you don't. Most people wouldn't. It's been playing in New York." Staring at him, Jill yelped, "Oh my god."

"He's perfect," Warren chimed in.

"Yes, I think he will do fine." They all had wide smiles on their faces.

"This is wonderful," said Ann Marie. "We'll make a great couple."

Mitch thought this was odd since they had just met. But things were happening so fast, and his life was so turned around that he said, "Sure," and they all laughed some more.

Doug cut it short. "Let's walk back to the Carriage House, and I'll get you a copy of the play. It's about a cowboy and a cheap dance-hall girl. Very touching love story and also funny. You're perfect to play this part."

"I don't know… Maybe I—"

"Come and walk with me." Doug was at the door. "I'll tell you all about it and show you the theater." He turned to the rest of them. "Mitch and I need to talk. You stay here. I'll see you all tomorrow at ten-sharp. And remember, in the theater, we are never late."

"Would it be okay if I finish my hamburger?" Mitch asked.

Back at his parents' house, he stayed up late and read the play. Twice. It was a little funny, but it didn't seem to make a whole lot of sense. He decided it would be foolish to get involved with these people because he didn't know anything about the world of plays. But in the morning, he thought it wouldn't hurt to go and see what this man Doug had in mind.

48

He arrived at the Carriage House before anyone else. The nine-teenth-century houses in front had long been torn down, and the row of carriage houses on the back street turned into shops. There was a coffee shop on one side of the theater and the Flowers for Life shop on the other. A flaking sign above the door read, "The Carriage House Players." He was about to start back up the street when a tall thin woman wearing overalls and carrying a clipboard hustled past him to the door and pulled out her keys. "Are you an actor?" Mitch turned to her, but before he could reply, she continued, "Are you in the cast?... Anyone else here?" She opened the door. "Can you make coffee?"

He followed her through. "I think so."

She gave him a look. "Maybe I'd better make it. You get those chairs and put them around the big table on the stage. I'm Mary Lee Money, Mr. Ramey's assistant." At his blank look, she said, "The director. Who are you?"

"Mitch Ryan."

"Find the lights backstage."

Just then, several people crowded through the door, talking among themselves without looking at him, so he found the lights, grabbed chairs, and brought them down to the table. More actors arrived, and then Doug Ramey bounded in, looking more like a seedy high school teacher than what Mitch thought a director might look like, tweed jacket worn at the elbows and shoes scuffed. But for all that, he had enormous vitality and was much more alive than anyone else in the room.

They sat around a large table at the center of the stage, nothing more than a platform about a foot high at one end of a large room. "You all know each other, but most of you don't know our new lead-ing man, Mitch Ryan. Do you prefer Mitch or Mitchell?"

"Mitch is fine."

"Mitch is going to play Bo for us." Mitch's face flushed, and his throat dried up. Doug went on, "This is Lon Walters. He will play the bus driver. And you know Warren Oates, you saw him in the play. Warren has kindly decided to stay with us to play the part of Virgil and deprive New York of his presence." This made everyone laugh. At that moment, the dark and lovely Jill entered the room, awash once again with strings of gold hanging from her neck and circling her wrists. Led by Doug, everyone turned and gave her a loud round of applause. She made a deep bow, glided over, and sat down next to Mitch.

"Hello, handsome," she said softly, touching the back of his neck.

"Be nice, darling. Jill will play Grace, the owner of the diner."

"Well, you sure are beautiful, and I bet you'll be wonderful. Have they been treating you all right?" She continued to massage the back of his neck. It suddenly dawned on him that she had played the old hag witch in the play. "He's blushing," she chortled, turning to the others to make sure they noticed. "How sweet." She touched his cheek, and he was getting ready to bolt again when just then a young woman came rushing in with a flurry of apologies and took a chair.

Doug went on for some time about what a great privilege it is to be in the theater, how lucky they all were to be able to do what they loved. Mitch looked around at this group. They were different from anyone he had ever met, certainly different from anyone in the navy. Finally, Doug finished his spiel, quieted everyone down, and announced, "Okay, let's start."

The words on the page transformed into human beings talking to each other. The closer they came to his first line, the tenser he became. And the harder he tried not to shake, the more he shook. His voice, which was naturally deep, sounded like a toy tin whistle when he started to speak. Finally, stumbling and misreading several lines, he stopped and took a drink of water, stood awkwardly. The chair hit the floor. "I'm very sorry. It's obvious this is not for me." He picked up the chair, replaced it, and walked stiffly out the door. He was down the street when he heard Doug, "Where do you think you're going? We have a deal. You don't just walk out on a show. Once you commit, there's no turning back."

"This was a bad idea, I don't know what I was thinking."

Doug sat down on the curb. "Sit down for a minute. I want to tell you something." Mitch's face was burning. He was torn between disappearing down the street and obliging Doug, who was now patting the curb as if it was a sofa. Mitch sat reluctantly and took a sideways glance at the older man, then dropped his head down to his knees. What was he doing sitting in the street with this stranger?

Before Doug spoke, Mitch watched him look down at his hands, his face suffused with sadness. "Life is strange," he began. "You remind me of myself when I first went to New York. Many a time, I wanted to quit, and then I did. I left the city. I was never going near the theater again. But I couldn't stay away, so I came back, but I came back here, to Louisville. I'll never be what I dreamed of when I was your age, but I have enough. I would never have had this if I'd quit the first time I got scared or fucked up. You must never think that way." A big truck lumbered by. Doug lit a cigarette. Then he was all business: "First of all, reading has nothing to do with acting. So you can't read, fine, you'll learn." Doug's voice became more intense. "When we get the play on its feet, that's when the fun starts, and then with an audience, everything changes. You have something that shines through." He stood. "Come on back. Everyone thought you were doing fine and that you will be very good in this part." He then turned and walked back toward the door. Mitch watched him stride back to his home, the theater, and he heard an echo. "I'll never be what I dreamed of when I was your age…"

So he sat there, his heart racing. He looked after this man who had taken this time with him and was waiting for him at the stage door. No one had ever treated him that way, certainly not his father. A while ago, he had wanted to run, but now he rose from the curb and walked toward the theater. Doug smiled and held the door for him, then patted him on the back as he passed into the theater—forever.

The six weeks of rehearsal went by quickly, and Mitch began to relax. Warren helped by running scenes over and over with him. The older actor had black curly hair and a crooked smile that seemed to help him with the ladies, who Mitch noticed were very attentive around him. Mitch, with his limited experience, was beginning to sense when women were receptive and when they wanted to be left alone. Jill, he discovered, was married and supported a jealous husband who had no use for the theater or actors. Warren warned

Mitch to be careful. "She's dangerous." This only made him think he wanted to know a little more about her.

Doug kept talking about behavior: "Do less, do less," he said over and over. Whenever Mitch grew emotional in a scene, Doug would stop and give him something to do. Warren tried to explain some of these directions, but Doug told him to leave Mitch alone. "Let him find it."

Opening night, Mitch would have thrown up if he had been able to eat. Doug came to wish everyone luck and saw the state he was in. "Mitch, it will be fine. You're doing a great job."

"I can't do it. I can't remember any lines. This is no good." He felt like a whining kid and that everyone knew something he didn't.

"Listen, you were telling that hilarious story about what happened to you in the navy, remember?"

"That was all bullshit, Doug, I made most of it up."

"You could have fooled me. You're a born storyteller, and that is what acting has got to be. Controlled lies. Storytelling." Doug gave him a hug and turned to leave. "It's like telling a story in the bar to all your friends."

On his first entrance, he could hardly speak or say his line. His knees felt like jelly, and his stomach was in a knot. And then…the audience laughed! This wave of laughter came up to the stage, and his stomach unknotted. He began to laugh, and this made the audience laugh more. Mitch looked at Warren, his sidekick, and he, too, was smiling. Then over to Jill, playing Grace, and she was a glowing bright light. He saw her face and her large black eyes as she moved toward him, saying, "Sit down, cowboy, you must be hungry."

He responded with his line: "I want a quart of milk." And the audience roared. Mitch looked out at them. They were waiting for him to continue. He realized he could do anything. He was free.

At intermission, Ann Marie, who played the love interest, ran to him first with a hug and kiss. "You were fantastic, that was incredible!" Then Warren came over. "Great job, now you're getting it."

Murray, who played Dr. Lyman and had not said two words to him during rehearsals, came by. "Where did that come from?"

The whole cast was thrilled, telling him over and over what a natural actor he was. Doug appeared. "An actor is born. Mitchell, that was good. You were all great. Keep it up. We have one more act. They love it, they love you." Then he was gone. Gone but never forgotten: like a strangely familiar dream he, Doug Ramey, would always be there, forever holding the door of the theater open for Mitch to pass through.

Mitch was twenty-one years old and felt like he had finally come home.

CHAPTER 4

The Happy Prince
1953

"*HAMLET*? SURE, I'VE heard of it."

"Have you read it?"

"No, not really."

"Yes, I think you should read the whole thing. I have an idea. We'll play him very young and see how a boy relates to the death of his father and to his mother getting married to his uncle so soon after."

"His father dies?"

"He's murdered by his own brother, who then marries Gertrude, his brother's wife and Hamlet's mother."

"That's Shakespeare...I don't know."

"Read it and come and talk to me tomorrow at Cunningham's at noon. Do you have a Shakespeare? I took mine home, but I'll get it for you tomorrow."

"My mother loves Shakespeare. She has a big book of all the plays."

"Good, read it. See you tomorrow. Before you leave, set up for the children's play. It's at three."

They had been sitting in Doug's cramped office at the theater he had started after World War II. Books were jammed in the shelves and stacked knee-high on the floor. The place held the lifelong smell of cigarettes, the water cooler that didn't work in the corner, and a mangy stuffed crow perched crookedly on the top shelf, observing all the chaos. Mitch was glad to be there and felt that he would never leave. He loved being part of a community, keeping the place clean, and building the sets, such as they were. One day he'd even decided to paint the front of the building, which had been looking pretty funky. After considerable nagging, he convinced Doug to get some paint, then went to work, and it turned out pretty well.

But he wasn't so sure about doing Shakespeare. The language was a little too much to think about. Anyway, he would definitely read it, even though he knew it would be difficult. He decided to go back to his parents. Maybe his mother would let him use her Shakespeare. He'd been staying with Gretchen off and on since that first night. She didn't seem to mind and had even bought him a shirt.

He set up for the children's play reading at the theater. Then he walked down to the corner and caught the Crescent Hills bus. He was glad to warm up on the bus. As he trudged to the house on Ingle Avenue, he hoped his father wasn't home. Every encounter these days led to the same drill: why wasn't Mitch in college? The street was quiet. He stopped on the porch and looked out to the wide side yard with the fir tree at the far end by the alley. This yard was the only part of the place that had any meaning for him. The house, which had been a farmhouse in an earlier day when it stood alone, now leaned to the left looking none too sturdy and was out of place surrounded by a subdivision of modern homes.

From the door, Mitch saw his mother sitting close to the coal fire in the grate. It was the only place to stay warm in the drafty old house. He closed the door. She turned, took him in, and returned to the fire. "Well, well! The wandering minstrel." Her voice was tight.

"I told you I was staying downtown for several days," Mitch replied with as much neutrality as he could muster. He walked into the hall toward the kitchen. "Dad here?"

"On the road."

"Can I make a sandwich?"

"Of course. Why not? I'm not sure what's there."

"You have a copy of Shakespeare, don't you?" he called from the kitchen, waiting in front of the icebox.

"Yes, why?"

"Can I borrow it?"

"No. You cannot."

He took a deep breath. "Can I read it here tonight?"

"I doubt it. It would take a year to read it all."

"I only need to read one play." He fished a piece of cheese out of the icebox and a slice of Wonder Bread from the basket.

"Which one?"

"Doug's doing *Hamlet*, and he wants me to read it." There was a long pause. He waited. Nothing. He took a big gulp of milk out of the bottle and went back into the living room. "Mom?" Holding him in the doorway with her eyes, she stood and went to the bookcase. She took down a large book, thumbed through the pages, stopped, and read, *On Fortune's cap we are not the very button...or the soles of her shoe.*

"What's that mean?"

"It's from the play. Hamlet and his two treacherous schoolmates Rosencrantz and Guildenstern are fencing with words."

"I think I better read it. May I?"

"Of course"—she thrust the large volume into his hands—"but it does not leave this house." She turned back to the fireplace. "Read it slowly. Read it out loud."

In his back-porch room, he plowed through the words. After several hours, he began to understand some of the language. He sensed his mother waiting in the living room but was pretty sure she wouldn't come back there. He continued. Some of the passages were a large mouthful, some were contemporary, sounding like nowadays, and others he couldn't follow even when he read them over several times. He heard a sound and turned to see her at the door.

"Where are you?"

Mitch flushed, stuttered, and sat up on the edge of the bed. "The king's just welcomed Rosencrantz and Guildenstern and told them to keep an eye on Hamlet. I'm trying to find out about Voltimand."

"He's the ambassador to Norway." She had a tea towel in her hand and was swinging it like a cowboy ready to rope a cow. Her face was open. She looked young. She tucked the towel into her belt and startled him by doing a little jig and slapping her foot Irish style. For as long as he could remember, he'd never seen her so full of life. She laughed, he laughed, she laughed, then they both laughed together. "What do you think so far?"

"The part with his father, you know, the Ghost, seemed a bit far-fetched."

"Oh dear, you have to remember that in those days, the Elizabethan times, everyone believed in ghosts, and they were very real to the audience." She came in and sat beside him, "Also, a woman alone…" She paused, and he watched as she seemed to fall back somewhere into the past. "Especially a queen, almost always married right away to protect herself."

"You know a lot about this play."

"My father read *Hamlet* to me when I was a wee thing, and your father read it to me when I first met him." She gave a small laugh. The picture of his father reading Shakespeare, and to his mother no less, seemed almost impossible to believe. Her voice was deep and throaty. *"What a piece of work is a man! How noble in reason! how infinite in faculty! in form and moving how express and admirable! in action how like an angel! in apprehension how like a god! the beauty of the world! the paragon of animals!"* She stopped, shut her eyes, and turned away. Her voice changed when she started again. Mitch sensed the sadness: *"there's a special providence in the fall of a sparrow. If it be now, 'tis not to come; if it be not to come, it will be now; if it be not now, yet it will come: the readiness is all…"*

They were both quiet. Mitch made a movement toward her, stopped, caught between embarrassment and an impulse to touch her in some way. But before he could move, she reached out and patted the heavy worn book. "I love Shakespeare," she began and then, sensing his need, moved away to the window. "I fell in love with your father when he read Shakespeare to me." When she turned back to him, her face was so different that he hardly recognized her. Her cheeks were full of color, and her eyes wide and alive. "My father read also. Fate that I should meet a man who loved Shakespeare and loved to read. Now my son is a reader." She slowly floated to the door. Mitch didn't want her to go. "Are you going to play Hamlet? Oh, no? But I think maybe you should." She turned to go.

"Stay, Mom, and read some more." She shook her head, smiled, and then, almost to herself, said, "He was for all time," and was gone.

His face felt hot. Why didn't he tell her the truth that he thought Doug wanted him to play Hamlet? He launched into reading again. When he came to the part his mother had quoted, he was amazed at how modern it sounded. And then when Hamlet tells Rosencrantz and Guildenstern why he has lost all his mirth and love of life, a strange sensation crept over his body. He read that section all over again. How could those old words be so heartbreakingly true?

He stood and stretched. I can't do this. These are smart, witty men. Why, he wondered, unaware that he was hitting on the age-old question, why doesn't Hamlet just go and kill the son of a bitch? Why does he wait? There must be some deep reason why he waits and waits. Mitch sat back down on the bed, contemplating this. He dropped the huge book on the floor and fell asleep.

He opened his eyes next morning to see his father staring down at the Shakespeare on the floor. Charles picked up the book, weighing it in his hands, then opened the large volume. Mitch kept watching his father. The man's lips were moving. A warm feeling of what could be called love moved up into where his heart was, "What are you reading, Dad?"

Charles slammed the book shut. "You reading this?"

"Yes I am." What play were you reading, Dad?

"I was looking at the pictures. If you are going to live in this house, you have to pay your share. Also, you can't just drop in whenever you feel like it. Are you looking for a job?" Holding the book, he said, "What play are you reading?"

"*Hamlet*." Mitch thought of what his mother had told him about his father reading to her. "You know the play, don't you, Dad?"

"Sure, everyone knows *Hamlet*. Your mother is the expert."

"Can I ask you a question about the play?"

"What?'

58

"Why doesn't he avenge his father's murder?"

Charles, still holding the Shakespeare, looked down at Will's picture on the cover. Then with a harsh slap he put it in Mitch's hand. "I'm sure I don't know. Maybe he grows up and decides it's not worth it. Maybe he decides to get an honest job and mind his own business. And another thing: if you're going to read Shakespeare, I'd wait awhile before getting involved in the tragedies…read some of the comedies."

"Did you really read *Hamlet* to Mother?"

His father turned away, then back. "It's all just words on paper. Something to divert you from what you should be about, which is getting a job and supporting yourself."

"Thanks, Dad, that's a help."

"Don't get smart."

"Sorry."

"There's some eggs in the kitchen." His father left.

Mitch hadn't meant to be smart with his father. He had truly meant what he'd said. His father had indeed helped. He sat on the side of the bed and the familiar feeling of hopelessness that always filled his exchanges with his father seem to have disappeared. They had exchanged about something instead of the usual orders and argument. Then he slowly dressed as he prepared to meet Doug. He couldn't wait to get back to the sanctuary of the theater.

Walking to the bus, the image of his mother reciting Shakespeare was vivid in his mind. Last night, I find out my mother knows *Hamlet* by heart, and today I find out my father knows the difference between the tragedies and the comedies!

* * *

He stopped in front of the little Carriage House. He wondered at how in a short time he had become so attached to this one-hundred-year-old building and all the actors? How? Inside there was Doug. "I want you to play Hamlet. Don't worry, we can work on it for two months. We'll open sometime in March."

"This is not for me, Doug. I'm a hick from Kentucky, and these are very sharp men. Maybe I could play the gravedigger." Doug was quiet for a few seconds. They were sitting in Cunningham's Bar and Grill at Doug's table. Doug seemed to be here almost all of the time. Mitch wondered if he had a home. He certainly never mentioned a wife or family.

The older man looked at Mitch and thoughtfully sipped his beer. "How little we know ourselves. You can do this, but it will be hard work. Also, you will be doing Hamlet many times in the years to come, if you wish. You have to take singing lessons for breath control, and we will go over every line until you understand it." Mitch started to protest, but Doug held up his hand. "No more talk. Will you try to do this with me?"

Mitch waited, suspended for a moment. "Yes."

"Good, we start tomorrow. Have a beer."

Mitch had a sinking sensation in his gut. What am I doing? Reading his mind, Doug took his hand. "Don't worry, it will be fun. Are you going to be with your folks or in town?"

"I'll be staying with Gretchen most of the time. Do you know, people think you live at Cunningham's? Do you have a house? Where do you live?"

"My wife and I live in Clifton above a beauty parlor she owns." Mitch wanted to hear more, but Doug sat silently, his shoulders sagged, and Mitch thought he seemed sad.

The silence felt good. Sometimes all the talking could weigh you down. He relaxed, and the quiet moment seemed to last a long time. "I would like to meet your wife sometime."

"Yes, maybe. James, could you bring me another beer? So what's your main question on reading it for the first time?" Mitch felt a strange wave of fear edge in on him. "Well?" Doug waited.

"I don't know. I didn't mean to be fresh, asking about your wife."

"No, son, it wasn't taken that way. She's just not very social. Now you must have a question about Hamlet, everyone since the beginning has had one."

"Okay, why doesn't he avenge his father's death?"

"See, you are an actor and you've started working already."

"Well, my mother knows *Hamlet* by heart, and my father knows the comedies from the tragedies, and he said he doesn't avenge his father's death because he grew up."

"Your father sounds like a thoughtful man. There's not an easy answer, many factors to consider. Tonight, read the scenes after he comes back from England very carefully. Don't get caught up in the gravedigger."

Mitch walked toward Gretchen's to tell her about Hamlet and watch her face when she heard the news. In the doorway of his mind, he saw his mother, wanted to run home, and let her know he was Hamlet. He pulled his jacket up around his neck and sat on a bench in St. James Court, lit a cigarette, and began to ponder what was in store, Jesus, just to learn the lines. The wind started to blow and a light rain started. He stood up to look in his pocket. Twenty-three dollars. He ran through the cold January rain to a bar near Gretchen's place and ordered a whiskey.

Hours later, he stumbled out of the bar and headed to Gretchen's. She wasn't home, so he sat on the stoop of the old Victorian rooming house. He must have fallen asleep because he woke up as a sleety rain turning to snow floated down on him. He retreated, freezing, to beneath the covered porch, walking up and down and pounding his arms around his body. Maybe he should just go back to the bar. What strange turns his life was taking? Who would have thought that *Hamlet* would be the thing that could bring his family together? His father reading to his mother, like an old photo.

Gretchen came running up, her face aglow from the cold, sleet in her hair, and gave him a large loving hug. "Oh…drunk? Are you okay?"

"I'm going to play Hamlet."

"Of course you are, but you have a few years before you need think about him. Come in and I'll give you a warm bath, Sir Hamlet."

He learned the four soliloquys, and because he went over them many times, they became part of him. Doug told him his instinct to give them an action was right and also told him it would be better to rein them in. Not to "tear a passion to tatters." The scenes with the dialogue were much harder and were a mess. The pace took some adjusting. Mitch found reserves of energy that Doug somehow knew were there. The scenes with Rosencrantz and Guildenstern came easier than most but took much work. The scene with Gertrude scared him. The actress kept touching him. She was a very sexy young student, only one or two years older than him. Doug didn't help him with the closet scene. He told him he was on his own and doing fine. Mitch felt abandoned. He kept pleading and then got mad. But just at that time, Doug, who had been working most of his time with Mitch, was obliged to start focusing on the rest of the cast. Mitch realized to his chagrin that without Doug's support, he knew nothing, not even how to rehearse. It devolved into a despair that lasted for weeks until Mitch, discouraged beyond redemption, determined he had to quit, only to have Doug pull him back and not too gently. "You have come this far, and you are good, so suck it up. Remember to be there in each scene and don't think about what is coming up. Listen to the other actors!"

Mitch put one foot in front of another, certain he was headed for disaster. Then the wardrobe came. And the props. What a joke. It looked like a dress-up for a third-grade party.

Doug never panicked or raised his voice. He was a steady hand and brought them all around to opening night. They all stood backstage like frantic bees ready to flee. Doug had gotten the university to let him use the theater where he had done *Dark of the Moon*, provided he cast a number of university drama students. It was a beautiful old theater—real dressing rooms, a green room, and a draw-up front curtain. Mitch remembered standing on the stage for the first time and the feeling of awe at the impact of live theater. But this opening night, that feeling was nowhere to be found. He was absolutely naked, and they were going to be throwing rocks at him as soon as he opened his mouth.

In Hamlet's first scene, he sits for a long time before speaking. This made Mitch uncomfortable in rehearsals. His mind wandered. He remembered that his father called before the play to tell him his mother was sick, and they wouldn't be able to come. In that span of time, he realized he was not only playing Hamlet, the prince of

Denmark, but also the boy whose mother married right after his father died.

He began to relax in his royal chair, glancing at the audience, his body filled with energy. Suddenly he saw the people sitting in the audience and heard Claudius drone on. Then his first line came out of him as if he had never said it before. "A little more than kin and less than kind." He felt everyone in the audience somehow knew *Hamlet* and was ready for the journey. At that very moment, he began to understand why Shakespeare was great.

Everything went better than he had hoped. The first act applause was thrilling. When he came to the closet scene, the sexual vibrations were enveloped in anger and outrage, and the first level of that scene was uncovered. Once the play was over and they took their curtain calls, the largest audience he had ever seen clapped and cheered. He was drenched in sweat and high as a kite. The party was beginning backstage.

When he walked over to the green room, his mother was standing there. His father had called earlier and told him she couldn't be there but seeing her there sent a shiver through his whole body. "I thought you couldn't…"

"If you could get me a cab, I need to get home. Your father didn't make it, but I had to come. It's not every day your son plays Hamlet." She sank down on a chair by the stage door. Mitch waited for more. He could feel the pulse in his neck. He waited. Nothing. After a few moments that seemed endless, she looked up at him. "It was good to hear the great words," she said almost to herself. "You reminded me of your father when I met him." She reached up, touched his cheek. Her hand held such tenderness that he blushed. The inner connection between Gertrude and his mother startled him—strange new feelings.

All he could do was wait for any sign of praise. When the taxi came, he walked her out and helped her in. She looked up through the open window. "You did fine, but you need to do better." Then she rolled up the window, and the cab pulled away.

Mitch stood silent, watching the cab drive off. In an instant, the tenderness he had felt a moment before fell away, leaving in its wake a sharp sting in his heart. He sat on the bench by the stage door and brought both hands to his forehead. After a moment he went to join the party.

In the cab, Genevieve put her hand to her mouth to quiet the sobs. I didn't need to say that to the boy. A flutter of envy made her blush: the long struggle of her life, the years of writing—some good, some not so good—always rejected. Had it come to this, jealous of her son, proud and jealous at the same time? She rolled down the window and let the cool night air wash over her face. She thought of *Hamlet* and how it was threaded through her history. She had been only ten years old when her father read the play to the family. She could still hear the heavy timbre of his voice as he filled the house with…*bloody, bawdy villain! / Remorseless, treacherous, lecherous, kindless villain! / O, vengeance!* Her body shivered, and she involuntary groaned, "O, vengeance!"

The cab driver turned his head. "The play was that bad, huh?"

She recovered quickly. "As a matter of fact, it was very good. Do you know *Hamlet?*"

"Sure, he's that guy who wonders if he should be or not."

"Yes, you're right. Well, my son played Hamlet, and he was good."

"That's great, lady, you must by very proud."

"I am." She turned to the wind and felt a sweet breath of recognition, the delicate thread between her son and her father. To have this given to her now was important and attention needed to be paid. "Oh god, why did I say that stupid thing to my son?"

The cab pulled up at the house. Inside, Charles was sitting in the dark, smoking a cigarette. "Well?"

"Why aren't you in bed?" She turned on the table lamp beside him.

"How was it?"

"He was very good."

"I should have gone."

"They play another two weeks."

"Yes, yes, yes, I'll go."

"I'm going to bed. I'm dead tired."

"I'll be there in a moment."

She turned. "He reminded me of you when you used to read to me."

"Jesus." He put out his cigarette.

"Seems like another life."

"It was."

"I was very proud of Mitchell."

"Did you tell him, Genevieve?" She had turned away so he couldn't see the terror on her face. "I'm going to bed," she said as she left the room.

Charles stared into the darkness.

In her bedroom, she slowly undressed and lay down. Let out a long sigh and whispered, *"On Fortune's cap we are not the very button...or the soles of her shoe."*

The paper the next day reported, "Shakespeare did his part. The Carriage House Players did not." And it went downhill from there. Mitch had let them all down.

Doug found him in the rehearsal room. "That critic, of course, was right. But what counts is the work. Never forget it. It's a process, and nothing matters but the doing. We have ten more performances."

CHAPTER 5

Barter Theater
1956

MITCH RESTED HIS head on the window of the bus. He loved the early evenings in these mountains. The sun shone on the tops of the hills, leaving the slopes in muted greens and grays with the occasional splash of color from a red barn or a patch of sunflowers. Then as they started up a grade, he saw a sign: "Abingdon, VA-41 Miles." Things were happening fast. Less than three years away from the navy, and here he was, trying to push himself into a professional theater. An old tension grabbed at his back during the fourteen-hour bus ride, and he had begun to lose his nerve.

He didn't know what to expect when he reached the Barter Theater. He hadn't heard from Robert Porterfield, the owner, who at the audition had said he would let Mitch know because "I want you in my theater." Doug offered to call the man for him, but Mitch wanted to see this through on his own. What did he have to lose coming here? He'd go on his own to see the man, and if it didn't work out, he'd visit his sister in Richmond. The bus kept climbing then started down. The mountains rose around the wide valley as the bus descended.

He brought the photos from *Hamlet* out of his ragged leather bag, the same old bag that had belonged to his grandfather, the bag that Mitch's father had given him when he went into the navy. He looked at the pictures, musing on the wonder of Shakespeare. Now, farther and farther away from Louisville, he felt himself diminishing, like he was nothing again. *Who am I kidding?* came the harsh interior voice. *I'm not an actor, not really.* The sense of value Doug had infused in him began to ebb, and Mitch feared it would disappear entirely. Everything he knew, he knew from Doug. How would he know where to start without him?

When the bus pulled into the station at Abingdon, he entered the tiny lobby. Behind a smudged ticket window, a woman with her hair in curlers was eating a banana split. She didn't look up. A bad sign. He continued through the door to a street that turned out to be Highway 11, the main drag of Abingdon, and the thoroughfare from Knoxville to Richmond. He approached a white-haired gentleman sitting with his face to the sun in front of the bus station. "Excuse me, but could you tell me where I might find the Barter Theater?"

The man looked up, tilted back a little in his chair, and folded his arms across his chest. "Just take the road east. Theater's across the street from the Martha Washington Inn. About a mile."

Mitch thanked him and turned to go, but the man continued, "Or you can turn left at Jackson Street—named after General Stonewall Jackson, who was raised near here in Wytheville—and go to the top of the hill and turn down Hinckley Lane to Barter Road and follow that to the back of the theater. Little shorter that way." He stopped for a breath and leaned forward for more conversation, another bad omen, but before he could get started, Mitch had thanked him and escaped.

The worn leather bag bumped against his leg. Maybe I'm crazy to show up without being announced. He imagined Porterfield telling him to get lost. "I said I'd call you. Sorry, but we don't need another actor. Are you even in the union? This is a professional theater, you know." Porterfield probably thought Mitch's sending all those cards was stupid. When he had auditioned in Louisville, Porterfield had asked his name. When Mitch had mumbled, the theater owner had shouted, "I didn't hear you. Always let them know your name!" So Mitch had sent a card every day on which he had written the same thing: "My name is Mitch Ryan." By the time he reached the theater, he was about to bolt right back to the bus station.

His spirits were unsettled even more when he saw a large marquee covering the whole front of the theater and tall double doors leading to the auditorium. This was the real thing. In glass-enclosed windows on either side of the doors were posters that read, "*The Tempest*, by William Shakespeare." There was someone in the box office as he approached and a vacuum whirring somewhere inside.

"Yes, can I help you?" A young woman with shoulder-length golden hair could be a good sign.

"I'm looking for Mr. Porterfield."

"What's your name?"

He found the courage to say, "My name is Mitch Ryan."

The young woman burst into laughter, "So it's you. You're famous all over this theater. We wait every day to see if another card will show up. Come on, I'll take you to Robert." He almost felt like giggling, but most of all, and to his great surprise, he started to relax as he followed the young woman through a small lobby to the top of the aisle. In the bright houselights, he could see that the walls were hung with heavy red velour and the seats covered in the red cloth as well, with gold numbers on the armrests. The stage curtain was up, revealing the most elaborate set he had ever seen, huge jagged boulders with lifelike trees and a sweeping red sky that filled the whole stage. Farther down the aisle, a man vacuumed the carpet that matched the seats and wall hangings. The man turned around. It was Mr. Porterfield.

He turned off the vacuum and looked at Mitch for a long time, trying to place him. *Oh god, he doesn't remember me*, Mitch thought.

Finally Porterfield blurted out, "Honey, where have you been? I had a part for you in *Tempest*, but you weren't here." Mitch had forgotten the deep, rolling Southern accent. He stammered something about not hearing from the other man.

"Speak up, honey, you have a large voice—let it out!" He walked up to Mitch, took his hand, and smiled. "I knew you would come. I was sure of it." He loomed over Mitch and continued to hold his hand. Mitch tried to disengage but could not. Porterfield just kept staring at him until finally he boomed out, "You hungry? Let's go over to the inn and have some supper." He turned to the young woman. "This is Mitch Ryan, our new leading man. Mitch, this is Anne Williams. She runs the box office."

As they walked to the inn across the highway, Porterfield asked, "You did a production of *Bus Stop*, am I right?"

"Yes, I did it for Doug in Louisville."

"You also did *Hamlet* just a while ago?"

Mitch stumbled, so surprised that he knew but could say nothing. He just gaped at Porterfield.

Well, you did, didn't you? All he could say was, "Yes!"

"Our next show is going to be *Bus Stop*. Do you think you'd like to do it again, or is once enough?" With a wink, he clapped Mitch on the shoulder. Mitch began to feel heaviness in his limbs. He stumbled again on the stairs to the large porch of the Martha Washington Inn and went down to one knee. What's happening to me? This is going too fast. He had nothing to hold on to, no frame of reference. Yet he recovered and saw himself walking through the large doors of the inn.

The Martha Washington was the most elegant place he had ever seen. The dining room had large floor-to-ceiling windows, and the falling sun made dappled shadows through white lace curtains. Well-dressed patrons dined around tables, each of which held a large bowl of flowers. The waiters were black, and one came up to pull out Mitch's chair. Everyone knew Mr. Porterfield. He called them all by their first names, to which he always added "Honey." They approached a large table with the whitest tablecloth he had ever seen. Mitch played with the silver and found it weighed a ton. The cups were so thin you could almost see through them.

Porterfield crashed down in the carved walnut chair. "They have the best candied pork chops you will ever taste. Also, divine fried chicken. I'm having the pork. Of course, it's all very good. Nobody can cook like Jasper."

"The pork sounds good." Mitch hadn't eaten anything but potato chips since the day before.

When they were finished with their meal and having coffee, Mr. Porterfield brought up money. He pulled out the list of productions that were to be done that summer. Besides *Bus Stop*, several other plays needed a young male lead.

"We have a great company, most from New York. There are several good solid local actors you'll be happy with too."

Mitch didn't know how to take this information. Was Porterfield telling him something about the season they were presenting, or was he referring to Mitch being in it? He felt better now that he had eaten but was hungry to know where he stood.

"We will talk about joining the union later—actually, you don't want to be in the union because they don't let you work in nonunion theater. This restriction will knock you out of a lot of experience that a young actor needs, honey." He turned to the waiter. "George, honey, can we have some spoon bread? And tell Jasper he did a fine job again."

"Yes, sir, Mr. Robert. I'll tell him."

"Jasper and I grew up together. He looked after my father's farm, and now he's a superb chef. Jasper cooks and his boy serves."

Something about that statement gave Mitch the willies. He tensed and his ears burned. It reminded him of Mr. Brooks back home running his construction company, saying, "I treat my Negroes good." *Jesus*, Mitch thought, *I get sick of this white-over-black shit that's all around*. It's the only thing his father ever got really mad about, and it was what Mitch admired most about that distant man.

Mr. Porterfield pulled him back with his big smile. "So, young fellow, as long as you are here, you will get room and board and, say, twenty dollars a week. How does that sound?"

Well, it sounded a little like he was being taken in as one of the slaves of the Porterfield enterprise. But he would have done anything at any price, as long as he could stay here. "It sounds fair."

After dinner, Porterfield took him to the Barter Inn, situated on a large hill above and behind the theater. He was shown his room, told where to find the dining room, and that breakfast was at seven, after which Porterfield took him to the office to review all fifty-five postcards Mitch had sent. A whole wall covered with "My name is

Mitch Ryan." Mitch was embarrassed and started to stammer some stupid apology. Porterfield laughed. "I loved it, honey. Don't ever let them forget your name."

Later, alone in his room, Mitch sat down on the bed and let it all sink in. All he could eat and twenty bucks on top. On his way! And going to do a professional play, a play he already had done and felt good about, plus several more. It sent tingles through his body as he lay back and let out a large laugh, then jumped up, went to the mirror, and spoke out loud at his image, "Porterfield had planned all these plays without an actor to play them. What if I hadn't come?"

Great grand thoughts raced through his mind. He was awash in gratitude. Then a sinking feeling in his gut: who would be acting with him? Professionals, from New York! Oh Jesus, they would see right off that he didn't know what he was doing. He jumped up and out of the room, down the hall to the front door. The whole building suddenly seemed damp and musty, like the Market Hotel whorehouse in Louisville, with paint peeling off the walls and some of the floorboards loose. Outside, however, was a beautiful garden with peach trees. A brick path wound down to the road. He lit a cigarette. It was evening, and the night-blooming jasmine filled his Being.

"Want a drink, young man?" said a gravelly voice behind him. He jumped and turned to see a figure sitting on a bench—a weathered-looking man wearing a train engineer's hat and holding a pint bottle. He looked like a character from another era.

"I don't mind if I do," he said, glad to take his mind off the incursion of New York actors. The man handed him the bottle, and Mitch took a large gulp. It burned going down, sweet like fruit.

"Peach brandy. Make it myself. I'm the Colonel. I take care of things around here." His nose was pockmarked, and the skin on his neck rippled.

When Mitch told him where he was from, the man exclaimed, "Louisville! I worked out of Louisville for the old Louisville and Nashville Railroad when I was about your age. Rough town back then. Yes, sir!" Warming up for a long conversation, he cradled one knee in his hands and settled in. He told Mitch about the people who lived here at the Barter Inn besides the actors. Mrs. Hilton, the widow of James Hilton who wrote a famous book called *Shangri-La*, was crazy about Mr. Porterfield. "Pretty sure he's after her money. Likely to get it too."

"What's Porterfield like, Colonel? He seems a strange fellow."

"You have no idea. He started this theater years ago and kept it going because he don't pay anybody and always seems to come up smelling like a rose. He's the cheapest bastard that ever lived, won't fix the inn, and cleans the theater himself because he won't hire a janitor."

"Yeah, he was vacuuming the aisle when I met him."

"See!" The old boy laughed and laughed. Then he told Mitch about the Penn sisters, who lived in a large house across the road. The one sister could be seen at the top-floor window now and then. She had been jilted on her wedding day and hadn't been out of her room for forty years. Mitch loved listening to this old bird. He would find out later that this town was much stranger than anyone could imagine.

At last, the two of them grew silent and sat there, taking in the night. When Mitch finally staggered back to his room, feeling more than a little queasy from the peach brandy, there was a script of *Bus Stop* on his bed with a note pasted to the cover: "Welcome, 'Your name is Mitch Ryan.' The Colonel is the biggest liar in the state of Virginia."

CHAPTER 6

What's a Movie?
1957

MITCH ACTED IN all the plays that summer and fall: *Bus Stop*, *Picnic*, *Dark of the Moon*, *The Rainmaker*, and more, including *Cyrano* and *Twelfth Night*. But nothing could compare to that first day in the professional theater, June 11, 1955.

The first reading of *Bus Stop* included the full cast onstage in the *Tempest* set. Porterfield made a speech similar to the one Doug had delivered on that first day of Mitch's life in the theater, only this was a louder and more florid version and seemed to go on forever. As Mitch watched their leader Robert Porterfield, the great Southern patriarch, very much in control, with the vanity pouring out of his big red face, turned slowly, fixing his gaze on each fellow cast member in turn. Everyone seemed tense, their faces frozen masks, and in a moment of clarity, he watched these masks change from one attitude to another but never open. When they finally started the reading, his nerves kept him alert, for he knew what he was going to bring, and that gave him a confidence that surprised him. These New York actors were very slick and had what he thought must be the professional touch. Their masks would morph, depending on whom they were talking to and what they were feeling, but when they were reading, the masks fell away altogether. They were good.

It was as if he were outside looking in at a world apart. He had had this sensation before, and it only intensified his sense of not belonging. Their voices were somehow lighter and more relaxed. But his sense of otherness disappeared when he started to read, the familiar words taking him to a place where he felt grounded and focused, and there was no place else on earth he wanted to be.

"That was great—you're so good in this part!" the woman playing his love interest told him animatedly after a quick kiss. A delightful lightness filled his head. The joyous company of actors all repaired to the café across the road at the Martha Washington Inn, everyone jabbering and glowing with a sense of promise and anticipation that Mitch thrilled to.

Many drinks later, he lay in bed in his room, far from sleep. He lit a cigarette, then went out and walked down through the garden to the back of the theater. He tried all the doors, but they were locked, so he clumsily climbed in an open window at the side of the stage door, went up, and walked to center stage. The stage light threw his long shadow like a giant Mitch out across the seats. Feeling the power of the stage and the empty house with the balconies like royal boxes, he became aware in some magical way of the ancient tradition of the theater. His voice was soft when he started: *To be, or not to be, that is the question, / Whether 'tis nobler in the mind / To suffer the slings and arrows of outrageous fortune, / Or to take arms against a sea of troubles, / And by opposing end them?*

He stopped, a disturbance roiling up within him. I wonder, do I have a mask? He sat down in the middle of the stage. What was this turbulence he felt? All the energy of the day, the reading, the cast, the acceptance of everyone, seemed to dissolve, and he was left with what seemed to be nothing. He was helpless without Doug. Wanted him here, needed his help, his support. He was nothing without that. Was it possible? Could who he thought he was be different from who he actually was? It must be so. It must be so. He sat on the stage floor for a long time with no will to make a move. Go where? At last, he shimmied back out the window and walked slowly up the road toward the Barter Inn, lonely and terrified and excited all at the same time. It was too much. He sat on the bench in front of the Inn and tried to relax, threw his head back, and watched the clouds as they moved across the sky. It reminded him of the Loews Theater back home with the moving clouds in the ceiling. In his bed, he was wide-awake, so keyed up he would never sleep. Where was he? What was he into? Tomorrow they would start. Did he have enough to face this group of actors from New York? I will have to find the courage, and I will. He finally fell into a fitful sleep.

The morning brought an anxiety he couldn't shake until he entered the breakfast room and was greeted by the young woman who was to play his leading lady. She was warm and friendly and continued her praise so that all of last night's attack faded with the magical glow of recognition. Mitch recovered and went to work, and the play was a great success.

During the regime of dedicated work over the next year and a half, Mitch did learn some things. That living with the praise and encouragement of the director and the cast and most of all Mr. Porterfield shaped him and allowed him to grow a persona much to his liking, and this contributed to making him the leading man of the company as well as a great favorite with the audience. But every night, he fell asleep with the question, *Do I really belong?*

In the fall, Porterfield called him to his office. "Honey," he announced, barely containing himself, "you've been cast in a Hollywood movie called *Thunder Road*. And that's not all. It's starring Robert Mitchum, and it will be shot just up the road at Ashville." Porterfield almost shouted the news in his excitement.

The casting director for this film had come to see *The Rainmaker*, in which Mitch was playing the title role, and he had also brought Mitchum. Later the casting director told him that Mitchum's lone comment at the performance, after telling him to get this boy for the film, was, "Jesus, why were they all talking so loud?"

A movie, resounded through his mind, *a movie—someone wanted him to make a movie!* Twenty-three years old and he had thought he would not do anything but plays all his life, do the classics, and become a great artist.

At the Barter Theater, he had been in every play for the past two years and was all set up for the 1957 season, and here he was suddenly thinking about the Academy Awards and wondering what "a five-picture deal" would look like—not that he was even sure what a five-picture deal was. His only knowledge of Hollywood and Beverly Hills was from movies like *Sunset Boulevard* and *What Makes Sammy Run?* Malibu came to mind from the photos he had seen in magazines, and he thought that might be a fine place to live. He actually thought he would wait till he reached Los Angeles to see what kind of car he should have.

Mitch had tried to be nonchalant about it all. "Well, that seems fine with me."

Porterfield laughed. "I should think so, honey, and you can show a little enthusiasm, if you please."

So Mitch let out a yell and gave Porterfield a big hug. "I'll be damned. A movie!"

"Now wait a minute, you still have to do the winter tour when the movie's over."

Mitch was walking out behind the inn, up a rise that led to a view of the long chain of Blue Ridge Mountains. He loved this route and tried to walk it every day. As he climbed higher and higher, he had a conviction that his life was taking a right turn. Gone were the grand thoughts and aspirations to learn the great roles in the great plays. He hadn't even seen these aspirations leave. He breathed in the fresh mountain air and started to run to the top of the ridge overlooking the town and the wide valley. He then galloped down the far side and at the bottom tumbled into the lush grass and rested, staring at the sky. Then he picked himself up, straightened his jacket, and trotted back to the inn.

The trouble started the first day on the set. The company was shooting the entire film at a country store outside of Ashville, North Carolina. Mitch had a two-page scene with Mitchum that very first day. He had learned the lines before he arrived but couldn't remember them and kept running them over and over. He sweated and paced in the sandy lot behind the toilet, which for some reason was called a "honey wagon." They were shooting all up and down a closed-off county road. He had never seen so many people standing around talking, drinking coffee, and seemingly doing nothing. A young pretty girl wearing a bandana and carrying a clipboard found him and asked his name and what part he was playing. She was the assistant to the assistant to the director, a very laidback young man wearing riding boots and a Western ten-gallon hat. He sat in a tall chair most of the time and pointed in different directions after looking at his script.

Mitchum came out of his Winnebago, looking very much like a member of royalty surveying his holdings. Mitch had a sudden strong sense that he somehow knew this person intimately. Mitchum didn't exactly glow, but he certainly had an uncanny, irresistible magnetism that you could almost feel, and as Mitch was to learn, Mitchum carried this everywhere. He was the same with a lumberjack as he would have been with the queen of England. He was always himself.

As Mitchum sat in a canvas chair drinking a beer, several rough men crowded around him, and all joined in a loud laughing exchange. They looked like they had known each other a long time, and Mitch imagined that they had done many movies together. He felt a surprising longing, wondering what it would be like to join in. Robert Mitchum was clearly in charge of the film set. Everyone came and consulted with him.

Over a couple of hours, four or five men lay down what looked like railroad track, and several other men put a small jeeplike contraption on the tracks, and then others carried in a large camera and attached it to the small jeep, which they called a dolly. A cameraman climbed onto a seat so he could look through the camera, and a very large man pushed the whole thing from way out in the road to the porch and then pulled it back again. They made this move several times. Then they called the actors and did the same thing three or four more times while they spoke their lines.

A fresh sexy young girl and a younger boy with greasy hair did a scene two times with the camera. Mitch was amazed at how moved he was to hear the assistant director call, "Quiet on the set," and then the cameraman say, "Rolling," after which another man shouted, "Speed!" So quiet now that Mitch could hear birds from different directions and a tractor up the road shutting off. Then the director, almost in a whisper, said, "Action." The sweet voice of the young girl rang out, and a hundred men and women stood still and listened. Then the director called, "Cut. That was good. Let's go again." The whole scene, done twice, took five minutes, but the setup had taken two hours.

"Who's playing Jed?" Mitch heard the AD ask. He started to raise his hand, then thought better and moved toward the set to enter a completely new world. Mitchum slowly stood up, looked around, and said something to the AD, who pointed in Mitch's direction. The movie star then walked straight toward him, growing larger with each step so that Mitch felt he must be shrinking, with nothing to hold on to. Through the cracks and complexities of his short life poured all his insecurity and terror as he stood there quaking. When Mitchum reached him, Mitch found they were the same height. The star stood for a moment that seemed like an hour and finally said in his unmistakable growl, "Always remember, son, I'm Big Mitch and you're Little Mitch." Then he broke into a warm smile and a wink. "Shall we shoot this fucking thing, or would you rather rehearse?"

CHAPTER 7

Across the Great Divide
1957

THE MOVIE WAS finished. Mitch sat on the bed, looking down at the tattered suitcase his father had given him. His father. He went back to the first day he met Mitchum, when the star had covered for him by blowing his first take because he saw how tense Mitch was. This made him relax and feel better, but when Mitchum said, "Great kid," he had felt a warm glow all over and looked away, suddenly shy that this man, a star, cared about him. This was the feeling he had never had and always wanted with his father. Several others had joined in with praise, and he suddenly belonged. Now, getting up and crossing to the window, he could see the bus that was loading up, taking the crew and some of the cast to the airport.

After that first day of shooting, he had been invited to dinner and got drunk, sick, and embarrassed. But Mitchum made light of it, and almost every night after that, Big Mitch took him to dinner. He told him he had to learn how to drink. "I will teach you. Not necessarily to be able to drink like a gentleman but to master it and to enjoy it." These evenings he looked for all day. A bond seemed to be growing, and he smiled, almost not daring to think that Mitchum cared about him. Suddenly Mitch felt a terrible loss that made him grab his bag and go out and down the hall to the elevator. Many of the west coast actors in the film had told him he should go to

Hollywood. "You'll work all the time in LA," they said. Gene Barry, a veteran of many films, told him he would be foolish not to come out.

He could take the bus to Hollywood, but he had to pause about his commitment to the Barter Theater and to Mr. Porterfield. He had assured Mr. Porterfield he would come back and finish the fall season. He was to do Marc Antony in *Julius Caesar. I come to bury Caesar, not to praise him.* Stepping out of the elevator and into the lobby he went over and sat down by Tim, Mitchum's stand-in.

"You guys leaving today?" Tim didn't answer. Mitch's face flushed, and he felt more alone than he ever had. He grabbed his bag again and headed for the door just as Julius Caesar Mitchum came out of the elevator and announced to Tim he was going to drive back to Hollywood and Tim should come along. Then turning to Mitch, "I hear it's real cold around here in the winter and worse in New York. You're welcome to come with us. Nice and warm in California. Oh, yes, best to come with me to sunny Cal than go up to freezing New York."

Mitch nearly fell down, moving after him. "Yes. Yes, I'd love to come."

The Ford Motor Company had given Mitchum a Lincoln Town Car in exchange for using nothing but Fords in the picture. The sleek black vehicle sat there like a jungle animal.

At last, they were ready, put the gear in the trunk, and piled in, Big Mitch in front with Tim, Little Mitch in the back with George Fenwick, their technical advisor on all aspects of moonshine.

That first day they dropped Fenwick at his house, about thirty miles away, and he insisted they come down to his still and take a taste. After several hours of "tasting," they were all lit up pretty good. He said they'd better eat something at Millie's Rib House, and so they drove another twenty-five miles back into the North Carolina woods. No one seemed to be in a hurry, and Mitch figured at fifty miles a day it would take around two and a half months to get to Hollywood.

Mitchum told, on request, several stories of his escapades, which brought laughter all around. Soon he turned to Little Mitch and announced to the assembly, "I found this boy in a little theater in rural Virginia." Then he became very fatherly. "Little Mitch was very good, at least he talked like a human being, but he was constipated and had no shoes, so I bought him a pair of shoes and a laxative, and then I had to teach him how to drink. The night after the first day of shooting, we were out drinking and our boy here did everything wrong. He drank too fast, was drunk too soon, and then threw up all over the waitress, but under my tutelage, he's showed marked improvement since."

Far from being upset or embarrassed, Mitch basked in the attention. It was just what he'd always wanted from an older friend. His father.

Near dawn, they were put in a room with several beds. Mitch lay there in the semidarkness, thinking about the story the movie star had told about him. A story that made him feel the way he did when Doug recognized him as something more than a hole in the air. He was a breath away from believing he had earned being accepted. Even in his alcoholic stupor, he sensed something important and pitiful about this need to belong, but it faded in a moment, as did Mitch himself. The next thing he knew, a large steak-and-egg sandwich was being wafted under his nose. The breakfast Mitchum had cooked up.

"Let's go, kiddo, we're on the road." They drove for the next couple of days, often stopping to drink and eat, with Mitchum heralded wherever they went. He was nothing but gracious and generous to everyone.

Kansas is forever. Looking at the endless sky, Mitch felt a release and a joy entirely new to him. In front of them were endless flat vistas of the great American plains. A million shades of green and buff reflecting off the fields washed themselves out in the glare of the sun. Mitch fell asleep in the back seat, and the next thing he knew, Mitchum opened the door saying, "Look at this," then walked away.

Mitch slowly pulled himself up in the back seat and saw they were near the top of a long rise. Mitchum was leaning against a rock wall at the crest of the hill. Mitch walked up behind him. A huge vista opened up. On the horizon, he didn't know how many hundreds of miles away he saw a long range of ragged mountains, all white and shining in the sun. He was silent. The Rockies seemed to suddenly and dramatically rise up from out of the ground.

"Going west, there are no foothills. First time is the best." Mitch watched him walk back to the car and didn't recognize the feeling that took hold of him. Acceptance.

Driving on toward Denver, the mountains loomed taller and taller. These were anything but foothills. The next stop was going to be Vegas…at the Sahara. The marquee read "Frank Sinatra" in huge letters, and below was "Louis Prima and Keely Smith in the Lounge."

As they sat down in the luxurious coffee shop, Mitch watched several men unlike any he had seen, wearing sleek silk suits with matching tie, pocket handkerchief, socks, and white-and-black shoes. These men gathered like members of a club, pulled up chairs, and rapped about movies and Sinatra.

"Let's go." Mitchum rose, heading for the door.

"Where?"

"Los Angeles." By now, it was dark, and they stopped at a small hotel and bar on the highway several miles the other side of Vegas. Mitchum said he had to be somewhere, that he was taking the car and would be back.

They went to the bar, a quiet, dark smoke-filled lounge with a door at the backlit up by a neon "Poker" sign. A sinister-looking man shouted from across the room, "Tim, you bastard, what you doing here?"

"Oh, Jesus!" Tim said almost to himself as they walked over to the man's table. "If Bob finds out he's here, we'll never get to Los Angeles. Hello Charlie, this is Mitch Ryan, he was on the picture with Bob." Mitch recognized the man when they got closer. His square face and unmistakable deep voice were familiar to him from many films. He was also so drunk it took him several seconds to raise his glass to his mouth, hold it in front of his lips, then after a pause, take a small sip, and just as slowly put the glass down. Mitch needed a moment to find a name to match the face: Charles McGraw. He had played one of the assassins in *The Killers*.

Then that voice: "Where's Big Nuts, is he in town?"

"He went to see Frank. I'm not sure he'll be back."

They had quite a few drinks, during which Tim kept hinting that maybe McGraw should go to bed. By now Mitch didn't want to drink any more. He was getting fed up with this trip and beginning to have second thoughts about Hollywood. There was no glamor to any of this, and the fear of what might be waiting for him in Los Angeles didn't help his uneasiness. What would he do there? Where would he stay? Porterfield and Mitch's own promise to come back and work hovered in the distance. Mark Antony was a solid reality, and this dark, smelly bar was a shallow substitute.

After about an hour, Mitchum came through the door. McGraw shouted and jumped up but promptly fell across a chair. The movie star pulled him to his feet like he was a kid and gave him a big hug. "Charlie, I heard you died, but I see you're just fine. Too bad."

"Never been better. Let's get drunk and go to the Grand Canyon for breakfast." Turning to Mitch, he said, "If you've never had breakfast at the Grand Canyon, you've missed a lot."

So it went for hour upon hour. Mitch never in his short life had seen anyone drink like Charles McGraw. The more he observed from the conversation sidelines, the more disconsolate he grew. He had nothing to offer while the two veteran actors bloviated endlessly about their past. The stories, meanwhile, were getting old and strangely repetitious. It seemed like everyone who came into the bar—old stuntmen, locals, people on their way back to Los Angeles wanting a drink or a last try at the slots—stopped by their table. Some Mitchum knew, and others just swung by. The movie star told the bartender to put it all on his tab.

Mitch was wrecked. Tim said he was going to bed. It looked like they were going to spend the night. No one could drive, so the plan was to get going in the morning. The people thinned out, and the waiter brought the check. The young actor from Kentucky grabbed it and grandly announced, "I'll handle this." To pay this bar bill, Mitch felt, would restore in him a shred of confidence. The few who were left stared at him. There was a slight pause.

"You don't have to do this. We could split it." Mitchum never let anyone pay.

"I'll get it, Bob!" Mitch insisted. That was the first and only time he had called Mitchum by his first name. Mitch looked at the bill. The total at the bottom of the fourth page was $948.89.

"You want to borrow some money, kid?" Charles suppressed a laugh.

"I'll handle it," Mitch replied evenly. He had about thirteen hundred dollars from the movie. With a hundred-fifty-dollar tip, that left him with just a hundred dollars to make his fortune in Hollywood. Three mornings later in Los Angeles, he woke up and found an envelope by the bed with his name on it. There were eleven hundred-dollar bills and a note.

"When you strike it rich, take me to the Grand Canyon for breakfast. Good luck, Little Mitch, from Big Mitch. PS. 213 657 9872. This is the number of that agent I told you about, Paul Wilkins. Call him."

Mitch didn't. He spent some of the eleven hundred dollars on a bus ticket back east. He didn't say goodbye or leave a note.

CHAPTER 8

Father
1958

THE LIGHT FROM the small window behind his desk fell on the green piece of paper in front of him.

Bastian Brothers Company
Advertising Specialties
Max Abrams, President

I'm sorry, Charles, but we can't afford to keep you on salary. You're welcome to continue on commission. Come and see me on the 12th. I'll be in town for two days. I'm sorry, kiddo.

Max

Charles stood at his desk, allowing the thing to sink in, and remembered a phrase from some forgotten poem, "to care and not to care," pain and freedom at the same time. He stared at the large featureless room where he had worked for the last twenty-six years and then at a floor near the door. He never bought that rug.

He picked up his pen, sank down in his old swivel chair, and opened the middle drawer. He rooted around for his stationery among the order blanks and random notes on faded yellow paper jammed into every corner. He pushed aside a penknife, some old ink pens, a few coins, and a hefty paperweight with the American flag buried down in the crystal. He found his stationery and underneath a letter dated April 1952 from his son. He picked up the flimsy paper with that sad ambivalence he'd always felt about this boy.

"Dear Dad, it's great in Japan. It's so different and the navy is swell. I'm doing well and getting used to navy ways. I'm a gunner's mate, which is a somewhat important job."

Charles let the letter fall back into the drawer and stood up to look out the little window behind his desk. The street was empty except for one man walking up to the corner, then a car turned into Freemont Street and glided by. The sun had been out earlier, but dark clouds were coming from the west. No need to write Max back. To hell with it. He walked to the closet, stopped, looked around again, then picked his coat out of the closet. The ragged lining caught his eyes. He had always been most particular about his dress out of the necessity of the sales job, but he hadn't cared for some time now. As he looked at his face in the mirror by the door, he saw a shadow of a life. "I used to care," he muttered, put his coat on with a shrug, grabbed the raincoat, trudged down the stairs to the street, and waited for the usual bus at the corner.

On board, he sat down next to a heavyset Negro woman who held in her lap a collection of packages wrapped in brown paper. While reading her newspaper, she spoke aloud, "This country is going to the dogs, but what do you expect with a general for a president." She grumbled and shifted to allow him more room. Something about her beautiful face and dark chocolate skin relaxed him.

"It'll be okay." He had not voted for Eisenhower. "How do you know I'm not a Republican?"

"Oh, honey, you got Democrat written all over you."

"What gives it away?"

"You're riding the bus, for one thing, and you got an honest, tired face, which means you does work for a living."

"Well, I don't work for 'a living,' and I'm not a Republican or a Democrat," he replied with a tired laugh. "No, I'm now a man of leisure."

A red-faced man swung onto the bus, saw the black woman, and said, "What're you doing sitting up here, momma? Go get on back, where you belong." Charles felt heat rise to his neck. The black woman looked straight ahead. "Did you hear me?" The man's voice was louder. Charles wanted to disappear. He could feel her body like a giant rock slowly relax as she turned to the man with a sweet, gentle voice.

"The driver said it was okay, on account of it's hard for me to move, I'm so big."

"Well, I don't give a damn what the driver said, you don't belong here. Go on, move."

"You can't talk to her like that."

The man leaned into Charles. "You keep out of this if you don't want a lot of trouble."

"It's okay, mister." The woman rose and lumbered to the back.

When Charles stood to let her pass, he found he was beginning to shake with that familiar twist in his gut whenever he backed down from anything. He climbed off at the next stop even though it was a mile from his house. "Jesus, it's not right." He watched the bus grow smaller in the distance.

His breathing slowed as he walked toward home. The late afternoon was sweet and warm, smelling of rain. He was still trembling after the violence of the bus but as he walked on the calming effect of the air brought him to a quieter mood, and his shoulders sank down out of his ears. No more traveling. No more sales. Hard to believe it was over. Gone the car, gone the expense account. What would he tell Genevieve?

At Franklin Avenue, he went into Millers Drugstore and bought a fudge royal ice cream cone from the boy behind the white marble counter. Doc Miller wasn't there, thank God. He liked Doc, but since his wife had died, he had become the kind of talker you couldn't get away from. Turning into his street with the ice cream cone, Charles thought how much he loved fudge royal. He let himself smile, remembering how Mitchell loved it too.

He was walking slowly, not wanting to get home to the small house he'd shared with Genevieve for twenty-three years. What would he tell her? They lived in a simple middle-class neighborhood, where he had cultivated isolation. They both had. Perhaps that was what they had in common. For years he'd kept a garden in the small side yard, enjoying his tomatoes and the watering they needed every evening. Now the little tract was bare, and he couldn't remember how long it had been that way. Could he start a garden again, beans and maybe tomatoes? He could still do that.

Suffused with a sense of freedom he had not felt since he was a boy, he took time to marvel at the old maple trees lining the street, how much they had grown in all those years. He finished the last of the ice cream and started to play with the air, stretching his arms and pushing both hands through it, feeling the texture, drawing it into his lungs until he felt lightheaded and had to sit down on the front step of the Shanebacklers' long walk. The Shanebackler cat came down the walk and rubbed against his arm until he stroked the purring throat and felt the breath of early evening all around him.

"What brings you down our street, Charles?" He hadn't heard the approaching footsteps. Mr. Griffin, who lived in the next block, stood with an umbrella, peering down at Charles.

"Just enjoying the fading light." He hoped Griffin would move on. He had never cared for this smug man, but they had been thrown together a lot when their sons were younger. "You know it's not raining yet, George."

"I thought I felt a few drops. What an evening. Humidity! It'll rain soon." He lowered himself to the step beside Charles. "How's Mitch? I hear he's gone on the stage."

Charles took a moment to decipher "gone on the stage," after which he summoned the presence of mind to reply, "Yes, he's been playing around with acting down in Virginia at some theater. Forget the name. But no, he's looking over several universities for the fall."

"I don't know whether you've heard, but our William was accepted at the firm of Stewart and Wilkes." Now Charles understood why the man had sat down. "They're the most prestigious law firm in the Middle West. Take only the top students." Charles could hear what Griffin was saying but felt a vague pain in his chest and leaned forward.

"You all right?"

"Fine, little indigestion"—he slapped at a mosquito—"great about your boy—big job, just swell."

"Well, it's a good thing. I'm out of here before I get soaked." Over his shoulder, Griffin said, "I think William's finally going to marry Helen. We'll announce it at the party on Sunday. Did you get the invitation?"

"Not yet, maybe it came today, but you know Genevieve has not been feeling well."

He listened to the steps click on the pavement as Griffin faded away. At that moment, a misty drizzle began to fall then turned into a full summer rain. He started to stand, but before he could move, he felt a sharp sickening pain in the middle of his chest. Froze. Lowered back down. Counting his breath: one...two...three... Everything was closing down around him. The wet bricks in the walk shone like varnished artifacts. Four...five... The Shanebackler cat raced across the street to another yard. The pain was gone now, but Charles was afraid to move.

The rain came down in a cloudburst then stopped. Soaking wet, Charles left his watery tomb and slowly moved toward his own house. The rain started again in earnest. He climbed the stairs to the porch. As he reached the top step, his wife opened the door. "Charles. It's early. Why are you home?"

Charles was trying to take off his raincoat. "I left early. I was sitting on the Shanebacklers' stoop. Started to rain. Did you see the sun through the rain?" He finally shook out of his raincoat. Without a word, he walked through the door, past his wife, past the sagging sofa and the windup record player, into his room, and sank down into his old easy chair.

"Do you want some tea?" Genevieve brought him a towel.

"No."

"We have an invitation from the Griffins. A party for William."

"I know. I saw Griffin up the street. Rather be boiled in oil."

"William was Mitchell's best friend, and you will be sooner or later."

"Will be what?"

"Boiled in oil." She left and walked back to her little workroom.

For several hours he sat in the dark with only the light from the hall. He knew she wouldn't disturb him, too busy with her endless writing. Not that he minded. She stayed away from him, and he did the same with her. In the half-light, he could still see the picture of the happy young couple on his desk, taken before their marriage twenty-six years ago.

These two people were strangers to him. What will we do for money? What will I tell Gen? He picked up his drawing pad and a pencil from the table and made a pass—black line on white paper. He stared at the paper then drew a face with Negro features.

CHAPTER 9

New York
1958

THE GREYHOUND BUS becomes his home. Mitch couldn't remember what day it was. Maybe he had finally stopped punishing himself for being the jerk he had been, catching that last-minute drive to California. A narrow escape. He didn't fit there. He belonged in the theater. By the time the bus reached Memphis, he knew he would have to make up his mind where to go. He could go back to the Barter Theater in Virginia but not to see his mother or father. He couldn't bear their judgmental silences.

In Nashville, he opted to take the bus to New York. He knew from the Barter Company that New York was the center of the theater world in the United States, and he needed the theater after the depressing road trip to LA. He cringed at the thought that all he had done was drink his way across the country.

With his new resolve, he planned to go to New York and then return to Barter for the fall tour. To celebrate his renewed dedication to the art of acting, he bought a beautiful scarf at a shop in the Nashville bus station. He flung it around his neck and let it drape down over his corduroy coat, making him feel very much the image of a portrait he had seen of the great nineteenth-century actor Edmond Kean. He paid eighteen dollars for this bright symbol and carefully counted what was left of his money: $173.

He arrived late on a Tuesday night, called the number he had been given and was told where to show up. He walked up Eighth Avenue to Forty-Seventh Street, turned east, and there at the end of the block saw a great shimmering nimbus of light that shot up and covered all the low-hanging clouds and flooded down again to fill the street. Behind him, Eighth Avenue was dark and gloomy compared with what lay before him. The light came from Times Square. He moved toward the light. Passing the marquee of the Ethel Barrymore Theater, he saw "Night of the Auk" in three-foot-high letters and announcing that Claude Rains was starring.

At Broadway, he stood with his ratty suitcase and paper bag full of dirty laundry, stunned at the life in the street. Pedestrians sped by, propelled by the kind of energy he longed to experience. Amid the profusion of the lights were restaurants with people coming and going, taxis honking, jammed together in a yellow river. Moving up Broadway to Forty-Ninth, he passed another theater, the Edwin Forrest, then continued up to Fifty-Third and back over to Eighth and past the Broadway Theater. On this marquee was "My Fair Lady" with Rex Harrison and Julie Andrews, stars of the legitimate theater.

He ran across Eighth and then back down to Forty-Seventh to the address he had been given and rang the bell. His host was Frank Lowe, whose roommate John, it appeared, had just arrived. Mitch was impressed when he learned that John was an actor in a play on Broadway. They told him he could bunk in the big living room. That seemed fine to Mitch. Then they tried to outdo each other telling him everything anyone would ever want to know about New York.

Mitch was inclined to go out and walk some more through the theater district, but his new friends were reluctant to release him from their stream of pointers and opinions. So early in the morning before either of them was up, he wrote a letter to Mr. Porterfield asking if he could borrow two hundred dollars and assuring him he would do a bus-and-truck tour sometime that winter. Then he headed out.

Through Times Square, he came to Shubert Alley and the Music Box, the Imperial, the Broadhurst, the Golden, the Shubert, and finally the Booth Theater, smaller than the others and looking like it had been there forever. Mitch was almost dizzy at the flood of images that came to him as he stood there in front of that legendary venue.

He pictured Doug sitting in Cunningham's years before, holding court to anyone who would listen. "In the two centuries before this one, the great actors did all the great parts until they died." Then Doug would pound on the table. "There were no distractions, no movies, no goddamn TV, only the power of the theater. The actors even had their own theaters. The great Edwin Booth would play in New York for months and then go on the road. All the big cities. Small ones too. That's impossible today, but the theaters are still there." Doug would spin out the names and deeds of all the greats: Booth, the greatest. Kean, Jefferson, Irving, Ellen Terry, Duse, Forrest, Sarah Bernhardt—all immortal. John Barrymore in this century, not forty years ago, played Hamlet. But the theater is not the same, yet it's good enough for you, Mitch. And he would name the names. Some Mitch knew and others he didn't, but that didn't matter. Doug had driven his passion into Mitch's heart, and now here he was, standing in front of the Booth, knowing with every breath he took that this was where he wanted most fiercely to belong. Only one day here, and already he knew he would do anything to stay, to work. He wanted to be a great actor. I can be a great actor."

When the money came from Mr. Porterfield, he found a place on Thompson Street, a walk-up apartment sharing a toilet in the hall at twenty dollars a month. Sitting on a milk carton in his Thompson Street palace and watching the cockroaches flitting around the walls dampened the euphoria a bit. When he went to the one window and tried to clear the smudge from the pane, he looked out on a crumbling brick wall maybe five feet away. The only way to see what was happening at ground level was to open the window, but that proved impossible. He surveyed the gloomy room and then, with a grand movement, swept up his new scarf, threw it around his neck, and marched out the door declaiming, "Once more unto the breach."

The subway entrance was right at the corner. He heard the noise of the train down the dark tunnel and a blast of wind, then it thundered into the station like nothing he had ever experienced. The sign in the window read, "RTD Coney Island." They clicked along for a long time, people pushing in and out, and then the train rose up out of the tunnel to an elevated bridge, with the Atlantic Ocean stretching into the distance. He was suddenly back in Chicago with his mother and father and baby sister, vacationing years ago, riding on a train above Chicago's downtown loop with a view of Lake Michigan. Now the ocean's reflection of the morning sun brought back that day, sitting on his father's lap, and wondering at the large body of water. He had not remembered that happy feeling in years.

He stood up, balancing in the jostling train, and walked to the end of the car. He wiped his eyes and leaned against the door. The train stopped, and he ran out of the car to the far end of the platform. When he recovered, he walked down the stairs to the boardwalk, watching his step.

He felt the wind getting stronger, and the sand flitted at his face as he sat on a bench, trying not to dwell on what was lost forever. He gulped in the fresh salt air as two old Jewish men wearing heavy coats walked over and sat on the same large bench as if he weren't there. He listened to the rhythm of their conversation, not understanding half of what they said, as if he were in a foreign country. *Well*, he thought, *I am in a foreign country, that's for sure. No one knows me. But they will!*

In due time he found the actor hangouts, got a line on the tear-off sheets that told what acting jobs were casting, and began to make the rounds as best as he could figure them out. He searched out Downey's, a bar on Eighth Avenue that actors frequented, and stood in the little entranceway looking at the glamorous, happily noisy crowd until a young man came up and said, "You going to eat or drink at the bar?" The bar was to the left, all dark wood and three people deep. He glanced at the menu. Way out of his price range.

The man on the door, watching him, said, "Gilholey's down the block has a cheap glass of beer, and you could sit all afternoon."

Mitch was humbled and grateful for the man's kindness. "Thank you."

A new life was happening fast. The days swept past him, exciting, unsettling, and exhilarating. He loved sitting in Gilholey's and listening to actors trying to top each other with stories. He met an actor drinking there who told him to see an agent named Archer

King. Mitch looked him up in the Yellow Pages, and when he walked into Archer's reception area, he could hear a man through an open door on the opposite wall singing, "I got the son in the morning and his dad at night." Mitch relaxed and sang at the top of his voice. "Gotta dance…gotta dance, gotta dance."

Archer was a jumpy fellow, always moving, always talking. He popped out of his office. "Gene," he said to Mitch, "I'm glad you're here. I've got a great idea for your next picture: you're an American painter in Paris, you fall in love with a French girl, give up painting— you were lousy at it anyway—and take up singing and dancing. I'm Archer King, your new agent."

This man, King, had a great heart and loved actors. He represented mostly men, all good actors. Right away, he got Mitch a reading for a play *Whisper to Me*, by a Southern writer, Greer Johnson, and starring a wonderful actress who was also Archer's client.

The reading was at the Provincetown Playhouse, where Eugene O'Neill did his sea plays, a fabled place that was at the heart of the off-Broadway movement of little theaters all around Greenwich Village. The O'Neill shrine was small and reminded Mitch a little of the Carriage House Theater in Louisville. He stood just inside the entrance, overtaken by a silence tinged with an awe akin to a prayer. Eugene O'Neill had worked here, his plays first seen here.

Six or seven actors all around his age were milling about. One of them walked over to Mitch. "You'd better sign in, and the sides are on the table." He pointed toward the end of the room. Mitch had no idea what sides were, but he saw that they were dialogue from the play. One scene. He looked them over and read to himself several times till he began to sense a direction. More actors came in, and slowly the six ahead of him finished, and he was called into the small theater. He read. A tall, elegant man walked up very close to him and in a quiet voice said, "Could you be a little more sultry? Remember, he's a Southern man-boy and vain about his body. Give it another try. Mitch, is it?"

He read again and was more comfortable. Then the director said thank you, and Mitch felt he must not have been interested. When he didn't hear anything for two days, he figured that was that.

Then the phone rang. The voice of Archer King. "You got the part—you're on your way. Congrats!"

Mitch put the phone down and walked to the window, stared at the brick wall, regained control, then moved back and picked up the black receiver, "Well, it's about time. I've been in town two months."

"Listen, you young jerk, this does not ever happen. Count your lucky stars!" Archer was almost shouting. "Come to the office in the morning, and I'll take you to breakfast." Thus began his long relationship with Archer King.

CHAPTER 10

Mother
1958

GENEVIEVE LOOKED DOWN at the letter on her desk: "Your style is fine, and it's a worthy piece, but not for our publication." She had received letters like this many times. They always brought with them a renewed sense of determination, but today there was a difference. She opened the cabinet, saw the large file of rejections, and with a weary sigh buried this one with the others.

July. The heat left her in a stupor all through the middle of the day. Now, at five o'clock, she sat down with her iced coffee and biscuit in the only place in the small house on Ingle Avenue that really suited her. Next to the bedroom, a little alcove had been added some years back, meant to be a dressing room, now her dressing room, only ten feet square. Windows had been installed on three sides by a well-meaning Charles. It was difficult for he was no carpenter and complained all the time, but she was grateful, nonetheless. She could close the blinds and feel protected and safe, or open them when she was feeling expansive and wanted to let in the light.

Almost every time she looked at the small bookcase attached to the back of her desk, she thought of her father. Originally it had been built by him, for his rare-book collection and his three volumes of Shakespeare, out of red oak with three inlaid shelves and an elegantly carved lip at the top on which he had carved: "To Thine Own Self

Be True." It arrived from the farm with Genevieve's loving care. The Royal typewriter sat in the middle of the desk with sheaves of paper stacked on each side, clean to the left, typed to the right. In-between her desk and a bookcase made from cinder blocks and oak planks was her Morris chair, where she sat with her hot coffee every morning and her iced coffee in the afternoon. Here she worked and here she sat.

Since Charles had been let go from his job, he seldom left the house. Their two children were gone. Daughter Maggie had married and moved to New York. And they had received a card from California some months before saying that Mitch was moving to New York. That had been his only communication for at least a year.

As evening moved in, there was still no sign of cooling. Today's rejection letter did not drive her back to the typewriter. She sat and stared at the machine. Lately she had a frightening suspicion that her work was no good or, worse, that all her creative life was mediocre and had no meaning. For thirty years, she had believed the short, simple episodes of life and the journals of her travels telling a story of gentle thoughts and plain actions belonging to ordinary people meant something. But what was the use? What was the reason for all her aspirations? Who cares about ordinary people and the stupid way they live? The publishers were right.

She picked up her coffee then put it down. With her spoon, she took a huge vengeful bite of the blackberry preserves her daughter had brought her from New York. Delicious. She took another. *Fat. Fat! Fat! I don't care. Damn. Must get my mind clear.* Maggie had visited from New York and left only yesterday. Genevieve had found, to no surprise, that there was nothing much between them and felt relief when at last her daughter departed.

She wandered to the window and watched the lowering clouds. Rain will cool everything down. Maybe I should be more receptive toward Maggie, Genevieve scolded herself. At least she makes an effort, nothing from Mitchie. She smiled at what she used to call him. "Baby Mitchie." Baby Mitchie!

The rain came, a light drizzle. She took her glass and what was left of her biscuit into the kitchen, stood at the back door, and watched the sun streak through the clouds, sending golden shadows across the yard. She reached into the pocket of her apron to get a cigarette and inhaled deeply.

Genevieve needed to talk to someone but saw no point in talking with Charles in his room down the hall. They hardly spoke. He mainly sat doing nothing. She knew he was depressed. She had tried to get him to paint, knowing how he had lived to paint at one time. He would tell her, "It's nothing." They would argue, and finally she gave up.

Well, back to work. Working will help my mood. In her little cell, she looked at the paper in the typewriter: "Chapter 12, 1933: First Year of Marriage." When they had first met at the Cincinnati library, Charles was sweet and wonderfully charming. She pulled down a large black album from the top of the bookcase and laid it on her lap. With that feeling of going back to better times, she opened the heavy cover. On the first page was a smiling young Charles standing beside her, a large sign behind them that read, "Mammoth Cave," and on the page handwritten in ink the word "Honeymoon." In the photograph, she was wearing her reddish synthetic fur coat, and he a suit, tie, and hat.

Whatever happened to that coat? She had loved that coat Charles had found for her. She put the book away. She looked down at the typewriter. As she slumped in the chair, she hit the keyboard one key at a time, harder each hit and harder until she was pounding on the poor old machine. She pulled her hand back, then up to her mouth, then gently touched the keyboard. *I love this.*

A cloudburst landing on the tin roof made her jump and shook her out of her reverie. She watched through the little window behind her desk the glittering silver mist gather around the two acacia trees in the side yard. The rain was majestic. She loved the rain. It didn't relieve the heat, though, more oppressive now, her blouse sticking to her. She took it off, drooping breasts through the camisole. She had always been proud of her breasts and always knew her face was plain. "You have beautiful hair," had been the bane of her youth.

She heard the telephone. Who could that be? Walking down the hall, she tried to remember the last time someone had called. "Hello," she echoed into the heavy black receiver.

"Aunt Gen, it's Chucky. Is Uncle Charles there?"

"I'll get him." She went to the study. "It's your brother's boy."

Charles walked to the phone. "What happened to your shirt?"

"The heat."

"Pretty racy."

"Didn't think you cared."

She watched from down the hall as he listened for a moment and then brought the receiver down to his side. He held his arm there, but she couldn't read what he was feeling. She heard a voice from the phone but couldn't understand what was being said. Finally Charles raised the phone. "I'm here, Liam...Are you all right?"

Genevieve watched. Charles waited and then said, "I'd like to come. Thank you, but I'll pay for the plane if I do. I think Gen will come too. Mitch is in New York. I'll tell him. Do you need anything?... Goodbye, Liam."

Charles put down the receiver, walked back to his room, and sat in his chair. Genevieve came to the door.

"Molly died."

She watched his face. "Poor Liam."

"He wants us to come to New York."

"With what? Sell the house for tickets?"

"He offered to pay."

"Well, I'm not going."

"Neither am I."

"Maybe you should. It's your brother...You were devoted to Molly."

Charles raised his head and stared at her. She turned to leave. He reached for his drawing pad. "Gen?" Something in his voice stopped her at the door.

"What?"

"Nothing."

"What?"

"Stay awhile."

She turned back, touched her hair. Charles looked down and picked up his drawing pad again. "It's a long time since we read any poetry."

"A long time."

"Shall I read some?"

"Not now…maybe later." She left.

He sat alone in the dark, his eyes wet.

In her room, Genevieve sat on the bed and lit another cigarette.

I wonder if he knows that I knew about him and Molly?

CHAPTER 11

Live Television
1959

NOTHING HAD PREPARED Mitch for what he saw that night. One evening during rehearsals for *Whisper to Me*, he had gone to see *Children of Darkness* at the Circle in the Square. When the play ended, he had to take a good while before moving again. Standing in front of the theater, he did not know what to do. Just then, the leading actor, George Scott, came out of a side door with several others and headed across the street. Mitch was caught between wanting to run to him to say something and being paralyzed with fear. Walking back to Thompson Street, he stopped every block or so, trying to puzzle out what Scott had done to bring this play about prison life during the French Revolution so stunningly alive.

Scott, in white makeup and black wig, had played a sinister lord who bought and sold people, had totally dominated both stage and audience. Mitch wondered just what magic had set this actor's performance apart from anything he had ever seen. For one thing, he had a terrifying voice: "Stop!" Mitch shouted, echoing a line from the play. "Don't touch that."

His senses charged, he started to obsess about himself—what people might someday say about his own greatness, whether he, too, might move an audience that way. "Stop. Don't touch that!" He stood stuck in an attitude under a streetlamp and tried to remember another line…Yes! "Death is nothing." Then again, with more volume: "Stop, don't touch that! Death is nothing."

"Death is everything, I've been told," came a voice from the dark across the street. "Think it over, sonny, before you try anything desperate." Mitch jumped. A tingle shot down his spine. He turned to the voice but could see nothing. He looked up in a panic. There was just the dark swirl of the midnight fog. He was alone in a dark street—no people, no cars, just black buildings, vacant warehouses, and silence. In the immense emptiness, there was something otherworldly about that voice. He had a sense that nothing was real, that everything was an illusion.

He steeled himself. "Death is nothing," he announced again. This time no answer, just a faint echo, and then in an instant, he moved off down Sullivan Street and turned left on Bleaker and then to Thompson. *Is this all an illusion, a life in the theater? Am I giving my life over to a paper-thin art form, saying someone else's words? What am I? Nothing? No more than a fluke.* But Scott was no fluke. "Stop, don't touch that. Death is nothing." He moved on the balls of his feet, sweeping down the street like a dancer or a musketeer getting ready to fence.

At home, he took an apple, lay on his single bed, and thought with joy about the power of acting. The words might be someone else's, but the life was in the body electric of the actor. He found himself calculating what parts he could play with white makeup and a black wig. There was no sleep. About three in the morning, the illumination came to him that the power and greatness of George Scott was the engine that was driving him. "Stop, don't touch that." And then, "Death is nothing." He lay there until a faint glow of light told him that morning had come again to save him.

Rehearsing the play took on a different tone. Although the actors were good, the process seemed flat compared with what he had witnessed. He found he was bringing some of Scott's mannerisms into the rehearsals until the director said for him to tone it down a little.

After they opened to not very good reviews, Archer arranged an audition for *The United States Steel Hour*: a live television play starring George C. Scott, the very actor he could not stop thinking about! He almost ran to Archer's to get the script, then bolted into Central Park and read it over.

At the audition, he recognized several actors from film and television. Still, he thought, I can only do my best. He read and thought he did all right. The director didn't even look up. He got the part. Archer was flabbergasted.

On the first day of rehearsal, Mitch was early and waited by the door while the others filed in, greeting each other like old friends. They took their places at a large table, but no Scott. Mitch still waited at the door. Then Scott breezed past him without a glance, strode to the table, and took his seat after giving the leading actress a warm hug and shaking hands with the director. Mitch found the only place left, right across from him. He was about to say something, maybe about *Children of Darkness*, but just then, the director said, "Let's start," and Mitch missed his chance. The few scenes he had with Scott made him feel as if he had to hold on to something or else be blown away.

Live television rehearsed for two weeks. In this case, rehearsals were downtown at a studio above Ratner's, a legendary Jewish dairy restaurant on Second Avenue. During that time, Mitch continued showing up for his play at night. The day before the airing the company moved to the ABC network studio on Broadway in the sixties. When they moved uptown to ABC, Mitch was totally lost. A TV studio is nothing like the theater. Moving from one set to the other with the assistant director timing the actors to make the action work for live TV was unnerving. This had nothing to do with theater. The cameramen were the gods, bossing everyone around.

Every time they went through a scene, Scott added another layer, his choices always a surprise. Mitch was challenged and noticed he was more nervous with George Scott than he had been with the Mitchum who'd driven him to California.

The director paid little attention to Mitch, who learned from the crew that this man was not popular and would fly off the handle now and then. "Move to your right. No, your other right. If you want to be in this shot, you'd better get over by the door." Mitch had been loose and relaxed downtown but not here. They had two days, one for camera blocking and the next for technical rehearsal, dress rehearsal, and then the show.

The first day they started at seven in the morning, and after ten hours, he realized with terror it was five o'clock and they were only halfway through. He had to get downtown to do the play. It had never dawned on him there would be a problem, and he suddenly realized there might be one the next night too. He went to the assistant director.

"Why the hell didn't you tell me?" the AD yelled, giving him a piercing look before stomping off to get the director.

"He can't fucking leave. Fuck his play." The director threw his script and kicked his chair. "They must have a fucking understudy!" Then he shouted across the stage at Mitch, "What the fuck did you think you were doing? Goddamn it, kid, get on the phone and tell them you're not coming."

The director flung himself back to his chair. The cameramen, all five, left their cameras and went to the coffee table. Around the set, the crew and actors stood very still, looking anywhere. Silence. Mitch, feeling the heat spike through his body, awkwardly stalked toward the exit door to the studio. "Bullshit."

He was pushed to the side. Scott himself was rasping in his ear, "Knock it off," and whisked him into his dressing room and threw him on the sofa. "Stay here and don't come out." Scott left. Mitch sat.

Scott came back, poured Mitch a drink of whiskey, and sat down, laughing. "Don't worry. Everyone is on your side. I've known this director for a long time. He can't help it. He doesn't handle shock well. He will talk to you when he calms down. Do you have an understudy?"

"Yes, but he's not very good."

The older actor stared at him for a moment. "Are you?"

There was nothing to say when George Scott asked a question like that. Right then, Mitch realized there was a price for being in the theater. He wanted to quit, and at the same, he wanted to be great. Scott pushed the phone at him. "Call and tell them the story. It will be fine. When we start again, swallow it, and go about your work. I know everyone else will do the same." He left.

Mitch called the theater. The director of the play was upset, and Mitch kept saying, "I'm sorry," then he told him about tomorrow night. *Goddamn, Mitch, what the hell will we do?* He cursed some more, but finally, what could he do?

When Mitch went out to finish the camera blocking, everything was just as Scott had said it would be. Nothing happened. The director blocked the rest of the show and gave him several directions in a normal voice.

The next day was worse than a nightmare. Doors broke, guns didn't fire, props were lost, and lines were missed. He forgot where he was at one point and earned a string of curses from the booth. Five cameras covered the sets. He thought a scene with Scott was going well when he heard, "Cut!" Cables to the cameras were fouled. As the dress rehearsal went on, there was more noise offstage than on. The director came roaring down, screaming at everyone.

The chaos ended at seven, with two hours until the program went live to all America—the longest two hours of Mitch's life. How would this ever work? No one seemed prepared. He could feel the anxiety and tension of the set through the dressing room door. The thought of leaving his room to get a drink of water was unbearable. There was a knock on the door. The director.

"Come out a moment."

Mitch took a deep breath, pretty sure he couldn't be fired at this late hour and stepped out. They took each other in for a moment. Mitch was trying to get the nerve to say he was sorry when the director spoke. "You're doing a great job. I wanted to know. Also, kid, you stick with this, and you'll have a very good career."

Mitch watched him walk away to the booth and felt himself relax. "I'm really sorry about yesterday," he called to the retreating figure.

"It's nothing."

At that moment, the floor director called, "Places, please."

Waiting on the set for the play to start, Mitch felt that powerful beginning of an explosion when a human being is being pushed into a high risk that feels like life or death, even if he knows it's only a play.

Then Scott came onto the set and stood looking at Mitch, as calm as if it were just another day. "Good luck, Mitch. Let's have a hell of a show."

When the AD hit Scott with the countdown and waved signal, and the red light stayed on the camera, and Scott barked his first line, the miracle happened. Mitch relaxed and did the part. He had always been amazed when this happened, ever since that first night, in his first play, *Bus Stop*.

When it was over, he felt as if he'd come through a war. Everyone was talking at the top of their voices and laughing.

Mitch saw Scott leaving and, fearing he might never see him again, ran over and blurted out, "You were great in *Children of Darkness.*"

The actor turned and didn't speak. He broke into a crooked grin and clapped Mitch on the arm. "We'll do a play one of these days." Then he walked out the door and onto Sixty-Sixth Street into the world of the audience.

A week later Mitch's sister called to tell him his father had had a serious heart attack and he needed to come home to Louisville.

CHAPTER 12

Death
1959

GENEVIEVE LED THE way up the steps of the small frame house, turned, and watched Charles follow, step by step by step, until he reached the porch and sank into his rocking chair. Frail body hunched over, arms folded on his lap, he tried to rock, gave up, looked out into the night at a nearly full moon, and listened to the duet of locusts and crickets, one chop-chop, the other click-clicking.

The air was soft as velvet to Charles as he sat on his front porch. The fireflies in the side yard gave everything a special depth, like an outdoor Cincinnati beer garden he'd once visited. He knew he was forever complaining about what life had dealt him, but tonight he was grateful to be alive. He loved his yard, green and lush most of the year, and now, tonight, this one night... Well, maybe this is what life is about, being alive with the locusts and crickets and fireflies and the warm air. Just to be alive.

He was weak and surprised that the doctors had released him from the hospital. After a massive heart attack, you'd think they would want him around. He had insurance. Oh, well, doctors... He looked at the rotting top porch step. Should get that fixed. Maybe do it himself? He shouldn't have quit selling. Downhill after that. He missed driving from town to town. Not the people so much, but the lonely two-lane blacktop roads, the old broken barns, rolling farms, and the sleepy hamlets that always featured a welcoming tavern or two.

Back in the kitchen, Genevieve took a glass of cold water out of the refrigerator. Why had they let him go from the hospital after only four days? The doctor said he was fine and would do better at home, but Genevieve felt it was because they only wanted the bed. The terrible experience that night, before the police came, when she'd found him lying on the floor face down. At first, she thought he was dead, but then he gagged and threw up. She had called the emergency police, cleaned up the mess, and held him until they came. And now, after four days, they send him home. Well, doctors are supposed to know. "Do you want anything, Charles?" Genevieve looked through the screen door.

"No, I'm fine. Come out and sit with me."

She made her way out and sat down on the top step where light from the streetlamp fell over the porch. He studied her. She was putting on a little weight, and the thick red hair was streaked with gray. "Come and sit here." He indicated the other chair.

"This is fine. How do you feel?"

"I think I feel better." He put his hand on his chest.

She leaned back on her elbows. Charles tried to rock, and the chair moved a small squeak. They sat. Charles leaned toward her. "It's nice out, not too humid, wisteria's full a little early." He looked at her face in the dim light, hoping she would look toward him. "Hear the loon?"

She looked out through the blue-gray light dotted with thousands of fireflies and listened to the slow scratch of his rocker. She lit a cigarette. "Mitchie should be here sometime tonight. It's what Maggie told me on Friday when she left."

Charles took a careful breath, squinting at his wife's smoke. "He's twenty-seven years old. I would think you could stop calling him Mitchie."

"He had a ride part of the way and then was going to take the bus. I think he told Maggie he would be here by Tuesday." All that could be heard were the noises of the night and the silence in the distance between them. "He was doing a play and couldn't leave until

Monday morning. 'The show must go on,' they say," and she gave a chuckle with a hint of hysteria.

"Don't smoke around me."

"Sorry." She didn't stop but instead pulled herself up and went down to the gate and looked out at the night. "I thought you were dead."

He stopped rocking. She came back to the stoop. They sat there with the light from the streetlamp falling across the porch. He could only see her profile. After a while, "It was a good thing you came home, or else I would have been a goner." He breathed a strained sigh. "When was Mitch here last, two years? Three?" Charles fighting for breath was more upset with his condition than not remembering when his son had been there.

She waved the cigarette at the bugs. "Damn mosquitoes. You ever wonder why he took up acting? 'Course, he would be artistic coming from my family. My father was something of a poet and could have been a good actor. He always recited Shakespeare around the house and knew all the famous speeches." A light breeze lifted a few strands of her hair.

Charles grunted, "Yes, yes, we know, we know."

She rose again to go down and lean on the front gate. "He was tall and very good-looking."

"I thought your father was a drunk."

"And died fifty years ago, and not from drink! Don't worry, Charles, Mitchell got your handsome features and my father's height."

They both turned to the loud hoot of the Ohio Valley loon. "He's telling us to shut up." Charles slowly creaked up and stood there on uncertain legs. "From Mitch's letters, it sounds like the boy is doing well. I think I'll try to walk to the corner."

"Is that a good idea?"

* * *

Mitchell smelled the endless gas fumes again as he boarded the Greyhound bus. He unloaded at Pittsburgh, the first leg of the trip back to Louisville. All the endless bus trips during his life came back, starting with the cross-country trip from California, leaving the navy. Remembering the stop in the Great Lakes brig was the standout. Ah! The Greyhound bus!

The phone call from his sister: "Dad had a terrible heart attack. Mom wants us to come home."

"Is he okay?"

"He's alive. The doctor said he might not recover."

Louisville was the last place in the world he wanted to go, whether his father was dying or not. There was that vague feeling he had about his father. A wasted life? He thought of his own as he tossed and stretched most of the way on another bus trip that would take forever.

The daylight was fading as Mitch left the Greyhound to take the city bus to Crescent Heights. Then he walked down through the darkening streets toward the house. He watched the familiar swarm of beetles and moths around the streetlights, all diving and chirping like a crazed army of creatures from outer space. He walked slowly, his body relaxing, marveling at his old friends the maples that lined the street.

Five years since he had been home, but it seemed longer. He sat down on the front step of the Shanebacklers' long walk and looked up through the trees. A marmalade cat came down the walk and rubbed against his arm. His mother had had a marmalade cat when he was a boy. Feeling…feeling. He could have let himself go and indulge in this feeling of loss. Instead, he lay back, brought the cat onto his chest, and held on to the nervous animal until it howled and he let go. At last, he stood and walked on.

He stopped again in the alley that ran down along the yard of his house. He could see his parents across the side yard, sitting on the front porch. He waited. His dad was in his rocking chair, his mother on the step. Who were these two people? He fished out and lit a cigarette and thought about leaving. At that moment, his dad rose slowly and walked down the stairs, out the gate, toward where Mitch stood in the shadows. His mother sat on the top step and watched. Should he run? The son waited. He didn't think his father could see him as he barely shuffled forward. The last time he was here, his father had seemed hale and strong. They had had several arguments, and he left before intended. All he could remember about his life in this house was arguing. When Charles came to the corner of the alley, he stopped, looked at his son, and smiled. Mitch thought for a moment he was looking at an old man, a human being heading toward death. Then the old man's smile faded, and he became Mitch's father.

"Hi, Dad. You can't be too bad, up and walking around. Maggie told me Mom said you were 'near death' in the hospital."

"Well, you know your mother. She was just hoping. I'm surprised you came. What are you doing in the alley?"

"I think I'll walk up to Miller's and get some cigarettes. Be right back, unless you want to come."

"Let's see how I do, son." Mitch hadn't heard "son" for a long time. Once upon a time, the word would have meant something. They walked on to the corner and turned up Cannons Lane toward Miller's Drug. He looked back to see his mother watching from the porch. Neither of them spoke. The shuffle of Charles on the sidewalk was the only noise. Mitch, staying beside him, felt like a giant. When they reached the store, Charles fell onto the bench by the door. "Get me a lime Popsicle."

"Not fudge royal?"

"Doctor said no ice cream."

Mitch went in. There was Mr. Miller behind the counter. Everything the same as when he was a boy—the dingy mirror behind him, the little wooden half door to the pharmacy, all the drugstore items stacked on one side of the room and women's cosmetics all down the other. Mr. Miller even looked the same, wearing the same shirt and green celluloid visor. "Mitchell, you're home! My goodness, it's wonderful to see you." Mitch remembered he always spoke in superlative clichés.

"Yes, it's nice to be home," he said, sounding like a line from a bad movie. "Could I have a pack of Camels and a lime Popsicle?"

"How are your folks? I know your dad's in the hospital."

"No, he's out. Must be okay, the Popsicle's for him. He's on the bench."

"He's okay? That's wonderful." Another bad movie line from Mr. Miller this time.

Mitch came out with the cigarettes and sat down next to his father, who took the Popsicle and began to struggle with the wrapper. "Let me help, Dad."

"I got it." Mitch turned away. At that moment, they both knew why there was such a divide between them. They looked out across the street and the railroad tracks beyond to a sparse stand of trees. "All gone now. Remember the big woods when we first moved here? Look at it now."

"I don't remember much of those early years. Isn't that strange? Why would I?"

"Tell me what you've been up to. I understand that show business is a tough way to go." Then, flinging away the popsicle wrapper, his father asked, "How come we never hear from you?"

"I write from time to time."

"Christmas. You got some kind of a backup job to take care of things?"

Mitch walked out to the road, still looking to the woods. "I do remember when I ran away to those woods, and you called the cops."

"I would never call the police. It's not in my nature."

Mitch stared at him. "Dad, how bad is your condition? Five years ago, you seemed young for your age. Now you're having trouble walking."

"I'm not dead yet." Mitch sat at the end of the bench. "Just a clogged artery. I need to rest and learn to eat right is all, and neither will be easy with your mother." He struggled closer to his son on the bench. "The reason I asked you about a job and money is because sometimes…" He was trying to get his thoughts in order, and then he stammered on, "Just making ends meet can keep you from going after what you really want." He stopped and half-heartedly sucked on the Popsicle. "I wanted to be a painter at one time…" He stopped again. "Loved to paint, still do, something about the smell of linseed oil and turpentine… Well, it just didn't work out that way. Money… had to…money." He was having trouble breathing.

"I know what I want, Dad." Mitch stood up. "This is hardly the time for advice. Let's go back. I think you need to be in bed."

Charles looked away, and they waited alone in front of the hissing neon sign in the drugstore window. Finally Charles, barely audible, said, "Go ahead and see your mother. I'll be there in a minute."

"Don't you think I should stay with you?"

"No! Go, god damn it."

Mitch backed up and moved away.

Later, after his father had fallen asleep in the living room, his mother sat by the fire. Mitch listened to the click of her knitting needles and recognized the old look of rage on his mother's face. But now there was also fear. Her hands trembled as she fumbled with the yarn. "What am I going to do when your—"

"I'll help you, Mother. Anyway, he's not going to die."

"You'll help? When did you ever help?" She twisted the needles in her lap. "Nothing. You have done nothing to help this house. Ever! Your father worked at that rotten job for twenty-seven years. Then what? They let him go, fired him, and what did you do? You left town without a word. You're too self-centered to work. All you do is play around with this theater business. You failed in school, and they threw you out of the navy." She began to cry.

"Mother, I had to get to that job in Richmond, that's why I left so fast." He leaned on the mantle and looked down into the small grate, now black and empty. "I called and wrote the next week. You're not being fair."

"Fair! Nothing is fair. You think life is fair? Life's hard and stupid, and people are hard and stupid. If you won't stay and help, it's better if you don't come around."

He went out and slammed the door. The wind caught the screen door with a loud smack.

"What was that?" Charles shook awake from his chair by the fireplace.

"Mitchell. He said he'd be back. Are you hungry?"

"No. Think I'll go to bed."

Charles took a long time to get undressed and into his pajamas. Everything came off with great effort. Genevieve wanted to help, but he wouldn't let her. She brushed her hair and lay down on the bed, waiting.

"I hope Mitch does well." He fell back on the bed. "People like him…he's so friendly. Everyone likes him. He's a good boy. Jesus, I'm tired. I was never liked much." Tired.

"You shouldn't have gone on that walk."

"It's out of my hands. The boy will do what he has to, I suppose. Whatever he ends up doing, I hope he sticks it out. I wish to God I'd stayed with…" There was a long silence.

"Good night, Charles." She turned off the light.

He looked over at her face, soft in the light from the street, and wanted to tell his wife he loved her. The grip of fear took him, the thought of life seeping away. *That time of year thou mayst in me behold / When yellow leaves, or none, or few, do hang / Upon those boughs which shake against the cold, / Bare ruined choirs, where late the sweet birds sang."* What would we do?

She opened her eyes. "Was that Shakespeare?" He was asleep.

Mitch went to Shelly's Bar and Grill at the corner. It'd been a fixture since he was a kid. Old man Shelly was now dead, but his son ran the place. Still the same, same smell and dingy lamps with red shades on every table. Nothing ever changes. He had several drinks but didn't want to get drunk, so he went for a walk around the old neighborhood. When he was sure his parents would be asleep, he returned to the house, crept to the sofa, and tried to sleep himself.

Genevieve awoke. Low moans, then a long exhale of breath. Charles moved slightly, then was still. The darkness was profound. Genevieve lay as quietly as she could ever remember, waiting for the next breath. It never came. In the silence, not allowing the possibility that he was dead to enter her mind, she heard the old house creaking and the wind rattling the windows. Those were the only sounds. Then suddenly she struck out at him, pushing him off the bed. "Goddamn you, Charles! Goddamn you!" The noise of the body hitting the floor brought her bolt upright. She ran around the bed, fell on her knees, and took his heavy head into her lap. "Oh, Charles…" She wept then, very quietly. Softly through the tears, she said, "Never, never, never, never, never. Ah, what would we do without Shakespeare?"

She stayed holding him until light, then she reached up and lowered a pillow down for his head. She finally raised his head off the floor and pushed the pillow under. Then she went to the living room and put Mozart's Piano Concerto No. 23 on the record player, cranked the handle, then sat on the sofa near Mitch, who was sound asleep, and touched his back gently. He awoke and looked up at her.

"Your father is dead."

They both looked to the bedroom, then at each other.

"I'll call Sis." Mitch sat up.

"You better call Uncle Liam too." Then Mitch put his arm around her, and she lay her head on his shoulder.

After a while, he disengaged from his mother and went to the phone. At the bedroom door, he paused, then went in. He was startled to see his father on the floor. Embracing him under his arms, he lifted him with great effort back onto the bed and folded his arms over his chest. In life, he had never held him as much as he did now in death. White peaceful face of a man he never knew. His eyes rested on his father's painting of Falstaff that had hung on the bedroom wall for as long as he could remember. Suddenly, somehow, he understood he was deeply related to this man, his father, and all he was came from him. He wanted to tell him that. He knelt down by the bed. Too late.

* * *

After the funeral, Mitch stayed with his mother for several weeks. There was no sympathy, no charity, no feeling from him for her. Behind the numbness, there had to have been damned up a sea of feeling, but for some reason, he could not locate or recognize that secret sea. He finally got her to talk about meeting his father for the first time. Yet still, Mitch was unmoved. Nothing she said seemed to have any effect on him. He tried to understand if what she was telling him was in her writing. If he could get her to talk about the writing, that would be one step removed from her suppressed hysteria that was frightening him. But she flatly refused. "It's nothing to do with the way I feel, it's just a book. Oh! Goddamn, I'm suffering, can't you see." She went into her alcove and slammed the door. He heard the sobbing. A deeply human conflict was stirring in him as he laid his face on the door. When he turned away, on the table by the bed, he saw his parents' wedding photo. Genevieve and Charles.

Out on the front porch, he stood feeling the nearly unbearable contradiction he had always felt from these two people and that there was nothing in him that could open to a woman who had lost her husband and was alone in the world. As he stood there, looking out to the empty street truly lost, his only relief was at the bar or the theater. He was isolated from the entire human condition and, at the same time, completely removed from any knowledge of his own condition. There was no access to this pain so deep that all he wanted to do was run.

Mitch went to the Carriage House to find Doug, the founder of the Carriage House Players was in his little office at the theater. At the entryway, Mitch watched as his mentor sat in a disquieting slump and didn't look up when the door was pushed aside. "You too, what's the matter with people?" Then Doug noticed him and smiled. "My boy!" he said and came to him with a warm hug so full of love and goodwill that Mitch felt shame pricking at his tears. He told Doug all he had been up to but never mentioned that his father had just died. Doug did not seem well himself, but the old man dismissed the question with a hardy laugh. "Meet me at Cunningham's in an hour, and we can chew over old times."

Mitch went to see Gretchen. At her apartment, another woman told him she had married and moved to Maryland. Back at Cunningham's, there was no Doug. He waited an hour. Still nothing. Then back to the theater, where all was locked. He realized he had no number for Doug and no information about any of the actors from five years before. Nothing in the phone book—several Rameys, but no Doug. It was like a dream of death. Mitch returned to the theater three days in a row, but there was no one to be seen. On the third day, looking up at the small sign swinging on rusty hinges, "The Carriage House Players" in faded paint, he lowered his head to lean on the heavy oak door. Time to go back to New York.

"I'm leaving."

His mother raised her head from her book. "Where?"

"Back to Barter or New York. I'll write and let you know."

"Goodbye. Yes, write. Wait, give me a kiss." He moved to her, and she raised her cheek.

He left a letter for Doug in the theater mailbox and took the Greyhound to New York. A dream of death.

CHAPTER 13

A Touch of Baptist
1960

MITCH WAS RECOGNIZING his mistake in giving up his Thompson Street luxury apartment to move in with the actress he had met at the Barter Theater. Because this actress was an activist, while he, Mitch, was becoming a drunk. This evening she was watching the presidential election. He was staring into the wall.

This big political moment for the country had made little impression on him, mainly because he couldn't find a job and had no money and had been drinking more or less since he had arrived back in New York. His father's death and the hopeless time with his mother had left him with a sense of despair he couldn't shake. In the kitchen, he poured a glass of vodka, went back, and fell onto the sofa.

She turned from the TV. "Why do you drink so much? Why? Do you know?"

He looked out the window, thinking he might jump, then laughed. "Well, I lost my parents at an early age and was raised by aborigines." His mother's face came into view, that strange tortured look she had when she told him his father was dead. "Sorry, never mind."

He started to leave, but she grabbed his hand. "Where are you going?"

"For a walk. I'll be in later."

"You used to like me. Stay," she pleaded. "Don't drink anymore." Her openness made him drop his head, and he turned away feeling like a man with no skin. Moving was hard, standing still was impossible. He couldn't sit for a minute without vibrating. In fact, he was in constant movement.

The TV blasted. "It all hangs on Illinois…a difference of four thousand votes with 50 percent of the precincts counted…Kennedy ahead…"

He stared at the screen. "My father died a month ago. I was never close to him. He left with no reconciliation." He looked at her in silence then left.

At the Shamrock Bar, he downed several whiskeys. Having no place else, he went back to the young actress's apartment. She opened the door. "I'm very drunk. May I come back, I…" She moved to him and took him in her arms. He clung to her. She got him to the bed, gently pushed him down, and lay beside him while he sobbed.

The next morning when he awakened, he thanked God she wasn't there. He packed his bag and, not knowing which way to turn, went to the bus station for a ticket back to the Barter Theater. It was the only place he could call home. He was twenty-eight years old and had no idea who he was or what he was doing. The closest thing to feeling was a longing for the comfort of affection and what he would call love and thought this place was at least close to that. Although no one would be there, no actors or any work, only the caretaker, that old moonshiner called Colonel, and maybe the owner, Mr. Porterfield.

As the bus neared Abingdon, he could see outside the window the skeleton trees and desolate brown mountains, a far cry from the lush summers he had known. Off the bus, it was bleak cold, but he felt easier here than in New York. He moved into his old room at the Barter Inn.

Jack Daniels became his companion. He fancied himself a tortured Heathcliff, reading Victorian novels and sipping bourbon. To complete the fantasy, he found a full-length black eighteenth-century overcoat in the costume department and went for long walks in the freezing woods wrapped in its folds. The cold drove him into the local gin mill on more than one occasion. He was aware of the scenario he was acting out, wallowing in self-pity. In a bar, nothing seemed unusual.

He struck up a friendship with the wife of the local preacher. She had red hair, she hid in a tight bun, and she wore no makeup. They had started talking one day after church. The bars being closed on Sunday, he gravitated to the only theater in town, the Baptist church. Everyone was welcoming, and when they all started to sing, the sound of the human voice gave him an unexpected thrill.

Then the preacher started in on sin and damnation, and everyone got carried away. He wondered at how seemingly intelligent people could buy into all this mumbo jumbo. When the preacher finally finished and was standing at the door shaking hands with the congregation, a handsome woman stood by his side. She held Mitch's hand and welcomed him while the preacher pumped his arm. "Welcome, stranger." He looked back at the woman, who was watching him. Their eyes met, and she smiled.

He went back the next week, and after the service as he was standing out front, she came over to him.

"Hello, are you one of the actors? I'm Mrs. Coward, but you may call me Louise."

"Yes, I'm an actor, but nothing is going on now, and I'm glad I came back to the Barter." She had on a simple wool coat and print dress that showed off her figure, and she wore a large hat with a feather. She was older than his twenty-eight years, maybe early thirties. "What do you think of our little town?"

"It's quiet and peaceful, and that suits me at the moment."

"Yes, everyone needs to find peace in their lives."

They stood looking at each other. She dropped her head.

"I like your hat."

She laughed and blushed. She must not get many compliments. "Where are you from?"

"New York." He wanted to stay with this woman but turned and started away. "See you!"

"We have a Bible class tonight, and you would be welcome."

"Well, maybe. What time?"

"Eight."

He slowly walked away to his little room at the Barter Inn. He didn't go to the class, but he did go back to the church, realizing he wanted to get to know this woman better. He needed some relationship with a woman. No thought to consequences. He told himself he just wanted some exchange, some warmth.

Two days later, he went to buy some whiskey and do some shopping, and there she was at the Piggly Wiggly grocery. She invited him to sit down in the coffee shop and started right in. "You seem to be in some sort of pain about your life. I would like to help and, if you will let us, it's all possible through Jesus Christ our Lord." As she grew more passionate about Jesus, her body got engaged, and when she clutched her chest, her breasts moved under her flowered dress. Her hair was still in a bun, but strands kept breaking free and floated down around her face, settling in her mouth from time to time, at which point she would pull them away and tuck them behind her ear. Mitch, slightly aroused, didn't know where to turn and hardly heard the words.

Suddenly he said, "You know, I think I could be a good Christian. I have always had a good feeling toward the church."

She smiled and sat back in the booth, relaxed for the first time. "Thank you, Mitchell, you will not regret it." At ease, she was even more appealing. He leaned forward, wondering what he was doing, what he expected. Nothing could happen. He looked at her breasts again, then down.

"I'm very happy." Her eyes were on his. "Jesus is our Lord and dear friend and is waiting to fill you with his eternal light." She would say "our Lord" as if he were their personal savior. Mitch began to doubt his decision to be with this woman. "Coming to church you are already doing, but you must participate in the Bible class on Sunday at eight."

"Wait, can't you and I go over the lessons of the Bible? I must say I don't follow what is being said from the pulpit—not to criticize the preacher, but I'm a little slow."

"Well, after church, you and I can have a talk and you can ask me any question you wish. Also, we can have tea with Albert, the three of us. He's really a wise and dedicated man."

He did want to spend some time with a mature woman, and he had no illusions about this coming to anything, but he'd rather keep her husband out of the room. He liked the way her lips demurely pouted when she would pause and the movement of her body when she gulped in a deep breath.

But it wasn't long before Mr. Porterfield told Mitch he had found him a job in a winter stock company in Pennsylvania. "Son, you can't stay here and do nothing. You are a young man, and you need to be working at your craft. You have too much talent, and you can't let it rot. Work, that's the most important thing in life. It will also keep the demons away. Be back here the first of June."

Mitch packed up and was ready to go to the bus when he thought of Louise and figured he should say goodbye. He went to their house, just behind the church.

Both hands went to her hair in an involuntary move that was very sexual. "Oh! I'm so sorry you're leaving, but I feel you are with Jesus now." She stood in the open door, and he could see the shape of her body from the light behind her. She was wearing her flowered print dress, the uniform that showed off her body, and he had a feeling she knew she looked good.

"I'll see you in the summer. I'm pretty sure I'll be back. Mr. Porterfield says he needs me."

"I know he does." She put her hand on his arm. They were close, and he felt her warmth. She had been standing, holding the screen door, and now she moved out and brought her hand down and took his.

"Well..." He moved to kiss her cheek.

She turned as he approached and brought her mouth to his. He froze and let the rich warmth of her lips move over his.

"God bless you," she breathed and disappeared into the house.

On the long bus ride to Pennsylvania, he kept coming back to the kiss. Maybe that was one of the demons to which Porterfield had been referring.

CHAPTER 14

New York Theater
1964

LATE MORNING. MITCH reached out to feel the warmth of her body. She wasn't there. "Jesus!" He opened his eyes and threw the pillow across the room. Always that sinking panic when he woke. He lay there watching the green gauze curtains blow over the bed and heard a sound coming from somewhere outside the bedroom door like a baby crying, then he remembered the little poodle in the kitchen. He rolled over and slowly edged to the side, swung his legs off, sat up, looked around the elegant East Side apartment, and called her name. No answer. The crying continued. He stood up. A little shaky on his way to the window. The curtains flapping around him, he looked down to the street. All he saw were the tops of trees. It could have been anywhere but New York. He opened the window, heard the city, and felt alone.

"Jane? Jane, where are you?" He leaned against the doorjamb. Was she hiding? The little poodle whimpering in the kitchen was suddenly quiet. From the bedroom door, he spied the sexy red-and-white striped dress she'd worn last night lying on the elegantly carved chair. He remembered her soft body—not the great reception of *Twelfth Night*, not the opening night cheers, not the party on the stage of the Theater in the Park, not waiting up for the rave reviews, not the late-night walk down through Central Park—nothing but her body. He picked up the silk dress from the chair and brought it to his face. The long sensual night seemed longer ago than just a few hours.

He looked for a note. What was the time? He wandered through the dressy, feminine living room with the overstuffed cream sofa and Persian carpet, then made the long lonely trek into the kitchen to find a bottle of whiskey and pour himself a drink. He looked down at his only friend. "What do you think—should I drink this before breakfast?" The pooch cocked his head. "I'll take that as a yes." He downed the whiskey and chased it with a glass of water. Breakfast. He felt more himself, showered, dressed, kissed the dog goodbye, and went down to the street and out the front door of her apartment building. He was enveloped by the trees that created a green canopy up and down East Sixty-Third Street.

A motorcycle blasted by, leaving silence in its wake so that for a few rare moments of quiet in New York, Mitch was back with the trees of his home in Louisville, the maples and oaks down every street. Then the deep sound of the city again, and he told himself that Sixty-Third Street was nicer than his place on the Upper West Side, which he liked well enough, but this was a rich street. Yes, he liked his new place and had money now and had even bought a sofa, but this was, he said to himself again, a rich street. Good, nice, better than Louisville.

"Beautiful day, isn't it, son?" It was from an old Jewish man wearing a yarmulke as he walked past.

"It is," Mitch offered. When the man was gone, he added to himself, "A beautiful day." Mitch followed him down the street and watched the man stop and pick up some trash to drop in the bin at the corner. The man put him in mind of his father, cutting the hedge in front of their house and saying to everyone who passed, "Beautiful day" or "It's going to rain" or "Not too hot." Charles Ryan trying to be friendly was always touching to him. There were so many simple things he could tell his father now. *I love you, Dad. Thanks for every-thing*, would be something to say. Too late. His father must have felt many things. He never talked about feelings. A few more moments passed, then he saw the apartment building across the street and realized that thinking about the past made him totally blind. The picture of his father in front of the wood-frame house where he had grown up was what he was seeing, not what was there in front of him. Like a dream, important, but he let go and walked to Park Avenue and hailed a cab.

"What time is it?"

"One o'clock on the nose. Where to?"

"Eighty-second and Amsterdam, drop me at the Triple Inn." One of his favorite bars because, like Stanley's, his downtown bar on Avenue B, it did not cater to show business. So he called the place his uptown bar because he craved the anonymity the same way he needed the constant attention, but he let that riddle go, too, and chuckled as he noticed the hack license on the back of the seat.

"I see you're Irish."

"Yeah, you?"

"My grandfather came from the old country."

"Let me guess: You're an actor."

Mitch's voice smiled. "How did you know?"

"I can spot what a guy is at first glance. You're a good-looking kid and you got long hair and a good voice—therefore, you're an actor."

Yes, it was finally true. He had auditioned for Joe Papp, the founder of the New York Shakespeare Festival, joined the company, and had worked there for the last three years after what he referred to as his "nervous drunken breakdown at the Barter Theater in Virginia." The New York Shakespeare Theater was lively and attracted many of the finest actors from the large pool in New York. The company performed summers in Central Park and winters touring the state. Mitch had performed *Macbeth*, *Twelfth Night*, *Tempest*, *Antony & Cleopatra*, *Winter's Tale*, and *As You Like It*. When he finished with *Twelfth Night* in the park, that would be all. Time to move on. He had been auditioning for as many plays as he could. He was beginning to love the process and learned most of the scripts before he went to the theaters to read for the parts. He never slept. Of course, he must have, but sleep didn't matter because he loved what he was doing and he loved the life. When he'd first returned to New York those few years earlier, he had slowed down his drinking but lately had stepped into the fast lane and was going at it harder than ever.

He stood on the sidewalk, taking in the sweep of the park from Eighty-Second Street to the tall hotels on Central Park South, thirty blocks away.

Inside the Triple Inn, he stood for a moment appreciating the glorious temple. The bartender was the only person inside the once opulent but now run-down establishment. The rich old wood bar still had a stately presence, and Mitch breathed in the coolness. Empty bars felt like home to him.

"Hey, Jimmy, give me a beer."

He was meeting with a director later to talk about a Broadway production, so he didn't want to drink too much. A Broadway show with a film star attached was a big deal. Mitch had to admit he was excited.

His friend Mel, "the only Jewish alcoholic in the world," walked in off the street. Mel would always be there, for he had money enough that he didn't need to work. Short, with a bullet-shaped head, an irritating style, and a voice that cut through you like a stiletto, Mel reminded Mitch of a prison guard he had met in his navy days.

"Have you read *The Spy Who Came in from the Cold*?" Mel climbed onto the barstool, his legs not quite reaching the floor. "A double vodka, Jimmy. A supreme work of art, the best book I've ever read."

"The best?"

"Without a doubt, period! And I include all the classic novels, even the Russians." He took a big sip. "The one exception is possibly Camus's *The Stranger.*"

"Well, I hope you write a long letter to the *Times* telling them all about your find."

"Okay, spend your life in a cocoon, you illiterate asshole. You still doing that babbling you call Shakespeare?"

"The Immortal Bard." Mitch turned, his back to the bar. "As a matter of fact, I'm going to see about a play today—a play on Broadway. A play in straightforward American words." Mel was sweating. His face glowed first blue, then orange from the neon beer sign. He was always edgy with anger or desperation, and Mitch recognized and understood this and found he liked being in that kind of company.

"What am I doing sitting in bars!" Mel let out a moan. "You meet nothing but losers avoiding the real issues of life."

"You know..." Mitch paused. "The world is a chaotic mess where no one listens to each other. The bar is an ordered universe. Can I have another beer, Jimmy? The only place I know where a man can quietly reflect on the, as you say, real issues of life. The saloon is a place of debate where you can exchange with your fellow man."

Mel applauded. "That is so much bullshit. But it was real pretty."

Mitch smiled into his glass. He was only half kidding.

Alan Mixon came in and moved up to the bar as if he were afraid of it. "Gladys is looking for you," he said to Mitch. "She needs to talk to you today." He said it like it was a vital secret. Gladys Vaughan was a director, and Alan her assistant.

"Is she at home? Let me buy you a drink, Alan."

"She's at home." Alan shrank back from the bar even more. "How can you drink in the middle of the day?"

"It takes a lot of willpower, Alan."

Mel laughed. "Give me some more vodka and ask this man to leave. He's making disparaging remarks about drinking."

"Alan, it's not good form to come into a bar and advocate not drinking," Mitch added, at which Alan left.

Mitch walked to the phone and made a date with Gladys for later in the day after his audition. He said goodbye to Mel and walked out and up to Eighty-Ninth Street, then into the park and down to Central Park South. At Columbus Circle, he hailed a cab and went to the audition.

The offices were in an elegant brownstone on Thirty-Eighth Street. The waiting room, which must have been a parlor in years gone by, was wood-paneled, understated, and luxurious. A handsome woman with gray hair and a young face asked Mitch if he wanted anything. "No, thank you."

He sat down and took in the pictures on the walls of famous actors: Marlon, Eva Marie Saint, Groucho Marx, and a poster of

Bonnie and Clyde on the wall behind the desk. He stood, stretched, and moved to the door. He wanted to leave. In these situations, he felt that familiar contradiction he wore like a cape: *I can play in this league. So why am I nervous?*

The woman's voice brought him back to why he was there. "Are you sure I can't get you a water or something?"

His mouth was dry, and he craved a drink. "No, thank you, I'm fine." He moved to the desk. "Who else has been in for the part?"

"Do you really want to know?

"You're right, I don't."

"You're in the Actors Studio, aren't you?"

"Yes, I am."

"I thought I've seen you there."

"You're an actress then."

"Yes, Arthur lets me work for him and gives me plenty of free time to audition." The phone rang. She gave him a beautiful smile. "You can go in now, good luck."

The tension in his neck made him stop and take several deep breaths. As he moved into the next room, his back straightened, his head tilted up, and he immediately relaxed.

Arthur Penn was at the window and standing next to him was a woman with startling blue-green eyes and a large golden face. If he hadn't known she was a famous film star, he would have guessed. She moved toward him, her hand out. "Mitch. Do they call you Mitch?"

He looked her in the eyes and held out his hand. "Miss Remick, Mitch is fine."

"I thought you were great in *Twelfth Night*. You look younger than you do onstage." He blushed, and she noticed. "We both were there for the last preview. Great notice. Did you have time to read our play?"

"I…It's great, I love the part."

"Would you read a few lines with Lee?" Arthur Penn asked.

"Sure."

She brought several pages to him, and they both read. He now felt on solid ground, that secure feeling he always had when he entered the work. He could tell when a reading went well. Mr. Penn was happy and said he would "be seeing him," and that was it. Mitch said goodbye to the beautiful woman and was ushered to the door.

He walked down Thirty-Eighth Street to Fifth Avenue and boarded a bus. All his doubts were gone. To be on Broadway with a movie star would fulfill all his dreams and put him in the class of actor who could make choices about projects. At Fifty-Seventh Street, there was a traffic jam, so he started walking the rest of the way to Gladys's. Still, in the fantasy about the sudden elevation of his career, he nearly stumbled over a homeless man sitting on a piece of cardboard on the sidewalk.

"Got a buck for an old army buddy?"

Mitch was so startled that he gave him a few coins from his pocket. He stared at the man's face, grimy with dirt. In the recesses of his mind, there was a vague image of his father, with dark clouds lowering all around. Then as from a long distance, he heard, "You look like you might be good for something." At that, the street man came into focus. Mitch couldn't tell if he was young or old. He kept scratching his beard, but his gaze was steady. Mitch spun away, walking fast to the corner, but the voice hit him like a baseball. "What's your hurry, brother?"

"Don't call me brother."

Mitch stopped, shaken and stiff with anger. "Jesus!" Suddenly the day turned dark. A large drink would take care of this. In one of those Madison Avenue bars, where everyone is dressed up even in the middle of the day, he ordered a whiskey and felt better instantly. This Broadway show was in the bag.

Gladys lived in the ground-floor apartment of an old brownstone on East Eighty-First Street off Third Avenue. She had directed him the previous year in *Winter's Tale*. He loved Gladys not in any sexual way but as a friend and colleague. He felt safe and comfortable in her apartment, with its high windows and generous light.

"You don't want to drink," Gladys protested when he asked for one, "You have a show tonight."

"Okay, fine. Wait till I tell you the news."

"What?"

"I had a meeting with Arthur Penn about his new play on Broadway, and I read a couple of scenes with guess who?"

"Whom."

"Lee Remick, and we were terrific." Mitch watched Gladys fall onto the sofa, her blond hair covering her face as she buried her head in her hands. "What's the matter, aren't you pleased?"

"Oh, Jesus. Of course, I'm happy as hell. It's just that Joe has given me the go-ahead to do *Othello* with James Earl Jones and you."

Mitch sat down, unable to speak for a long while.

"Two jobs. This is not right." He went to the kitchen to get that drink and came back. Gladys hadn't moved. He sensed her disappointment. "Maybe I won't get the Penn show. It would simplify the problem."

"Oh, you'll get it." She looked ready to cry. "And you must take it."

Gladys, Mitch, and James had been talking and working on *Othello* for at least a year with the hope of bringing the masterpiece to Papp's New York Shakespeare Festival. Now what...Only street sounds and a cloud passing by the sun changing the light.

"I'm going to the theater. I'll call you later." He kissed the top of her head.

"Mitch, you must take the Penn play."

"I can't think about it now."

That night after the show, when the actors left, he sat in his dressing room for a long time with a glass of whiskey. Billy, the stage manager, came in. "You going to spend the night?"

"Sorry, I'll get going." He finished his drink and left via the outdoor amphitheater they had been performing in all summer. He stopped and looked up at the two thousand seats, remembering his initial impression four years before, when he had first arrived. The thrill and power of a theater in the open air, the history of the Globe, and the Greeks and how much that ancient family meant to him—all that he had learned from Doug Ramey, who had spent so much time with him at the beginning and to whom he owed everything. Mitch sat down in the first row and looked up at the stage with the lake behind. Dear Doug. He'd never had this.

"I don't want this choice," he said to the stage, heading out of Central Park to the Triple Inn. Iago or whatever was bothering him would wait till tomorrow.

He woke up on a bench in Central Park. The morning traffic sounded like a waterfall. His limbs ached, his mouth felt like cardboard. For a moment, he wondered how he had ended here. He remembered pronouncing last night at the bar that he would never do anything but Shakespeare for the rest of his life. Slowly now, he sat up and made for the street. Fifth Avenue and 103rd Street, twenty blocks north of the Triple Inn and on the other side of the park. He hailed a cab and went to his place, took a bath, and called his agent.

"Well, are you sitting down?" Archer was using his matter-of-fact voice. "Penn wants you to do the play. Hot damn, we're on our way. Hallelujah! Meet me at the Russian Tea Room. I'll buy you lunch and anything else you want."

"Not too early."

"What the fuck is the matter with you? Are you hungover?"

Mitch didn't realize how off his game he sounded. "I'm fine, just stunned. I'll see you at two."

"You are the luckiest actor in town, god damn it," Archer was now almost shouting. "Don't fuck this up."

"You're right, Archer. See you at the Tea Room."

He wandered around the streets of Manhattan for the rest of the morning, stopping at several bars, hoping for an answer. He went over every possible turn until his brain went numb. He remembered Lee's bright face and the curve of her neck. Doing a play with a cinema queen or doing Iago with the best Shakespeare company in New York was a choice he had never imagined.

Archer leaned in across the small table in the classically elegant Russian Tea Room. Mitch became more and more calm, listening to Archer's reasoning to take the Broadway job. Then Mitch gazed around the imperial old-world tsarist Russian room and said, "I'm going to do *Othello*. Tell Mr. Penn I'm very honored and sorry, but this commitment comes first."

Archer was speechless for three seconds. "You can't play Othello! He's fucking black, for Christ's sake."

"Blackface."

"Don't be a smartass. You're kidding. Tell me you're kidding."

"Put this on my tab."

"Tab? What tab?" Archer followed Mitch to the door. "Are you going to blow this opportunity of a lifetime?" They were out in the street now. "What the fuck is the matter with you? You do this, you're a bigger loser than I thought. For what! A two-hundred-dol-lar-a-week art job? 'Shakespeare!' Jesus!" Mitch kept walking, Archer shouting after him, "You're stupid if you do this. Don't do it!"

Mitch was down the block, walking nowhere fast. Was he making a mistake? *This agent has got some nerve telling me what's smart. Loser? Fuck him!* He felt better. Free. Choice! He never wanted a choice ever again in his life. He walked east toward the river.

CHAPTER 15

The Golden Age
1964–1969

THERE WAS A deep inaccessible place within Mitch that served to both protect him and keep him at a distance from fully realizing his promise. It was the inability or refusal to care, to love—and deeper than that, the abiding sense that he was not worthy of love or anything else that was truly good unless he could invent a persona that would be acceptable to everyone. There was a powerful drive inside that he could never share with anyone, that no one knew anything about—least of all himself—because he was not even aware that a hidden voice was ruling him, telling him he always needed to be acting, always needed to keep his guard up. This way, he would always be recognized and accepted and incognito and anonymous.

There was a shock in reading *Othello* that first day. As the great transcendent language came flowing from all the actors, Mitch knew instantly that Iago's very life depended on his ability to deceive those who trusted him. Oddly uncomfortable to identify with this character who needed to be recognized and believed. Iago's lies had to be flawless. Mitch was to act out his own persona right there on the stage. James Earl Jones as Othello was a powerhouse and deserves all the credit he got for his great Othello.

After the reading, he left the theater and headed for the nearest bar, marveling at how he instinctively understood Iago so deeply.

What a fantastic challenge to explore the ins and outs of this man in hell, to move inside a vicious villain, this "Honest Iago." Then after the first drink, out came a confession, said to no one and everyone: "It's always dangerous to delve too deeply into something that is better understood in action, in the doing I am, therefore Iago is!"

He sat as if waiting. Then a sense of loneliness swept over him, and underneath his invented persona was ancient longing, something important had been neglected and forgotten.

Drinking became the answer, or at least the placeholder answer. Drinking brought him into the immediate distraction—a play, a woman, a lie, a mock of himself performed in a bar. Why would the dark wood and dark light of the bar be so comfortable? Why would he be more at home and alive there than anywhere else, even the stage? He told himself he loved the drinking life. He also loved the theater. To him, they seemed to go together, and he did much of both. But only in the bar or when working on a play did he feel most alive. The complete exhaustion after three hours of *Othello* left him drained and ready to forget the horror of Iago and give himself up to debauching.

Mitch murdered himself that summer and came into his own through the shape-shifting of embodying Iago. He allowed his essence to die and this invented persona to live.

The Greeks

They were eating from platters of succulent Greek food and listening to a Greek band, made up of a violin, drums, and an instrument called a bouzouki, playing music that sounded both ancient and modern. Mitch hadn't much liked this music when he'd first heard the strangely familiar strain, but since being imprisoned by the Greeks for three months, he was getting the feel of something old and forgotten.

They were at the Egyptian Gardens, a Greek restaurant just off Eighth Avenue. The Greek invasion had started when Ted Mann, producing director of the Circle in the Square, told Mitch that Michael Cacoyannis, the famous Greek director, was coming from

France to direct a Greek play by Euripides, along with Irene Papas, the equally famous Greek actress, and he asked if Mitch was interested. "You will have to read for him."

"Sure." Mitch recognized the two artists as being world-renowned and the actress one he had admired in an award-winning film. "Oooo—her." Mitch looked up. "Well, well, well!"

"Forget it, she'll chew you up and spit you out."

Mitch spent the next few days reading *Iphigenia at Aulis*. He knew next to nothing about the Greek plays, so he cut down on the drinking, telling himself this was important, that this director and actress represented a whole different world—ancient, primitive, profound, a world that existed five hundred years before Christ. Mitch tried not to fantasize about what doing this play could lead to. Many things. Streamers of hundreds of scenarios developed that he had to shake himself to drop. He kept drinking coffee, pacing up and down his railroad flat, running downstairs to grab a sandwich and beer, tearing over to the park to eat, and then running back to the apartment. Anyone watching this display would conclude that he was mad, acting like a hysteric.

The day of the audition came. Why was he such a mess? He'd auditioned many times before. "Get a hold of yourself, Mitch," he said out loud as he walked down from the train toward Bleaker Street and the Circle Theater. He stopped, ordered a drink, held it in front of him, then put it down, moved to the door of the bar, stopped again, and went back. "I am who I am, and this is an audition for a play I'm sure is not worth all this anxiety." He drank the whiskey.

At the audition, the actress was sitting with the director in the house, and Mitch, onstage, couldn't see her but heard the vibrant accented voice. "Nice to meet you." He had studied Agamemnon's long speech from the first act. As he performed, he sensed he was rushing and slowed down. Then all of a sudden, he was alive, and the stage was his, the words, and Greece was his. When he finished, there was a long pause. He could hear muted voices from the dark. Then the actress stepped into the light, as if making an entrance. He couldn't move. She had a powerful dark, tragic face, black eyes, and the most luscious long black hair.

"That was good." She took his hand.

"Thank you."

"I'm Irene."

From the house: "The producer will call you."

As Mitch let go of the actress's hand, he found something both strange and familiar in her eyes, something that sent a shiver through his body. More than approval, the look said, "You are good and you understand." As if obeying a cue, he left her and came down to where the director was sitting. "Can you loan me twenty dollars? I'll give it back to you on the first day of rehearsal." The little Greek director was so taken aback that he pulled out his wallet and gave him the money. Mitch heard the actress's low laugh as he said thank you and left.

In the street, he stopped under the marquee, then quickly moved down toward Thompson Street and stopped again. He still held the twenty-dollar bill in his hand. Had he blown his chances? He started back to the theater, then thought of Stanley's bar, his warm, cozy home. That's what he wanted, more than anything, a drink and a story. He held up the twenty and addressed the marquee aloud, "Well, if they hire me after this, I know I belong."

Somewhere in all that coming and going was a dim recollection that Mitch had made a deal with himself and the devil. His wild drunken persona had been creeping up on him for some years, so if this kind of joke, this cheap whim, could destroy the possibility of taking this next step, then that's the way his fate had to be, and that's the way he told the story to his cohorts, waiting patiently for him at Stanley's.

The story about hitting up the famous director for twenty bucks was all over town in no time. Mitch started the legend that first day, and soon the legend became his myth.

The run was a great success. The actress and director received great press. Mitch and the rest of the cast were mentioned. The chorus of the twelve ladies of Athens was given special mention.

But during rehearsals, everyone was frustrated, the actress included. The whole cast suffered at the hands of the legendary Greek director. He had a definite vision of how he wanted the play done and, though Mitch thought he was right, he went about it in a way that simply didn't help actors. He had no understanding of how American actors worked, nor did he care. He was abusive to the twelve talented women of the Greek chorus and gave line readings with a cringing pathetic emotionalism. Mitch had seen *Zorba the Greek*, the director's triumphant film, and his excellent *Electra*, so the man clearly knew what he was doing.

Mitch had no problem with him. He was following Doug Ramey's ancient advice to "never argue with the director." They got along fine. Irene, however, saw this as a sign of weakness and took Mitch in hand. "You are a wimp." She was planted squarely in front of him and ablaze with her marvelous passion. "You need to be a man. You look like a man. Now you must learn to act like a man."

Mitch was an apt pupil as she taught him many things, and he reveled in every moment. She taught him Greek dances and how to eat oysters, how to love Greek olive oil and make real Greek salad, how you never kiss on the mouth until after you make love, and many more interesting ancient Greek practices.

In rehearsals, she was having a hard time with the English. "You speak it very well," Mitch consoled one day when she quit the scene in frustration.

"I hear the words in Greek and then translate them into English. English was not made for passion. You can't use your force. The power won't come through. The language is no help." He felt he shouldn't mention Shakespeare. "Why don't you do it in Greek?"

She looked at him for a long moment, then backed up and stood very still. She was wearing a light green dress patterned with darker green flowers that buttoned up the front. On almost any other woman, the frock would have looked plain, but on her, the dress radiated earth and sexuality. She slowly started the long speech of Clytemnestra to Agamemnon. The Greek language coming from her deep throaty voice startled him, vibrating, frightening, and beautiful, and as she spoke, she completely changed, and so did Mitch. Her face assumed a form that was primal and terrible. She fixed her eyes on him, and in response, he backed down to the edge of the stage. She was like a wild animal. The Greek language went right to the bone. Mitch felt alive with a sensation that traveled up and down his spine, and when she finished, she was right up against him and then burst into tears, grabbed him, and held him for a long time. "So sad, so sad, the world."

Now, eating from platters of Greek food and listening to a group of Greek actors and writers talking politics and dishing the United States, he was getting a little pissed off.

"The CIA is behind it all!"

Mitch felt like every Greek in town was there—Irene and the director, who wrote the music for the Euripides play, another Greek film actress, in town doing the musical *Never on Sunday*, and several friends of hers. They talked endlessly about politics, freely dumping on America and then the takeover, the overthrow of the democratically elected socialist Greek government by a CIA-led putsch. Mitch, drunker than he wanted to be, felt he should say something in his country's defense, but what? Maybe he should just leave.

"It's this US government that turns into fear and loathing at the smell of communism. They're willing to sacrifice a whole country to keep what they call world stability. Now they've turned all of Greece over to a bunch of gangsters." Irene took a breath as Mitch pushed up. "Where are you going, dear boy?" Irene took Mitch's hand.

"I'm going to leave because you people make me sick." He felt himself getting carried away but couldn't stop. "You come over here and work and live off the fat of the land, the United States of America fat of the land. You take the money, and the whole time you degrade the greatness of this country and the great principles upon which it was founded."

There was a long moment of silence. They all turned and looked at Irene. He wasn't sure what he had said, but the rejoinder rang in his ear like the Pledge of Allegiance. When Mitch turned to go, Irene stood and applauded, and they all joined in, following with a loud round of bravos. Mitch was pulled back to the table, and they all announced, "He speaks!"

And as the lyrical Greek music swelled, Irene raised his glass. "To the great young American patriot."

He was to have ten more months of glorious penal servitude with the Greeks before he was released.

Moon for the Misbegotten

A cold sweat in bed, tangled in his sheets, Mitch's annoyance grew as the phone continued to ring. No way to stop it. He answered. Ted Mann, from the Circle: "Can you come and see me? I want to talk to you about a project."

"I'm sick as a dog. I drank some bad booze last night. Could I come by tomorrow?"

"For Christ's sake, you're thirty-four years old. Grow the fuck up and get over here."

"I'll see you in the morning." Mitch hung up.

In those days, he was living in a Tenth Avenue walkup. Plenty big enough and better than Thompson Street, it seemed to fit both sides of his persona: one, knowing that he was doing better, and two, the fear of failure because he was a fool to think he could live in this world that worshipped success. The place marked his battleground because all the would-be actors and broke drunks felt free to flop at "Shay Ryan." Mitch was never sure whom he would find there in the morning. He fell out of bed and went to the bathroom. In the mirror, his tongue was covered with large red welts.

"I think I should take some vitamins," he muttered. Watching the image of his face in the mirror, the gloom of his apartment, his red eyes, and his pale skin forced his head to involuntarily lower until he bumped the sink. Then he pulled himself straight. "I need more than vitamins." He rubbed his face with hot water, then brushed his teeth, dressed, and took a cab down to the Circle.

When Mitch walked into the office, Ted was talking on the phone, so he sank into the big leather sofa and waited. Ted hung up and plowed ahead. "I'm prepared to give you one of the greatest parts ever written in one of the greatest plays ever written. When are you going to stop acting like a jerk?"

"You want me to play Mother Courage?"

"I should throw you the fuck out. It's a great part in a play that I love and is dear to my heart. I know you are serious and can play this part. It's O'Neill! I'm going to do *Moon for the Misbegotten*." Mitch fell silent. Ted went on. "I want you to play Jamie Tyrone and Salome Jens to play Josie. I'll direct. We can start in a week or so, and I want to open before the summer." Ted climbed out of his dark leather chair, went to the bookcase, and pulled down a book, a play. He opened and read: "That young man is playing Othello better than I ever did! That from Booth the greatest actor of his day or any other. And it was true! And I was only twenty-seven years old! What the hell was it I wanted to buy, I wonder. Mitch, you could have all you want out of the theater if you don't throw it away. Do this part and take care of your life before it's too late."

This was a play Mitch loved and thought would never be done, at least not with him. A monumental play. He went to the window and thought of a drink. He was overwhelmed by what the older man had said. Finally, he said, "Thanks, Ted, that really means a lot to me."

Ted waited.

"I mean that, I'm very touched that you want me to play Jamie."

But Mitch was even more thrilled—and terrified—than he realized. He went to a bar next to the Circle to have a celebratory drink. Then he had another. But the drinks didn't relax him as they usually did. He felt hopelessly lost. The idea of playing O'Neill in New York was staggering. He couldn't help thinking Jamie belonged to Jason. Mitch had seen Jason Robards's interpretation in *Long Day's Journey into Night*. Such comparisons were entirely stupid, he knew that, but there it was. Then it hit him. Ted had never directed a play, and why wasn't he letting his partner Jose Quintero direct? Jose was a brilliant director. This was a mother of a play, and without help, he wasn't sure he could to it. He called his friend Salome Jens.

"We can do it. We'll help each other." She tried to reassure him. That calmed him. She could always do that. "Meet me at Joe's. I'll buy you lunch, and we can talk. Don't drink."

He didn't tell her it was too late.

Going uptown to meet, having not seen her in several months, he was hungry to be with her. She was the most extraordinarily beautiful woman, with a powerfully strong body, a radiant presence, and a large classic Slavic face you might find on propaganda posters for early Russian communism. She was a great friend, and he loved her very much.

"It was for the best that we never got together," she always said. That was their running joke, that they had never been single at the same time. They talked about the play and how much they loved O'Neill and how difficult the challenge would be. Then with a big smile, Salome leaned across the table to him. "But we can do it, and it will be a dream to play."

An actor named W. B. Braden was to play the father, and several days later, they all read the play in Ted's office. At the end of the reading, there was a long silence. They would start the next morning. They knew they were in the presence of a great play.

The rehearsals went as well as could be expected. Ted was a serviceable enough director. At least he knew what the result should be. But that wasn't much help on a day-to-day basis. For Mitch, the results didn't matter nearly as much as the process. Salome knew all about the process, and when Mitch forgot, she reminded him. He could count on her. The play, as O'Neill tells us, is a play about forgiveness. The struggle unfolds with long acrimonious exchanges between Josie and her father, after which James Tyrone comes wandering in, up from his morning drinks at the local pub. As things progress, the relationships between father and daughter and Josie and Jamie become enmeshed in layers of recrimination and manipulation, culminating in James Tyrone's confessing a memory that has haunted him for years.

Each day after he finished rehearsal Mitch would have a drink with Salome, then go to a village bar and head home early. He had hardly noticed that beneath his enjoyment of playing Jamie, something buried in him was the key to the character: the character's guilt over his dead mother and his desperate need to be forgiven. That thought bubbled up from time to time, but he'd just dismiss, deny, and put it away.

* * *

Every time Mitch came to the long scene where the dialogue plainly told him that this was a confession, he would joke or fake the emotion. Jamie knows deep down that Josie loves him, but not until he's drunk enough can he confess this degradation that has haunted him and ask to be forgiven. In Mitch's mind, the confession had to be delivered via Jamie's coverup as the slick Broadway sharpie. What O'Neill called for at the end, he would tell himself, was far too simpleminded, too "on the nose." But the truth was, Mitch didn't want to truly play this horrifying scene. Salome pushed him to go deeper, but he would shrug the commitment off with "I'll get it later." Yet it haunted him, and the amount of alcohol he drank was in direct proportion to his repressed thoughts about his own mother and the way he had treated her and how she would reduce him to tears and how he would, by this, be driven to lacerate her in a brutal way—and then crawl back for forgiveness and never be released. His circle of pain was just too extreme to go there. He couldn't go there in the play or in life.

The play was well served, and everyone thought O'Neill would have been pleased. Opening night was thrilling, and the reviews were great for Salome. Mitch received a nice mention, but no more than that. He knew he just could not give himself to that terrifying scene at the end of the play.

One night several weeks after they opened, Mitch was walking to the train from the theater and for some reason didn't wish to visit a bar or join the endless talk there. He passed by several watering holes, and when he arrived at his apartment, he lay down on the bed. He couldn't stop going over the play, and his mother kept coming to mind. Having spent most of his introspection on the failure of his relationship with his father, he had never pondered much on his mother.

He left the bed, poured a drink, and went to the window. He watched the few cars cruising down Tenth Avenue. A voice came to him saying that he was not being true to his acting at a deeper level. Still, he thought, here he was in a hit show, so why torture himself trying to blast down into this murky private world? Better to leave that no man's land alone. At that moment, he saw a vivid image of the sadness and disappointment lined into his mother's face. Surely, she carried that in her heart as well. His memory cleared, and he envisioned her sitting in front of the fireplace in their small home in Louisville, heard the deepness of her sighs as she dealt with a depressed and half-drunk husband and a thoughtless son. He remembered her face when he came home from the navy in disgrace and her face after his father died. Then overwhelmed with a wave of humiliation, he remembered that in a drunken fit, he had cursed her and left her weeping while he crashed out of the house to the nearest bar.

Over the years, he had worked to erase her until she was nothing but the shadow of a memory. Now, standing at the window in the darkened apartment, he wanted to cry, to have some release, but the conflict was too great to discharge.

The next day as that scene came up, something suddenly triggered the visions of the previous night. In the scene, Jamie is sitting next to Josie on the steps as he starts telling her the story of his train ride back to New York from California. He could see his own mother's face, her lovely red hair, and he began to weep as he entered the confession, sorrow falling into him like a stone. Knowing he was onstage, he took command of the long confession and, through the sobs, let himself feel how desperately he wanted her love and forgiveness. He became deeply aware of Salome's breasts and her lap where his head was lying. Their arms were around each other in an anguished embrace.

When the scene was over, and before the final scene of this most gentle and forgiving play, Salome came to him backstage and held him. "Wonderful, Mitch." Later that night, he walked all the way to his apartment, cherishing the one word, "wonderful," that he had received from Salome.

By the time he reached home, he was a mass of confusion, certain that the play had allowed him to confess, elated at the release and yet terrified that he was now sinking into a hole in need of his mother's forgiveness.

He ran up the stairs, burst into his room, grabbed the open bottle by the bed, and took a long drink. Then he sank down on the bed, a warm glow in his middle. Who needs to be forgiven? Alcohol was his confessor. Alcohol forgave. And for that, he always had Stanley's.

CHAPTER 16

Stanley's Bar
1968

MITCH WAS PUSHED by a chill wind into the park at Eighty-First Street, past the empty Shakespeare Theater where he had enjoyed five years of employment. Late fall and the stage was deserted, littered with faded red and gold leaves blowing through the arches where he had deceived Othello, charmed the forest philosophers, and menaced the world as the mad king Leontes. His shoulders sagged as he regarded the amphitheater, tall wings black against the bright sky, two thousand seats climbing up away from the open stage, and something sad and almost tragic emanating from the deserted theater that was nothing without the players. He spoke into the wind: *"Our revels now are ended. These our actors, / As I foretold you, were all spirits and / Are melted into air, into thin air…"*

As he walked out onto the Central Park Mall, the wind ripped down over the lake, blasting onto his face. He began to shake, though not from the cold. He didn't feel as bad as he should have for the amount of booze consumed the night before. Eating crossed his mind, but not for long.

In this theater world of New York, there was usually a friend to have a drink with anytime day or night and today, and he needed a friend, but he didn't want to go downtown to Stanley's Bar. He knew what would happen at Stanley's, so he avoided the disaster until he couldn't. Instead, he headed east through the maze of naked trees that were a thousand shades of black and brown. A splash of red caught his eye, a woman's hat as she darted through the trees. A glorious clear cold late November day, and as he hurried east, that same crushing fear that he didn't belong, that he was a fake, began to take charge of him, to master him with the pain of an outsider. He was staring in a hit play, for God's sake, and there were offers of more work. He walked faster across Fifth Avenue, past Park and Madison, and slipped into a saloon on Third Avenue. "Short Bush and a beer."

"What ho! Mr. Ryan, my friend." Allen, the day bartender, in what he fancied was a stage vibrato, said, "I hear the new show is terrific."

"Yeah, doing well." Mitch downed the shot. "I know you won't come to see it, but if you do, I'll take care of the ticket."

"They tell me you play a drunk. How do you manage to pull it off?"

"Acting, acting, acting. 'Except my life, except my life, except my life.' Give me another."

"Did you see the poster in the hall?"

Mitch moved to the hall, and there hung *Moon for the Misbegotten* in bold red and black.

At his favorite booth in the window, he watched the people passing by, studying them as if they were a different race, all looking tired and worried. He tried to guess what they did for a living and fluctuated between vague contempt for humanity and a deep longing to belong.

He had taken to the dark O'Neill—a truly great play—but he'd been startled by the rave reviews. He never thought working on and in this play would lead to so much attention. He had gone six years straight without a break from one play to another. He still felt the cloud of fear seep into him when he remembered his experiences during that aborted trip to Hollywood. But in New York in the bar, he was safe. He relaxed. "The time is out of joint," he said to Allen.

"Seems fine to me. Time is what it is." Mitch signaled for another. "Starting a little early, aren't you, Mitch?"

"Make it a double." He thought about Stanley's and felt the danger but pushed it down and away. He paid the bill, left, and hailed a cab to the dive that was his home away from home: Avenue B at the bottom of the world.

He'd gone for drinks at Stanley's ever since first coming to New York. It was a small dark bar that brought solace to the drunks of the Lower East Side. Lately, artists and the flotsam of the West Village had discovered the hellhole and migrated east. He loved Stanley's mainly because no one there knew or cared about what Mitch did or who he was. In Stanley's, everyone was on an even footing.

As usual, he left the cab at Fourteenth Street and walked down to Stanley's. Several bums sat on the curb, smelling of whiskey and rotten clothes. Tall, angular, faded tenements lined the two blocks down to Twelfth Street. The entranceways resembled dark mouths leading to the squalor inside. Maybe in the Bronx or Harlem, there was a more trashed street. Yet he was much more comfortable here than he was uptown. He was at home in the squalor because that matched how he felt about himself.

The building that housed Stanley's stood on the corner and had been built as a tenement for the Irish a hundred years before. Stanley lived on the top floors. A sign hanging over the door at one time had read, "Stanley's Tavern."

He pushed open the heavy wooden door. Two men sat facing out from the bar, behind them a large mirror and rows of bottles. Stanley himself, in the back of the bar, looked like he had never been anywhere else. To the left was a dark, gloomy empty room with a hall leading to the back. To the right were three windows, their panes smudged with grime and cigarette smoke.

One of the men watched Mitch as he made his entrance and progressed through the tables up to the bar. Stanley poured him a shot of rye and a glass of beer. The man who had been watching said, "Well, well! If it's not Mitchell Ryan, that great O'Neillian actor, star of Morning Becomes Afternoon."

A listless laugh went up from the shorter of the two men, a dark Greek with a classic face, and he said to the taller man, "Have you studied or even listened to any of Mozart's sonatas?"

"Of course I have, and they are very fine," said the first man, "but you can't put them in the same class as the concertos. There's no comparison. The complexity alone of a Mozart concerto far outweighs any sonata, Mozart's or Beethoven's or whoever the fuck writes one."

Mitch drank in the conversation as it droned on. It could have been any day, any time in Stanley's, just one ongoing, unresolved, and endless conversation. The music expert was Lou Popjieff. The Greek was Charlie Jeremiah. Lou was tall and gaunt with steel-rimmed glasses. Charlie was short and thick like his fisherman ancestors. "How's the play going?" Lou asked.

"Don't change the subject!" Charlie slammed his fist on the bar.

"It's like going on a large drunk every night from eight to eleven. Sort of imitating life. You want to see it?" Mitch leaned both arms on the bar.

"No, I get hydrophobic in crowds."

"You mean claustrophobic, you dummy," Charlie spoke to the listening world.

"No, I mean just what I say: theater audiences make me foam at the mouth. As do—pardon me, Mitch—most plays."

Charlie resumed his defense of the sonata. Mitch went to the toilet and stood staring at the wall, dirty with names and numbers written above the commode. Back in the bar, Lou and Charlie, nose to mustache, had switched to Kierkegaard and "infinite resignation." How appropriate. Mitch shook his head in awe, picked up his drink, moved away to a table.

"What's the matter? You look blue." Stanley took the chairs off the tables in preparation for the morning drunks. Mitch looked at Stanley's wrecked face and was flooded with feeling for this worn man who had been serving drinks and kind words to lonely men for years.

"No, I'm fine, all I need is another drink."

"Well, we can handle that."

Mitch laid his hand down on the table scarred from years of men pounding their glasses as they sweated and wept out their stories. He drank all day and night and finally passed out at one o'clock

149

that morning on a cot Stanley kept in the back room for these kinds of emergencies.

He woke up as the light started to fill the greasy window at the back of the storeroom. He washed his face in the men's room at a small sink with a large crucifix hanging on the wall in place of a mirror. He came out and sat down at the end of the bar. Lou was on his usual seat and Stanley right where he belonged as if no time at all had passed. Sitting next to Lou was Mike Cherry, who rented a room upstairs and tended bar on weekends.

"Here he is. The iceman cometh," Lou announced.

"What would we do without O'Neill?"

"Want a drink, I suppose?" Stanley leaned in. "That was quite a show you put on last night. About ten o'clock yesterday morning, I asked our actor if he was okay, and he said he was fine." Mitch looked for his money. "Give Lou and Mike something."

"Thank you, Mitch. Say thanks, Lou." Mike slapped Lou on the back.

"An actor springing for a drink—will wonders never cease. Well, Mitch," Lou launched in, "it is we who should buy the drinks. You were fine last night, I can't say enough. Did all of *Hamlet*, most of it with song."

After several glasses of ale, Mitch ventured to a small glass of whiskey and felt much better. Somewhere inside, he knew that yesterday's attack was a run for the hills, but he told himself that today would be peaceful and calm. Important, now, to pay attention and be careful with the drinks, to space them at intervals to maintain the proper meditative state.

Several others ambled over and were worked into the select group. The talk moved from topic to topic as if these men were public intellectuals, heavyweights, plumbing the mysteries of life's truths. There would be long silences and slow, unhurried dissertations. Mitch joined in from time to time, but mostly he was quiet.

At about two or three o'clock, someone brought up the subject of food and was shouted down. Several patrons left. Mitch was just considering that it might be time to leave when the door swung open. A woman stood framed in the light. She would have turned heads anywhere, but in this dive, she glowed like a vision. All in white, with a form-fitting top and a long flowing skirt. She had an open Slavic face and honey hair. A full-length mink coat was draped over her shoulders. She walked up to the bar between Lou and Mitch and slipped the mink around Mitch, saying, "I'm looking for Stanley," in a voice that was husky honey.

"That's me," Stanley stammered from behind the bar.

"You're very well thought of uptown, highly recommended by a friend and coworker of mine," she said, not glancing at Mitch, "so I thought I'd come down and see for myself. Can you make a martini?"

"What's in it?" Stanley was braced for the unknown.

"Vermouth and gin or vodka." The bar audience was riveted.

"We got no vermouth."

"I'm Salome and I brought my own." She pulled a bottle out of her black silk purse.

Stanley's voice was shaking with formality. "This is Lou, he's a musician, and Mitch here's an actor." She looked at Mitch and laughed.

"What do you do uptown—Salome, is it?" Mitch asked, knowing full well what she did uptown and wondering what this great actress had in mind, coming all the way down here to Stanley's Bar.

"You act, Mitch? What play are you in?" She smelled like fresh cream. "Who wants a martini?" There was a listless groan from the assortment of tired rotgut drinkers spread around the smoky room.

Ducking the question, he played along. "Can I keep this coat?" as he ran his fingers through the fur. He was flattered by the visit but also annoyed that she would intrude on his hideout. Performing together in O'Neill's *Moon* for nearly a year did not give even this close friend and artistic cohort permission to look into his hidden life of destruction.

Still looking at Mitch, she said, "Can you make a martini, Stanley?"

"Well, how hard can it be?"

"Stanley, would you allow me to make everyone a martini?" She turned to the room. "Everyone must have a martini. Who will join me?" There were, besides Lou, Mike Cherry, and Mitch, several regulars plus Charlie Jeremiah, who had just come in.

The men sitting at tables muttered in unison, "No thanks."

"Of course you'll have one. I'll pay."

"I've never had a martini. You, Charlie?" asked Lou.

"Oh, sure, many times when I was in the Foreign Service. I'd be honored to join you. I'm Charles Jeremiah." He bowed gallantly.

"I'm Salome," she called as she went around behind the bar, "I'll do the honors. How about you, Mitch? Now where is the shaker."

"I'll stay with rotgut, if it's all the same to you." He watched her, all in white, the dress clinging, her long legs. What a glorious body.

"You don't have to call it rotgut," Stanley turned and grunted as he threw down the bar towel. Mitch had forgotten he was sensitive.

Salome did a masterful job with the martinis, and Stanley found some halfway suitable glasses in the back. She mixed the drinks and served each man, charmingly, flirtatiously, and then said, "We must all dance, and I see a jukebox. What's on it?" Nobody knew, nor had anyone listened in recent memory.

"Lou, you said you were a musician. What do you play?"

"Well, I play the sax, but not for a while. I've got one, it's in Mike's apartment, upstairs."

"Go get it right now. I must have music, and I must dance! She started to move her hips in a slow grind and pulled Stanley out from behind the bar. He turned away as she moved up against him and fled to the back in embarrassment. Mitch went up to her as she slowly moved around the tables and blocked her way. "What do you think you're doing?"

"What's the matter, Mitch? Someone stealing your thunder, losing control of your little kingdom?"

"What do you want, damn it?"

"You'll see…more shall be revealed."

He went back to the bar, catching a look at himself in the mirror. His face was red and blotched. He felt dirty.

Lou was back with Mike and three others. "Play!" Salome commanded.

Lou started to play his classic golden sax, a little shaky at first but slowly better and then quite good. Salome danced with all the men. She even persuaded Stanley to do a turn. When she was done with everyone but Mitch, she moved alone. Her dress caught the light and transformed Stanley's broken remains of a bar into a glimmering dance hall. Mitch watched it all with a slightly amused feeling of wonder at the sheer nerve of this woman.

Finally, she came to him. "Come dance."

He wouldn't leave his perch at the bar, but she pulled him off the stool.

Mitch took her in his arms. She was almost as tall as he and a terrific dancer. Her body was hot. At first, he held her at arm's length, but she slowly pulled him close, her lips close enough to whisper in his ear: "Archer is looking for you." She waited for his reaction. "They want us to go on the road starting next week for the Theater Guild and play all the great cities." She pulled back to watch him with such delight that he burst out laughing. "So will you come home with me now and let me pamper you so you will be wonderful in the last week of our O'Neill in New York?" Then a radiant smile and a big hug. He laughed again.

The whole bar applauded Mitch: "Gentlemen, this woman is pleading with me to marry her. What shall I say?"

CHAPTER 17

On the Road Again
1969

ALWAYS MOVING, ALWAYS restless, his life had the texture of a butterfly. No. A butterfly was too peaceful and seeming content. In his movement he was more like a mosquito or a horsefly. On the train down from New York with the cast of the touring company of *Moon for the Misbegotten*, he felt he would rather be anywhere but on the road. He needed a break from O'Neill's dark side. The quiet first-class ride through the idyllic Maryland countryside was lovely but no antidote to his wondering inner world. All the long trips he had endured in his short life came flooding into his distracted memory. To California with a movie star, Greyhound bus back east. Several bus tours, *Rainmaker, Julius Caesar.* There were more, but arriving in Washington cut his nightmare short. They checked in and dispersed to the rooms. For the next months, he would be living in a hotel. A strange wonder a hotel—everything done for you, soap, thick towels, anything you want brought to your room. This first stop of the tour was Washington, DC, at the grand old historic Ford Theater. He spotted a bar on the way into the giant lobby of the hotel. First stop.

"Maybe you had better take it easy until after we open." Salome sat down beside him.

"Yes, I'll be all right. Just blue and don't know which way to turn. I think I'll go for a walk."

"I'll come."

"No, could I be alone—you don't mind, do you?"

"Sure, I understand." But she couldn't, for all her profound empathic genius, so for the first time, she was truly afraid for Mitch.

He walked down Pennsylvania Avenue past the White House, all lit up, and thought of Kennedy winning the election, and now he was dead, and his brother was dead, and Nixon was the chief. He walked all the way to Georgetown and back. All night he walked, stopping at an occasional corner bar for a taste, and finally went to sleep on a bench out in the National Mall.

When he awoke, disoriented, he saw a group of schoolchildren running across the Mall toward the Washington monument, all shouting, young and full of life. He sat looking up the Mall past the monument. With the noise of screeching and yelling the intrusion of long-ago school filled his memory. Just then, he was startled by a vicious shout off to the left: "Give me that or you will be sorry, you little rat!" He turned and saw a bigger boy pushing a smaller one. Images of the playground at his grade school and Jackie Parsons came before his inner eye. "No, you dumb shit, you don't want chocolate, you want vanilla." Traces of school memories intruded into his mind, reminding him how he ran away that day and how he always failed the challenge, the demands of school.

He got a rental car and drove out into the Virginia countryside. Dark clouds hung low in the sky, sucking the color out of the green and gold farmland. He stopped to study a crumbling barn that had been red once upon a time. It started to rain. He raised his head and let the big drops splash on his face as he leaned on a split-rail fence beside the road.

He put his hand on the top rail and began to saw his body once, twice, and over the fence like an imitation of some ancient Olympic hurdler. Then he broke into a run across the field as if his life depended on getting to the other side. Or was he running to escape from something. He slopped in the mud through the pouring rain, up a hill, across another field, trampling on the growing life, and finally sat on another rail fence that bordered a dense wood.

He panted out the words: "To…be…or…not…to be." What if everything ended now? What if he wasn't here anymore? Was this the time to leave? *To…go…or…not…to…go.* "What would we do without Shakespeare?" He climbed up on the first rail, then to the top rail, just wide enough for him to keep his balance, and started to walk down the fence. "You see," he shouted to the wind and rain, "I'm not afraid—this is who I am, not that foolish act of myself." He lost his balance, fell into the mud, and lay there, free and happy. Everything suddenly familiar like being back on his grandmother's farm, lying in the cornfield out behind the barn when the rain started that day, and he wouldn't move. He'd heard them calling but said not a word. Five years old. So calm with the rain on his face, knowing he belonged much more to the rain, the corn, and the mud than to anything else in his world. Now in this all-new rain Mitch sat up and watched, through the drizzle, the clouds open and the sun peek through. "The clouds methought would open and show riches Ready to drop on me…"

He didn't want to be anywhere else in the world at this moment. His body was as light and free as if it could float up to the sky, just as it'd been behind that barn thirty years before. And in this forgotten field, that small boy and he were the same. A "boy eternal" moment.

Then the magic was gone. He stayed still, waiting, then started to thrash around and slap his hands in the muddy water. "Singing in the rain, I'm singin' in the rain, what a glorious feeling I'm happy again." He rose, soaking wet and covered with mud, danced back to his car, imitating Gene Kelly as best he could: "I'm singin' and dancing in the rain."

In the front seat, he studied the red barn being lashed by the storm. He shut his eyes and listened to the rhythm of the rain, the thrilling moments lying in the mud still very much with him. He slept, then awoke with a jerk, and consulted his watch: 4:00 p.m.

He drove back to town to the theater. He parked the car, pulled the bottle of whiskey out of the glove compartment, entered the stage door, and climbed up to his dressing room.

What had happened out there in the rain? What had left him with the calm, fresh feeling that things would be all right? The transformation had the markings of a miracle. He didn't recognize what he saw in the mirror. He was different. For a moment, there seemed to be a stranger looking back at him.

Salome knocked and came in. "Jesus, we were worried. You all right?"

"Want a nip?"

"No, and you don't need one either. It's opening night, you know."

"There's no business like show business! I'm fine and liable to get better." She started to leave. "Sal, I love you, you know."

"Sure." She left.

He was looking forward to the play. The work saved him.

Most every night during the tour across America, he and Salome would go to the bar nearest their hotel after the curtain and drink. He was lucky to have her. God knows what would have happened if she hadn't been there. He wanted to share this new feeling of peace and calm with her, but how could he describe these feelings, and would she understand? They had faded some since the run in the rain. An illusion, maybe. In any case, he never did share with her or anyone else his inner journey and its deep joy. All that was left of that moment in the field was an interior vibration that would come sometimes when he was onstage in a quiet scene, and there was that connection between him and the audience. Energy would flow from them to him, and he could send it back.

The show toured America—Chicago, St. Louis, Dallas, and Denver. In each city, he found fresh depths in the role. After having delivered several hundred performances in New York, his experience on the road seemed totally different. He was humbled to find a powerful theatrical tradition in the playhouses of these towns. Some of the theaters were very old and had been hosting roadshows out of New York for at least a hundred years. Standing in the green rooms or on the stage, he would reflect on the past and the great actor-managers who had toured the country, back to Kean and Booth, Irving and Barrymore, and also O'Neill's own father, James. Those days were long past, and the theater didn't offer that kind of life anymore.

This would invite in Mitch the gloom of a missed opportunity and what might have been. Such is the alcoholic mind.

At last, the play made its way to Los Angeles, the world of the movies, a world he was about to enter.

CHAPTER 18

The Wild West
1969

MITCH WALKED THROUGH big glass doors leading into a three-story entrance hall with a spiral staircase winding its way to the top, hallways running off on either side flanked by windows flooding California light everywhere. He asked the receptionist for the office of Landers and Roberts, followed her directions, and sat down to wait while a good-looking young woman at the upstairs desk went to tell them he was here. Bobby Roberts and Hal Landers were the producers of *Monte Walsh*, the film he had just been hired to do. Walter Beakel, an old friend who became his Hollywood agent, had urged the two producers to see *Moon for the Misbegotten* two nights earlier.

Roberts came down the hall, holding out his hand. "Mitch. Bobby Roberts. May I call you Mitch?" He didn't wait for an answer. "Great to have you in the movie, everyone in town was after this part. But when we saw you, we knew right away you were the guy." How had they got an illiterate cowboy of the 1890s out of the drunken O'Neill Broadway character he was playing on the stage.

"Come." He started down the hall. "He's waiting to meet you, and Jack just showed up." Mitch knew "he" meant Lee Marvin, but who was Jack?

Into the office and right in front of him was Jack Palance. Behind him, sitting in the window, was Marvin. They seemed giant men, and Mitch felt he already knew them, the way you feel when you meet celebrities.

"What do you understand about Eugene O'Neill's problem?" Marvin did not even look up.

"Jesus, what kind of a question is that?" Jack came to Mitch and grabbed his hand. "What the fuck do you know about O'Neill?" Lee sniped at Jack. "Did you ever do one of his plays?"

"As a matter of fact, I...Oh, to hell with it. Good to have you here, Mitch. Don't listen to this asshole."

Lee burst out laughing. He had a tragic grin on his enormous face and long shoulder-length pure-white hair. "Tell us about Shane, Jack."

And before Jack could say, "Fuck you, Lee," Marvin went on: "You're right, I'm an asshole, but I still want to find out about O'Neill. You want a beer?"

Mitch didn't know why he was surprised that Lee Marvin knew anything about O'Neill and had an interest in O'Neill, and Mitch would like to find out about his interest, but being in this situation with two movie stars, all he said was, "Maybe he drank too much."

"How much is too much?" Marvin talked in questions.

"Hardly any is too much for you," put in Jack, "I'm surprised you're still alive. Well, got to go, see you in Tucson," and he was out the door. Lee handed Mitch a beer, and as if on cue, in came a tall, lanky man with a white beard who looked like a Civil War general.

He was followed by a dark, sexy woman who went straight to Lee. "I thought you were not going to drink today."

"Mitch, this is Bill Fraker, the director, and this is Michelle, the cunt." Then Lee went back to the window, turned, and smiled at the audience of three standing there watching him. Mitch looked at Michelle and observed her barely perceptible humiliation morph into a tough-manager attitude. A shock at the casual way this brutal line was thrown and the quick absorption by the woman generated in Mitch all the terror of his whole life. He had been on guard, but now he realized he was in enemy territory and must be very smart. "We have to go," she announced to Lee. "We're late and you need to do this. *The New York Times* is staying at the Beverly Wilshire."

"All of them?" Lee said over his shoulder as they left. Roberts quickly consulted with Landers, and then they hurried after their star.

"I saw the second act of the play last night," Fraker offered when they were gone. "You were great. That is some part. I'm a cameraman and I'm going to direct this movie." Fraker went to the desk and picked up a script. "Have a look at this. I'm getting some terrific actors from New York. You may know some of them, so I'm not worried. Just take care of the acting, and I assure you, you'll look great."

The next evening Mitch was backstage at the Lindy Opera House, standing in the hallway leading to his dressing room when the producers, Roberts and Landers, and Fraker walked in the stage door. They were pale.

Roberts burst out with, "Did you get fired from *A Man Called Horse*?"

"Yes, I think I did. All I did was a costume call. Then I was told not to go to Arizona."

"Were you drunk at that call?"

"Yes, I'd been drinking. Why?"

"Jerry Henshaw, the head of production for the studio that's financing this movie, also did *A Man Called Horse*.

There was a long pause. As Mitch looked at the three angry and disappointed faces, the memory of the quiet peace that had touched his life in the rain that day in Virginia allowed him to swell with courage and realize he had a way out of this horror they call Hollywood. He had spent a sleepless night after he confronted Salome with the news that he would be leaving the show at the end of the run in Los Angeles and watched the sad disappointment fill her beautiful face. He also remembered the costume call in a flash. He had been drunk out of his mind. There would be no way he could do this movie now to his great relief.

"As I remember it," Mitch said, pulling himself together, "I told Archer King, my agent at the time, to get me out of the movie. I did not want to play an Indian who speaks no English."

All three of them seemed to turn a slight shade of green.

Just then, Mitch's agent, Walter, who'd set up the deal, came running down the hall. "I just talked to Meyer and he says not to worry. Lee wants Mitch to do the movie. Lee and Mishkin are going to talk to Henshaw in the morning, and we should all be there. But not you, Mitch."

After they left, Mitch walked from the theater to the hotel where the *Moon* cast was staying. On his way, he bought a paper and a pack of cigarettes and did a little jig as he waltzed up the street. He laughed. Everyone in town wanted this part? Well, they could have the whole movie. That's how sure he was that Jerry Henshaw would never hire him. He met Salome at the restaurant across from the hotel. "I'm not going to do the movie, and I'm very happy about that. I would not do well out here and certainly not in Arizona."

"I thought they wanted you."

"The producer who fired me from *A Man Called Horse* wants no part of me."

Mitch didn't drink that night. Later in his room, he was suddenly overcome with waves of joy, the likes of which he'd felt only as a child in the cornfield of his grandmother's farm and again when he'd run in the rain those months ago at the start of this tour. Stupid to have ever entertained this movie idea, he was an artist. Stupid to leave a show he loved that had eight more weeks to play in four cities. A form of art he had spent fifteen years working hard to master. But now he was free. What a miraculous escape! He went to bed alone and slept like a baby.

The next day Walter and Bobby Roberts came to his hotel and found Mitch in the coffee shop. "It was no contest," Roberts said, "Meyer and Lee were great."

"It was pure Hollywood," Walter added. "You should have been there. I hadn't heard such good bullshit in a long time." A thickness came over Mitch. He couldn't speak. "Well, say something," Walter hollered, almost jumping up and down. "What do you think of that, you lucky son of a bitch?"

"He couldn't let go of the coffee, then spilled it all over his pants," Mitch managed. "Very good, Walter, thank you. I've got to get to the theater. Thank you both for everything." As he fled Roberts, see you in Tucson!

So at the end of the week, they closed *Moon*. His understudy would do the show until they could find someone from New York to take over. He said goodbye to Salome, who was happy and not happy. He was sick to leave this play and doubtful when Walter told him what a great step this movie would be. "You can always return to New York and choose what you want to do, but this way, you can have two worlds."

Mitch knew somewhere in his gut that this was not true. "I have trouble with one world. How can I handle two?" He flew to Tucson, Arizona, the next morning.

Mitch stepped off the plane in Tucson into a hot, dry desert wind. Walking toward the terminal, he looked out at the gold and mauve mountains that ringed the area. The sky was immense, the clouds a brilliant starchy white. As he walked across the tarmac, taking in the vast sky and feeling the warm wind, the tension began to leave his body. Filming in this beautiful spot couldn't be too bad. At the gate, he saw a craggy-looking man, a genuine cowboy, who could have been an Indian; he was so dark.

"Mr. Ryan?"

"Mitch, please."

They shook hands, and the cowboy introduced himself as Leroy Johnson. So this was the famous stuntman, nearly as legendary as Marvin himself. He wore old jeans and a blue shirt under a ragged deerskin coat and a sweat-stained hat that seem to suit the myth. He had an animal sense about him, alert, calm.

He walked Mitch toward the luggage carousel. "We only been here three days, and we're already two weeks behind." Mitch laughed. "All the drivers were sick and hungover, so they asked me to get you." His huge sinewy hands picked up Mitch's two heavy bags as if they were empty. Mitch also noticed he had a conspicuous limp.

"How'd you hurt your leg?"

"Horse fall, he rolled on me. Let's go." As they drove off, he said, "So you're from New York?"

"Yes. Marvin and Fraker saw me in a play."

"I worked in New York some years back, did stunts and horse stuff for Dennis Weaver. I forget the name of the show if I ever knew it. You do plays? Hah. What play?"

"It was called the *Moon for the Misbegotten*."

"*Misbegotten*? What does that mean?"

"I think it means sort of, well, a kind of misfit." Mitch suddenly found this was a strange talk to be having with a stuntman he'd just met, and also, Mr. Johnson was speeding in and out of traffic.

"Yeah, that makes sense. Worked on *The Misfits*, did Gable's horse stuff. Jesus, what a fucking collection of loonies that bunch was. They took the cake." Mitch mentally ran down the list of actors in that movie, some of the best in the world. This stuntman was a tough customer. "They told me this is your first film."

"I did a film twelve years ago with Robert Mitchum."

"You know all about it then. You know the score." Suddenly Mitch was out of his league, and he knew it. "Can you ride a horse?"

"No."

"Well, that's something."

Mitch couldn't tell what he meant. The man's genuine smile belied his comment. Suddenly he, the stage actor from New York City, was in alien territory and realized this job would be a challenge. What he did know was limited but had to do with playing a role. Now he had to find a role that would let him into the world of Leroy Johnson.

Leroy's driving was just short of reckless, but behind the wheel, he was as still as a deer in the woods. Mitch ventured, after a violent swerve that just missed a truck, "Jesus Christ!"

"Don't worry, son, I'm only reckless with other people in the car."

"Well, that's a relief."

"Ah-ha! That's a good one, son."

The cast and crew were staying at a rambling motel that Mitch found out later had been the home for movie crews and actors for some thirty years. The place smelled of soap and disinfectant. Leroy told him to go to the office. "You're expected."

There he met the assistant director, a burly red-faced Irishman with a cowboy hat perched on his huge head. "Here's the cast list, a shooting schedule, the call for tomorrow, and some money. Costume and makeup call tomorrow. No shooting."

He went to the bar and sat down beside a tall, very thin man who looked like a cowboy. "Name's Mitch."

The cowboy looked over and, in a raspy voice, pronounced, "Actor," as if describing a disease.

"Yes, does it show?"

"Very much. I'm Fred. I drive the camera truck and other odd jobs."

Mitch was curious what the trait was that nailed him as an actor but decided to let this mystery go. In fact, Fred was an "expert" on everything, which Mitch learned later was common to all drivers. When he finally escaped away to his room, he lay awake till early in the morning, wondering again what kind of world he had entered and what he thought he was doing here.

At 5:00 a.m., he rolled over and tried to imagine what the day would be like. In the lobby, the AD pointed to what he called a "stretch-out vehicle," and Mitch climbed in with nine people he didn't know. When they arrived at the set, he was dumbfounded. They had built a whole town—hotel, saloon, livery stable, hardware store, and main street with houses. Farther over a rise was a working ranch with corrals, a large barn, bunkhouse, and scores of horses.

He had sense enough to tell Pervus, the wrangler who was to give him riding instruction, that he knew nothing about horses or horsemanship. Pervus didn't tell Mitch a thing about what not to do. Like all good teachers, he spoke only about what Mitch should do, and he kept it spare and simple. Within an hour, Mitch was catching on and began to ride up the road and dismount. He practiced the dismount and the mounting with more ease. Leroy rode up. "If you live long enough, you might get the hang of this."

Mitch loved horsemanship, rode every day, and soon he looked like he'd been riding all his life. He was given a holster and a two-and-a-half-pound .45 Colt six-shooter revolver. Since he was supposed to be a quick draw, there was no end of embarrassment when the gun went flying as he tried to draw the six-shooter out of the holster, inspiring a nickname, the Lincoln Center Kid, which stuck. He understood where that nickname came from. Hostility turned to shrewd humor. This was classic cowboy humor, and he loved and understood that this approach to life went back to Mark Twain and Abe Lincoln. He had to win them over, so he decided to play the person they wanted him to be, the tenderfoot who had to be initiated.

Sometime in the first week, Mitch became aware of a beautiful redhead who was a stand-in. Her name was Lynda. He had always been struck by red hair. He walked up to her early on in the shoot. "You look great on that horse, like you and he are one."

She gave him a pitying disdainful look. "You're going to have to do a lot better than that. Of course we're one, we were raised together." Later at the bar, she bought him a drink. She had a baby boy and a missing husband. She was a real cowgirl, and he was intrigued. She was completely unlike the actresses he knew and a tough drinker who loved marijuana. He saw her every day. They became good friends, and he liked her two-year-old son, a sweet little hellion named Tim.

Things were happening fast, and he forgot the theater. At night he would feel stricken and ask himself what he was doing, playing like a kid with six-shooters and horses, but he pushed the guilt away and slept like a baby. Drinking was fun again, and the desert sun blasted the hangovers into oblivion.

Each day he would study the cowboys and stuntmen, study how these master craftsmen handled the saddles and all the tack that belonged to the ancient culture of horsemanship. For Mitch, everything was new, a whole new way of living, not just the film-acting or camera technique but the very real old world of the cowboy.

That first day he walked around the set and down to the end of the town where a huge barn had been constructed. At the entrance, in silhouette, he could see the many "hands," handling the horses and washing them down, then walking them to the corral to "turn them out." He felt a kind of longing as he walked over to the fence. "Hello, I'm Mitch."

A ruddy young hard-looking cowboy turned his head. "Sonny. What part do you play?" Everyone knew he was an actor. He had on his wardrobe and had thought when he reviewed himself in the dressing room mirror that he had looked pretty authentic.

"It's the part of Shorty."

"Hey, Mickey, here's your actor."

A tall, lanky cowboy about Mitch's build shifted slightly from his reclining position at the other end of the barn and raised his hat from over his eyes to look in their direction. "I'll do your stunt work." Mitch walked over and introduced himself. Mickey, still lying there propped up against the barn, raised his hand. "Can you ride?"

"I'm learning."

"Well, don't worry, I'll handle all the rough stuff. I think we'll shoot the bronco-breaking scene in a day or two. See you at the bar tonight. You can buy me a drink." Then he leaned back and pulled his hat back over his eyes.

The young men were strong and graceful, while the older ones were getting fat and profane. All of them, he learned, had Leroy Johnson's sense of humor. And every last one had nothing but scorn for "the art of acting." As time went by, Mitch learned by keeping quiet and watching to see what was needed. He found out that you're treated well by the stuntmen and cowboys if they like you and if you live up to some secret standard like riding a horse at full gallop through a bar.

These cowboys had their role to play and had been perfecting an identity from the last century. Mitch later learned that some of the most thoughtful of them, like Leroy, had highly developed bullshit meters and felt acting—when they bothered considering acting fakery at all—was nothing more or less than being real. And if you were trying too hard to act, you were a phony. This logic made sense. The rough wood houses and the wardrobe and the guns and the horses and the desert and the mountains did most of the work creating the reality of the 1890s male-dominated West, filled with violence and bravado and tinged with twentieth-century right-wing ideology. Mitch loved it.

Late in the week, the company drove about seventy-five miles out to Patagonia, down near Mexico. When a film company moves, there is a great caravan of stretch-outs and pickups and semis with large cranes balanced like prehistoric animals. Cattle trucks carry the livestock, and a huge chuck wagon feeds the hundred fifty actors and crew—several camera crews with electricians, grips who lay the track for the cameras and build platforms used by the director, painters and greens men who move bushes and take out trees, stuntmen and real cowboys who wrangle the stock, and the twenty or so actors and their stand-ins. Stand-ins who do just that for the actors during the lighting and camera preparation.

The gathering place was the chuck wagon, where everyone hung out when they weren't needed. Leroy was the leader, and Mitch, fresh meat, was the butt of most of the jokes when they realized he wasn't sensitive about being a tenderfoot.

"Well," Leroy pronounced one day as Mitch walked up to the gang, "well, it's the Lincoln Center Kid. Well, kid, we all now know what your real name is."

"What's that?" said a barrel of a man named Bear Hutchins, who had been a bodyguard for gangster Mickey Cohen. "His name is Mr. Only. It's printed on his dressing room door. I seen him come outta that door, and it was plainly marked 'Men Only.' Is that an Irish name, Mr. Only?" The whole crowd laughed.

Then on cue, another stuntman piped up, "Tell us about them, what do you call them...*plays*, Mr. Only?"

"No, no!" Leroy gave the cowboy a shot on the back. "His name's the Lincoln Center Kid. He likes that handle, and I think we should honor his feelings. Well, tell us, what is a *play*, kid?"

Mitch, on the spot, ate his instant Irish fury. He knew this was an absurd question, and the truth was obvious, but of course, he couldn't say, "You boys are a play, and not one of you has the slightest idea that you're in one of the greatest tragic plays of all time." He recognized these men for what they were, living as they could, trying to preserve proudly some semblance of what was past and gone. A pulp fiction that had transformed the century of exploring and settling of the real Old West into this gaudy pageant completely made up and populated by people like them, with their rehearsed parts, played out day after day.

Suddenly he was sad. What a sordid spectacle. The Lincoln Center Kid fit right in with this farce. In his mind, he had betrayed the theater, and their faces reminded him of when he was a boy watching the bullies taunt Donald Coward, who was bald because of scarlet fever. He looked at the faces, now, of these strange hard men, smirking with twisted smiles and full of bitter humor, and finally, sensing danger, Mitch came out with, "Well, a play is when you have to do your own stunts. That's the reason there are no stuntmen doing plays." Silence, then they heard a loud clapping and turned to see Marvin standing back of the chuck wagon.

"Don't, whatever you do, hang around with the stuntmen. They're nothing but a lazy bunch of bums. All they do is stage fights and get paid for it. They try to make a big show of falling off horses, but any idiot can fall off a horse," he said this with an evenness and bite that Mitch felt he really meant.

Marvin walked away, and all the cowboys moseyed back to the barn. Mitch stood alone. He was a hybrid and knew he didn't really belong anywhere right now, not the theater, not the movies, not the West, nowhere. In order to survive, some action would be necessary.

His opportunity came sooner than he expected. On the third day of the shoot, they were to film a sequence where, in response to an accident with one of the wagons, several cast members—Mitch included—were supposed to run and mount their horses, which were tied to the hitching post in a close row, and then ride out fast. Leroy told the director to be careful because if you run at horses, they will get jumpy. Well, on "Action," four actors and stuntmen heard the crash of the wagon and ran to the horses. Mitch's horse reared and broke his tie before Mitch could mount him, but Mitch, the kid from Lincoln Center, seized the moment, as the horse came down, by grabbing the horn. When the horse took off, Mitch ran alongside the animal and somehow swung himself up into the saddle and, hugging the horse's neck, took hold of the reins and brought the creature under control. The shot was a mess, but Mitch's action created a ripple among the stuntmen and cowboys. No one said anything, but after that, things were different. He began to feel accepted. Later in the bar, when several stuntmen bought him a drink, he mused, *I see you have to nearly kill yourself to get in this club.*

Most of the days in the Sonora Desert were a hundred ten degrees, but in the evenings, a gentle orange blossom breeze flowed through the outdoor bar at the snappy Desert Inn. Several months of this caused Mitch to relax into a new rhythm, leaving New York and the stage and his fate a distant memory.

Every night before they drank too much, he and Lynda would walk out into the desert and watch the sunset. She had been raised in the desert and often said, "I can't imagine any place better than this that could soften the soul and give you such a glow." After the grueling hot days, this was a meditation to walk out behind the inn and to watch the sweep of sky go from light blue to mauve to several shades of indigo, finishing in deep purple and finally black, except for the billions of stars. This is when he fell in love forever with the desert. At the same time, he fell in love with that beautiful woman and her trouble of a son. Just what a full-blown drunk needed.

He worked all summer in Tucson and drank a lot with everyone, mainly with Marvin, who took to Mitch and wanted him around. He was a little afraid of this man who had a way of acting, so you never knew to whom you were talking, his changing personalities, and his cast of characters.

At last, the shoot was over, and the company was heading back to Hollywood, the entirety of Arizona, the film, and the desert all fading to black. He felt a great sadness when Lynda told him, "I could never live in Los Angeles."

"I hate Los Angeles too, could never live there, and anyway, I'm going to move back to New York."

"Oh my god, if there's one place worse than Los Angeles, it's New York." They laughed, then she kissed him and left. He watched her climb into her old truck, wave, and drive onto the highway. He walked to the edge of the parking lot and watched that dirty gray-blue truck disappear around a curve.

Arizona had been a superficial interlude as he later learned all location shoots were, and when the company came back to Hollywood to finish, all was different. He was cut adrift and had little to do to finish the film, but he was on call, thrown back into a town he didn't know. He sat in his hotel and realized he was the same lost person he had been, but now with no role to study, and the only way not to take stock and look into himself was to drink. He thought of going back to New York, but in the end, he stayed in Los Angeles. He found an apartment on that stretch of Pacific Coast Highway, cheaply made and not worth what they wanted for rent, but there was a balcony, and the ocean was beautiful. Walter helped him buy a car so he could get around. He remembered the long-ago dream he had had when he went on the trek across the country with Robert Mitchum. "Buy a fancy car and live in Malibu." Well, here he was. Holy Christ! He found he didn't care for the ocean. It was cold, and he never went near it but to walk up the beach. That closed him in on one side. On the other was PCH six feet from the front door. He was trapped. His only escape was to drive somewhere into Beverly Hill or Hollywood. This lasted a very short time. The bars were much too fancy for him. He at last found the bars in Malibu were much more to his taste and moods—dirty and run-down.

Everything started to come back in on him. He realized he was the same lost boy he had always been. Without the theater to guide him and dig deep into his inner world, he was nothing. He would drink himself into a dangerous state and risk driving home. I must get out of here. Go back to New York, he would say every night as he tried to sleep.

One night when he was lying on the bed without getting undressed, the phone rang. What was that? Must be the Circle in the Square. It was Lynda. "I find I miss you. Do you think Tim and I could come to California?"

"You want to stay?"

"Yes, at least for a while."

"It will be fine. I wanted you to come all along. It makes me very happy."

And he was. He almost fell down the side stairs, down to the ocean, and ran out into the lapping surf. Then he remembered he hated water, and the Pacific was cold as hell. He laughed; he howled.

He forgot as if they had never existed the theater and New York and any dream or need to work again in the theater arts.

Lynda and her son Tim came to live with him. They bought a bed and several chairs and set up house. She loved the sea and swam every day. Tim was thunderstruck. He had never seen the ocean and stood for a long time just staring. They settled in, and it was peaceful, and Mitch, if not happy, was content with the way things were.

Walter called and found him TV jobs. He did TV Westerns that fall, *High Chaparral* and several others. He and Lynda smoked grass and drank not a lot but steadily. So it went from month to month, and then it was almost a year, and *Monte Walsh* opened in New York to not very helpful reviews. He was invited to the premiere but wouldn't go. He didn't go near the reason, which was buried deep in his clouded psyche. Everyone took turns blasting him for not going. The producers called and were upset. Walter was beside himself. Even Lee Marvin came by and wondered why and ended up saying, "Whatever you want." There was such a deep need to murder all that would lead him to responsibility for his life and a terror of this responsibility to take his place and be a grown-up.

Slowly the alcohol began to take over. By the end of the year, Mitch astounded himself at the volume of alcohol he was drinking. He drank all day. Sometimes he and Lynda would go to Topanga Canyon to a compound where Will Geer lived. They drank and watched their doper friends Matt and Tom get high. These boys had good-natured fun with Mitch at the expense of booze. "Dope will get you in touch with the higher nature. Whiskey will kill you," Tom would say, slipping into a catatonic state.

This is the way Mitch lived. In the late spring, Walter called and announced, "You are a lucky son of a bitch. You have been cast in a big movie to be shot in Spain. With movie stars."

CHAPTER 19

Spain
1970

WALTER HAD SENT him a telegram: *"It's all over town. Even as much as I try to downplay it the producers are really pissed off and want to bury you. We'll work it out. Walter."*

Mitch tried to make sense of it, tried to get past the first line of defense: it hadn't cost them any time—what difference did it make to them if he drank as much as he did?

The stewardess appeared. "Can I help you?"

"You can have this champagne. Do you have any saltines?"

"Yes."

"Also, bring a vodka, please."

"You're not going to join the other...?" The actor up front was blasting away, and everyone in first class was wondering what could be done.

"No, I don't know him. Don't worry, I'll be fine." Suddenly he was bereft. The three-year-old child in him, his constant companion, was telling him, *You're done for. You will never play in the sandbox again.* Then came the four-hundred-year-old voice: *"The undiscovered country from whose bourn / No traveler returns..."* Between him and thoughts of suicide, Shakespeare's voice. Life.

Whenever his thoughts went in that direction, he would dwell on what it would be like not to be here anymore. This thought disquieted him just enough to prompt him to have another drink. The vodka came, and as he sat listening to the hum of the engines, he reviewed the past several weeks.

Had it only been two weeks since he had arrived in Madrid to do *The Hunting Party*? The elevated ego that comes with being in a big film in Europe had pumped him up in his first-class seat, drinking champagne all the way from California to New York and then from New York to Spain.

Almeria was a sunbaked medieval village in southern Spain on the Mediterranean. From the window in his hotel room, Mitch could look out over a beautiful orange and violet garden past the azure sea to the distant coast of Africa. A fortress built by the Moors during the great Christian-Moorish wars covered the hills above the town.

One night about a week after they had stormed into Almeria, Oliver Reed announced, "We must have roast pig." The roast-pig restaurant had been built in the fourteenth century with fierce stonewalls and high arching windows. From where they sat, they could see two large ovens around which brightly dressed cooks prepared the pig, then slid it into the flames on metal spatulas. Mitch watched the flames. This was an exotic, strange country. The dark, strong people, handsome men, and beautiful women stirred him.

Standing behind a wine bar were two women dressed in identical black, an older one with deeply etched lines in her face and a younger, taller one with beautiful light chocolate skin and deep black eyes, whom Mitch correctly assumed to be the daughter. Mitch found himself powerfully drawn to them, wanting to hear them talk, to find out about their lives, and to get away from the loud table of would-be cowboys. As the roast pig arrived on several large platters, Mitch walked over to the Spanish women and met the younger woman's eyes. They connected, and there was a sense of primal danger as she held his gaze. He remembered Irene, the intense, intoxicating Greek actress who had taken over his life years before. The two women had the same eyes. Finally, she looked down and brought her hand to her lips for a brief moment. The older woman turned to her but said nothing.

He asked for a glass of wine. A small man he hadn't noticed came from around the partition. "What kind, señor?"

"What do you recommend?" Mitch asked the younger woman, regarding her steadily. The older woman turned to him, and with the same eyes, but eyes ablaze, said, "No! England!" The young woman said something harshly to her mother, then looked at Mitch and slowly, as if caressing the words, added, "Señor, quiere Bodegas Emilio Moro Tinto." Her voice was low, and as her lips moved, he felt a quiver through his body.

He took the bottle the man offered him. "Put it on the bill." At the table, he looked back at her. She was watching him.

Mitch returned to the roast-pig place the next night and then the night after that to see the young woman again, each time having no idea where to start to contact her. He was getting increasingly obsessed. She was elegant, inaccessible, and yet near enough to possibly approach, despite the mother perpetually standing guard. How to break the barrier of culture and language?

His last night in the film, Mitch showed up again. He was drunk and realized he was causing a stir among the waiters and the fierce little man who served the wine. But he didn't care. He stood at the counter, unable to read the look on the young woman's face, but when she didn't look away, he asked her to come and sit with him and enjoy a glass of wine. At this the mother said something to one of the waiters, and the little man came to him and asked him to leave.

"I'm not doing anything—just want to talk and visit with her." Mitch tried to hide the desperation in his voice.

"Please leave, señor."

Then, irrationally, stridently, his voice going up several notes: "No, I won't. I'm not doing anything!"

One of the waiters put his hand on Mitch's arm. "Please… leave."

Mitch jerked free, and then suddenly, two Guardia Civil state policemen were standing in front of him. "Please come with us."

Taken by surprise, he flushed with anger. "What for, what's the charge?"

"No charge. You must leave."

"Why? I'm not doing anything."

"You must leave," they repeated more emphatically.

"Goddamn, this is stupid—I'm going to eat." Mitch headed for a table.

But the Guardia now had him by the arm and were moving him toward the exit. Mitch, needing deeply to be heard, resisted. This was a mistake. The policemen threw him out the door. He landed on his knees. For a moment, he felt utterly removed from reality and imagined he was in a movie. It all seemed important, though, and he kept thinking, I'm not doing anything. He considered various lines of dialogue but determined that it would be more effective to remain silent and on his knees. The two giant policemen then politely asked if he needed a ride back to his hotel. He shook his head no and shifted position, so he was sitting in the street. As the Guardia walked away, standing in the doorway were the Spanish waiter and the wine procurer, staring down at him. Getting himself up, Mitch, humiliated, felt like a Jean Gabin character in a film noir. Sick drunk, he walked off and awoke later on a bench near the water. The sea was calm, and the sky had a tint of rose.

The police, it turned out, reported the incident to the producers. No one said anything until the morning, when he was fired. It never crossed his mind that he would be making the producers nervous. In retrospect, of course, he could clearly see how they would be. They sent the assistant director to give him the news, a sweet-faced young Spaniard who loved classical Spanish music. "I'm sorry, but I'm told to say this," the AD intoned, reading from a piece of paper: "We have no alternative but to fire you. Signed, Arthur Gardner, producer."

All Mitch could say was, "Why?"

The young Spaniard smiled. "Well, you, Oliver, and several Spanish horsemen trashed a little restaurant not far from here. You called Miss Bergen an unmentionable name and told the producer to go fuck himself when he wanted to talk to you about your drinking. And it's very bad news to get mixed up with the Guardia Civil."

"Is that all?" Mitch was mentally starting to pack. "Do I get a ride to the airport?

He was sleeping when they finally landed in New York where he had to change planes. He considered going into the city but thought better of it. New York seemed a long way off as he recalled his early glory days there, full of promise. Who was that boy? Who is this man? Two different people, two different lives. The irony struck him as he sat in the American Airlines VIP lounge. He remembered the opening night of *Othello*, then *Moon*. He pulled himself up, ordered a drink, and with both hands on the bar, stared down at the vodka. He took a sip, spun around, and realized his knuckles were white from holding the glass. Jesus! All he could think to do was slink back to Los Angeles and hide.

It was 11:00 p.m. when they landed in LA. He took a cab to his Malibu apartment near Big Rock. Lynda was glad to see him, and Tim jumped into his arms. Mitch was touched. He'd never thought he would ever have a son. He kissed his beautiful 1969 chocolate brown Pontiac Firebird. He was half-drunk and dead tired. It was nice to sit on the little balcony with Tim on his lap and watch the ocean with Lynda telling him everything would be okay and him knowing she didn't believe what she was saying. He fell asleep in a sea of self-pity.

The next few days were one long drunk. Lynda saw to it that he ate at least once a day. He wasn't very amorous, but she was sympathetic.

On the fourth day, he was feeling better and told himself he wouldn't drink today. The doorbell rang. Who could that be at nine in the morning? It was Walter, his agent.

He was smiling as he breezed past Mitch, sat down, turned, and regarded him with an impish grin that didn't fit his usual brusque manner. "Sit down. I have a miracle to relate to you." Mitch sat down on his unmade bed. "Sometime in the late evening yesterday at the Grand Hotel in Almeria, Spain, several producers and the director of *The Hunting Party* decided to fire the actor who replaced you…and hire you back."

He waited for Mitch's reaction, starting to laugh. "Seems Oliver would not work with this actor they had hired, and since they had two good weeks of film on you, it was cheaper to bring you back."

A large rush of relief tore through Mitch, and he sat dumb-founded, his fluttering hands betraying his excitement. Finally, he said, "Can we get more money?"

"You asshole, this is the greatest coup in the world! This never happens, and it saves all our butts." Walter was ecstatic. "God bless that Limey bastard. You have to get back as soon as possible. There's a plane for New York that leaves at noon to get to Madrid tomorrow and then down to Almeria."

When Mitch arrived at the Grand Hotel in Almeria, he was hailed like a conquering hero. Oliver gave him a great big hug and whisked him off to the bar, where the rest of the cast gave him a rousing cheer. Candice hugged him and said, "You may call me any-thing, anytime." Don, the director, shook his hand. Then in came the producer. Mitch went up to him and apologized. The man was gracious. "Glad you're back, son." Mitch tried not to drink, but that was impossible because drinking was the reason he'd been brought back.

During the next few weeks, everyone took credit for Mitch's return, all but the person who had actually been responsible. Oliver never said a word, but he didn't have to. He had his drinking buddy back.

CHAPTER 20

The Beginning of the End
1971

STRADDLING THE HORSE in the narrow chute with the calf tie in his teeth, the rope in one hand, the reins and the saddle horn in the other, Mitch was having second thoughts about doing this shot. The director had said that all he needed was a medium shot of Mitch's cowboy character coming out of the chute.

Slim, standing at the back of the pen, leaned in. "It's a good thing you're dead drunk. You can't possibly get hurt. You might get killed, but it won't hurt a bit." Slim had been a real rodeo clown before he'd become a featured character actor.

When the director called "Action," the crew simultaneously turned the calf loose and opened the chute. Mitch's horse tore off after the calf as Mitch threw the rope and went with it, sailing through the air, finally landing on his back. He lay there, the wind knocked out of him, as James Coburn, Gentleman James, who was playing the lead in this rodeo movie, jogged over and helped him up. "Can you have dinner with me tonight?"

Mitch looked up, a damned odd time for a dinner invitation.

"Meet me at the El Toro around eight. You all right?"

"Yeah, I'm fine."

Just then, Ross Dollar-Hyde, Mitch's drinking pal and roommate, came along with Slim, who was staggering with laughter. "That was a beauty of a roping. You nailed that calf like you been doing it all your life. It was a miracle. Look." Ross pointed down the arena. There was a cowpoke taking the lead rope off the calf, and Mitch's horse was standing, well trained, waiting. "How did that happen?"

"You threw the rope, and somehow it landed right. The next thing to learn is to stay on the horse after you make the throw."

This rodeo movie was called *The Honkers*, but Mitch couldn't get anyone to tell him why.

He took ribbing all afternoon, and when they quit, he and Ross headed for the bar. They walked in and noticed four or five pretty girls sitting around a table. Ross went right up. "What you old hides doing? Mitch and I are going dancing later. You all want to come?"

"Get away from here, Ross Dollar-Hyde, and get yourself a bath. You stink."

Ross laughed and went up to the bar.

"Kill any steers today, Ross?" the bartender was primed for Ross as he sidled up.

"I sure would like to kill that blonde over there."

"Ross, you couldn't get laid in a whorehouse with five hundred dollars."

"You jackass, when I was world champion, I had to beat 'em away. 'Sides, I'm an *actor* now, so show a little respect. I've got lines. As a matter of fact, I got more lines than Mitch. He writes 'em for me."

Mitch looked at this broken-down cowboy, knowing he was in the film as a favor to his old friend Larry Mahan the gaffer. He felt a stab of guilt, for he himself had been hired the same way by the producer of *The Hunting Party* as a favor to his agent. After finishing the nightmare in Spain, no one would hire him, so Walter had done a job on Arthur Gardner, who had then taken him on. He had no real part and had to make up his own dialogue. He was living on borrowed time, and he knew the bill was coming due.

"Ross, let's go down to Mexico tomorrow. You got the day off, and when you got the day off, so do I because we're a team."

"Goddamn, I'll go! You're a great pal, Mitch, and light up any movie. You would have been a great rodeo hand." Ross's big hand landed on Mitch's shoulder. "You're like a son to me, boy."

Mitch felt sad and was touched by the big cowboy. "You're a waste of time, you big ox, and cut the father-son crap."

"Well, I could go into your lame horsemanship and your shoddy acting but I told the producer, 'Keep him, I want him in all my movies.'"

"Why is that, Ross, 'cause you know I can't stand to be around you?"

"Well, there ain't no one else can stay with me in the drinking department. A guy needs a partner, and I never seen a man drink like you."

Mitch jumped up and stood on the bar: *"I know you all, and will awhile uphold / The unyoked humor of your idleness: / Yet herein will I imitate the sun, / Who doth permit the base contagious clouds / To smother up his beauty from the world..."* The women turned, shouting hurray and clapping loudly.

"That's the talk," shouted his drunken friend. "Damn right we're going to shine tonight, I can feel it in my bones." Mitch sat down on the bar.

"Jesus, Mitch, get off the bar."

Then Ross played serious. "Don't you just love the educated way he talks? That's Shakespeare, you know."

"Well, tell Shakespeare to get off my bar."

Mitch was watching the ladies as they resumed talking about whatever five girls talk about. He listened to the warm laughter of these handsome and sexy country cowgirls, confirming to himself how he loved women. As Ross and the bartender jawed at each other, Mitch jumped down and became very still inside, all the outer noise having gone silent. Women...women seemed to understand something a man can't ever know. They carry an essence and are born with a native intelligence that a man has to look for and earn. I should have been a woman Mitch mused out loud. *"Give me my robe, put on my crown; I have / Immortal longings in me: now no more / The juice of*

181

Carlsbad's grape shall moist this lip... "He started to laugh and poured his glass of whiskey on the floor.

"Jesus, what the hell, wasting good booze. Are you nuts?"

"Ross, I'm going to have dinner with James. He wants to tell me something." As he left, he looked back at Ross, who was shouting a string of cowboy cuss words after him. Wouldn't Ross jump out of his skin if he announced he would prefer to be a woman?

At the only good restaurant in Carlsbad, they sat at a table in the corner. After ordering, James paused, looking a little embarrassed. "I hope you don't mind, I was talking to my agent, Meyer Mishkin, who's been told about your drinking. As you know, he handles Lee also, and he called me to get the latest story, and I told him what I felt and saw."

"I'd feel better if all of you would just leave it alone."

"Let me finish, and then you can say what you want or leave. I'm told you are a very good actor, and you're going down the drain fast. Believe me, when Meyer says this, it's true. There is no reason for you to be in this movie. It's nothing. But here you are, and if you can clean up, finish the movie, and get some help when you get back to California, you'll be fine. I say this as a friend and hope you take it the right way."

Mitch's face burned, and his throat was dry. He felt the anger begin to rise, but he managed to simply stand up, say thank you, and leave.

The beds were turned over, the mirror broken, the chairs smashed to pieces, and all stacked in the middle of the floor. He remembered very little of a horrendous drunk the night before. Ross was passed out on the floor. With the three thousand dollars he was going to give Lynda, he paid for the damage, finished the movie, and caught a plane to San Francisco. Walter had found him a film because an old friend of Mitch's from Louisville who had come Hollywood and done well wanted him. And this old friend had helped him in his first play fifteen years before!

War and Peace. The boy was reading and taking notes. The stewardess asked, "Drink?"

"Ginger ale."

The boy hadn't heard and was so absorbed in the book that Mitch gave him a poke. "Drink?"

"No, thank you." He returned to his book.

Mitch thought of those several years when he was doing bus-and-truck one-night stands for the Barter Theater. With nothing to do all day on the bus or in the motel, he had learned to read the classics. His mother had always told him about Tolstoy and the Russians, Thackeray, and more. She read Dickens constantly. He never paid any attention and looked on reading with scorn. But then one of the Barter actors was reading Faulkner's short stories and encouraged him to try them. After which came the flood of other great American writers—Hemingway, Fitzgerald, Thomas Wolfe, and Mark Twain. When he found Steinbeck, he spent a year reading and rereading every book of his—*Grapes of Wrath*, *Of Mice and Men*, all of them—and once he'd discovered the beauty of reading, he would stop at bookstores in the little towns they played in order to buy more. He studied the boy in the next seat as he turned the page, and there was something familiar…

"You studying the Russian writers?"

"Yes, I am. Do you know them?"

"Not well, but Dostoevsky will wake you up. Have you started in on him?"

"Not yet. My writing teacher says to read Tolstoy first, then Dostoevsky, and before I put down one sentence, he says, I have to read all of Dostoevsky."

"Are you a writer?"

"I want to be. I've started to write small things. You know, put little brief scenes together. I would love to be a writer. I can't think of anything that could be grander than to be an artistic prose writer."

"Yeah, it would be something, to be artistic. Well, good luck." At which point, Mitch turned to the American Airlines magazine. He could not muster any defense against the deep depression that was sucking him down. Time for a drink. He hit the stewardess's call button.

No sooner had he landed and started this movie, which was being shot all over San Francisco, Lynda called to tell him his mother was seriously ill, and the doctor in Louisville had said something must be done, and he should come at once. She gave him the doctor's number.

"Doctor Evans?"

"Yes?"

"This is Mitch Ryan. It's about my mother."

"Well, she's very ill, the last stages of diabetes. She's home but will need to be taken care of and soon will need to go to a care facility or given an around-the-clock nurse."

"I suppose that should be done."

"Who is going to see to that?"

Mitch hung up and sat on his bed in the Earl Hotel, trying to find some spark of compassion or anything else remotely related to the realm of feeling. An unconscious distracted dream, in the depths of his mind, of a black and ugly quagmire of self-hate and sickening self-pity was pulled up by an ugly faded blue sofa he hadn't noticed before. When they wrapped two days later, he flew to Louisville and brought his mother to Los Angeles.

CHAPTER 21

Genevieve Ryan
1972

SHE PULLED THE heavy clock out of the cardboard box, positioned it on the mantle, and looked over to Mitch, who was sitting on the couch. Her son looked pale, was in obvious discomfort, and smelled of alcohol. She watched him, the weight of centuries in her eyes, and when he suddenly looked up, she turned away and lovingly stroked the sturdy oak body of the clock that had been in the family for as long as she could remember. She had brought the ticking keepsake as a living testimony to her past.

Mitch was perched between packing boxes on the faded blue sofa when he caught his mother staring at him. He knew why and didn't care. His vision blurred the clock on the mantle into a Madonna. It stood tall in the dark-brown frame, like hair surrounding a large white face. He couldn't make out the numbers but remembered this clock from when he was a boy living with his mother and father on Ingle Avenue in Louisville, Kentucky, a hundred years ago. Breathing thick and needing a drink, he looked down at his gray hands, trying to still them as if they belonged to someone else, and half-listened to his mother droning on.

"Well, at least there's a mantle. I'm not sure about this neighborhood, and the kitchen is too small. Is your kitchen the same, Mr. Kline?"

Elderly Mr. Kline, a Jewish man who lived in the building, had been helping her move in for several days. "Yes, yes, much the same."

"I like that there are plenty of windows, good light. There's nothing wrong with the plumbing and no leaks in the roof."

"What are you talking about, Mother?"

"Nothing, dear, you just sit there and rest. You had a hard night, I can see." She stood across from the sofa, leaning against the mantle. She wore a baggy black sweater over a white shirt. "My son is an actor, Mr. Kline. An artist. Acting is an art, isn't it? Maybe the highest form of art, he tells me. You have to *suffer for your art.* Isn't that so, Mitchell?"

"You should know, Mother."

Genevieve observed herself in the wall mirror. "God, I look a mess." She turned, waiting to be contradicted. No one said anything. Mitch remembered his mother as a handsome woman, but years of pain, of the soul and body, had left her with a sharp tongue and a bitter closed face. Decades of carbohydrates had left her fat. "Well, anyway, here I am, for better or worse, Mr. Kline, in Santa Monica!"

"Yes." Mr. Kline waved his arm around. "It's a lovely apartment, Genevieve." He sat on a straight chair in the archway between the kitchen and the generous living room. "May I call you, Genevieve?" His thick glasses made his eyes look enormous.

"Mrs. Ryan will do until I get to know you better, Mr. Kline." She sighed with a sad smile. "What a place to end up. I'm so tired." She kicked at Mitch's foot as she went back to her packed boxes. "My son brought me here against my will, all the way from Louisville, Kentucky. Had a horrible drive, took longer than the first settlers. I won't fly, you understand, much too dangerous."

"Mom, that's not entirely the truth."

"How much longer will this life go on, do you think, Mr. Kline?"

"Much longer than we have a right to expect." Her son leaned forward and put his face in his hands.

"That sounds familiar, dear. What play is it from?"

"You're the dramatic one."

Mitch could see that Kline, bewildered by this exchange, had been rendered mute.

"I think of things like that now. Dying… Do you think about dying, Mr. Kline?"

Mr. Kline caught Mitch's eye and nodded toward the woman, hoping Mitch would jump in and say something, but he, her son, never knew how to be with his mother. Staying above water was the best he could do. He was damn sorry he'd come here today. Trying not to drink on the drive across the country had been excruciating, even though he carried a bottle in the trunk for emergencies. In Los Angeles, he'd been met by the news that Lynda had gone back to Tucson, suffered a breakdown—he assumed it had been brought on by his drinking—and taken Tim with her. Mitch tried to call, but she wouldn't answer. His agent had left a scathing message, and on top of all this, he now had no money or job. So he methodically made up for the lost time by drinking day and night. His breathing was coming in shallow gasps, but he was able to remember the bar across the street.

"What sort of work do you do, Mrs. Ryan?" Mr. Kline didn't like the way the son was limping toward the door.

"I write—are you leaving, Mitchell? So soon?"

"I really should get going."

"An artistic family, what is it you write?" Mr. Kline's voice tried to keep the son in the room.

"Well, if you must know, I'm working on a journal of the end-less trip I made here from Kentucky. My son, Mitchell, came to res-cue me in a truck, a big orange truck. Isn't that right, Mitchell?

At the door, slipping out quickly, Mitch paused. "I didn't know you were writing a journal, Mother. That should be a hell of a story."

Genevieve held back and turned on the boxes. "I must get unpacked."

"What a good boy to do that for his mother," Mr. Kline jumped in.

She gave him a withering look. "Do you have any children, Mr. Kline?"

"I have a daughter in San Francisco. My son was killed in Vietnam. You said you never cared for people, but your boy cares for you. It's not good to be alone. Looks like he wants to be near you."

"What tripe, Mr. Kline."

"Mother." Mitch still stuck at the door.

"What?"

"Nothing." He turned his back to the room, still glued to the door. He wanted to defend the poor man, but it was too late.

"Mr. Kline," she savored the words, "you have been very kind to help me this week with the move, and I appreciate your thoughtfulness, but please don't give me advice. And if you will excuse me, I'm very tired, thank you."

Mitch still stood, head aching, hands shaking, wanting to be gone. "You don't have any whiskey, do you, Mother? We better have a drink, Mr. Kline." He tottered back to the sofa. "Jesus, Mother, what's the matter with you? Mr. Kline is trying to be neighborly."

"No, I understand," Mr. Kline said, moving, "you want to be alone. Sure, you're tired." At the door, he turned as if to say something, didn't, and left.

She waited, looking after the old man. "I have no liquor. Why do you need a drink?"

"Because it helps."

"I have nothing to give you for your disgusting habit. You're on your own." She picked up a small box. "This man drops in all the time. Please, Mitchell, tell him I guard my privacy."

"He's trying to be helpful, Mother, and you can see he's lonely."

"Oh god, everyone's lonely." Her voice snapped under the strain of lifting a larger box onto the Formica countertop. She managed to pull the container open and started to take out the collection of figurines she had gathered over the years, placing them on the shelf between the kitchen and living room.

"I think I'll be going. Mother, are you hungry? I could go get something."

"Not hungry. It's morning. You're not going to drink now?'

"Forget it."

She pulled a small frame out of the box and sat down. She was having trouble breathing. "Your father drank in the morning near the end. Here he is before he became a drunk." Looking up, she caught Mitch observing her. She put her head down. Her hands started to tremble. "The damn doctor was exaggerating. I'm fine. I just forget to take my medicine."

"Christ, Mother, you were half dead when I got there. The doctor said it was dangerous for you to live alone."

"Oh, that stupid doctor." She handed the photo to Mitch. "Wasn't your father handsome? He was a secret drinker, you know."

"I never noticed."

"He thought nobody knew, but everyone was on to him. You got his good looks. You look more like him the older you get." She took the photo back from him and went to the mantle. "Charles was sweet and gentle those first years," she said, suddenly coquettish. "He read poetry to me, can you imagine. Wasn't till later…oh well, all gone now." She dropped the frame carelessly face down on the mantle and returned to the box.

He watched her unwrapping the knickknacks with great care. Her movements, the turn of her head, how she stood with her weight on one leg—all so familiar. A quiet tenderness flitted at him. Suddenly all the years of resentment melted as if a great weight had been lifted. He realized finally he didn't know anything about her. He could see she was nervous, and he felt the same. He wanted to help. He couldn't move. She'd become slow and vague with age. They were quite a pair. He sat on the stool and observed her loving consideration of every item: painstakingly unwrapping first a gold picture frame with nothing in it, then a small Victorian figurine. The familiar bronze horse that had always pranced on the mantle at home. "Remember?"

He had to get out. He had to find some money. Call Archer. No. That's no good. Maybe Murray—he's got money. He had to get a drink. He leaned on the kitchen table. When the doctor had called from Louisville to tell Mitch his mother was seriously ill and needed looking after, Mitch had been drinking for several weeks and could hardly comprehend what he was being told. "She has no money, and she needs care. Your mother has diabetes. You are her son, aren't you?" So Mitch had gone to get her.

He found himself edging to the door again. The bar across the street called to him. The heat and nausea were making him weak. He retreated to the sofa, sat, and pushed on his stomach to relieve the pressure. Genevieve followed her son with quick glances. Wordlessly she showed him a small watercolor, a delicate, richly colored painting of a young girl with red hair.

"Is that you?"

"Yes. Your father painted that before we were married. Your father had been a good painter at one time." She laid her picture down gently and held up a green glass stone set in silver. "This was my mother's. Did I ever tell you? My father gave this to her when they met in Ireland." She paused and studied the stone.

Mitch moved back to the door and held on to the doorknob as if it would get away. His feet began to itch from neglected athlete's foot. He tried to scratch his toes through his shoes. He walked into the kitchen and ran a glass of water. The water activated all the alcohol in his system, and he started to sweat. "You want anything, Mother? Coffee?"

"Put the water on, please. Why have you been drinking?"

"It tastes good."

"That's a smart remark! I hate it when you're smart-alecky. Whatever became of that sweet little boy you used to be? You really shouldn't drink. You look like hell."

At the door, Mitch began to finesse his escape to the bar across the street. "Well, this sweet little boy has a present for you out in the car."

"Mitchell, are you all right? I'm worried about you."

"You're fucking worried about me? That's a laugh."

They were both startled, then quiet. He wanted to run to her, fall in her lap, and beg to be forgiven. Instead, he watched, watched her hand fluttering around her stricken face. He hung onto the doorknob as if it would escape. She sat lost in a dream of otherwise. After a while, she rallied and looked at him. "You mustn't talk to me like that, Mitchell. It hurts me. You know nothing about me or my life. You have never even bothered to ask."

"I'm sorry, Mother."

She looked off somewhere, hands quiet now. "A present...you have a present for me?"

"Yes, you'll like it, I'm sure. I'll go get it now." And out he went.

She sagged down onto the sofa, face hurting, hands starting to open and close, then stood. "Must get unpacked." She kneeled down and opened a large box. "*Oh!* God, I knew it. Goddamn!" All her china was smashed. Several select pieces had belonged to her mother. The rest was dime-store. "This is the end." She fell onto the sofa.

Outside, the white glare assaulted him, and his inclination was to get in the car and drive. Instead, he propelled his fragile body toward the bar. The trip from Kentucky had been an eleven-day disaster. Now he was back, drinking almost continually to keep enough alcohol in his blood. The bar was cool and dark. How he loved dark bars, especially in the daytime. He had a shot of whiskey and a beer and calmed down. Then he had another.

He left the bar feeling a little better. He moved to the car and carried the large box into the apartment. She stood when he entered and went into the kitchen. "All the china is broken. If you hadn't rushed me, I would have packed it right. What in God's name is that?"

"I got you a record player with a tape deck and everything."

"What did you do that for?"

He lay his burden down on the floor in front of the sofa. He looked into the box of china at her broken world. "I'm sure it won't play seventy-eights. The man at Woolworth said they don't make those kinds of players anymore. We'll get thirty-threes, and I'll get some new china. I already bought Mozart. They don't make seventy-eights anymore, Mother."

"I don't want the damn thing."

"I'm going to set it up anyway, if I can. I know you love Mozart. How about behind the sofa? It just fits on that table."

"Put it anywhere." Mitch felt the old tightness in his stomach. "Spending money on a record player when there's no need."

He was getting angry and increasingly sick. He had to go. He couldn't get the thing out of the box, and then he had trouble reading the volume of instructions.

She was sitting rigidly at the kitchen table, holding the jar of instant coffee. "There's certainly a better use for your money. I know you don't make enough for yourself, much less me."

"I help when I can. Cost plenty to get you here."

"You could have saved yourself the trouble. I did not wish to come to California. I was perfectly happy in my little home in Louisville, but I'm here now, and I will make the most of it, *if I am allowed.*"

"Throw the goddamn thing in the garbage then," he growled. "I'm leaving."

"Fine." She strode into the bedroom and slammed the door.

"Goddamn this old woman." He was beginning to shake on the way to the bedroom door. He knocked. "Mother, come out!" Nothing. He left.

She heard him knock and call to her and then heard the front door. She sat on the bed and started to cry. Then she wandered to the bathroom, picked up a towel, and slowly walked into the living room, trying to summon the strength to do something, even fix a cup of coffee. She sank down on the sofa.

He sat in his car. "Jesus!" There was a burning in his throat, and something was trying to come up. He went back to the apartment. When he came through the door, she was sitting on the sofa crying, holding a towel to her face. Mitch sat down next to her. She put her head on his shoulder. Her sobs quickened. When he touched her arm and felt her thin back, his heart opened a little, and there *it* was, the sad hopelessness that was always with him. "I'm sorry, Mother. Don't cry."

"No, it's me. It's me, Mitchie." She laughed through her sobs. Then she put her arms around his neck with a girlish giggle and held him in a tight embrace. "I haven't called you Mitchie for years." He stiffened at first, then slowly relaxed and held her until she calmed down. "I was afraid you'd left." Then, lightly she added, "I always loved you, you know that. I'll be fine. I want to be with myself now. I'm sorry I was cross." She stretched out to lie down so that he had to move out of the way. "Come for breakfast. I would like that." She smiled. "I'll make eggy in a cup the way you always liked it."

He was close to breaking down as he helped her lie back and covered her with a throw, then turned to the door. "I'll see you in the morning." His voice cracked. "Do you need anything?"

"No." She shut her eyes.

He turned at the door. Her face was relaxed, and for a moment, she looked like a young girl. He covered his mouth to stop the sob and shut the door as softly as he could. Outside he let the sob go as he ran to the car.

The scenes from her life came floating through now that she was alone. Her father tall and straight, smiling down at her as they picked wild blackberries in the woods on their farm near the river where she grew up. She saw him moving like a giant through the endless rows of corn and reading poetry—or was that her husband, looking disheveled as he stood at her desk in the library? Then they swam at Cherokee Lake with her children, Mitch and Maggie. The water seemed real, filling her mouth and spilling down over her chin, then a warm sensation, then a bright light. Then…

"Stupid. Stupid. Stupid life." Mitch composed himself as he sat in the car. He drove to the nearest bar and sat outside in the car. "Stupid. Stupid." The day was one of those white days in Los Angeles where the glare wipes the color out of everything. Finally, he went in and had a drink. Then he headed toward a bar in Malibu called the Cottage where he could always find any number of drunks to provide some gallows humor. He called this his home away from home. The Graveyard. His life right now looked pretty bleak: fired for being drunk and disorderly in Spain, then hired back. It made for a great bar story but wasn't funny anywhere else.

The firing had serious consequences. Plus, he had no money, and his wife was suing him. So here he was driving to his favorite shithole. He couldn't wait to get there. When his mother had put her arms around his neck, just a moment ago, to hold tight, that maternal hug broke through the shell of his pitiful life and gave him a sliver of hope. But a twinge of hope was no match for the Graveyard in Malibu.

The next morning as he drove with both hands clutching the wheel to have breakfast with his mother, he was as sick as a human being could be. He had not slept and had thrown up the scrambled eggs a lovely actress had made him in her kitchen somewhere in Malibu. He'd met her at someone's house, where he'd ended up after drinking for several hours at the Graveyard. When driving him back to his car this morning, she had told him she'd taken him to her place out of charity and that he had refused her advances and was listening to Mozart when she'd gone to bed. Somewhere near Sunset Boulevard, he was sick again. He pulled over and just managed to get the door open and his head out. He had to use a dirty shirt from the trunk to wipe his mouth and smear the last of the eggs off the running board.

He sat in the car at his mother's place, trying to figure out how to pay for her apartment. He maneuvered up the walk and into the front door, then to her place on the ground floor. He rang the bell. No answer. He rang and knocked. Still nothing. He fished out his key and let himself in. Dark. Parts of the record player were still strewn all around. She lay on the couch where he had left her, gray vomit on her chin. She was dead.

He lurched out to the car, took the bottle out of the glove compartment, stood a moment, then dropped the thing on the front seat and walked slowly back inside. He stood over her, looking down into her face. With a washcloth, he wiped the vomit away. When he finished, he felt he was in a movie. "We'll put the camera behind the sofa." He turned away in disgust. "Jesus!" Then he finished putting the record player together, sat down on a chair opposite his mother's body, and began to listen to her favorite Mozart—his Piano Concerto No. 21.

CHAPTER 22

Undertakers
1972

THE RINGING PHONE yanked him from the depths of his nightmare and dumped him out of bed, crawling and clawing until he finally found the instrument jangling on the table.

"Hello."

"Is this Mitchell Ryan?"

He hung up and traced his steps back to bed. The ringing began again one, two, on to ten times, then stopped. He lay there in a waking coma. He dozed off, and it rang again.

Endless journey back to phone. "Yes, what is it?"

"I need to speak to Mitchell Ryan."

"That's me."

"This is Marfori Brothers Funeral Home. We have had Genevieve Ryan's ashes for two months now."

"Oh! God."

"You are her son, are you not? What do you plan to do about them?"

"Yes, I'll be there this afternoon." He started to hang up. "Wait—what's your address?"

Had it been two months since his mother died? He had been in this apartment on Yucca Drive for a long time, too long. The last thing he remembered clearly was seeing her on the sofa, in the apartment in Santa Monica, with gray drool on her chin.

Christmas had come and gone, and God knows what else. There was no sense of time, only the sensation that time was no more. He sat on the bed, still holding the phone, trying to piece together the sequence of events the morning she died. Mr. Kline from down the hall had said he knew of a funeral home. Mitch, in a strange, detached panic, paced up and down the apartment until Mr. Kline's efforts to console him drove him out into the small yard. What to do? There was no one he wished to see and certainly no one he would ask for help. Wait. He had an AA friend, Pat Hogan, who was devoid of judgment and opinion. If he could help, the last rites would be simple. Mr. Kline called the funeral home, and they came, and Mitch called Pat Hogan. The funeral team arrived, led by a jolly, obsequious man who needed to know many things, which Mitch told him, the most important having to do with cremation. They left, and Mitch said he would follow. As they were putting Genevieve's remains on the gurney and moving her out, Mitch lifted the sheet and looked at the sweet childlike face. "The endless possibilities all gone." He dropped the sheet. Then Pat was at the door.

The emporium of death had the look of a preacher's house in small-town America—with soft plush carpet, deep chairs, and white lace curtains. They were told to sit and wait. Muted organ music floated from somewhere. After a while, the same fawning man asked if they wished to view the body. "No." The man looked hurt. She would be cremated right away.

Mitch and Pat sat. They were both quiet. Mitch was clouded by a thousand memories of his mother: her red hair, the most prominent image, floated in and out of his consciousness...her hug on the porch when he returned from the navy...taking him to grade school that first day...his shock at how she looked when he went to Louisville to get her...how she had put her arms around his neck the day before she died—this was most vivid of all. All of a sudden, Pat began to recite the Lord's Prayer. Mitch had never heard the words out loud.

There was a power that didn't seem to belong to any one church. "Forgive us our trespasses as we forgive…" He felt a flicker of compassion for the long sad life of his mother.

That had been two months ago. The clicking of the phone in his hand brought him back to the present. The rest of that day with Pat slowly came to him. They had walked down to a coffee shop near the funeral home. "Are you hungry?"

"I want a drink. I need a drink."

"No, eat something first, some eggs."

They sat in Tiny Naylor's, and he tried to eat. "My mother was a writer. I don't know why you should know that, but she wrote journals of all her trips, around the South mainly." He stopped and played with his eggs. "I remember when I was a kid, she would be in her bedroom writing away, and my sister and I were not allowed to enter or even knock until we were summoned. Now and again, she would have us in and read to us, Charles Dickens mostly. She loved Dickens. Some of her journals were good. One was published in the *Atlantic Monthly*. I think it was the *Atlantic*…The story was about…I don't remember. Well, good night, Pat. Thank you. I'm going back to Yucca Street.

Pat listened because he wanted to. Mitch had met this gaunt man on the set of some show or other. He had a sad Irish face and a lovely way of telling a story. He was a gaffer and a good electrician.

"I remember when she came to see me play Hamlet when I was twenty-one years old. She knew *Hamlet* by heart. She knew a lot of Shakespeare by heart. By heart? I wonder what that means. That night, she had been sick and called, saying she couldn't make it. But at the last minute, she must have changed her mind. She said she liked it and that I would get better." Mitch laughed. "Also, she wore her best coat and dress, the coat a fake fur that was two shades of brown. My father called it skunk. 'Genevieve and her genuine skunk coat,' he would say."

He stopped. It was as if Mitch had run down. "She had memorized whole passages of *Hamlet*. She would have been a good Hamlet."

"I think it's good for a man to talk about his loved ones when they're gone."

Loved one. Mitch guessed you could say she was a loved one.

Another silence with just the sloshing of the Latino washing the dishes and the waitress humming something familiar. "When I came home from the navy, I was terrified of the reaction I would get because I had a bad conduct discharge. I stood out across the street from our house. A warm, humid night and I remember the gardenias filled the air. Seemed everyone in our neighborhood grew gardenias. While I was standing there, my mother came out on the porch, looked over at me for a long time, and then waved. I waved back and then slowly walked up to the porch, and without a word, she put her arms around me and held me close. It was a shock. She never touched me or held me. Then she said, 'I saw you through the window.'"

"Thank you for telling me about your mother."

"I need a drink, Pat. Thank you for all your help."

"You all right?"

"Yes, I'm okay, a little nip and then home to sleep this off."

Now he was back in his room on Yucca Street months later, sitting on the bed, still holding the phone.

Two months. The funeral parlor man had said, "Two months." Jesus! He felt nothing. He realized he was totally bankrupt and had no idea what day or month it was. He had to get over there and get his mother today. He slowly rose up, went to the kitchen alcove, and poured a tall glass of vodka, then took the drink and himself to the broken-down sofa, sank into it, and slowly sipped his nourishment.

CHAPTER 23

My Old Man's Place
1973

HE WAS AWAKE on a mattress on the floor. He raised himself up on one elbow and saw a dim lightbulb swinging from a cord in the middle of the room, as well as a dresser, a mirror, a writing desk, several chairs, and a sleeping woman lying beside him. He fell back down and closed his eyes. There was a knock on the door, and someone called his name. He couldn't move. After a while, the knocking stopped, and in the silence, he dozed off again. Sometime later, he heard pounding again and then shouting. Staggering off the mattress, he stumbled toward the door. "Knock, knock, knock," he croaked, "it's the porter of hell gate. Who's there, in the name of Beelzebub?"

"Tomorrow, and tomorrow, and tomorrow, / Creeps in this petty pace from day to day," came a familiar voice from the past outside the door. Mitch opened up. "Bill, old friend—God bless you, come in!"

Bill Devane, looking washed and starched, peered into the room. "No, I haven't had my shots." As he walked away, back down the squalid hall, he called, "Meet me at the corner bar. I have good news for you."

"Be right there. What's the date today?"

"Monday, the twenty-first of March."

The last date he could summon was two months after his mother died when the funeral home had called, and that was after Christmas—yes, Christmas, he remembered. A generous landlady had knocked on his door that Christmas morning. A large woman, heavy on the eye shadow, her enormous body spilling out of her tight-fitting dress. He recalled her words with a shudder: "No one should be alone on Christmas, honey."

He looked around this place, not knowing where he was, sat back down on the mattress, and observed the woman lying beside him. Who was she? Somehow, he knew he must stop drinking. Knew that the free thrust and delight of life could come back, as life had over the years. He remembered that night at the Ford Theater, when he felt a freedom of mind and feelings and body, after sitting in the rain, then coming to the theater where he astounded himself and everyone else with a different level of performance.

But when Walter had confronted him with the depth of his illness, he had laughed and told him with deadly stillness, "After carefully examining all sides of the problem, I have come to the conclusion that what's the use? It's really not important. I always did my job in every movie, and that should be enough, I figure. Besides, it's nobody's business but mine. I'm not going to quit drinking anytime soon." Walter had called that "self-deception."

There are certain characteristics of a low-bottom drunk, aside from the obvious self-delusion that brings about a morbid and absurd worldview. This warped view of Mitch's was in powerful contrast to his need to be recognized, to be accepted. And now this conflict, which had been present his whole life, was only deepening and becoming more exaggerated as he sank further into his dispirited and defiant state.

He looked around again, trying hard to puzzle how he'd gotten to this apartment, to this floor, to this mattress. He remembered drinking with a friend who he guessed had brought him here. He had a rented furnished apartment of his own, on aptly named Yucca Drive, so he figured he'd better head back there, but then there was Bill waiting for him downstairs.

He rolled off the mattress, found his pants, and got out his wallet to see if there was any money. Surprisingly, there was. He looked down at the woman. She hadn't moved. Could she be dead? He put on his pants and went around the mattress to collect the rest of his clothes. He could see she was breathing. He knelt down and touched her face. She was warm, moved a little, turned over, and took his hand, curling the fingers into her body in a wonderful comforting unconscious movement.

She was not young and had a lived-in face. He let her hold his hand. There was a great need in this grasp, and Mitch resisted the urge to disentangle himself from her desire, so there he sat with his hand in hers which she had so fiercely drawn to her breast, the clasp surely a matter of life and death. A cloud of memories leaped up—his mother, Lynda, all the actresses, the dark lady of the sonnets in Spain…or was it Irene? He gently ran the back of his hand over her breast, and for a moment, the guilt fell away. He relaxed and became aware of his breathing. After what seemed like eternity, he finally pulled away, put a blanket over her, and left.

He ordered a beer and sat on an orange plastic stool in a run-down bar called On the Way.

"How did you find me?"

"I called Jackie, and he said he was drinking with you two days ago at the Raincheck, and some guy took you both to this creepy place to score some dope. Jackie told me where it was, and here you are." Mitch had known Bill from the early days in New York. They had spent years together at the Shakespeare Festival. He was a good friend—Irish, from Albany, New York, and tough.

"Ed is looking for you. He's doing a film, and there's a great part for you. Gene was going to do it but he won the Academy Award, so he went elsewhere. I said you were out of town, but I could find you. We start in two weeks in San Francisco. I suggest you quit drinking and eat something."

"You're in the picture?"

"Yeah, Michael Moriarty, Arthur Kennedy, and me," Bill laughed, "and you, too, if you can stop fucking up. Well, are you going to do it, get off your ass?"

"Bartender!"

Bill slid off his stool. "That's it, fuck you."

"What'll it be, lads?"

"Check. Give me a lift, Bill?"

In two weeks, he'd learned his lines and was with everyone in San Francisco, ready to shoot. Again, he showed up and did his job. He decided to drink only wine since the company had moved to Calistoga, California, in the middle of wine country. He was reluctant to ask Arthur Kennedy about *Death of a Salesman*, but one night at dinner, he did. He and Arthur had dinner together almost every night. "Your idea to drink only wine is fine, Mitch, but two bottles before dinner?"

"Drinking Mondavi Fumé Blanc is not like drinking alcohol."

"Then how come you're drunk every night before you eat? I'm amazed you can be as good as you are, the way you slop that stuff down. Are you hearing what I'm telling you?"

"It's not that I didn't hear you. I just don't care."

"I'm not so sure." Arthur cut into his steak.

"But I'll tell you what I do care about: *Death of a Salesman*."

"Have you done it?"

"Yes, I played your part."

"It's not my part."

"If you wanted to, I could listen to something about Cobb or Arthur Miller or the process."

"Well, all I can or will say is this…" And then he stopped. "But that was twenty-five years ago." As Arthur's face turned to utter melancholy, he looked off as if to retrieve a long-lost world. Mitch felt a deep rattle within him as he recognized that look. He took a long gulp of wine. Watching him Arthur returned to his fatherly dictum: "A short span in the scheme of things, twenty-five years, but it seems an eternity. Be thankful for the good things that are in store because there will be much slovenly crap that will fill your life if you don't remember Linda's line in *Salesman*: 'Attention must be paid.' And you, Mitch, are not paying attention."

And so the film went on. The Vietnam War was still raging, but Mitch paid little attention to "a stupid war" as he called it, while it ripped the United States apart, and Watergate, who gives a shit. He didn't care. He continued eating dinner with Arthur. Mitch wanted to hear more about *Death of a Salesman*, but the talk was always about the war. The film they were shooting focused on the contrast between a lifetime professional-killer Special Forces officer and boys who were drafted. It was the first picture to point out the terrible damage that senseless war had inflicted on the young men of that generation.

When the talk in the company invariably came down to the war, Mitch would walk off. At one point, Arthur told him to grow up and open his eyes. "You're the most ignorant and politically naïve person I have ever met." Mitch laughed, left the bar they'd been convening in, put in at his home away from home, and crawled into bed. He lay there thinking Arthur was right, but Mitch didn't know how to do anything except put his energy into the work. So he put it there.

He was everywhere as he became caught up in the filming, stayed late to watch the dailies, and made discrete suggestions. This was the first time in a long while he had done good work and, even more important, he felt good. Ed was very happy, and the producers were well satisfied.

Michael Moriarty, who played one of the young draft boys, did a fine job. Mitch had been in *Antony and Cleopatra* with him in New York and remembered him as a closed-off snob of an actor. One day while they were waiting for the setup, sitting on the veranda looking out over the beautiful gold and green hills of the Napa Valley, he was surprised when Michael started talking about his mother, who lived in Ohio. He didn't seem to be talking to Mitch, but Mitch was the only one there.

"My mother never showed affection. Ever." He stopped. Mitch looked over. Michael didn't look at him but seemed to be talking to the air. After a pause, he continued, "She never hugged me or touched me…" He stopped again "Or even encouraged me in schoolwork or sports." Again he stopped. He had this halting way of talking. Mitch stood up. Michael went on, "She never once said anything about my choice of going into the theater." Mitch sat back down. Another pause. "I always wondered if she ever loved me at all. I think because

Arthur is playing my father in this same uncaring distanced way, I could use my feelings for my mother in relation to him. You study the Method, Mitch, what do you think? Is your mother alive?"

Mitch stood again and started toward his dressing room, then whirled back. "My mother's dead. Do whatever works for you, Michael."

He went to his dressing room, threw the first thing he saw, a glass, against the wall, sat down on the couch, and poured himself a large drink. Jesus. Fuck him. Why am I so pissed? He drank the whiskey and slammed around the room, then stopped and crouched down on his haunches when he felt the convulsion of sobs coming. He tried to stop, no use, pounded on the floor as he lay there until the sobs subsided into stifled wails.

Mitch was late for his call the next day, in a foul mood, and no one said anything to him. He shot his scene, left, went to a liquor store, and bought a bottle. The next day was scheduled to be his last. There were several car shots and a long shot of him standing in the rain in full dress uniform, a hunting rifle cradled in his arms. When he was done, he did not say goodbye to anyone, did not know anyone, did not recognize anyone, and did not recognize himself. He took a week to get back to LA. He would stop on the road at any anonymous roadhouse or lonely bar in some dusty small town and wonder what there was to stop him from ending this stupid useless life.

CHAPTER 24

Yucca Drive
1973

MITCH NEVER BOTHERED to collect his mother's ashes. He couldn't muster the energy to make a move from Yucca Drive. His street was in sight of the iconic Capitol Records Building, a shabby neighborhood just above Hollywood Boulevard where wannabes and has-beens began and ended. It was an alien strip as good as any in which to be alone and drink since they, the lost, seemed to be all in the same unmoored boat.

Madam Landlady, who lived down the hall, knocked and walked right in. She would drop in from time to time with a bottle of crème de menthe. He didn't mind. She was a good soul, simultaneously lonely and predatory. Today she brought her friend Mr. Herbert, a smallish dark man with thinning white hair and glistening black eyes that perpetually looked to be on the verge of weeping. He had been an extra since the silent days in the extravaganza *Ben-Hur*. "I drove one of the chariots, you know," he lied with pride.

"Don't start with that old story, for God's sake. Here, Mitch, have some of this, crème de menthe."

"I will talk about it, and also I'll tell Mr. Ryan the rest of my stories, if you don't mind. You're in the business, aren't you, Mr. Ryan?"

"You might say so."

"I had lunch every day, with Ramon Navarro—well, almost every day." He blushed. "I don't get around much anymore, but when I do get down to the open calls, they all know me, and I usually get the job, and—"

"Shut up, you old fool. You haven't had a job in twenty years."

"You shut it, you fat prima donna."

Mitch drifted off, their voices the babble of rain on a distant roof. He stared down, unsure what to do with the crème de menthe. Then he turned toward the window and saw the room as clearly as if a camera was panning the cracks in the wall and the peeling paint, up to the sill, and to the picture of Lynda and Tim, who had long since gone back to Tucson. He didn't blame her, but mostly he missed Tim. What a joke. He missed him the way you would miss your cuddly dog that ran away.

A mock protest from the landlady: "Mitch, you going to let him speak to me like that?"

Mitch stared at her. "Get thee to a nunnery…" *I have heard of your paintings too, well enough…you jig, you amble, and you lisp, and nickname God's creatures, and make your wantonness your ignorance.* He closed his eyes.

"Well, that sure sounds like an insult."

"No! No! I'm sorry. Don't listen to me."

"Come on, Ben-Hur."

Mr. Herbert gallantly took her by the arm. "That's Shakespeare, *The Taming of the Shrew*, you ignorant love of my life." Mitch's guests never seemed in a hurry, and he didn't care much if they stayed or went, but this time they filed out.

Hamlet reminded him of his mother. And he had always hoped he could be a caring father to Tim, but of course he didn't know how because he, Mitch, had never learned anything from his own father. What does, some kind of, what, forgiveness about your father and mother require? What catharsis of terror and pity? Could he love them? All the blame and resentment had been replaced by shame. He stumbled to the window and looked down on the street. Night in Hollywood, the menagerie of neon-colored lights all blended into a blur. He saw the odd assortment of ugly buildings, body shops, greasy spoons, and low-rent transient apartments, like seeing deep into the bowels of hell. The whole street seemed to have been thrown up as an afterthought so that every runaway from every city in America would end up here. While the Hollywood freeway traffic endlessly thundered past, thirty feet up.

He thought of eating, but the trip down to Dolores's Coffee Shop on Hollywood Boulevard seemed monumental.

So his life went, from week to week and month to month, as he dug further into isolation and disorder. He seldom bathed. Even his friends from the building started shunning him. He fell down the stairs one day, bruising his shoulder and spraining his right wrist. Calls came from old friends from New York who had moved out West, but he put them off, not wanting to be seen in this pitiful state. Such was his perverse pride, rather die than ask for help.

One day Walter showed up at chez Yucca with a list of people who would not hire him under any circumstances. He sat on Mitch's one chair: "I think I'm the only friend who still cares what happens to you. Would you please get some help?" Mitch sat mute, head down. Walter left.

After Walter's visit, Mitch woke up lying halfway off the sofa in his trashed room. He sat up. He worried about the rash all over his torso. Leprosy? That at least brought a weak laugh. He tried to get up off the stained rank sofa and fell back, his eyes level with the steel-framed window. He tried to judge his next move. He had been drinking continuously for many months, one day running into the next. "I'm thirty-eight, I think. That's too young to die!" he proclaimed in his Shakespeare voice, dramatically trying to stay upright. He found, in his self-imposed solitude that he spoke out loud a lot to the mirror or a chair. They had become his friends.

Matt Clark had given him some LSD. In a pill jar. Must be here somewhere...? "I don't care for drugs," he muttered, "but it might be a relief from the vodka." Moving like an old man, he stumbled over the corner of the Murphy bed and fell. He had never been able to get that bed back into the wall. He stayed on his knees for a few minutes, staring at the grime caked on his hands and wrists. The appendages looked like strange foreign creatures. He wet his fingers and wiped them across his wrist, leaving a dead white streak. He choked down a sob and then another. Self-pity is a wonderful pastime. *Come on, you ninny, cut the crap.* He rolled over onto his side and lay there a moment, then finally righted himself back onto his hands and knees, crawled to the nearest chair, and began to rummage in the coat thrown over its back, for what he couldn't remember. Oh yes, LSD. Still on all fours, he spotted a small bottle on the top of the half-fridge and pulled himself up.

Matt had told him one tab would make an elephant high. Mitch reasoned he would need more than an elephant would, so he took two. In less than an hour, he saw large black bugs on the wall. They didn't appear to be moving, but he took no chances and left. On the outside landing that led to the stairs down to the parking lot, he became aware of the "Hollywood Snakes" he'd heard so much about. Here they were, writhing at the bottom of the steps, waiting for him. He looked up to see them hanging down from the palm trees that lined the cracked plaster balcony. Strange, he wasn't afraid as he lay down to take a nap. He watched the raging fire across the parking lot, which, even in his current state, he knew was the Christmas lights behind the Chinese restaurant.

As he lay on the hard cement, he closed his eyes, and a profound silence came to him. At that moment, he realized that every human being in all the whole world was taking a breath at the same time. Every three seconds. And that proved to him that time was not what he had thought, and his father and grandfather, therefore, were somewhere, more than likely in the Shamrock Bar down at the corner. He'd head down there in a moment, he decided, but his father came walking down a long corridor and handed him an ice cream cone. Fudge royal. The light in the corridor kept getting brighter, bright white above and all around. No color anywhere until a reddish blob came into view.

"You're awake." He moved and tried to sit up. Strange images appeared. He looked at the plump nurse in front of him, a candy striper, with a tray of food. She was bright and cheerful with nice large breasts he couldn't help but notice.

"Where am I?"

"Here's something that should help. You must be hungry. You're going to make it now, but when they got you here, you looked like something the cat dragged in." She busied herself, putting the tray in front of him. "We've been worried about you for several days. It was touch and go. You were hanging by a thread."

"Stop!" he croaked. "I'm fit as a fiddle, and I'm going to pull through." She missed the joke. "What is this place?"

"Hollywood Community Hospital." She smiled her generic smile and reached for his hand in a touching way. "We all prayed for you."

He raised his hands. They were swollen. And his neck and back felt like a board. Touching his face hurt. He looked at the young girl's innocent face, and she smiled at him. "How long have I been here?"

"Three days. The police found you crawling down Vine Street." She left.

He pushed the tray aside, pulled out the IV, and stood up trembling. He found his clothes in the closet. When he reached for them, he saw his hand was swollen. His pants fell to the floor, and he had trouble standing after he'd knelt down to retrieve them. He leaned on the doorjamb and tried to finish putting them on. Then he made his way through the door.

A nurse ordered him back to bed, but he kept going down the stairs to the street. He called his friend Jane to come and get him and waited in a coffee shop on Hollywood Boulevard. He ordered coffee. Across the room, the images were blurred. When the coffee arrived, he took a sip, gagged, and spit it back into the cup. His hands were puffy and red, and he wondered what had happened to them.

Jane arrived, looking concerned, and sat down. She was a casting agent for small movies and occasional TV shows. She loved to take care of people. It was her strength and her weakness. Mitch had met her when he first came out to Hollywood.

"God, you look bad."

"I'm going to stop drinking."

Jane raised her eyebrows.

"No, I'm serious, and I need to stay at your place."

She went to the counter. She was caught in "should I get out of here or stay and help." She asked for coffee. She looked back at Mitch and slumped over his cup, his face gray and looking old. That brought her life's work to the ready. He needed her. When she sat down again, he looked at her open face and knew all he had to do was ask.

For the first time in his life, he felt ashamed to be taking advantage of someone who cared about him. He had used people for as long as he could remember. "I need you to help."

"You're a piece of work, Mitchell." She opened a sugar, wet her finger, and scooped some into her mouth.

A wave of nausea swept over him. "You're my friend, I hope you'll give me a hand. Can you take a week off, and we'll have a little vacation?" She didn't smile. He reached over to get some sugar.

"Are you really going to quit?"

Out the window, he watched a flock of pigeons spiraling in a long arc—another world beyond this pitiful farce in which he was trapped. "I have no feeling. Nothing. I care for nothing. It's time to stop and look for something to bring me back. To where, I have no idea." His head went down on the table.

She reached and touched his hair. All her maternal feelings were gathered in that touch. Recognizing these feelings, Mitch gratefully put his hand over hers, and they sat that way for some time.

"Let's go," she said finally.

At her sweet little one-bedroom in West Hollywood, she put some soup in front of him on the coffee table. He tried to eat, started to feel sick again, and stood up from the pink chintz sofa, but his arms and legs began to tremble, and his heart raced as he fell back down in a convulsion.

"Jesus, let me take you back to the hospital."

"No need, I'm just having a little withdrawal." He tried to stand again, fell down, got up, and staggered toward the bedroom. "Think I'll lie down for a while, be better with a nap." Shaking violently now, he blacked out and fell down again. When he came to, he tried to stand. Jane ran to the phone. He fell yet again and hit his head on the wall.

"Stay on the floor, god damn it. I'll get a doctor."

He watched as she moved in slow motion toward him, her mouth open and terror in her blue eyes. Warm blood slid down his face. That's all he remembered.

CHAPTER 25

Sober
1973

THREE MONTHS LATER, Mitch left the sober living house at five o'clock on a beautiful late summer evening. During his stay at Comfort House, he had learned to be silent. Being quiet turned out to be a great relief. He had never realized how much he talked. They told him to listen during the three meetings a day. As he made his way alone to Pico Boulevard, he thought of the hours of reading he found himself doing, and most of all, he remembered a poet named Rilke: "I live my life in growing orbits which move out over the things of the world." Well. I'm ready to move out into the world. The sun on his face and a slight breeze gave him a deep feeling of freedom and joy. He caught a bus to his old apartment. He had told no one he was leaving. Just like when he left the navy. There was no one to tell.

"All your things are in the basement," the landlady chatted him to the door at the top of the stairs. "I didn't hear anything from you, honey, so what could I do? Jesus, it's been three months. Where have you been?" Her voice still had the Eastern European accent, an echo from the past, and she wore the same dress he remembered from Christmas. The whole apartment complex seemed like a distant dream or a movie in which he had once acted.

"I'm sorry, what do I owe you?"

"Nothing, honey, forget it."

His feet remembered the way, and slowly he went down the staircase to the bottom, where a single lightbulb dangled like a small moon in the middle of the room. He recognized his belongings as he pulled an old lawn chair over to the pile. The worn leather bag his father had given him sat, like a weathered face, in front of a collection of cardboard boxes. The lines in the soft leather gave this paternal inheritance a life reminiscent of many an old drunk at Stanley's Bar. The thought of that familiar haunt brought on a wave of tenderness: still part of the myth, the conviction that a bar was the only place where a man could be comfortable and converse with his fellow man. The leather bag was a friend and the one thing, aside from his inner loathing, that resonated with a true past for him. How old was this horsehide heirloom? He touched the rough side, how many years? The bag traveled from Ireland with his grandfather more than a hundred years ago. Almost lost many times with no luck, Mitch was now thankful to see the old friend.

In the first box were some old photos of films he had made, along with several books—*The Possessed, The Adventures of Huckleberry Finn*, and an article from *The New Yorker* by Kurt Vonnegut on the state of writing. Underneath this literary level were a few soiled shirts wadded up with his boyhood baseball glove. In a stack of papers, he recognized his father's handwriting on a letter dated June 19, 1956. He remembered Charles Ryan's thick bond paper that he had used for important letters. Mitch smoothed the paper.

"Dear son, I'm happy to hear of the joy and fulfillment you are getting out of your acting. It was a great event to get your lovely letter. Your mother read it out loud to me. She made her usual remarks, but I know she was pleased. You talked about having a purpose in life and how that is the only thing that makes life worthwhile. Of course, that's important, but it can be hard if that purpose is blunted or taken away by circumstance. You have a gift. I have not been helpful in many ways, but I want you to know I care for you and have always loved you."

Sitting in front of the drugstore with his father those long years ago while the old man fought with the Popsicle wrapping, Mitchell Ryan, the son, had realized that Charles Ryan, this stranger, his father, was talking about his own failure to live up to his promise and was trying to warn his son. Mitch had to put his hand over his face for some minutes, then he took a deep breath and finished the letter.

"I know you will do well if you stick to it. Come and see us when you can. Dad."

He sat for a long time, staring at the collection of odd bicycle tires, rakes, and what appeared to be a horse harness hanging on the basement wall. At last, he stood up, put the letter in his pocket, and headed to the stairs. He stopped, went back, and picked up the bag, turned out the light, and climbed the stairs.

He walked down to the little triangle park that separated Franklin and Cahuenga Boulevard and glanced away from the liquor store on the corner. The early evening was warm, and a light breeze fluttered through the struggling tree in the center of the small park. He sat down on the one bench and took out the letter, still remembering his father sitting on the bench in Kentucky eating that Popsicle the night he died.

He put the letter back in his coat, then stood and walked past the liquor store along Franklin Avenue to Beachwood Canyon, watching the last rays of light filter into the dark-green foliage, welcoming the scent of night-blooming jasmine that enveloped him. When he turned the corner into the canyon, he heard a sudden laugh from a pool in a backyard and only then became aware of the birds chattering in the liquid amber trees lining the canyon. Then a car stopped at a light, and an old lady shuffled across the street as the light changed. She was wearing a shabby coat that looked like fur. He watched her take some time getting across Franklin.

Life had gone on as usual while he enjoyed his little vacation. Everything seemed normal and quiet. He watched the daylight fade.

CHAPTER 26

Born Again
1973

HE LEASED AN old ranch house about thirty miles from Los Angeles that had attracted his attention one day as he was driving the environs of Los Angeles. Off of Mulholland Highway, out past Agoura, he'd spotted an old place down in a hollow. There were several old live oaks hiding in a low building. The place needed a lot of help. Maybe they could help each other. He took the number off the for-rent sign and made a deal.

After he moved in, he found the place was a bit worse off than he thought. He found the front door wouldn't close. He borrowed a plane from a neighbor up the road, went to the hardware store and bought some tools—hammer, saw, paint, and varnish—shaved the door until it closed with ease, and spruced up the inside. One day he was trying to figure out the mystery of roofing shingles for the leaking roof in the back room. Shingles are an odd shape, thick at one end and tapering down to very thin at the other. He looked up from his study of the shingles to see a middle-aged man walking across the backfield from the woods. He came right up to Mitch, less than a foot from his face, then ran back some ten feet and announced, "You need help. I'm good at helping. I tell you one thing, wood shingles are against the law in fire-designated places, and this is a designated fire forest, all of Agoura is a designated fire forest, but it doesn't matter because everyone uses wood shingles because they look the best, and I know how to put them up, or down would be a better way to describe what happens to them when they're nailed to the roof." He said all this in one breath. "I can help, yes, help!"

Mitch, startled, asked, "What kind of help?"

"I can nail and paint, and I do it for free."

"Well, I don't need help. I can manage, but thank you."

"Oh, please, please, let me help, I have a lot of time. I'll show you how shingles are supposed to be on your roof, do you know how to put them down, never mind, I'm very good at it, I helped Mr. Goddard, who lives next door, when Mr. Goddard put them on, so I know how. Mr. Goddard wanted to pay me, but I work for free. I have plenty of money."

That was Melvin. He lived in a little house in the woods and received a pension every month from his family that he called "stay-away money." He had been designated "retarded" and seemed about five or six years old. But Mitch soon learned that Melvin had a surprising understanding of human action and a simple, clear knowledge of the way things were, and he, Mitch, wondered if maybe the "slow people," as they were called in some circles, weren't ahead of the rest of us.

This broken-down house of Mitch's in Agoura sat on two acres and was just what he needed to save his life. The old live oak tree that he sat under every day had become his best friend, until Melvin walked into his life. Melvin took the shingles out of Mitch's hand, climbed up the ladder, scrambled onto the roof, and turned back with, "Come up, I show. Bring rest of shingles."

When they were both up, Melvin said, "See, the thin part goes underneath, and you start at the bottom of the roof." He was agile as a cat. "Go get the nails and hammer. Did you get the right kind of nails? Roofing nails?"

In some mysterious way, Melvin relieved Mitch of the burden of self, like it says in the Big Book of Alcoholics Anonymous. Melvin came every day, and after running up to Mitch and then backing away ten feet, he would ask if Mitch was okay. Then Melvin asked, "Are you going to work today?" This trait of Melvin's was the most peculiar of a string of strange habits. He did the same with everyone. He just wanted to be sure you were paying attention.

Mitch hadn't worked for more than a year and wasn't missing Hollywood one bit when the call came from Walter. "Well, I think you have a job. How are you feeling?"

"I'm fine. What's the job?"

"It's a cop show, *Chase* it's called, for Jack Webb at Universal, and after he meets you tomorrow, they'll make an offer."

"Oh, Jesus, Jack and Universal."

"Go to the meeting at ten in the morning."

Mitch hung up.

Walter called right back. "Who do you think you are? You, Mr. Ryan, are not in a position to do anything but thank God and Jack Webb for this opportunity. Don't be a jerk. This is a good job and can lead to something."

"Sure, Walter, I'm going. Thank you, have a good evening."

"To hell with you."

"No, I mean it. I'm sorry. You know I care. I feel rotten."

"Get some rest." Walter paused. "Are you going to meetings?"

"Yes, don't worry, I'm fine. I'll be there in the morning."

"You better go." Good old Walter. He had remembered him.

Mitch was a stubborn man who was completely blacklisted because of his own behavior and hadn't been to an AA meeting in months. At his first meeting, he'd sat in the back with the only friend he knew who was a member. This man came and drove Mitch to a church in Hollywood where they held twenty-one meetings a week, morning, noon, and evening.

Mitch's usual mantle of being an outsider was draped over his shoulders, and he almost walked out several times, but a combination of not wanting to be noticed and being caught by something that was said kept him in the seat. By the time the meeting was over, he had relaxed and was greeted by any number of unlikely men from all walks of life, from a plumber to an actor he knew, and he was surprised to see all of them treating him like he was being welcomed back from the dead. As the months went by, this crowd of men helped him, and one or two became friends, but the smell of the program, the talk of God or a higher power, became a source of irritation and ignited a spark of defiance in him. So he didn't go back.

To be honest, he liked living alone in the country, with his new friend. When he was alone, everything slowed down, and the silence of this place allowed him to consider his life. Did he really want to throw himself back into the movie business? He had no idea what life could be or who he was or even what role he could play. In AA, there was much talk about being reborn and living a new life. Well, he did want a different life than the one he had been living, and this simple life suited him fine. If not for the money he needed to live on, he might have passed on all of show business entirely.

A short way from the house was the grand old live oak tree. Melvin told him it was at least four hundred years old. This was his tree. He sat down on the cool moss that sprawled out from the trunk. His mutt ambled up to sit and tucked himself into his master's leg. Looking up through those enormous tree limbs all green and full of life, Mitch pondered his situation. He would never have used the word pondering, but pondering it was, and in a deep and unaccustomed way. He saw clearly and maybe for the first time that he first had to have an aim for his life and then a plan. This was so foreign to him that he almost dismissed the idea as a stupid dream. He seemed like another person, having these thoughts because to Mitch, life had always been an accident. He'd reacted from his gut and formed his worldview from those actions. He laughed and, as usual, discarded any takeaways from his "pondering." He sank back to consider only the absolute essentials. He knew what he needed. What he needed was money. And where was he going to get money? TV in Hollywood.

He walked onto the Universal lot as nervous as he could ever remember being. He paced up and down across from the looming soundstages that seemed to go on forever, then headed back to the main gate. He stopped, stood for several minutes, then turned back and realized he didn't know where to go. So here he was, wandering through the lot, almost asking several people for directions but not quite managing the transaction. He noticed that every woman he saw was a "10." In fact, he had never seen so many gorgeous ladies in one place. They all resembled each other, but that didn't diminish his appreciation. Well, he reflected, he wasn't altogether dead. Finally, he managed to stop one young woman. "Excuse me, do you know where Jack Webb's production office could be?"

"Sorry, this is my first time here."

He looked into her eyes and saw terror. Suddenly he relaxed. "Good luck, don't worry. I'm Mitch."

"Thank you." She blushed. He put out his hand to shake. She hurried away.

He stood there, looking after her. Then he made his way up to the huge soundstages that surrounded the wide main street. He walked to the stage door of the first one. A heavyset guard sat on a director's chair drinking coffee.

"Can you tell me how to get to the Jack Webb productions office?"

"Down this street to Avenue J, turn right, and it'll bite you."

The outer door of a lush suite of offices with "Mark VII Productions" in gold letters above the door was intimidating. Below, in smaller letters, was "Mark VII, Inc." Today was the first time he had been out on a job since he'd quit drinking. There is nothing more private or intimate than a man's recovery from illness, and here he was in the most public place in America. He checked his tie in the glass door and buttoned his coat, then unbuttoned it. What would he do in the meeting? Let Webb talk. He couldn't talk about drinking. Funny, in the AA meetings, he would talk and laugh endlessly about drinking and his "sickness," but here on the outside—hardly a word.

He was not at all comfortable with seeing this man. Close to the surface was the sheer snob factor of working for Jack Webb, who had a reputation for doing popular stupid cop shows. But that was on the surface. He remembered Walter's words from yesterday: "Who do you think you are?" He tried to find some of his old confidence. Nothing. *Who am I? Jesus!* He checked his face and hair again in the glass door.

A beautiful girl behind the desk smiled and said, "You look fine, have a seat." His face flushed, and his whole body tensed. You would have thought he had been caught stealing something.

Jack came out and greeted him. "Mitch, I saw you in *My Old Man's Place*. You were good and tough and just what we need in this part." Mitch remembered the last movie he had made in what seemed to be the distant past. His mind clouded with memories of that time. Then he heard, "I would like to have gotten Kirk Douglas for this part, but the cheap bastards up in the tower wouldn't come up with the dough." Mitch looked blank. "No, no, I'm just kidding," and he led Mitch down a glass hall and into an enormous office.

"Sit down. What are you drinking?" He headed to a bar in the corner opposite the enormous empty oak desk.

This was the first time in his life it dawned on Mitch that he would be presented with a choice of whether to have a drink or not. He had always done what he wanted, never realizing there could be an alternative. When he didn't answer, Jack looked over and Mitch said, "Nothing right now. I have a bit of a gut ache."

Jack poured himself a big drink, went behind the desk, and sat down heavily. He looked familiar, but Mitch realized that aside from a rerun of *Dragnet*, he had never seen him in film. All he knew about him was that he hated hippies and had been honored by the LA Police Department. He had what looked like dyed black hair and a soft round face. There was something dangerous in his manner. His voice was the most revealing thing about him: raspy, sarcastic, deeply compelling, commanding attention.

"You spent a lot of time on the stage, didn't you?" He took a long drink, then before Mitch could respond, he said, "I never did a play. I began in radio." Raising his hand in a Caesar-like wave, Mitch assumed he was referring to the movie lot all around them: "Universal is a factory, and as long as we respect it for what it is, we can do pretty much what we want. I have. Let me give you a script before you leave. You're fine with me, but you have to meet Sid, the head of Universal, and tomorrow I want you to meet the kids that have been cast. Can you come at ten o'clock?" Mitch started to speak, but Webb turned away, walked to the window, and looked out for quite a long time. Then he lit his second cigarette, still with his back to Mitch. "I'm tired, this business is a fucking grind. You're just start-ing—I envy you." Mitch felt uncomfortable and wished he had taken that drink. The man turned back and smiled. "Well, if you do this picture, you're going to have to put up with me. I'm going to direct."

Mitch read the script that night: cops, cops, and more cops; his role was a tough police captain who ran a special squad of three men. One flew a helicopter, another mastered a hot car, and the third rode a motorcycle. He dropped the script on the floor and went for a walk.

He saw the moon through the large live oak trees and continued out to the road. There were several houses in this part of Agoura, none too close. He thought about the man who was to direct his life for the next month. He thought of going to a meeting. He drove to the movie-house in the mall. The marquee read, "A Place in the Sun." He watched Monty Cliff for an hour or so and then left because this American tragedy reminded him of earlier promises he had made to himself. What was the force that had headed him off in this direc-tion, so far from where he had started, and what he had told himself he wanted?

The next day he gave his okay to the three very handsome young men and was approved by the head of production for Universal. In a meeting a lot like a visit to the principal's office, the production boss told Mitch about the difference between films and TV. The looming shadow of his life for the next year brought back in vivid color the same impulse that had driven him to the discouragement that had made him run away and join the navy years ago.

He called Walter and told him that the day would have gone better if he had gotten drunk and forgotten the whole thing. Walter said, "Forget about it. You don't have to get drunk to forget about it. But you're in no position to turn anything down, and you would be an idiot to turn this down." He also said he was sorry, but he could get "no money" out of the contract boys at Universal because of Mitch's reputation for drinking.

He was playing the lead in a prime-time television show for three thousand dollars a week. What the hell? He was dead broke. It was a bad setup, but he decided to do it and keep his mouth shut. A small part of him realized he was lucky to be here at all. The larger part he kept under wraps until they started shooting when he realized the cop opera was far worse than he could ever have imagined.

Jack said, after the first scene, "That's good, but it's too rich, too much acting. This isn't Lincoln Center." Mitch was going to ask him what he meant by "rich" but decided life might be more fun to try to imitate Jack's *Dragnet* style. So he very slowly worked the deadpan of *Dragnet* into the proceedings. But still, he got from Jack, "Cut. Too rich, you're over the top."

They were the longest four weeks of his life. The young boy who played the fast-car driver on his team of detectives came up on the last day of shooting and said he was honored to have worked with him. Mitch mumbled something and hurried away. He had treated the boy with such contempt. Driving home, his relief at being done with the show was colored by the boy's generosity. What had he been doing? Walking around full of self-loathing and spitting on anyone who talked to him? Three weeks later, Walter called. "The network bought twenty shows, and you'll be working till next May."

What had he done?

CHAPTER 27

Eastwood
1974

THE HIGHLANDS INN sounded romantic to Mitch, something out of *Wuthering Heights*, but the inn turned out to be a motel. The first night Mitch went to bed and couldn't sleep. Ever since his meeting with Eastwood, first at his office in Hollywood and now just a few minutes before, here in the High Sierras, a paternal connection had been established, at least on Mitch's part.

He lay there a few minutes, then bounded up, pulled on his pants, and went out and down the hall. He heard Western music from the lounge, looked in, and saw through the smoke several cowboys standing at the bar. He watched for a moment, then turned away from his former life.

He walked outside across the parking lot to a large stand of pine trees and looked up at the endless dark peaks lit by the moon that circled the valley. He breathed deeply and began to sense a connection with his surroundings. The moon was there, the mountains were there, the parking lot, the pine trees, the warm wind—a new feeling, as if he had never lived before, and yet everything seemed ages old and familiar. A new kind of living energy filled his body and mind. He raised his arms and waved them around, turning like a dervish.

Awake, alert, alive, he walked back to the motel. He had been dead for years, dead with fear and loathing, and now he was awakened, resurrected, his sense of dread gone. He was a human being who actually belonged.

On the first day of shooting, the cast walked around the set in their Western outfits. The set was a work of art, built on the shores of saltwater Mono Lake in the middle of a huge basin formed by ancient volcanic eruptions. This "town" included a broad street and a working bar and stable.

Every day he felt renewed and couldn't wait to get to the set. Bob, a cast member who was also an expert on the natural history and recent history of the region, told Mitch everything he knew on the bus to location each day, and Mitch couldn't get enough of the history of these mountains and the men who had settled them.

No one had too big a burden in the film. They played together and, over several weeks, became an ensemble. There was a profound sense of camaraderie on the set, and further encouraged by the most beautiful setting imaginable, Mitch could relax, maybe for the first time, on a movie set or anywhere. He was almost two years sober and wondering how he had lived all those years under the cloud of alcohol. When he walked out away from the set to a bluff above the town on that sunlit day, Carson Peak towering fourteen thousand feet above him and the lake behind, he felt the gratitude of a man who had been saved from drowning.

After twenty shows for NBC, the cop series had been mercifully canceled, and Mitch had been called to meet the famous actor/director who was doing a Western to be shot in the High Sierras. Mitch met Clint Eastwood at his office on the Warner Bros. lot. He was in the middle of lunch, a big bite of sandwich in his mouth, but he welcomed Mitch, and they had a nice talk. Mitch was prepared to be intimidated, but the director was so down-home friendly that he relaxed. Mitch watched his face, open and generous with a ready smile. Mitch was comfortable almost at once, so unlike his experience with the TV show he had just finished.

"I got a bunch of good actors for this show," Eastwood drawled as he leaned back casually in his chair. He seemed unaware that most actors would line up to work with him. "Have you ever been to the High Sierras?"

"No."

"There's nothing in the world like them. They aren't as high as some ranges, but there's magic about them that never gets out of your blood." There was a softness in his voice when he spoke about the mountains as living beings.

Bishop, California, in the foothills of the High Sierras, lay in a low valley circled by mountains, white and glowing in the sun. The plane had twenty-five seats filled mostly with actors, some stuntmen, and the director of photography. Mitch had never been in a small plane before, and as it tossed around in the mountain passes, he started to feel sick. Finally, the plane lurched and started down, and Buddy Van Horn, who was Eastwood's double, woke up, took one look at Mitch's green face, and let out a big laugh. "Here, take this—it's a magic pill for throwing up." Then he settled back and continued, "Nothing makes me happier than a ten-week movie." Van Horn was about the same size as the movie star and very agile, like most great stuntmen.

The idea of dealing with stuntmen again left Mitch nonplussed, mainly because he was playing the town boss and would not be doing any riding. Van Horn seemed a different kind of man, or maybe the distinction was that Mitch had been half-drunk during those previous two Westerns, only two years before. Now that he was sober, things were different. Sober! He marveled when he thought of the volume of alcohol he had consumed in that last Western.

"It's strange to be in a Western and not ride, don't you think?"

Van Horn opened his eyes and looked up. "Gary Cooper didn't go near a horse in *High Noon*." Then he closed his eyes as if to say, "No more stupid questions." Maybe he wasn't that different after all. When they landed, he and Mitch sat together on the bus to the location.

Leaving the airport, the bus dipped down into a long green valley with horses and cattle clustered at various islands among the pines. Mitch was as excited as a kid, his face up to the window. After the bus rambled along the floor of the valley for ten minutes, it started to climb. He hadn't thought about what Eastwood had said about the Sierras until this panorama opened up on all sides.

He was brought back to the bus by the ripping noise of what seemed like the transmission and then a jerk as the driver geared down to make the grade. The mountains kept unfolding, growing larger and more imposing as the bus moved up into them. On all sides, the peaks rose and towered over the pass. Buddy nudged him to look back. The green valley they had just left was far below, in miniature.

After about forty miles of mountains on all sides, the bus turned down a side highway and then labored up a small grade for several miles. Right before the top was a large sign that read, "Oh! Ridge." At the summit, the bus stopped. There before them was a valley with a towering mountain across the way and a range rising like walls from two stunning crystal blue lakes. "Oh, Jesus!" Mitch was unable to contain himself. The spectacular mountains, lakes, and sky suffused him with a kind of awe, wonder, and gratitude that took him by surprise. At that moment, he understood that if he had still been drinking, he would never have been able to allow this natural intoxication to flow into and through him.

In the little village called June Lake were several motels, and on the main drag was a tackle and sport shop. An old lodge up on the ridge overlooked the town and the post office, grocery store, and the Tiger Bar. In front of the lodge on the ridge, the large sign read, "The Heidelberg."

Everyone left the bus and poured into the bar. It was Mitch's first time in a bar since he had sobered up. He sat, ordered a BLT and a root beer, and watched everyone mixing and catching up. Everything in the Tiger Bar was wood, with booths and a pool table at the back. He felt isolated as he sipped his root beer and waited for the sandwich. There was nothing to say. He didn't feel uncomfortable, just removed. The noise in the bar reached a crescendo with all the greetings and the sheer joy of having a good job. His sandwich came, and he ate in silence, then left and went looking for the motel.

"Where're you going?" came a voice from the door of the bar. It was Bob, one of the actors.

"I thought I'd find the motel." Together they picked up the luggage from the bus, checked in, and went to the makeshift office of the film company. Clint arrived at the same time and set down a large bag of groceries on a desk.

"Hey, Robert. How's Sissy? Good trip, Mitch?"

"She's fine. What's first tomorrow?"

"Oh, I don't know. We'll all go out and fool around on the set. Wait till you see what a great job they did."

Mitch watched him leave and felt a sudden fraternal longing. He walked out after him. Clint was putting his groceries in his truck. "Clint?" The man turned. "Thanks for having me on the picture. It's nice to have a job." Mitch stood there like a small boy, full of feeling.

"There's nothing like a ten-week movie to lighten a man's burden. See you in the morning." Then Eastwood climbed into his truck, and Mitch watched him drive away.

Back inside, Bob was looking over the "day out of days," a schedule of how the movie would be shot and had counted up the days he was to work. "On call almost every day. God, there's nothing better than a ten-week movie." Mitch smiled. In his former life, he'd have thought of a ten-week movie as a prison sentence, but for some reason, the calm and gentleness he felt now made him giddy, and he started to laugh, then sing, "A ten-week movie…is like a melody."

CHAPTER 28

Try Sobriety
1975

As he was finishing his second film for Eastwood, Mitch was cast in a TV series at Metro Goldwyn Mayer called *Executive Suite*, based on the film starring William Holden. He had felt strange about doing another long-running series since Jack and the cops had been quite enough, but mainly he hesitated because he was actually debating whether to return to New York and to get back into the theater. Somewhere in him, though, was a strange configuration of feelings that kept him in Hollywood—or was the commitment to New York intimidating? In any event, he took the job, good television with decent and talented people, but his heart was elsewhere.

One morning as he arrived at the soundstage of the *Executive Suite* series, on what unexpectedly turned out to be its final day, the second assistant director rushed up to him and declared, "You're late! They've started reading the scene, and Mr. Rubin is looking for you." Mitch looked at the young man. "Could you repeat all that while you're falling under a bus and get me a cup of coffee?" Then he walked to one of the many sets where the cast was blocking the day's work.

"Anytime, Mr. Ryan," said the director. Then he said, "Let's take a break." And the man ran off. Mitch wandered to the craft services table and poured himself a coffee.

"Where you been, smarty-pants," said the young actress playing his daughter. He looked around to see if his TV wife was close, but she was nowhere to be seen, so he didn't have to feel guilty, but he did.

He caught an inner glance of himself. Jesus, he was having a go at both of them, and it was suddenly sickening. He tried to walk away from the craft services table, but she followed him. "I thought you were coming by last night."

"Sorry, I was with my lawyer trying to figure out an angle on how to get out of this show."

"Oh, silly, you don't mean that. Can you come over tonight?"

He looked at her sensual face and wondered where this child had come from. "No. You're right. I don't mean anything I say."

The AD barked, "Let's set up for the first shot. That'll be your closeup, Mitch. You don't mind if we shoot backward?"

"Might be better."

They had just started to shoot when the producer entered the stage and whispered something to the AD, who then whispered to the director, who called, "Cut. Mr. Arnold has something to communicate to us all."

"I'm sorry to tell you the show has been canceled."

Everyone was struck silent, frozen in disbelief. Mitch had assumed the show had been picked up. They'd been on a roll, cranking out episodes beyond the original order of seven. Only moments before, the faces around him had been alert and alive with interest, tinged with an unspoken smugness that comes with having a show business job. Now suddenly, they had the aspect of mannequins.

An older actress who had been around a long time said, "Are you sure, Mr. Arnold?"

"Yes, that's it."

"Let me finish Mitch's closeup, anyway." The director was still not taking in the news.

"Why? They won't need it. What would we do with a closeup if we don't have the rest of the show? Save the stock and the electric bill." No one moved.

Mitch turned to the leading lady. "Time to celebrate! Can we all come to your house tonight for a party?"

"Go to hell, you negative son of a bitch."

"Testy, testy. Couldn't be happier to have this thing done with."

And with that, Mitch turned and left. As he walked out, the older actress followed him to the stage door. "So long, Mitch. Nice to know you. I was hoping if we'd run a little longer, you would have gotten around to me."

"Ruth, darling, you were next on the list." He gave her a kiss on the cheek, and she held him in a warm hug. "Goodbye," he managed, then it was into his car, leaving everything behind in his dressing room. He drove off the lot. At the gate, he pulled to the side, stepped out, and stared back at MGM, thinking of the glory days, Clark Gable and all the rest. He recalled that Gable had started in a play. *Maybe I'll go to New York*, he thought.

So there it was. *Executive Suite* was canceled in the middle of Mr. Ryan's closeup. The news became a joke around town for at least two weeks. But for the first time in a while, Mitch had money, so he paid off all the people he owed and settled with the IRS, and that left him with just enough to take a small vacation, so he went on a driving trip through the great barren Mojave Desert into Arizona. He started to relax but cringed at the memory of his recent disgusting behavior. Slowly the deep inner feeling of peace and freedom that had found him in the mountains had vanished, pushed out by fear-driven cynical behavior.

He headed toward the Grand Teton Mountains in Wyoming that he'd always wanted to see. As he drove the endless roads of the Arizona desert, he realized he hadn't really been alone since that year in Agoura, fixing his house, and this was his first time on the road since his hitchhiking days, when he'd left the navy. All alone, with no one to see or call.

Why had he never been alone these last years? He had needed people to drink with, and that pattern had been loosened but not broken in the four years he had been sober. He still needed people around. He couldn't blame Lynda for leaving again, but now that he was sober, he realized what a sick man he had been. He missed watching her with the horses and the way she would hum and sing to them. He knew this was love when he realized that she hummed because he had been a hummer all his life. Sadness lingered with him most of the time.

Slowly, all of Hollywood started to fade, then disappeared. The great expanses before him made Hollywood seem like so much clap-trap. He felt small in the face of the enormity of the earth and sky and found, not surprisingly, that he actually liked being alone. Suddenly he felt almost—dare he say the word—joyful, almost content. There was a freedom in not needing anyone and not thinking he had to do this or that or he must see so-and-so. There was nowhere to go and nothing to do. He loved it.

He spent three weeks driving from town to town all through Wyoming and Montana and then on to Idaho and down to Nevada. He began to understand how to slow down. He didn't have to move fast and didn't want to. If he saw a place he liked, he stopped. He was overwhelmed with the sky and the thousand shades of color in the forests. His father, on rare occasions, had spoken of the glory of color, mostly in the fall when the trees were red and gold. Now, during the summer, the trees weren't just green but blue in the sun and then a strange black-red that was full of light as darkness fell. Night was Hamlet's "majestical roof fretted with golden fire."

Doug and the great talks about *Hamlet* and acting. He realized he had never followed up on the deep advice about living he had gleaned from Doug. Doug had told him to go to college, even though he himself hadn't. He had told Mitch to be an educated man because to become a great actor you need all the knowledge you can acquire. "Life is an improvisation," he would say, and you have to be ready for what's coming, you have to have an aim in this life, or you'll be rolled over because life has an aim for you. Mitch pondered, *What is an aim?* Certainly not to be rich or famous. What could Doug have meant? Was he still alive? He hadn't been in touch with him for years.

He went around Las Vegas and headed toward Route 15, the road to Los Angeles. He passed the flashing lights of the roadhouse that seemed to be the one where he had spent a day and night with Mitchum so long ago. He stopped and went in. The first thing that struck him was the stale beer and cigarettes, smell of the past. When his eyes adjusted to the dark, he saw that what he had remembered as an upscale cozy bar and restaurant was actually a shabby wreck of a place. He sat at the bar next to a slightly intoxicated man with a Mack Truck jacket on and a Chicago Cubs baseball hat down low over his forehead. How strange that the glamour and good fellowship he had once felt here belonged strictly to the alcohol fumes of imagination.

"Ginger ale, please."

"My Gawd, I ain't never heard the likes—ordering a soda in a saloon."

"Well, I gave it up."

"My Gawd, why would you do that?"

"It seemed time."

"My Gawd. Oh, yeah, I get ya. I give it up too, every night when I go to bed."

"Makes sense."

"My Gawd, to stop for all time. My Gawd!"

Mitch wondered if he said, "My God" in every sentence.

"My Gawd, I knew a preacher give it up on Saturday night so he could pass the word on Sunday." He started to laugh, an unpleasant chortle. "But by Sunday night, he was back to normal. My Gawd, but he could put it away. Methodist!"

He stopped and threw watery eyes at Mitch, then said, "Another double, George."

This was said softly, right in Mitch's face, and George down the bar said, "Coming up."

After his drink came, the Cubs fan took a small sip, then in a soothing, deeply concerned voice, "I'm worried about you, son. My Gawd, it ain't natural for a man to not drink."

Mitch, in long-ago days, could have spent several weeks talking to this Mack Truck philosopher, plumbing the depths of all the absurdities of life. But now, he saw the pitiful waste and sadness in this man. "Thank you for your concern, and I will take it under advisement, but I must be going."

"My Gawd, did you hear that? Under advisement. You'd better think long and hard about the future, son. A life without the warm comfort of your choice of heavenly liquor is something else. My Gawd, gives me the shudders."

Mitch fell out into the harsh desert sun. Troubled and deeply grateful to be away from the lure of that hapless, hopeless life he looked to the west at the lonely stretch of desert between Las Vegas and Los Angeles. There is a difference, between heaven and hell, between the gold and green bear country, surrounded by the forests of Idaho and Montana, and this barren wasteland that lay before him. A fitting reentry into his beloved Hollywood, bleak and colorless.

He arrived home to the great joy of his dog and paid the house sitter. Thank God for dogs. They love you no matter what. There was a message from Lynda and Tim. "Hello, how are you, Dad." It was the first time Tim had called him Dad. He must get them back. He called. No answer. He talked to Walter. No movie or TV work and no hint of any.

He went to several AA meetings over the next few weeks, left early, didn't participate. "Addiction of the body and an obsession of the mind" sounded like so many words. Driving around the country carefree and with no responsibilities had been much different than facing what his life really was, here and now. At the meetings, he tried to count his blessings. He was still sober but had forgotten, if he'd ever known, that that wasn't enough. Since he wouldn't drink and knew very little about how to live sober, he slowly became a real bore to himself and the meeting, then before it was over, he'd be gone. One day he got upset in a meeting when an AA old-timer told him, "Mitch, you better get up and tell us how it is with you."

"No, I'm not talking today."

"It's a good idea to speak when you're asked. It always helps."

"No, nothing to say."

"You'll wake up drunk one day, son, and won't know how you got there."

"Fuck you!" Mitch stormed out of the meeting and stood outside the clubhouse, smoking and letting his rage cool. Pretty soon, his friend Jamie came out and asked him if he wanted to get something to eat. Jamie had been sober twenty-three years and had worked for the studios. He had a big square jaw and more lines on his face than corduroy pants.

"I'm sorry. I'm a jerk."

"Forget it." Then, over coffee, Jamie said, "You're in good shape, Mitch. Get your head out of your pocket. And always remember, getting really sober is a long process that only begins with quitting drinking. You're like me, like all of us—you will have to learn how to live and find some real values, but the most important thing for you is to decide what you want. These are decisions you will have to make sooner or later. How well you do in this program depends on your attitude." Mitch heard what he said. Later on, the words even began to make sense.

When he returned home, there was a message from Walter. "Where are you? There's a job coming, a great script. Call me— Walter, your agent, in case you've forgotten."

He sat down, tried to relax, lit a cigarette, and let the familiar swell of self-pity flow into him. Pacing around the room he thought hard about taking a drink. Then he remembered what the old-timer had said: "You'll end up drunk and won't know how you got there." At nine o'clock in the evening, Los Angeles was in full swing, and he went to bed. The film was called *The Hemingway Play* and shooting wouldn't start for three months.

And then the most extraordinary thing happened. He found the ape.

CHAPTER 29

The Hairy Ape
1976

MITCH WAS WALKING down Santa Monica Boulevard where it crossed Western Avenue in the east part of Hollywood, and as he took in the filthy street and gutter and the faded storefronts, it seemed to him that there was something familiar about the angle where Santa Monica Boulevard and Oxford Place came together. Crawling up his spine came strange goblins, dark and foreboding. Not since he'd lived in New York, committing walking suicide, had he been visited by the demons of his former insane alcoholic life.

He realized what it was: he might've been coming to Twelfth Street and Avenue B in lower Manhattan, Stanley's Bar could have been on the corner. Memories of those dark days stalked, no, shadowed him. He stood for a moment. You're sober now, and that life is over. *Walk faster, get into the theater, before your mind can overtake you.* He turned into Oxford Place toward the theater. The theater, which saved his life in those early days in New York, was going to do it again. Oxford Place, total trash, deserted buildings, could be the name of a street running in front of Buckingham Palace.

He had just turned forty and come to the decision that his "time was out of joint" and that he had better take a good hard look at the state of his acting. He hadn't done any theater acting—and not much good screen acting, for that matter—in too many years. His old friend Ralph from New York, who'd come to LA and landed a lead in a TV series, was starting a theater and wanted Mitch to join as "managing partner." Sounded like running things, Mitch thought, not his cup.

Inside, up an uneven flight of linoleum-covered stairs, he entered a comfortable, warm lobby with a large Persian rug in front of a dark oak bar. Beyond this was a surprisingly accessible theater with a three-sided stage very much like New York's old Circle in the Square and good sturdy theater seats. Sitting there on the stage before him, he recognized New York friends from ten years ago. As it turned out, there were to be four more managing directors besides himself, all distinguished actors: Donald Moffat, Richard Jordon, Gwen Arner, and Ralph Waite. Mitch had worked with them all. An ancient mystery caused Mitch to be transported back to New York and the Circle and allowed all the actors from that time to come into view. He stood in the doorway. From the stage, Ralph called, "Don't be shy, youngster. Come on up, we won't bite."

As he walked down the aisle and up onto the stage, his body remembered the joy of being in a theater and on a stage. He had never felt like he truly belonged on a film set or location, but on the stage, he had always felt at home. In fact, he was more alive on the stage than in his life on the street. All this came to him at that moment, as he remembered his vow to return to it, to his calling, to his real life. Then suddenly, everyone spoke at once. And then there were hugs and exclamations, and the family of actors picked up where they'd left off years ago, as if waking from a dream.

"We will have a season," Ralph planning and prophesizing, "and we will start with *The Hairy Ape*, by Eugene O'Neill. You, Mitch, will be the ape, and I will be the ape director. Then Gwen will do *The Kitchen*, by Arnold Wesker." Ralph always talked as if he were addressing a gaggle of marines. "Richard will do Howe's *Museum*, and Donald will do *Cock-a-Doodle Dandy*, by Sean O'Casey, and with any luck, I will participate in that production."

"Jesus, I thought I was a managing director, don't we have anything to say about the lineup?"

"What would you change, Mitch?"

"Well, for starters, maybe Gwen should play the ape."

"I thought of that, but we all agreed that you would be the only one to truly understand the inner workings of an ape. Especially O'Neill's ape." From the bare stage, love radiated through the empty theater.

They started rehearsals. When Mitch read the play, he was amazed to find that the part was completely written in a 1900s Brooklyn dialect and needed to be deciphered as you would a foreign language. Once he got his mouth around the language, he found he was dealing with a very difficult role indeed.

For a day or two, he had no clue how to approach this part. Sitting, smoking after rehearsal on the back fire escape of the theater, he looked down at the tangle of alleys in this decidedly unglamorous edge of Hollywood. He watched a man and a woman huddled together at the bottom of the fire escape, an overstuffed plastic garbage bag between them. The man handed her a brown paper bag, the top of a bottle just showing, then she put the glass circle to her lips and took a long pull. Another man just about Mitch's age but looking older poked through a dumpster. Broken people as he had been not so long before. Just because he hadn't had a drink in more than four years didn't mean he couldn't join that couple. They were waiting for him. One drink. There was something almost appealing about the deadly life he had once known. No feeling, no pain, no responsibility.

He watched another man pull a ragged blanket out of the dumpster and yet another man fished several greasy boxes out of the same bin. They looked like starving mangy animals. So he, Mitch the artist, smoked his cigarette and watched the combination of shapes in front of him: a square building with a broken wall behind the dumpster, the man putting the blanket around his shoulders, red bricks, green dumpster, a sad, crumpled man with blanket—all unreal shapes. What was real? Nothing real except breath. He studied the panorama for a long time and imagined the ape, self-willed, always himself, until—the fall. The ape is self-willed, and so was Mitch. The ape is terrified, and so was Mitch. The ape is enraged, and so was Mitch. Terror and rage had run him all those years of his drunkenness until God knows who he was now. Well, whatever he was, Mitch was human. The ape was human.

Once he committed to the part, day after day he found the place he needed for the ape, whose name is Yank. Yank has some of the longest and most poetic and complicated speeches written by O'Neill, and this created a towering challenge. Yet the deeper he climbed down into the part and allowed himself to see and feel the beast in his body, the more he found he still had the power to let his voice out and free himself of his physical bondage.

He went to the Griffith Park Zoo and watched the large ape there. As the creature stood watching him, he slowly moved and looked Mitch right in the face, measuring him. Mitch felt a chill and knew the ape was about to smack him for being insolent, and indeed after several moments, the ape made a violent movement to smash the reinforced glass, then bent over and swung his long arms back and forth. Later Mitch found that when his trunk was bent with both hands on the shovel, moving from the coal pile to furnace door, it was the same violent swinging movement the ape had made, back and forth and back and forth.

O'Neill had built the part so that nothing would make sense unless the behavior was absolutely on the money. So in the end, the very specific animal behavior Mitch had observed and incorporated to ground the role of Yank allowed him to soar.

On opening night in this small theater in a wretched section of Hollywood, away from any trappings and pretense, he was as nervous as he had been on his first opening night some twenty years before in Louisville. Then as soon as the stage lights came up and Yank started to speak, an inner calm took over, and he was back home. O'Neill's power of the verse and deep understanding of the man and the life of the world helped him. He remembered what Doug Ramey had said: "The work is what counts. The doing is what counts." He was back in the theater, he was back in himself, and he liked himself.

After the opening-night party, he left Ralph's house and drove to his little ranch in Agoura. As the glow of the opening faded, something like poison gas filtered into him. He pulled off the freeway and sat in the car. Sweating. Trembling. What was this? The obligation and deep meaning of this play were working on him. He was to bring Yank to life for ten weeks, every night. This was a good thing, he told himself. This is what he had said he wanted. Why was he afraid? Was life so difficult? Christ! What was at home? Lynda and Tim had left and were not coming back. He had asked her to reconsider, now that he was sober, but she had given him no hope. Was he starting over in everything or maybe just starting? What was this life for? To start over all the time, every day, one day at a time. He had felt so alive on the stage tonight. He had known who he was and why he was there. But now... *"Life's but a walking shadow, a poor player / That struts and frets his hour upon the stage and then is heard"*...he started the car... *"no more."*

CHAPTER 30

Hemingway
1976

THE DIRECTOR WOULDN'T leave. He had been fired, but he simply wouldn't leave. Mitch and the whole cast were standing on the set when the producer came out and announced he was going to finish directing the picture. They watched as the man who had just been fired went to the back of the soundstage and sat down in his chair. Mitch felt bad because he had begun to like the man. Now for some bizarre reason, this director continued to return every day, walking to the back of the stage and sitting down there. He had been asked to leave but would not. So there he sat, all through the shoot.

They had started with great hopes. The whole cast was excited when they heard this film was to be shot on a stage with four cameras. Mitch was to play the crumbling world-famous author, two other wonderful actors, Tim Matheson and Perry King, would play the younger Hemingways, and a famous stage actor Alexander Scourby was to play Papa. This was to be one of those rare times when every element served to make the project work. The screenwriter had beautifully crafted the film script from his stage play, bringing to life all the complexities of Hemingway's personality by depicting him at four different stages of his life as four characters who meet at a café in Madrid: a young Hemingway, wounded in the war; the Paris writer; the middle-aged world celebrity; and last, the old Papa. The magic of the characters and talent of the actors brought a deep conviction to each of them that lived up to a complete picture of Hemingway. This was the experience Mitch needed to follow *The Hairy Ape.*

The cast worked in a rare and magical way that seldom occurs in the making of a film. The four-camera platform brought to the project a semblance of theater, and the two-week rehearsal bound them together much as a play would.

But when the cast reported to the soundstage, they soon discovered the director's plan was, in fact, to use just one camera and then shoot closeups. The intricate planning necessary to utilize four cameras takes time, and he had done none of that work. However valuable his direction had been, what was needed now was a knowledge and mastery of how four cameras work simultaneously. So he was fired. The producer, who had worked with Orson Welles and had directed many plays and films, took over, but he needed to call off production for two days while he designed all the shots for four cameras.

Mitch, meanwhile, had been ready to shoot, and so when the new director announced the two-day delay, his silence was loud, and the director noticed. "Mitch, I need time to design the shots. I know we're all geared up and ready to shoot, but it can't be helped."

"I'm sorry. I'm ready, that's all," Mitch muttered, and he headed for the stage door, trying not to show how undone he was.

"It will be fine. You are fantastic in this part. You have no idea how good you are. Get some rest and work on those scenes with Alex."

Mitch ran out of the studio, passed several bars, then stopped at an ice cream store and devoured two large chocolate sundaes.

Later he sat at the dressing table with a stomachache and looked at himself in the mirror. Did the director mean what he said, or was he bullshitting? Mitch realized that despite everything he'd accomplished and all the work he'd done, he was still insecure. He suddenly knew why he drank. He opened the script and began to go over his lines. Then he threw the script on the sofa. He wants me to "work with Alex." What the fuck for? He studied himself in the mirror. Do I want to "work" with Alex? Why? Calm down, damn it, it's only two days. Alex. All right, I'll have dinner with Alex. I might learn something.

So it was dinner with Alex, who was playing Papa. They went to a little Italian restaurant on Sixty-Seventh Street. Alex said, "Smells of garlic. This is good." It did. And it was.

After they ordered, Mitch asked, "Do you still get this sickening attack of fear before you work? Sometimes I think it's not worth all this tension. It's just a movie."

"It's what life is," the older actor said. "Anything that one cares about and feels a responsibility toward is going to bring a pressure that can go into the work or be eaten up by anxiety. What was your father like?"

This unexpected question prompted a quick series of images of his father. Mitch saw him lying in his coffin, the image superimposed with the few times his father had hugged him, grabbing him in a bear squeeze, holding him for moments, then dropping him and moving off.

"Why did you ask that?"

"I don't know: fathers and sons. Hemingway's father, as you know, killed himself."

Mitch ate a couple of fast bites and dismissed the question with, "My father wasn't much help to me or anyone on any level, and he didn't kill himself."

Alex remained silent for a while. Then he said, "You're a funny duck. You seem to not need help, always coming across as being on top of things and capable of handling what comes along."

Mitch looked at Alex, the old-school actor morphing into an old-school psychiatrist. Alex, twenty or so years older than Mitch, had a great voice and brought a powerful reality to all the parts he played, but now he sounded preachy and tiresome.

"I'm good at burying the fear," Mitch admitted, then, to cover up, asked, "Does it ever fucking leave?"

Alex looked at him with a curious smile. "Waiter, could I have a brandy stinger?"

"Jesus, I used to drink vodka stingers."

"Only a crazed drunk would drink vodka stingers. No wonder you quit." He laughed. Mitch laughed too. "Well, I was a crazed drinker. I have often said I drank 'only fine scotch,' when, in reality, I would drink anything that was put in front of me."

The older man settled back and became quiet. "Well, you're right, your tension doesn't show. And no, it never leaves. Why do you feel so different when the show is over? Where does that deep relaxation come from when you finish a job well done? Also, I watch you, and you're able to overcome tension when you enter the part. That's the mystery. In your bones, you know that mystery. This part you're playing of the famous Hemingway is really nothing but a man who will drink anything that is put in front of him. How perfect for you! Hemingway had discipline in his writing, which I think left him later in life, and when we meet him at this stage, he's a shell of what he was. There is something organic that you already understand about what agony he is trapped in."

At home that night, Mitch thought about Alex. "You understand the agony trapped in the man," he had said. Alex had recognized some deep life truth in him, Mitch, and in Hemingway, and Mitch felt thankful that he had gone to the restaurant and smelled the garlic.

All the work they had put into the rehearsals was right there when they finally started shooting. The director had them do fifteen to twenty pages at a time. He blocked several scenes using the four cameras, ran the scenes, then filmed them. When necessary, he would punch in for closeups. They all had done live TV, and the process was satisfying to be able to experience again.

All through the shooting, the fired director sat and watched. What agony for him to stay? At first, his silent presence was unnerving, but the show pulled Mitch in, and he forgot about the ex-director. The new director was a wizard and had more energy than all of them put together. The relationships between the four Hemingway's worked. It was amazing to have the Hemingway's of different ages talk to each other, creating in the process such a singular complete picture of the man.

They shot for three days, and at the end, Mitch was in a wholly different state, transformed from where he had started. Alex had been right. He had experienced this lightness and joy before, but now he could be aware in ways that had been unavailable to him while he'd been drinking. He had a new feeling of himself, quiet and profound. As the four Hemingway's kept hugging, he was able to experience and recognize the joy with no barriers.

The fired director came over to him and took his hand. "You did a great job. I think Hemingway would have liked it." He stood a moment then walked away toward the exit. Mitch felt an impulse to go after him, but anything he might have said would have diminished the man's elegant gesture of recognition.

Bigger news had occurred during the project. Near the end of the film, Lynda had finally come back with Tim. She was happy, and this meant to Mitch that she had forgiven him. Tim was sullen and didn't want to be there—or anywhere, for that matter. When Mitch returned home after the last day of shooting, he went for a long walk with Lynda out through the woods across from his house. Young Tim was asleep. They had come back, and so had he, and this was a wondrous thing for Mitch, a miracle.

"Lynda, I'm glad you decided to come back, away from those cowboys, improve your 'lifestyle.'"

"Yes, it's good to be back, but now that you don't drink, you're so…boring." A long sigh. "I'd have sent Tim on to you but figured he needed me around also. Ah, it was always such fun when you'd disappear for a week at a time and then the joyous celebration when you'd finally stumble on home. I also loved it when you'd bring four or five of your mangy drunken friends home with you. Such great fun, watching you fall down or up the stairs and in the door. Don't you miss all that? Now, all you do is work, come home, and go to the movies, and sometimes you take me and buy me popcorn."

They were walking out through the soft, warm night, his arm around her. "Ah, you say such nice things about me." They watched the moon as it showed through the trees. His heart was light. He was beginning to understand the word sober, the idea of the word, the living of it.

CHAPTER 31

Electra Glide in Blue
1978

MITCH HAD DONE a string of ordinary movies in extraordinary places and for a long time had wanted to bring Tim along, yet school or something else had always quashed the venture. But now, while he was doing a first-class shoot in Texas with an important cast, he thought this would be the perfect opportunity for Tim to join him.

Setting aside his natural curiosity about new places Abilene, Texas, wasn't really revealing much to Mitch, so he was especially happy Tim was coming. Before he had left Agoura and his little ranch, he and Lynda had discussed Tim's visit. "West Texas is a fascinating place, they tell me," Mitch had said, "and he'll have a terrific time. He'll love it."

"Oh sure, Texas—fascinating, fascinating, the land of the America First boys, shoot-you-down-in-the-street bunch."

"No, dear Lynda, we will be in the bosom of Hollywood and isolated from the cruel world. Also, it would be a way for the two of us to get closer. Which needs to begin soon or it may never happen."

"Oh crap, Mitch, you need to be a father and work with him every day, not just take him on vacation to the glamour of a Hollywood movie set." But Lynda finally relented, and a plan was hatched. The boy was excited, and the three of them went out to dinner down in Malibu to celebrate.

Mitch picked Tim up a week later on a Sunday at the Fort
Worth airport. He was more than pleased to see the boy and felt
Tim was happy to be away from his mother and LA. They were, as
expected, both a little tentative at first. They stopped at the Rustic
Steak roadhouse, and Mitch watched Tim devour his twelve-ounce
burger as the tension slowly dissolved. Mitch had never known the
reason for this mutual unease, but he also never seemed to do the
right thing, so most of the time he found defense in ignoring the boy.
Now he wondered why. The youngster was so relaxed and seemed so
happy to be with him that Mitch felt he could let his guard down, so
he ate a French fry and passed the ketchup to Tim. "There's a dude
ranch that's not far from Abilene, I'm told. Would you like to go? I'm
not sure what we'll find, but how bad could the horses be?"

"Well, not as bad as Ronald." Ronald was a beautiful horse but
could never be trained out of his habit of kicking. "Remember the
time he wanted to get rid of you, and you flew right into the fence?
Mom thought you were dead." Mitch laughed, and Tim joined.

"That was my fault. Kicking was his."

"Remember when he kicked the horseshoe man who had hit
him with his crop? You ran him off with a long line of curses. I never
saw you so mad, except at me once or twice."

"Well, I can't stand anybody abusing animals."

"You were my hero that day, Dad."

Mitch blushed and ate some more fries then wondered if Tim
were putting him on. There was always something dark in the way
Tim smiled when he said, "Dad." Why feel strange when he was
called "Dad" as if the title was out of kilter? So he changed the subject as they went to the car and talked about doing movies on the rest
of the drive.

They hit it off that afternoon, and the next two weeks were pre-
cious to Mitch. Father and son for the first time. Tim would get up
at dawn and join the crew and actors on the ride to the set, where he
became an assistant prop man and accepted by everyone. He called
Mitch "Dad" many times those first weeks, and each time the name
and the sound of the word bothered Mitch, but he said nothing, for
fear Tim would close down.

One day the scene being shot involved a number of hippies in a broken-down stable. The director told Tim to get into wardrobe and join the kids who were part of the scene. He was so happy he ran over to Mitch's dressing room and burst in. "I'm in the movie, Dad, isn't that the best? I've got to get to wardrobe—do you think I should have some makeup?"

"Well, you could maybe…" Mitch started, but Tim was gone with, "I'll ask the director, he'll tell me."

Mitch watched as he ran off toward the set. The boy had called him Dad again. Why did that make him so uncomfortable? He could see his own father and maybe would always see him relentless and unforgiving when he had stood and said nothing the night Mitch, as a boy, had run away from home. But not only his father—the coolness of his mother and indifference of his sister also played with his soul. Now could he ever be a father? Deep once-buried feelings had been starting to surface, and as Mitch slowly studied them, he knew that foremost he needed to make peace with his dead father, to somehow forgive him for not knowing how to love. "Love." What did Mitch know about love? Haunted by the fear that he, too, would be incapable of being a decent father, he found that hearing himself called Dad somehow exerted a disturbing pressure on him. This, together with his need to have the boy love him, prompted a painful contradiction that was easier to just set aside and ignore. The ability to block out what he didn't want to deal with made life so much smoother. Denial was almost as good as drink.

The film they were making, *Electra Glide in Blue,* had started shooting three weeks before, and in the short time since there had been much offscreen drama, resulting in the writer-director being fired and the star taking over the directing and leadership roles. How this came to pass was unfortunately not all that unusual in the film-making world.

Mitch had originally met Rupert Hitzig, the writer-director, at the same time he met the star. He'd been hired, after which he and Rupert had flown to Texas together. They found they had much in common, the same interest in history and the great American writers. Rupert was a gentle man and after years of writing for TV he was embarking on his first directing job. He was nervous but had high hopes and had convinced a celebrated and accomplished director of photography to come on board.

Aristocrats are rare in Hollywood—a few authentic stars and directors, a producer or two, and several directors of photography. As DPs went, you didn't get much nearer the all-time top than Conrad Hall, whose eye and intelligence put him in a league all his own. At this point he was nearing the end of a long career.

The first glimpse Mitch had of Conrad the DP was on the *Electra Glide* set, a replica of a police academy, while Conrad was having a serious chat with Robert Blake, the star of the film. Tall, lean, darkly tanned, with bright black eyes, Conrad towered over the actor, every inch a king. They couldn't have been more different, with Robert Blake short, tense, always ready to fight for what he wanted. Mitch noted writer-director Rupert standing at a short distance, looking puzzled. As Mitch poured a coffee for himself at the catering truck, he picked up the increasingly heated exchange.

"Why, with all due respect"—Blake was closing in—"do we have to show the mountains when the scene is a tracking shot of the cops and their motorcycles?"

"Well, it's a movie about a cop, I know, but the images of the environment he lives in are important," Conrad countered.

Then Rupert stepped in. "I feel the shot Conrad designed serves the scene, so let's shoot it."

"Well, by all means, let's shoot the fucking thing." Blake stomped off to his dressing room. The DP went over to the camera. Mitch drank his coffee. And that's how this drama within a drama would continue all week. Rupert would block out the shot, and the star would attack the idea.

It was inevitable that something or someone had to give, and in this case, that role was reserved for Rupert. The classic great gulf fixed between the theater and Hollywood was never more vivid to Mitch as he went about his work on this project. The writer, given no respect, a mere appendage on which to hang a star's ego-driven impulses, was allowed little chance to breathe, much less go deeper into the script. Every time Rupert wanted another take, Blake would override him.

"Cut. Print. Next! That was fine and all we need." Further exploration would just be a waste of time and money. Rupert, thrown by this pushback, always chose the right battles, and there were plenty to choose from. Finally, the differences: what Rupert had written and what he envisioned were at odds with how the star wanted the picture to turn out. In almost every case, the star won out.

The end came early on a day when the desert temperatures headed for a high of a hundred twenty-five degrees. The heat hung like glue to the ground and rippled in waves, dancing over the trucks and bikes parked around the set. Rupert, Blake, and the producer were standing facing each other. Mitch, having heard a loud shout from Rupert, was now in the door to his dressing room.

"You can't do this—I have a contract, and I wrote the fucking thing! This is not only underhanded but completely illegal!" There was a strange silence, followed by the bang of Rupert hitting the side of the honey wagon and then pacing back and forth, with Blake standing by and saying nothing. They were all drenched in sweat.

"You tell me this asshole producer is going to direct my movie—well, fuck you both."

"Stop! Wait!" Blake jumped at Rupert and planted himself in the writer's face: "Make it easier on yourself and leave as soon as possible." Rupert stood there stunned, rubbing his arm and holding his forehead.

Mitch, sweat running into his eyes, was thrown back to grade school and, through the heat haze rising from the asphalt, saw himself standing watching a boy whining in front of the five bigger ones who took turns making cracks about the boy's prick. They had pulled his pants down. "Look at those skinny legs and tiny little pecker! What happened to your head?" Mitch had watched, horrified, unable to say anything.

A shout brought him back to the scene playing itself out in front of the honey wagon. The first thing he became aware of was Tim standing between two stuntmen. He hadn't seen him before and couldn't read the expression on his face, but the boy was looking right at him. First, Mitch went rigid, and then the sweat turned cold, and panic filled him. What was his son feeling? Blake was shouting at

Rupert, who was stumbling away toward his car, "Stay calm, Rupert, and don't make it worse for yourself."

"You are full of shit and you're a rat."

"You hear what I'm saying?" Blake charged after Rupert, his chest puffed out and the veins on his neck standing up as if part of a George Grosz drawing. Mitch, detaching himself from the humiliation before him, kept watching Tim and started to move toward him. Did he want to know what was going on in the boy? No. He stopped. Some of the crew tried to get away, heading behind the wagons or off into the sagebrush.

Mitch remained at the door of his dressing room, his hands shaking and his guts turning over. Then Rupert saw the DP and ran over to him. "Can you say something, Conrad?" Mitch kept watching Tim. Rupert pleaded, "Tell them it's part of the design, the way we set up the shots. We talked it all out. It was all planned!"

"There's nothing we can do, son. The producer is the money, and he'll take it and go. He doesn't care." Rupert moved to Mitch, who shrank back in the doorway. "What about you, Mitch? Is this right?"

"Connie's right," was all Mitch could say. Nothing else came out. He shot a quick glance at Tim, who was still looking in his direction.

"Get in your car and leave. It's the best thing you can do." Blake's voice turned Tim around. They all watched Rupert stagger to his car.

"Fuck you! Fuck you!" Then Rupert drove away.

Tim looked over at Mitch again, waited a moment, then walked away with the two stuntmen toward the barn. Tim's turn brought Mitch up cold and hard, a sharp inner gasp piercing his chest. And then, too late, he charged at Blake. "This is not right."

Blake turned on him. "He was a goddamn amateur in every category, writing and directing. All he showed me this week is that if he was left to finish the picture, it would be a mess." The actor had worked himself into a fever pitch. "I gave him every chance to prove to me he could handle the job, but he couldn't, so he's gone!"

"Bullshit, you gave him 'every chance,'" Mitch grumbled in his outraged mind and, helpless to salvage his shame, headed to his dressing room. He stopped at the door. Tim? In the room, he fell on the bed, sick to his stomach. Lying there, he saw the bottle of whiskey Blake had given him the first day. "Piece-of-shit movie, rotten fucking movie industry." He sat up, chuckled, then yelled at the ceiling, "Goddamn fucking AA!" Tim. What had Tim seen? He leaned on the dressing-room trailer wall and tried to save his pride. When he calmed down, he went to find Tim, who was sitting on the rail fence at the wide barn door. A cowboy was telling him a story about John Wayne and Mitchum in a movie he'd worked on.

Tim looked up. "Hey..."

"Hi, boys. Want to eat, Tim?"

"Sure." His face was a mask.

Mitch, feeling him out, ventured, "What a day."

Tim paused. "Yeah, Blake fired the director, the guy who wrote the piece." Then nothing.

They were quiet as they watched the grubby cook behind the counter and tried to ignore the grime and grease on the walls. Mitch resisted the lure of dwelling on the firing and bullying that was Hollywood. Tim ate but said very little. The tension hung over the table. Tim suddenly looked at Mitch. "Why did they fire him?"

"Well, they thought he wasn't doing the job. It was unfair and didn't have to be done."

"Why didn't someone speak up and defend him? Did everybody feel that way? Did you feel that way?"

Mitch looked Tim in the eye. "No. He was inexperienced, but he could have done the job with a little help. The people who put money into the film were afraid. Money people are like that. But you can't do a movie without money." He heard the hollowness of his voice as he watched Tim's impassive face.

At that moment, one of the actors walked into that sorry excuse for a dining room, so typical in the cheaper motels of the Southwest. "Tim, this is a great actor, Elijah Cook. This is my boy." He hated the way that came out. Blake followed right behind and asked if he could sit and join them. "Sure." Mitch studied Tim and again could detect nothing. "What's going to happen? Are we getting a new director?"

"How you doing, kid? Tim, is it? Having a good time?" Blake patted Tim on the back. "I was watching the dailies a couple of days ago, and who popped up—a future star! You looked pretty good, kid. Following in your old man's footsteps?" Tim glowed. "Jesus, this place is a dump. Bring me a coffee," Blake was shouting at the waitress. "I'm going to see if we can't get a better hotel for the rest of the stay."

The star was deliberately avoiding the subject, Mitch knew. He was relieved that Tim seemed delighted by the attention. Anyway, Mitch already knew the producer was to be the director in name, which meant Blake would actually do the directing. That was how it went in this system.

"Mitch, could we talk about those big scenes we have coming? I've got some great ideas." He was starting already.

"Sure." No point in speaking his mind. Mitch continued eating.

"We can talk tomorrow on the set." The star stood and turned to the other actor. "You getting everything you need, Cookie?" Now he was director and producer.

"Yes, I'm fine. Good to be here."

"Take care, kid. See you boys later." And Blake left.

Silence, then Cookie ventured, "Blake's one tough son of a bitch. I guess he fired the director. Well, he had to. As far as I could see, the guy didn't know what he was doing."

Mitch looked at his steak then pushed it away.

"Is that right?" Tim asked Mitch, the man who was supposed to be his father.

"I don't know, son." Tim kept looking at Mitch.

"Seemed like a nice man," Cookie continued, "but he was in way over his head."

Mitch rose. "I'm going to bed."

"You haven't finished your steak."

"I lost my appetite. Coming, Tim?"

"Yeah. Do you mind if I watch TV?"

"No, but I got to get some sleep."

Then Tim touched Mitch's arm. "Don't worry, Dad, people get fired in the movies all the time. Buck told me he'd been fired five times. Nobody meddles or speaks up. It's the way things are, so—"

Mitch stopped him. "Don't call me Dad. Call me Mitch. I'm your friend and pal."

As Tim looked at Mitch with a stone cut face. "It just came out, Mitch. Sorry."

"No, don't be sorry, no big deal. Forget it." But it was never the same after that. Mitch regretted bringing it up, started to get mad, and slapped his hand on the wall, but it was too late. Tim was gone. Just pouring coal on their smoldering tenuous relationship.

Mitch knew Tim was reading back what Buck had told him. He also knew that Tim was telling him exactly what he saw and how he felt about what had happened. Tim sauntered to the room. In the lobby, Mitch ran into the DP.

"Too bad about Rupert."

"It happens."

"Well, it should have been handled in a better way."

"How? There's no good way to fire someone. At least this was fast and a short pain span." The DP headed away down the hall.

Mitch followed for a step. "Jesus, what do you mean? The guy will have to live with this for a long time."

"I was talking about Blake." The DP disappeared into his room.

Mitch turned to the wall and became aware of a dingy painting hanging there he'd never really noticed before. Underneath, he could read in gold letters, "Cossacks Celebrate Victory Over Turks." The garish work portrayed a Cossack with a murderous glint across his face and eyes, terror among the Turks in a cage.

After weeks of hard work and long hours in the Texas desert, Rupert became a distant memory, a casualty of war. Mitch had a key role in the film and withstood the star's caprices as much as possible; he kept his mouth shut, pretended to listen, and then did what was necessary. The rare free time allotted with Tim passed. Nothing was different on the surface, but a fog of tension remained between them. The two traveled around to local ranches when they could. With a week of shooting left, Mitch had three days off, and they drove to the Grand Canyon. When it was time for Tim to go home, Mitch took him to the airport. They spoke very little, and Tim seemed to be pondering something.

"What's on your mind, Tim?"

"Nothing."

"No, there must be something."

"Nothing. I was just thinking about that director who got fired. Must have been hard for him, don't you think?"

"Yes, it must have been." Tim kept his eyes on Mitch.

"What? What is it?"

"Nothing." That was all. Tim said no more the rest of the ride. They parted with a tentative hug. "Goodbye, Mitch."

"Tim, I'm glad you came. I had a great time."

"Sure, me too."

Mitch watched him climb up into the plane. The slap of "Goodbye, Mitch" from Tim like "sweet bells jangled" or shattered. When the door shut, he turned and tried to straighten his shoulders as he hurried off the tarmac. Defeated, he felt he'd never gotten the bat off his shoulder and took three strikes without trying to work it out with the boy.

Finally, Blake pushed too hard, and Conrad the King let him have both barrels. In the last week of shooting, Blake said one too many things to the DP about the camera placement. "You don't know what you're talking about," the DP told him quietly. "You can fuck up all the actors you want, but keep your nose out of the camera department, and tell your 'producer' never to speak to me again, on the set or off. From the very beginning, you have behaved like a drunken Roman emperor. The way you fired the writer. The way you talk to actors. The way you handle the set." Conrad suddenly stopped as he became aware that in the deadly quiet, the whole crew had been listening. For a long silent moment, he looked deeply saddened, then turned and walked away.

Mitch, watching this, came over to Conrad. "That was poetry, Connie. I'm glad you told him."

"Who are you?" The DP bent toward him, the look on his face heartbreaking. "We both turned away when he fired Rupert. You never said a word, and I waited till the last day. What does that make us?"

Mitch backed away toward his dressing room. What could he have done? Well, it was over now, and the film was nearly finished, and there would be another one. In his dressing room, he went to the bottle of bourbon from Blake that had been sitting on the makeup table, waiting since the first day. He broke open the seal and took a drink.

When the whiskey hit his tongue, he gagged and spat it all out onto the mirror. Then he washed his mouth out, took a long drink of water, sat down, and stared at the wall. What can a man do when he can't take a drink? He can stare at a wall.

CHAPTER 32

Hell
1978

ONE CAMERA WAS on the roof of the barn, and another was aimed over Mitch's shoulder as his character watched a fellow actor riding a tired mule down the road, a menagerie of assorted animals traipsing alongside and behind. As they all turned into the barnyard, Mitch, who was playing the ranch owner, could see, straggling behind the mule: a dog, two peacocks, a duck, and several goats. The shot was supposed to track the mule and wagon and these creatures up to the porch, where there would be dialogue. Well, the mule spooked, reared, and threw the actor to the ground, after which the goats ran off, the peacocks flew to the roof of the house, and the dog commenced howling. Mitch laughed as he went to help the actor, who didn't seem to be hurt, and when he, too, started laughing, the whole crew joined in, over which the director's bullhorn boomed, "Cut!" and a loud cheer arose from everyone. Then the director barked, "That's a wrap, goddamn it."

Back at the hotel in the little town of Fish Creek, outside Prescott, Arizona, Mitch and some of the cast and several cowboys who handled the horses sat down at a big round table in the dilapidated dining room. The room was a rustic remnant, pictures of John Wayne on the walls testifying to a picture Wayne had apparently shot there years before, in case anyone had forgotten. Rambunctious remarks about the day were winging across the table when in came Leroy Murtaugh, the small-animal wrangler. "Look who won the pool today for efficiency. How come you're late? Had to run down those peacocks, did you? That was something to watch."

"Go to hell, Bill. I noticed you're real good at keeping that folding chair warm," snipped Murtaugh. "This director is crazy if he thinks that shot is possible," said one of the cowboys.

"I'll get it, and you can all be damned," Murtaugh bawled.

"Well, I was thinking as I was watching that Chinese fire drill unfold that we could use a few more," came from one cowboy.

"Yeah, Leroy," another cowboy piped up.

"Ain't you got a leopard?"

"Yeah," called another, "we need more varmints—how about some of those monkeys? I know you got a lot a monkeys, Leroy."

After the laughter, they all ordered, and Bill, the gaffer of the stunts, said, "The missus is coming down with the two boys. You got a family, Mitch?"

Suddenly everything went dark. Mitch reached for his iced tea, knocked it over. "Damn!" He started to mop up, then threw down the napkin, and fled out to the parking lot. What the hell was this?

Back in Los Angeles after the previous shoot, there had been little contact with Tim. He'd wanted to ask the boy how he felt now about the firing of the director but was afraid to open the subject. Despite their weeks together on location, they were like strangers now. The time never seemed right to talk, and with Tim rarely around or available, Mitch didn't push it.

Walking back to the restaurant calmed him down, and he thought of trying again to have Tim come here too, so they might repair what had been lost. Maybe, Mitch reasoned, he was making the whole thing up. Besides, Mitch really was enjoying doing this film—*Peter Lundy and the Medicine Hat Stallion*. He had a good part, an impressive part, and he was creating the kind of work of which he could be proud. The work gave him a quiet feeling of belonging and even leading by example. He wished Tim could be here to see this, so why not bring him over for a week or so?

Tim came, and for a while, there was a connection for which he, Mitch, had been reaching between father and son. Mitch took him everywhere and found him a horse. They went on several rides together, and when Tim wanted to learn to use a six-shooter, Mitch loved watching the wranglers having fun with him. On one of their days off, the head wrangler took them to his ranch. It seemed they could be friends. Tim had turned seventeen and looked older. He had filled out and was good-looking, blond, and tan. But much as Mitch wanted to get underneath the outer mask—not only Tim's but his own—he never could.

One morning when they were having breakfast at the chow truck, and Mitch was watching the sunrise over the dark mountains. "Ah! The desert at dawn. Nothing like it."

Tim, between bites of his egg-and-bean burrito, said, "Dad, could—"

Mitch stopped him. "Call me Mitch."

Tim pulled back. "Yeah, yeah."

"Sorry, Tim. It's just that I'm not your father."

"Forget it. No big deal."

"Tim, what were you going to ask me?"

"No, it was nothing."

"Come on, Tim, tell me. I'm sure it was something."

"It would be fun if Ritchie could come here."

"Tim, you understand this is a workplace and there can be no monkey business. I can work with you, but you have to impress on Ritchie that everything has to stay cool. I know you understand, but make sure he does."

"It'll be fine." He didn't want to call him Mitch, and he couldn't tell him why.

But Ritchie was a year older, and only too late did Mitch discover the marijuana. The company was shooting late, and Tim and Ritchie had asked a teamster going out to the set to give them a ride. When they arrived with much out-of-control laughing and a very bad act of trying to be casual, it was obvious they were stoned. Mitch, standing behind the camera ready to do off-camera dialogue, tried to laugh it off, then flew into an embarrassed rage. "Jesus, Tim, what do you think you're doing! Have you no sense?"

"Dad, let me explain. It's no big deal."

"Don't call me Dad—my name is Mitch, goddamn it! Get in the trailer and stay there until I find you a ride—you too, Ritchie! Jesus Christ!" This scene played out in front of everyone on the set.

Mitch tried to get Tim by the arm and take him to the trailer. Tim jerked away. "Fuck this." He tore off his leather jacket with the Indian fringe that Mitch had bought him and threw it on the ground. Then he ran off toward the woods, shouting, "Fuck this. Fuck you. Fuck everything."

Mitch stood there, the crew looking the other way. He was the one out of control, not Tim. "Well, you can't win 'em all," provoked a few weak laughs. Then he went into his trailer, sank into a chair, and put his face in his hands, remembering the time when his father had shouted at him, and he'd run away into the Finley Woods. Why didn't he want this boy to call him Dad? Why? Why in all the distorted exchange of relationships between these two would he deny the boy that? Did he hate the idea so much that he would lose himself?

Later, Milo O'Shea, an Irish actor in the film, brought a sullen Tim back to the set and took him to Mitch's trailer. He also had Ritchie in hand. He sat Tim on the bed and put Ritchie on a chair in the corner. "I found him easy enough. He wasn't far, sitting under a tree." He pulled Mitch aside. "Take it easy on the boy. He's hurt bad and awful angry about something."

Mitch watched Tim for a moment. "I lost my temper. I'm sorry." Ritchie let out a snicker. "You keep quiet, or I might really get mad."

"Come with me, boy," said O'Shea to Ritchie. "The men need to make peace."

When they were gone, Mitch sat opposite the bed. Tim twitched and kept scratching his arms. Mitch said nothing, waiting for something from the boy. They sat in their separate worlds. Strange to know exactly what was wrong with the boy and where he was hurting inside and not be able to do anything to help. The horror came to him like a light in a black room. He didn't want to help. The long road to living a useful life stretched out before them both. Finally he said, "Well?"

"Can I go home to LA?"

"Is that all you've got to say?"

"Yes."

Mitch put Tim in the car with Ritchie and told the driver to take them to the motel. They found three ounces of weed in Ritchie's suitcase. There was a plane that night. He called Lynda to pick the boys up.

When they were gone, he slumped in a chair and felt all the horror and curse of addiction. Now again, he remembered his last days of drinking and all the heartache. His face itched, and his body was rigid with tension. There was a knock on the door. The AD. "You want to join us and do this shot? We can do it tomorrow. There's plenty else to do with Mimi and the boy in the barn."

"No, let's do it."

CHAPTER 33

A Great Play
1979

"Mitch, wait till I tell you the news… I'm doing a revival of *The Price*, and I want you to play the cop… Arthur's going to be hands-on involved, and I told him about you, but he wants to see you in person… I'm so high on you I hope you can come read for him." Jack Garfein had said all this in one breath.

"Wait a minute, when and where? I would love to do it and also meet Miller, but I'm here and you're there."

"You must come to New York."

"Jesus, when is this going to happen?"

"We want to start in early March and open in April sometime. Are you working on anything? We'll start in the little Harold Clurman Lab Theater, and if all goes well, we move to Broadway."

"I finish the picture in two weeks. Let me think about it, and I'll call you back tonight."

"Oh, and Mitch, we don't have any money. You'll have to pay your own way, but we can put you up while you're here. When we move to Broadway, of course, there's a new contract."

"I don't care about the money. If I can think my way to doing it, the money is no problem."

"Great. I'll hear from you tonight. You were born to play this part."

"Yeah, yeah, that's what they all say." Mitch put down the phone, stepped back, did a little two-step, and sang, "Give my regards to Broadway / Remember me to Herald Square / Tell all the gang at Forty-Second Street / That I will soon be there. Yeah!"

Lynda came in the door, flushed and in her riding gear.

"I'm thinking about doing a play in New York. What do you think?"

"Not much."

"You and Tim could come for a couple of weeks. It'll be fun."

"We'll see." She peeled off her boots and went toward the bath. "Tim is missing. He didn't go to school and he's nowhere to be found. Ever since he came back from Texas, he's been totally gone. When he's here, he won't talk or answer questions. What the hell happened in Texas?"

"The boy's out of control, and I don't know what we should do. There's nothing you can do with a boy who won't ask for or care about help."

"Well, you better do something, don't you think? Running off to New York is not a good idea." And she was gone again.

He had finished the film in Arizona and was now back in Los Angeles shooting yet another movie of the week. Tim had kept to himself during this time after he and Richie had been sent home. He would answer in one-syllable words and avoid contact with everyone. Not a word to Mitch. Mitch knew Tim was taking drugs and wanted to confront him but could never bring himself to speak to the boy, could never trust himself. There was always that fear of losing his temper or worse of Tim losing his. He'd realized some time ago he was afraid of him in the same way he feared his father. Tim stayed out of his way, and that made it easier for Mitch to put off any action of his own.

Now, as Mitch looked for a copy of the play, the significance of Jack's call deepened. To be in a play in New York. An Arthur Miller play. Jack ran an acting school in New York but spent time out in California, and they had worked together on Strindberg's *Miss Julie* with an eye toward mounting a production. Jack was a pure theater man whom Mitch thoroughly enjoyed. To work on this play in New York would be something.

He found the play in the bookcase on the side of the fireplace. As he started looking through the script, he recalled seeing a production years before and admiring the powerful acting and Arthur's great dialogue. Looking in the mirror above the fireplace, he couldn't help but smile at a dream come true. He recalled the pride he'd experienced doing *Death of a Salesman* in Boston, inspired and imbued with Miller's ideals. How the playwright could transmit the importance of being held accountable for your life, being willing to pay the price. Willy Loman's wife's stunning pronouncement seared right into him: "Attention must be paid."

Willy and Biff. Fathers and sons. He leaned on the mantle, his chin on the back of his hand. Jesus. Tim. What a mess, life imitating art, or the other way around. He went out and walked through the oak grove. There was such a deep bond between him and the three five-hundred-year-old live oak trees that stood in a triangle behind his house. When he had told some people that he would sit between them and feel a moving vibration passing from the oaks through him, they all laughed, so he stopped telling anyone. He was forty-five years old and had been sober for six years. Sitting quietly, the wise old trees began to talk to him. There was a soft breeze. What was he? He tried to wrap his arms around the grandfather oak and felt the life. His arms stretching out didn't move halfway around. Who am I? An actor—no! A man of parts. Who? What was he? He didn't know. This play was important. But what could he do about the boy?

Then he saw Tim walking down the lane and into the house. He ran to the porch and through the door, and there stood Tim.

"Hi, Daddy, want to help me with my algebra? Yes, I'm loaded."

"Where've you been?"

"What do you care?"

"I care. Your mother cares and worries."

"How much do you care, Mr. Ryan—35 percent? More? I would say less." Mitch moved to him and slapped him in the face. Tim was so stunned he sat down and brought his hand to his cheek. "More than 35 percent. Wow, I never would have guessed, Dad."

"I'm sorry, Tim." Mitch was shaking. His face burned. He couldn't move.

Tim rose slowly and started for his room. "Sorry? Sorry? Sorry? This is sickening." Mitch stood like a steer that had been shot but hadn't fallen over.

A few minutes later, Lynda came out. "Did I hear Tim?"

"Yes, he's in his room."

"What did he say?"

"He said he needed help with his algebra. He's full of dope, and I slapped him. I'm ashamed, but it's impossible." He started out.

"Where are you going?"

"For a walk."

"Don't you think we should talk?"

"Yes, but not now."

"The little man who was never there," she shouted after him.

He walked all the way to the Old Place, a restaurant two miles down Mulholland Drive. He didn't drink, but he sure wanted to. He ate some clams. Lynda was asleep when he returned home.

Mitch had a week off from the movie, so he flew to New York and read the play on the flight.

Lynda had screamed at him, "Think, god damn it, what you're doing."

"Just for a few days, play won't start for another two months."

"Play! *Play!* To hell with the play. What's a play? Nothing! This boy is in a lot of trouble, and we have to take some action!"

"When I get back, we'll go see a counselor."

"Oh, fuck! You are so full of shit. The boy needs a father, and he needs to be paid attention to."

"Attention!" The word hit him like a hammer. His body went stiff. Then with a German-officer click of his heels and a smart about-face, he walked out and slammed the door, went to his car, and sat. "My life. It's my life."

It was a long trip to New York. As he sat in the plane, he let himself be jerked around from one degree of rage to another. He paced to the back of the jetliner and was told to take his seat. He tried to watch *The War of the Roses* on the TV screen but couldn't focus.

A "Welcome to New York" message greeted him above a large picture of Ed Koch, all oily smiles, looking down on the airport throng. He hurried through the terminal and found a cab. All the frustration and helplessness he'd felt about Tim was drowned in the excitement of the idea of the city and Arthur Miller and the play. Great to see Jack, who took him to dinner at Sardis, and thrilling to be back in the atmosphere of the theater. The next day he met Miller. The man's whole life could be seen in his face—the agony of his plays, his marriage, the House Un-American Activities Committee— all in the lines etched there. There was recognition between the actor and the older playwright. Nothing you could see, but each of them knew something about the other.

He read well and was getting increasingly absorbed in how the part should go. He stopped himself several times and went back. At the end, Miller came down to the stage.

"That was good. I like it that you were rehearsing and not trying for a performance. If you will do this part, I would be much obliged."

Arthur Miller was asking him to do his play.

"Yes, I will be honored."

CHAPTER 34

Malibu Jail
1979

TIM LEFT THE car, walked into the bushes, and relieved himself. He thought he saw the tree in front of him move and walk around. Wow! Have to get home and…what? Finish essay for school tomorrow. A joke. Where was he? Whatever Ritchie had given him was conjuring alarming fantastic images. He was used to calming down his nervous energy with marijuana or heroin, but whatever this was did the opposite.

He held on to the tree trunk, finishing his business and then, still holding the trunk, tried to edge down, then turned around and, almost falling, pushed his back into the tree trunk and inched down onto the mossy ground and put his hand in the piss. "Damn!"

Shaking. He looked up, watched the full moon through the treetops, and wondered how he was going to get up. He couldn't see the car. "Hello! Hello, Ritchie?" Nothing. He tried to remember the subject of the paper he had to write for school. *Goddamn, I have to finish with the fucking school. I made it this far.* He felt sick. There was a terrible taste in his mouth, no food. He tried to get up, fell back, hit the tree with his head, rolled over, and curled up and went to sleep.

He dreamed that he woke up and saw his stepfather, Mitch, standing on a large podium high in the air with dead fish hanging down the sides. Panic! He tries to crawl away…he's on an island…

from a boat way out in the water his mother is yelling and beckoning to him. "Come on, you can make it…"

He woke up and stumbled back to the road. No car. They were gone. Ritchie wouldn't have left him. Tim sat down in the middle of the road and put his head on his knees. He had to believe Ritchie would be right back. That he'd just gone to get a beer. Tim closed his eyes. The next thing he knew, he was being nudged in the back, with someone shouting, "What the hell do you think you're doing?" He could see nothing but red flashing lights.

Mitch received the call from the sheriff's office just as he was leaving to go to Warner Bros. Since the slap and Mitch's return from New York, the boy's hostility toward him had reached a pitch that now called out for intervention. For a moment, he considered how a day in jail might teach Tim a lesson, then he changed his mind. This was Tim, not him. The boy was only seventeen. He called the studio and said he had an emergency.

He was to fly to New York in a week to start work on the Arthur Miller play and still had two more days on this film. Lynda had gone to Tucson to see her mother, hoping that in her absence, Mitch and Tim could begin to repair their relationship. Mitch called her. "Tim is in jail. Maybe you should come home."

"Jesus, oh God. What happened?"

"I don't know."

"What do you mean you don't know?"

"I just got the call, and I'm going to the police station now."

"I'll leave at once."

As Mitch entered the small courtyard of the police station through an iron gate, he realized he was angry as hell with Tim and with himself. He had tried to be a friend to Tim and even made a pitiful attempt at trying to be a father but had to admit he'd been an utter failure. He had loved Tim as much as he was able, and he had tried, but there was something about the boy, something organic that turned him away. He was afraid of Tim in the same way he had been afraid of his father. Either Tim or himself would invariably say the wrong thing, and an argument would spark and combust. He knew Tim used dope and that he, Mitch, was powerless to stop the boy.

Mitch hadn't had a drink in six years, and it scared him knowing Tim was doing some sort of dope. He had tried to play the policeman but hated that. Would he never be free of the wreckage of addiction?

The old Malibu jail on Pacific Coast Highway was still the same, a charming old building, made of dusty bricks, built in 1923. He knew the place well, having spent several evenings there himself in the past. This was hardly a joyous reunion, but there might have been a bit of nostalgia if not for the circumstances. The boy had been arrested for possession of drugs. Jesus! The officer who had called had said Tim had been sitting in the middle of Mulholland Drive when the police picked him up with no ID and, not believing him to be a minor, had brought him to the lockup in Malibu.

Thank God Mitch didn't know the officer on duty. Maybe they were all gone. How many years since he'd been locked up in this jail?

"Well, well, what brings you to our fair establishment," came a faintly familiar voice from the next room. Sheriff Graves was a Malibu icon with the silver hair and tanned face of a movie star.

"It's my stepson."

"So that's who that boy is? Man, the kids these days." The sheriff went behind the desk and opened a large booking ledger. "You'll recognize the cell. You've been a good boy for how long?"

"I was never a good boy." With some satisfaction, Mitch watched the sheriff's face lose its playfulness.

"I'll see about getting him released to you right away."

"What the hell are you thinking, arresting a seventeen-year-old boy?"

"Jesus, at seventeen, they're capable of committing felonies. Had no idea. Boy wouldn't talk or say anything. Stoned dumb." Sheriff Graves pulled a bunch of keys out of a drawer and headed to the back of the main room. "You can't blame the arresting officer. He found a number in the boy's wallet. It turned out to be yours, they told me."

"Forget it. Let me see him."

Graves gave him a look, then opened a large door, led Mitch down the hall, and passed him into the lockup.

Tim sat on an iron cot in the middle of a cell.

Mitch stood looking at the boy, and as he moved to the cell door, all the years of waste filled his brain like crawling spiders. He half turned away.

"Hey, Dad. Oh, sorry, Mr. Ryan."

"Hello, Tim." Mitch had to look at him. The boy's look twisted from a sardonic smirk into an impish smile. Face strained, eyes bloodshot, everything about him looked hunted. Mitch stood transfixed, the bars of the cell between them.

"Did you notice the bars in this jail are painted blue and the walls are green? The light from that window gives the tiles a beautiful shade of gold. You've been in lots of jails, right? Are they all this colorful?"

Mitch's palms were sweating. He was struck, maybe for the first time, at how mature Tim appeared. Even red-faced and worn-out, he had an intimidating air of worldliness. They regarded each other warily, and then Tim turned away.

Mitch saw himself younger for a moment and flashed on crashing around anonymous bars, through long nights, followed by harrowing recoveries—everything he did not want for this boy. Leaning back against the wall opposite the cell, he pushed down the sickness in his gut and loosened his tie. Tim walked deeper into the cell, his back to his stepfather. Mitch felt helpless as he watched the boy shaking and sweating.

A tall detective in a dark blue suit came into the corridor through a large steel door. "The release papers will be ready in a few minutes. We need to ask you a few questions, Mr. Ryan."

"Do you want anything, Tim?" Mitch regretted the question as he spoke.

"No," Tim replied the twisted smile, "they take good care of you in the famous Malibu jail. An hour ago, I asked for a glass of water, and nothing."

"Mr. Ryan, the sooner we do this, the better," said the detective in the blue suit. "I'll send in some water."

Mitch walked up to the bars as close as he could get to Tim. "I'm sorry, son."

"For what?"

Mitch watched the boy hug himself and rub his arms as if he were freezing, then he began to rub his face violently with both hands.

"Tim, are you all right?" Mitch turned to the detective. "Is he okay?"

"I'm fine! Just get me out," Tim shouted, looking back at Mitch for a moment, then turning to the corner of the cell and standing with his back to them.

Mitch's face flushed, and he darted a look at the officer, who looked down. What had he done that the boy could feel such anger? He backed slowly through the steel door to sign the papers. Then he sat on a bench outside the station-room and looked out on a lovely garden of vibrating color. The sea was there. He could smell the salt air. He took in the lush roses that went halfway around the police compound, red and yellow against the dark green of the ivy, crawling over the brick wall, out of place around a jail. He leaned his face into his hands. He longed to be normal, do his acting, putter in his house, and not have to fuck around with a doped-up kid. How simple life might be if he just walked away. He's not mine—not my responsibility.

"We have to take your boy to the hospital. He's having convulsions, some kind of withdrawal," Sheriff Graves moved to the desk, talking to the air.

Mitch leaned against the concrete wall. "Oh, Christ."

"He told me he was using heroin." The sheriff got on the phone. "This is Graves. Yes. I want an ambulance at the jail, going to St. John's." He hung up and turned to Mitch. "He's a sick boy, but I think he'll be all right."

"Should I come with you?"

"No, you'd better stay here for now."

Mitch slumped down on the bench. He ran his fingers over his forehead and pressed his thumb at the temple, vaguely aware he had used this gesture in countless movies.

Later, when Mitch told the policeman at the hospital who he was, the nurse let him into the sterile white room. Tim stood at the window in a hospital smock, smoking a cigarette. When he saw Mitch, he walked shakily to the toilet and flushed the butt. "I'm fine.

Why did they have to bring me here?" His voice was calm, but his face was chalky white.

Mitch went to the window and looked out on the street that led away from the hospital. The jacaranda trees were in bloom, creating a deep purple maze as far as he could see. He wanted to point to the glorious bloom, wanted to let the words come to him, but he waited a moment too long, and Tim slammed the bathroom door.

The policeman stuck his head in. "Everything all right?"

"It's okay, thanks." Mitch stayed at the window, his back to the room, looking down to the street. He reminded himself that he was going to New York to do a play called *The Price*. Price! What was the price for life? He started toward the door, hesitated, then kept going out of the room. When he saw the policeman in the hall, the price of life didn't seem too high. He couldn't leave the boy. He went back in. At the closed bathroom door, he said quietly, "Tim, come out. We need to talk." There was no response. "Tim, heroin can kill you. I know what this is like. Tim? Tim?"

"I don't want any help."

"I spoke to your mother. She's worried and wants us to talk about this. We all need to sit down and talk, don't you think? She'll be back from Tucson today."

Mitch waited, then returned to the window to follow a fly as it walked up the glass pane. He could not relax his clenched fists.

Tim opened the door. "Oh, fuck, this is sickening." He raised his arms above his head and threw them down in a gesture of despair as he collapsed on the hospital bed.

"You think your mother's not aware. The school reported your using on campus." Mitch forced his fists open. "Talk to me. Please let us help...Let me help."

"What help? You never help. You say let's do this, do that. You never ask what I think—what I want. You try to run me like you run the fucking movie set and everyone."

"Get me a coffee, would you, Tim? Get this, get that." He turned over to lay on the bed face down.

Mitch stepped back toward the door, his fists closed again. In the middle of the hospital room, he trembled at the depth of Tim's rage. In the hall, he asked the officer to call Sheriff Graves to bring the release forms. Back in the room, he sat on a metal chair and waited. Tim's look was right at his face as if studying who he was. Suddenly he was a boy, a sweet contrite boy who knew he had just frightened his father. Mitch felt a great need for Tim to forgive him, to come and put his arms around him.

Instead, the boy threw himself off the bed, walked to the wall, and stood with his back to Mitch. After a long silence, both suspended in their own hells, Mitch said, "They won't let you go till morning." Tim did not respond. An image loomed, a tunnel stretching back to when Mitch, after having run away from home, stood silent in front of his father.

The following morning Mitch and Tim drove home in silence, Tim looking out the window, saying nothing. Every now and then, he would run his hand through his long blond hair and rub his face. The drive from Santa Monica to Agoura took nearly an hour, but not a word was spoken. When the car stopped in the lane between their house and the corrals, Tim jumped out and ran past the barn to the woods behind. Lynda was nowhere to be seen. Mitch watched him go, then walked up to the large covered porch and sat down heavily in his rocker. His dog Murphy came over and sniffed him, then flopped down across his foot. Mitch was proud of his ranch. He loved the smell—a combination of dry pine, manure, and alfalfa. For the first time in two days, the tension in his shoulders gave up.

He heard Lynda's taxi and walked to meet her as she moved toward the gate. A light breeze caught the chimes hanging at the corner of the porch. She stopped at the yard gate and looked around at the old oaks down the lane with the horses beyond, then walked over to the corral and reached out as the horse pranced over looking for a treat. "I can't sell Sweetheart. I thought I could but I can't. Is Tim here?"

"No."

"Where is he?"

"I don't know."

"Oh my god. I thought you got him. You mean he's gone again?"

"No, he's around. I picked him up this morning. He's walked into the woods. Or up on the mountain, more likely. He'll be back before dark." He watched her go up on the porch and sink down into one of the big ranch chairs.

"What can we do?" She looked weary and seemed fragile. The dog came over to her, wagging his tail, and began to lick her hand. "Murphy, stop! Go sit down." He kept licking. "This dog is so spoiled." She kept petting him. "Why was he in jail? What son of a bitch would lock up a seventeen-year-old boy?"

"He was loaded and sitting in the middle of Mulholland Drive."

"Is that a flip answer?"

"No. He wouldn't talk. They thought he was older."

"What are we going to do?"

"I've talked to a man who runs a school up in the mountains at Running Springs near Big Bear. It's called Cedar School, a lockdown, way high up in the wilderness. I think it's what we need to do." Mitch stopped, aware that his voice was thin and frightened. He wasn't sure at all.

Lynda stayed silent.

"I've thought about the AA program, but he's not ready. Maybe later, but now he needs a total commitment to getting well with professionals. It's a sound place recommended by several people I know." He paused. "I don't know what else to do."

"I think we've done enough."

"It's not all my fault."

"We've both done the damage." She headed into the house. The blurted bitter words hung in the air.

Mitch held in his anger as he walked down and leaned on the wooden fence of the corral. Christ, lockdown school was a drastic measure, but something had to be done. His big gray General came over for a treat and nuzzled his hand. If it weren't that he had signed up for the film of his life, he would get on his horse and have a long ride. He wanted this boy to disappear. He didn't need this. He wanted to flee. A panicked tightness in his gut reminded him of his drinking years and of his own father, again.

Lynda came down to the fence. They stood looking past the barn to the mountains. "I'm sorry, Mitch. We shouldn't fight. We need to do something."

"Yes."

She walked down along the fence to the shade of the large oak tree at the end of the corral. "I love this place." She opened the door to a large shed. "We need a new tack room."

"There he is." Mitch pointed to the far end of the meadow. Tim was walking across the large expanse of pasture behind the barn. His head hung down as he moved slowly, like any country boy dallying so as not to do his chores.

The breeze had stopped. The harsh California sun glared a relentless shimmer onto Tim's image as he moved toward them. Mitch watched Lynda as she ran up the lane to meet him, feeling empty as they embraced. He knew he had to act. There was no way he could live like this with a sick child on his hands. The school was the only option. Mitch walked back to the porch. He looked back at them, holding hands and smiling, and he was brought up short, seized with a longing mixed with tenderness. Then the moment faded, and he wanted them gone.

Tim didn't look at Mitch as he slowly came to the porch with his mother. "I'm sorry…" He still couldn't call him "Mitch." "Thank you for getting me out."

"It's okay, boy. How're you feeling?" At that moment, remembering himself at seventeen, Mitch saw only a shy lad who just wanted to belong. The vast history of fathers and sons was beyond movement. He stood helpless.

"I'm tired. I think I'll have a nap," Tim said, walking up the stairs. He turned back to his mother. "Thank you for not getting mad, Mom. I know I can do better, and I will try. Would you mind if I went to my room?"

"Darling, of course not. I just want you to be happy and take care of yourself. I love you so much." She took him in her arms, and he received her with a low sigh, then pulled away.

"I just want to be alone for a while."

Mitch sat down on the step. Lynda watched her son walk up the stairs and into the house. "Oh my god." She covered her face and began to cry. "He's so removed, it's horrible."

"He's loaded, Lynda."

"Jesus, this is so stupid—why don't you do something! You're hopeless. You run off to New York, you're never here, no wonder he's a mess, oh God. I'm sorry, I don't mean to blame you. What can we do?"

He fought back his rage at her outburst. "He can start at the school soon. I'll drive him up after I talk to them. By the way, it costs three thousand dollars a month." And he walked out to his oak tree.

CHAPTER 35

The Price
1979

"MITCH, COULD YOU and Fritz have dinner with me tonight?" Arthur Miller stood at the edge of the stage. Mitch dropped his script, and when he stooped to pick it up, his glasses fell out of his coat pocket. Arthur smiled. "It's just dinner, Mitch, don't worry." And he walked to the back of the theater, where he and the director, John Stix, were working on the notes.

Mitch, still on his knees, "Sure, where?"

"'Frankie and Johnnie's, okay? After the shows start, eight thirty."

"Great, see you there." Mitch retrieved his script and glasses. He was going to ask what was up but stopped himself. "Come on, Joseph, I'll walk you out." Joseph was playing the old Jewish furniture buyer in the play. They had been working for a little over a week, and the rehearsals were not what Mitch felt they should be.

They walked to the corner of Forty-Eighth and Broadway. "Not a nice man." Joseph Buloff was small, with a big voice and bigger ego.

"What do you mean?"

"You see the way he stuck the needle in you back there? He's not a nice man."

Mitch had felt hurt from Arthur's remark that went way back to his never measuring up, but he didn't dwell on his past weakness. "Have you worked with him before?"

"Oh yes, I've done this play forever. Eight hundred performances in New York and on the road, and also I did *Death of a Salesman* in Yiddish. He was there all the time, getting in everyone's way." Joseph was a famous Yiddish actor. He knew where every laugh in *The Price* came, and in the middle of rehearsal, he would say, "Hold for the laugh, youngster."

Mitch took it for a while and finally asked him if they could wait for the audience before they waited for the laugh.

"That's a good one, sonny."

"You see the way he sits with the director," Joseph said, walking, "in the back of the house and whispers to him, and then the director gives us notes as if they were his? He won't let anyone do his job."

At first Mitch was excited to have Arthur there but after several days he changed his mind. It was exactly the opposite. The first reading of the play at the table had a classic feel. But when they started blocking—way before Mitch had a chance to try things and search for the core of the part—and an actor would stop and ask a question, Mitch noted John, the director, deferring to Miller, who would explain what he wanted. His input always made great sense, but Mitch felt he would like to find his own way first and ask for help later, if needed. He tried to adjust and listened and tried to take Arthur's help but couldn't. He realized he worked in a different way, and he didn't understand what he was being told. He couldn't recognize the result until he experienced the full power of his feeling and thought, and that would take time. Being told what was needed may well lead to the right result. He just didn't know. Scotty Bloch, Ms. Bloch, playing his wife, and Fritz, his brother, weren't the least bit upset by what Mitch was trying hard to ignore. On the contrary, they were excited to take the suggestions and seemed eager to put them to work. He had begun to doubt himself.

Walking to Broadway, Mitch wondered why Joseph would badmouth Arthur. He saw what the old actor was doing. He was a sweet-looking little man, but there was something dangerous about him. Mitch couldn't imagine him as Willy Loman. Mitch thought Iago would be a better part for him. He was a special actor with an old-school Borscht Belt flavor that didn't seem to fit Willy. "If I were you, I wouldn't go to dinner with him. He'll talk your head off all about himself."

"Well, I'll take my chances. Arthur did write the play and must feel strongly about how it should go."

"I wouldn't be so sure about what he knows." The cab came. "He's not a nice man."

Mitch laughed and held the door, then started out for Fifty-Seventh Street, where he was staying at Jack Garfein's apartment. During the walk, his mind was clouded with Joseph's words. He bumped into someone, grunted, and moved on.

"Mitch!" It was a friend from the old days, Tommy Sig.

"Tommy."

"Jesus, you here in town and with the man—I hear he's at every rehearsal. What's he like? It must be something. I'm heading down to meet Ben at Allen's. Come and have a beer and we can have dinner. Oh! Right, I heard you quit. What's it like?"

"Not as much fun. Miss crawling out of Jimmy Ray's on my knees every morning at 4:00 a.m."

"You can have a Coke."

"No, but I'll drop in one of these nights. Got to get going. See you." He hurried on to Garfein's and slammed the door as he entered. He called the lockdown school in California where Tim had been taken.

"Hello, can I help you?" a severe female voice said.

"Yes, Mr. Jenkins, please."

After a moment: "Jenkins, here."

"This is Mitch Ryan, Tim's father." The word hit Mitch with a montage of images, Tim's face full of anger, Tim's harried haunted look when he sat in jail. Mitch worried that the boy's resentment had only deepened after the fit he'd thrown when he realized he was being locked away in a reform school, however beautiful and nurturing the place seemed.

"Yes, Mr. Ryan, I'll get him."

"No! Wait! I want to hear how he's doing first. Is he okay?"

"Well, he's taken to the place. A very talented boy, and after the first several days of 'acting out,' he's settled in. Even in group therapy, he started talking almost right away. He's working in the drama department, and he's a natural. But that's no surprise."

Mitch, suddenly realizing this man might talk all night, said, "Great. Could you get him? Sounds like he's making the grade."

"You bet. I'll go get him now."

He wanted to hang up and leave, but he also needed to stay and listen to the boy and judge for himself how he sounded. After a long while, with people talking and doors closing, he heard, "You tell him."

Mr. Jenkins came back on the line. "I'm sorry, Mr. Ryan, he won't come to the phone."

"Jesus! It's that bad?" Mitch felt stupid for letting this slip.

"No, that's normal. He wants to do what he has to do without feeling pressured by a parent—not that you would, but this is what's in his mind, I'm sure. You might write a letter with your feelings." There was a pause, and then, "Thank you. Anything else?"

"No, that's about it." Mitch hung onto the phone, wondering who he was and why he was trying to help. He felt like a robot with no will of his own. Still gripping the receiver, Mitch picked up the book that was on the bed—*For Whom the Bell Tolls*. He had planned to send this modern classic to Tim. He dropped the useless thing into the trash.

Mr. Jenkins said, "Mr. Ryan, I'll hang up now." And he did.

At 7:30 p.m., Mitch headed out for Frankie and Johnnie's. When he hit Fifty-Seventh Street, the bad taste of the last several hours was gone. He'd put Tim out of his mind. He was good at that. Great to be strolling down through the city, with the sun still shining. His heart felt good, and his distress about Arthur seemed stupid. Arthur was our great American playwright, he told himself, and he, Mitch, was part of that greatness.

He came down Sixth Avenue to Fiftieth, then over to Times Square, past Birdland, where he had visited the first year he came to New York, then on down to Forty-Seventh, taken in as always by the hundreds of billboards pulsing with lights, and then he was pulled down to Forty-Second Street. How shabby the rest of the square looked, down there, with porn theaters and panhandlers dotting the landscape, the garbage in the gutter, and the broken people, the fringe humanity that recalled Avenue B and Twelfth Street, the home away from home of years-gone-by Stanley's Bar. And still the hopeless state of the people wandering the streets of the square or camped out on their cardboard still inspired a weird family familiarity in him.

Turning away with a certain reluctance he walked down Forty-Fifth toward Eighth Avenue to Frankie and Johnnie's, which was upstairs above the Theater Bar. Looking down into his old drinking hole through the large glass window he saw the habitual patrons sitting in the same places they'd occupied some ten years ago when he had left for Hollywood. He recognized several actor colleagues and Mosley, the bookie who lost his shirt in 1969 when Joe Namath beat the Colts in the Super Bowl. There was something sad about that picture, for all its continuity.

Arthur Miller and Fritz Weaver were at a table by the window overlooking the Broadhurst Theater, and when he arrived, they hardly stopped talking as he sat and studied the menu.

"No, no, not a simple thing," Arthur was in full swing, "this facing the 'price' you have to pay for the choices you make in life. There is a great turning point in every life when you are mature enough to face the price life is demanding for your choice. Your character, Fritz, came to this understanding some years before. He accepted the price as the loss of a brother. Victor—your part"—he looked over at Mitch—"has never come to this and irrationally fights the pressure exerted by his brother to confront his life. Your part is the American dilemma. No one is willing to pay the price."

As he went on defining the characters and their actions in relation to the great movements threading through American life, Mitch became uncomfortable enough to think about a drink. Always at times like these, when he was asked to use his mind at the exclusion of his instinct, he rebelled. Several years later, he would discover that he had, in fact, a good mind, one that could collaborate with and serve his intuition well, but at the moment, he felt with his whole

Being that no one had the right to fill actors with the message of a play. Actors were meant to serve their characters. The writer and director had to worry about the bigger picture. So he said nothing and ate his dinner, nodding at the right times. He tried to join in occasionally, inappropriate as he believed the conversation was for actors at this stage of the process, but he felt outclassed, and that was the problem: he just wasn't smart enough. His neck was getting tight, and his gut was churning. Every time he ventured to say something, his dinner mates seemed to merely tolerate his contribution. Finally, he made an excuse and left.

He walked over to Times Square and then slowly up to the apartment. All the magic he had felt about being back in New York had evaporated. He wanted to get back to stupid and simple TV movies. At least they didn't pretend to be anything but entertainment. Still, the thought of Hollywood depressed him even more, and Arthur was right in wanting the play's deep symbolism to be understood. Mitch told himself he was acting like a stupid kid. He was having dinner with the greatest playwright of the American theater and acting like an ass. So Arthur "didn't know" how he arrived at a part, Mitch didn't know either, but he needed to be open and keep searching.

Jack was home when he arrived. Before he could say howdy, Mitch tore into him. "What am I doing here? The director parrots Arthur's orders and pretends they're his. Fritz and Scotty talk endlessly about beats and motive—Jesus, that's not the Method. This was all your idea, Jack."

"Mitch, what's happened?"

"I had dinner with Arthur and Fritz. They were analyzing the play." He fell onto the sofa. "This is not good."

"Mitch, shut up and listen to me. You're scared because you haven't done a play in New York for ten years." Jack was pissed. "I want you to think about what you're doing. You have the potential to be a really good stage actor. There are very few who have that potential. You are in a position to be in a great play and have a nice long run in New York, where almost all actors in the world would like to be. So go to bed and remember that, though Arthur is a great playwright, you don't have to have dinner with him or listen to his worldview. Do your work, and you'll be fine."

"Well, don't you make it all sound rosy. I wish it were only that simple. I'll just put my shaky emotions and neuroses on hold and dance through the play."

"I would suggest you keep quiet and listen to everyone around this production, and especially Arthur, who may know a thing or two more than you about putting on a play. Form your own conviction about how this part should be done. Remember, you will be the one up there, the incarnation of what Arthur has put down on paper."

"You're talking like a producer, Jack also a friend. Thank you, pal. I'm going for a walk."

"And I'm going to bed. See you in the morning." And he gave Mitch a big hug.

Mitch walked up to Central Park and felt like he might be okay. He sure had needed that pep talk. The night was sweet and warm for April. The trees were sporting tender little leaves, and the park, with its old-fashioned streetlamps, could have been the film set for a 1900s period piece. He half expected Fred and Ginger to come dancing down the walk. He had scared himself to death earlier. Like he'd been on a ten-day drunk that had, luckily, lasted only two hours.

Everything was fine after that. He did listen, and he reserved his comments for the shower or the long walks he started taking. Everyone became pretty good at what they were doing, and by opening night, they all felt like they were in a hit. Arthur seemed pleased. "Be good tonight. You are fine," Arthur said to the cast.

Opening night, his friend Lee Marvin and wife, Pam, were in town and came to the theater. Mitch was surprised and flattered, and when Lee came backstage, his presence filled the space. "You were grand, Mitch," he said and complimented the rest of the cast. He loved the show. When he introduced Lee to Arthur, the two men sized each other up in a way that made Mitch uncomfortable, and he retreated to his dressing room.

Lee said, "The play was good, Arthur."

"I'm glad you liked it. Why are you in town?"

"I'm promoting a movie."

"A Western?" Arthur said.

"What else?"

"I didn't know you could ride."

Lee gave a little chuckle. Lee called into the dressing room, "Mitch, let's get some supper."

This otherwise polite exchange had somehow called to mind a scene from *Who's Afraid of Virginia Woolf?* Lee wanted Mitch to go to dinner, but there was an opening-night party, and Mitch felt obligated to the cast to show up. And now here he was, in the middle. He begged off both in the end and rode the subway to Coney Island, where he sat on the boardwalk in the cold wind from the Atlantic.

About a week later, he received a letter from Arthur Miller thanking him for his performance in the play and telling him he'd more than fulfilled the part. "Mitch," the playwright wrote, "I would be happy to have you do any of my plays."

What an ass I was and am, thought Mitch.

CHAPTER 36

The Chisholms
1979

MITCH WAS SITTING in a motel restaurant drinking coffee in the small town of La Junta, Colorado. A pall familiar to him, following him, slowly bubbled up, that strange haunt or disease that resurfaced intermittently to keep him off-balance, restless, and sadly empty. He reread Arthur Miller's letter, reminding himself that the words were real, that his success had truly occurred. He longed to be back in New York rather than here, back where he had felt alive, doing that play with those people, an artist doing what he knows and loves. He faced the self-pity that had shadowed him and recognized the self-centeredness in himself that separated him from the true values Arthur Miller embraced and by which he lived.

Mitch watched, among the few patrons, an old man in overalls with a face labored and strong with character, to whom the waitress brought a plate of brown gravy covering God knows what. "I'll be with you in a moment," the waitress said to Mitch, ducking behind the counter.

He was interrupted by the arrival of a tall, impressive, familiar-looking man, carrying a large bulky package. "You must be Mitch Ryan," the man said, and he recognized Robert Preston, one of the stars of the twenty-part TV series that had brought him to Colorado. "Welcome to Colorado," Preston said. "We've been on the road since

October. We started in Illinois. Guess they told you we're following the exact path of the wagon trains that came West in the nineteenth century, only it's taking us a lot longer."

"Nobody told me anything."

"Well, you'll catch up. Here's a present. Rosemary wanted to give it to you herself, but she went to Denver to shop." This actor was a large man, bigger than life and always seemed to speak at the top of his voice.

Inside the parcel from Rosemary Harris was a worn wide-brimmed hat with a round crown and a fur band tied around it. Mitch stood and appraised the hat, then put it on. "That's the ticket. Looks just right. Rosemary researched the thing herself, seems you have to wear it whether you like the fit or not. Look me up later, and I'll buy you a drink." Then he was gone. Mitch sat still wearing the hat and looking out at the nearly barren alien desert of eastern Colorado. Mitch asked himself, as he seemed to do in every new place and situation, what on earth he was doing there. He took off the hat to study the shape. "Jesus!" He put it back on.

The waitress came up. "Well, you look like a New Yorker in a ten-gallon hat."

"Do you think it'll work? I'm playing Ward Bond."

"Nobody could ever take Ward Bond's place. You want something?"

"A piece of apple pie with ice cream, thank you." He smoothed Miller's letter and folded and carefully tucked the artifact into his pocket. Whenever he found himself in a new place with a new job, worries about his self-worth settled like a slow-moving weather front. *I should have stayed in New York.* The pie arrived, and at the same time, a rumpled man in an expensive suit came up to the booth and introduced himself.

"My name is John Ehle, and if you take off that ridiculous hat, I'll join you." He had a wonderful rich Southern accent, Virginia or the Carolinas.

"Please do," Mitch relieved his head of the hat. "What do you do in the film?"

"Nothing. I do nothing with film. I don't like film." Before Mitch could respond, the man went on, "Have you eaten here? What's good?"

"I just arrived myself. My name is Mitch. I drove from Denver. I thought all of Colorado was in the mountains, but this desert is impressive."

The man laughed. "I think you're an actor, am I right?"

Mitch still didn't know what to make of him, so he said, "No, I'm not an actor. I came here for the waters."

"'But we're in the middle of the desert.'"

"'I was misinformed.'" They both laughed, bonded by Bogart.

John was a writer and married to Rosemary, the leading lady on the wagon train. Thank God he would be with them for several weeks. They would and they did become fast friends. John had a great wit and was not afraid to talk about the big ideas, life's meaning, and human purpose. Mitch was ripe for this, having previously avoided—more like run from—questioning the deeper aspects of life. Sure, he had come across such questions and quandaries in the great Shakespeare plays, but he had focused on them merely as they might inform his character and then only during performance, to be dismissed later over a lineup of whiskies. Now, stimulated by John's thought-provoking explorations, Mitch could see that there was more to life than being locked in his own limited misguided worldview. As he listened to this man of ideas, Mitch grew calmer and more relaxed, and slowly the recurring question, "What am I doing here?" became less a cry of despair and more a prompt to investigate, dig deep, and examine.

At breakfast the next day, John looked at Mitch. "What are you reading, do you read much?"

"I read a lot at one period of my life but mostly was influenced by characters and plot—Dickens, Hemingway, Camus. In Camus, I always felt a larger view of life. He seemed to be asking questions, but I could never see exactly what questions. I avoided most of the universal questions, except, well, what am I doing here? That one does dog me now and then."

"Now and then—well, well." His new friend smiled. "Have you ever asked, 'Who am I?'"

"Well, yes, I'm…" Mitch realized he didn't know how to answer that question.

"No need to answer. Have you thought of the many layers of your own question, 'What am I doing here?'"

"No, I just always seem to ask that question when I arrive at a new location."

"Yes, that's part of it—that's one layer. The other and much more vast level is 'What am I doing here on earth?'"

In the middle of the night Mitch realized that the question, like the reason for being on earth had been there all along in him, just not articulated.

One afternoon later in the filming, when he had no call, Mitch and John were sitting in the motel restaurant, a typical American motel coffee shop, weak coffee and grease. Mitch had spent every evening he could with John. This day John was quieter than usual, just smoking. Mitch didn't remember him ever being without a cigarette. Now he watched his beautiful, thoughtful face.

After a silence, John spoke, "What do you want, Mitch?"

"I don't know. I've had the chicken-fried steak, which gave me indigestion, and that, I was told, was the best on the menu."

"No, no, what do you want?" Something in his voice made the question seem important. He was looking at Mitch, calmly waiting, when after a moment, Mitch started to say something. John stopped him. "This is a serious question."

Mitch paused, his mind racing. He had, in fact, first wanted to make his usual glib remark, but that would no longer do. He remembered the recurring theme that plagued him. At last, under John's steady gaze, he said simply, "I don't know."

"That's a start. We don't know. Socrates said a long time ago, 'An unexamined life is not worth living.' Let's eat."

Mitch was used to putting his sensibilities on hold, always ready with a story or a joke to take control of his place on the set and to keep the crew happy, a clown of sorts, like the fool in *King Lear*. His life was an ongoing accommodation, a semblance of living. But since John had asked, "What do you want?" Mitch had felt deep in himself, and at the strangest times, a longing that would suffuse him, a longing for "more." More of what? These feelings came at different times, however, and were always covered over with the act he'd practiced all too long and perfected all too well.

Days later, Mitch was doing his imitation of John Wayne for the stuntmen. "Dance, pilgrim," as he fired the blanks in his .45 at the feet of one of the stuntmen. Everyone laughed. The security guard came running around the wagon. "Don't worry, Sheriff, I got 'em all under control." When the guard started to get mad, everyone laughed, and he joined in.

Mitch walked over to the chow truck. His friend John was watching him. "You are an ass." He took Mitch by the arm and moved him to the back of the truck. "Why do you toss away your life's blood on these jerks? They're eating you just as fast as you can throw yourself at them. You're dead, and soon it'll be too late, and you'll never know who you are or what you could have done because if you don't care, no one else will." He started to walk away, then turned back. "I'm leaving. See you sometime. Come visit me at my farm in North Carolina."

John left soon after. Mitch regretted his friend's departure, but he didn't change. Not at first. He saw no need, but even more importantly, he had no idea how. He couldn't recognize that what John had said was true, that he trivialized his life with his need to be accepted at any price, that this desperate grasping drive to belong colored every action. This man, his friend, who had called him an ass, had somehow thrown him into doubt. And out of the hurt of John's words, Mitch sensed a growing freedom that gradually, over the weeks, allowed him to get more interested in his life. Bit by bit, he could relax his constant striving to be what he thought they would expect him to be.

CHAPTER 37

Of Mice and Men
1979

THERE ARE DRY periods in the life of an actor, and this was a bad one. No work for eight months, six of which went to the writers on a much-needed demand in the form of a strike. Mitch spent his owed tax money hoping for work that didn't come, so now he had no money when the long-dreaded letter from the IRS arrived.

"What do you mean, you didn't you pay your taxes?" asked his agent Walter in complete wonder.

"I was hoping to get several jobs, I'm sure you remember, that didn't work out."

"Jesus, you are crazy—do you have any idea how much interest they charge? The bill triples every hour, you idiot. You'd better talk to them and work out a plan."

"Yes, that is true, I am never wise. I will make a plan." He hung up, and the phone rang almost at once. "Robert Blake." The memory and poison of their previous experience together came back up in his throat, and Mitch almost hung up on him too. The very voice of the star of *Electra Glide in Blue* brought back all the sad business of that time and even, to Mitch's surprise, the physical nausea. But then he heard *Of Mice and Men* and paused. And he remembered he had no money. "You're really doing Steinbeck's book?"

"Yes, you play Slim."

"Charles Bickford's part?"

"Yes, I'll be using the Lewis Milestone 1939 script. Needs a little work, but we can handle that. I'll send it to you. See you later in Dallas." Mitch took a deep breath, a deep breath, on the way to the bookcase, and down came *Of Mice and Men*.

"Jesus, rewriting Steinbeck." He opened and read, "It ain't no lie. We're gonna do it. Gonna get a little place an' live on the fatta the lan'."

Somewhere in Texas, Blake had found a wheat field. The day was gray, and as Mitch looked out across the tallow-yellow grain at a huge spectacularly ugly threshing machine, far out in the middle of that sea of wheat, he felt Steinbeck was there. He could see the book coming to life: wheat being harvested, and a large wood at one end, and the ranch house, bunkhouse, and barns at the other. Magnificent set built in two weeks to look as if the wood and paint had been there for years. This was worth having, a set you could be proud of because everyone was working for next to nothing. The money had been spent on the production.

The first day he had to sit on the huge threshing machine and drive the beast into the shot. The crusty old farmer who owned the device told him what to do. The man had a deeply lined face and chomped on a plug of tobacco, a copious glob of which he'd spit out every now and then. He was blunt and seemed to know a lot about everything. Farmers are like that. His life seemed useful.

As Mitch finished his first run, with the old boy sitting beside him high in the cockpit of the machine, the veteran slapped his leg and let out a loud, snorting laugh. "Well, young fellow, that was downright handy. You pick it up faster than most, but that's no cause to get cocky. This is a dangerous animal."

Mitch laughed back. He looked down to the ground. "I'm not worried about that, but I may break my neck getting off this thing. How do you do it?"

"Same way you got on, sonny."

When they hit ground, Mitch asked the question he had been holding back. "You ever read *Of Mice and Men*?"

"No, I never did. When I was a young man, I saw Burgess Meredith, I think, do the film of it. I don't remember much except it was a little corny, like a lot of picture shows."

The AD walked over. "Want to try one, Mitch? Everyone's ready."

The first scene of the shoot, and they needed several takes, mainly because Mitch could barely control the monster apparatus he was driving. The farmer had warned him.

Back at the hotel after the first day, Mitch heard that the producers had contracted Art Carney to play old man Candy. Mitch was looking forward to meeting him and watching him work, having enjoyed him in *The Odd Couple* back in New York years before and as the unforgettable sewer man of TV's *The Honeymooners*. But when the aged actor arrived at the hotel, he was drunk. Everyone but Mitch figured he would sober up in the morning and be ready. Mitch knew different as he helped him to his room. This was a worn-out, deeply ruined man. As Robert and Mitch put him to bed, he slurred, "Too many lines. We have to cut most of it down…not needed, all that verbiage." Then he passed out. Blake cursed and left.

Mitch stood watching a dead man, his face pale, with just enough breath to keep him alive. Vivid images of lost drunken nights and pitiful, pitiless hangovers flashed through him as he walked to his room. He fell on his bed, a rising tide of sadness creeping over him. Then he got out and down past the bar, waited in the dark, then walked out to the parking lot and down to the highway. The wind was moving the trees that lined the road, and the night was cold and clear. He looked up to the "majestical roof fretted with golden fire." Centuries-old melancholy descended on him as he contemplated the curse of life-destroying drink. Carney embodied this curse completely. Mitch had forgotten his coat. He sat shivering on the fence across the road. *"The air bites shrewdly…"* He went to bed.

In the morning and for the next two days, they—Robert mostly—tried everything with Art, from bucking him up to threats, but nothing worked. Mitch sat with him for a while on the second night, after he had been fired. "Doesn't matter to me, Mitch. Nothing can be done with these old bones. Feel bad for the picture, but there're plenty of good actors who would die to play this part. I'm going to die not to play it. Would you hand me the cough medicine?" He took a long pull. "Ah! That's better."

"So that's where it was, in the cough syrup."

He smiled. "Yup." His face was red and blotchy, with the look of a lost child. Mitch saw himself, sitting like this poor man, head down, all hope drained. He saw up close in freeze-frame what he could become.

Art was flown back to New York, and Lou Ayres replaced him. Mr. Ayres was the oldest man, Mitch figured, he had ever seen. But he was a spry one who took hold almost from the start. "I did my first movie in 1929, and I've been in more films than anyone," he answered when someone asked him how many films he'd done.

The next day they started shooting the old man's scenes.

"Speed! Rolling! Action."

"He stinks, Candy, you got to put him down."

"No, I'll keep him outside, he'll be fine."

Mitch, as Slim, came over and sat down by the old man. "He'll be better off, Candy. The old dog is suffering. I'll do it if you want." Looking into the eyes of this old actor, Mitch could see the endless agony of life and death. He watched him take as long as he needed to agree to have Slim kill the only thing he loved.

The weather in March was cool and rainy for Texas, and the sky was low, the perfect setting for this bleak story of the harshness of life in the Great Depression. Steinbeck had created such vivid characters that the cast could only silently absorb their power, and all of them did good work. One night near the end of the shoot, Mitch was sitting in the bunkhouse set with Whitman Mayo, a black actor.

"It's amazing how Steinbeck has infected us all," Whitman said.

"I almost didn't take this job."

"Why wouldn't you jump at it?"

Mitch sighed, "Blake."

"He's different, don't you think?" Whitman knew something. "Are you changed?"

"Must be Steinbeck. I almost didn't come either. How the tenor of life changes when you give yourself up to it." That's what Whitman knew and Ayres and Steinbeck.

When they finished the film, no one wanted to leave. They were mostly quiet that last day as they waited in the lobby. Several at a time took the stretch limo out to the airport to catch their various planes. Mitch drove back to Los Angeles alone.

CHAPTER 38

The Two Medeas
1982

ON THE RIDE to the campus, Mitch was reminded after all these years of the glorious rich green in this part of the world. Forests and farms backed up to each other. He recalled his impressions back then, on coming into these highlands for the first time, deeply convinced he had found his life's work, here in this lush part of the world. How could there be a working theater in this wilderness, he'd wondered, all of thirty years ago?

Samuel, the boy who was driving, a tall fellow with the face of an introspective eager young intellectual, said, "I've seen several of your movies, and you were super, but have you done much stage work?"

Leslie, the girl who was with him, said, "Oh, Samuel!"

Yet the boy had spoken with such respect that no offense could be taken. "Yes, I've been in a few plays."

The boy was keenly interested. "What range? Do you deal in the avant-garde or more classic? I'm studying European theater of the twentieth century myself." Mitch smiled and remembered a young man's earnestness.

The boy continued to ask Mitch the names of the plays he'd done, at which point Leslie broke in, "My God, Samuel, can't all this wait till you read the program?"

How long since he, Mitch, had been around young people who loved the theater and were eager to learn? Mitch leaned forward. "Tell me what you're working on. You must be doing a production."

"Yes, we're all working on *Hamlet* for the year's final."

"What are you playing?"

The boy smiled, blushed, and admitted, "The First Gravedigger."

And he, Mitch, was transported back to Louisville thirty years before. Clear as a glass of water, he remembered being in front of Doug Ramey and answering, "I think the Gravedigger is what I should play—anyone else in *Hamlet* is way beyond me." He smiled at the memory: "Whose grave's this, sirrah?"

The boy, quick as a wink: "Mine, sir."

"I think it be thine, indeed; for thou liest in't."

"You lie out on't, sir, and therefore it is not yours..."

Mitch laughed with hidden joy, "What's next? I forget."

"You must have played Hamlet."

"A long time ago. The old Gravedigger's a great part and key to the end of the play."

"Did you ever play that part?"

"I wish I had."

They had picked him up at the small airport not fifty miles from the Barter Theater, where he had begun, and now they were almost at the University of Tennessee.

The Media Project had started six months before. Mitch had received a call from Archer King, his New York agent. "I pitched you to Whitehead, who's directing, and Zoe, his wife, remembered you from *Othello*." Archer couldn't resist adding, "Aren't you glad I talked you into doing Iago all those years ago? I told you it would pay off!" Would Mitch be free, the producer asked, to come to Tennessee to play Jason in *Medea* for two weeks, then open and play a month at the Kennedy Center in Washington, and then, maybe New York? Mitch had said yes. "And, oh, Judith Anderson is also going to be in the production."

"Wait a minute: two Medeas?"

"You can handle it."

They were on the campus now, pulling up to a large brick building that looked like anything but what it was. Over the entranceway in bold chiseled letters was the name "Clarence Brown Theater."

What he was not prepared for was the beautifully appointed physical space and the professionalism of the students in the Drama Department. Those building the set were allowed to come to all the rehearsals, and they didn't miss one. The cast was treated like royalty. Mitch began to feel charged up. He felt younger every day. The students had prepared an ambitious presentation for the cast. The kids varied in talent but were all splendidly wild in their attack: *Golden Boy* and Lorna Moon, *Electra*, *Becket*, Tennessee. One young man, who played Hamlet with a light-sensitive touch, stood out in particular. His name was David Fallon, and he came to Mitch the second day asking if he could be of service.

"Are you an actor?"

"Well, I would like to be."

"What are you working on?"

"I take several scene classes and a History of Theater course."

"No, no, what part are you working on? What part do you want to play more than any other?" Mitch surprised himself with this question, then he realized, "You're playing Hamlet, am I right?"

"Well, I'm trying." The boy thought a moment. "I see that you played Iago. I think that would be the greatest gift an actor could ever have. To play all of those great parts Shakespeare wrote. I see that it'll be impossible for me to pull Hamlet into anything worth the play."

Mitch looked into his young face as he tried to get his breath. "I heard you this afternoon. You will be fine." Then he made some excuse, found his way out of the building, and walked toward his room. He walked fast. This boy reminded him of how he had been in Louisville with Doug Ramey. Mitch had almost forgotten that bracing, wonderful sense of aliveness, that feeling of worth, of belonging to something greater than yourself that comes with the theater.

When Mitch met young Hamlet the next morning, the boy asked if he had said something to offend him. "Far from it. No, what you said is something you should hold on to, and if you do that, you will do well. As for being offended, I want to thank you for saying what you did. It made me remember something important."

Five weeks in Tennessee. He was looking forward to digging into the play and working with the two colossally talented women, one who had made Medea her own and another who'd be taking the titanic role now. Indeed, *Medea* was Dame Judith's. She owned the rights to the Robinson Jeffers translation and had been solely identified with it for all of forty years. Until now. Dame Judith Anderson's idea was that Zoe Caldwell play the role, while she would play the nurse.

His first rehearsals with Dame Judith left him in awe. Her voice was unique, and her range so astounding it took his breath away. But Zoe was every bit her match and watching the two giants stretching themselves and exploring depths of their characters was nothing short of mesmerizing. The real magic, however, was witnessing Miss Anderson slowly build the inner core of the nurse—the pausing and the starting of a speech over with subtle modulation, all the while keeping an eye fixed on Zoe. The two would huddle from time to time and whisper, now and then getting heated but always ending in a warm hug and then plunging back into the work. These two Medeas guided Mitch to a performance that made him feel alive again and more content than he had for months, perhaps years.

A smart and sophisticated audience enthusiastically received the play. The students held a big party for everyone the night before the production left for Washington. They had all—cast, crew, students— had the time of their lives. The fifteen students who had worked on the production each offered a touching farewell, and Zoe brought them each a present.

In Washington, the play was a great success, and as the end of the run neared, the cast was asked if they were available to follow the show to New York. All agreed. That night Mitch was the only sober person in Robert Whitehead's suite.

On opening night at the Cort Theater on Fourth Street, Mitch was not alone in feeling the excitement of the crowd. There is nothing in the theater that can compare with an opening night in New

York when the stakes are high and you have a play you know is a masterpiece.

The final curtain came down to a standing ovation, and the following party at Sardis was something out of a dream, with rapturous reviews appearing at 1:00 a.m. Zoe and husband Mr. Whitehead positively glowed, and after Judith made an entrance worthy of the queen she was, she graciously ceded the floor to Zoe, the prize of the evening—Miss Zoe, who would receive a standing ovation every night of the run. Mitch had an inner glow as he stood at the side and watched the ladies have their night, but the calm that was part of him, now in these days, brought his every wish and aspiration to life. As he looked at the crowd, flocking around the two Medeas, no one knew that this was his night above everything.

Once the opening-night reviews had been read, he left quietly, slowly walking up through Times Square and all the way into Central Park. Suffused with a sense of worthiness and fulfillment, of accomplishment and belonging, he realized that nothing came close to what he was feeling now, in this city, in this play, with these people. This was indeed rare, this flood of wonder and gratitude, and for once, every part of him was ready to receive it.

A routine soon developed. Mitch would trade off with the actor who played Creon in walking Miss Anderson to her hotel after the play each night. On those nights, Mitch and the Dame sat in the bar at the Warwick Hotel on Forty-Fifth Street, a short cab drive from the theater. She had a double vodka and Mitch a root beer. As she sipped her drink, she looked over her glass provocatively and said in her deep immortal voice, "I never trust a man who doesn't drink. You mean to tell me a strapping worldly man like you will not drink with a woman?"

"Well, I'm sorry, Miss Anderson, I don't drink." He considered unveiling the horrors of his suicidal alcohol-drenched days but thought better of it. His mind strayed a bit, though, to the blessing of his narrow escape and how facing his life was taking its time. How learning the simplest things, like listening to another person or being generous with one's fellows, was also, sometimes, fiendishly hard to do, off stage, and somehow rarely rang true for him. He still felt that hole in the center of his gut. Suddenly, aware Miss Anderson was asking him a question, he refocused. "I used to drink quite a bit—too much, really—so I thought it better that I stop, and if you had seen me, you would agree, Miss Anderson."

"Oh, for God's sake, call me Judith. In England, they call me Dame Judith. I don't really care if you drink or not," she slurred several words, putting him on alert. "What I asked is how did you get such a trained voice? Most American actors pay little attention to voice production."

"I always thought it was what was needed to play the big Shakespeare roles." He was about to continue but saw that his ward's shades were already halfway down. She was wonderful company and told electric stories as she flirted, but then…She habitually had two large vodkas, during the second of which she would start to fade and get slurry. This would be Mitch's cue to walk her to her room. She would kiss him good night and say every time, "If I were only one year younger." He would then walk up to his sublet on West Seventy-Third, marveling that Dame Judith was eighty-one years old.

In a fit of bittersweet joy, Mitch stopped on his way home, sat on a bench along Central Park West, and breathed in the cool night. What a strange jagged path his life had taken. But then, unbidden, came the familiar haunting ghosts of broken promises, devastations, and betrayals. And now followed the dark melancholy of his life in Los Angeles with Lynda and Tim. A life that was gone, which had intruded from time to time despite the fact that he made sure he was working too hard to allow a family, any family to have a hold on him.

This time, however, Mitch's taking a job in the East had been too much for Lynda, and she'd packed up and gone back to Tucson. "You're going to do a play in New York and be gone a year? Well, fuck you," delivered with the finality of a person who has finally given up. Tim was still up in the lockdown school. He was curt on the phone and didn't answer any letters, so Mitch had quit writing. A strange purple tragedy, this off-again, on-again relationship with Lynda and Tim—yet somehow it suited him. Someday, he convinced himself, he would look into it, but now was never the time.

Mitch never connected his tension and fearful longing to this turning away. Easier, instead, to be consumed in the struggle of how to manage everything and everyone. He now realized that he had no life except for the stage. And now that he was in New York and in a hit, this could be the way back. But as he skimmed over his life, he suddenly remembered John, whom he'd met in Colorado, and what he had told him: "Be serious about your life and don't throw it away." Strange how something so important, something that could have such an effect on your life, could be so easily dismissed, so easily lost.

The only time he felt alive was when he was acting on the stage, and he had deserted that. And for what? Now that he was back, he would never again abandon Lear's "great stage of fools." He jumped up, walked to Seventy-Third Street, climbed the three flights past the sterile walls, and entered his small apartment. How wonderfully lonely this tidy place was. He fell onto the bed, not bothering to undress. Complete darkness but for a slice of light coming through the window blind. As he floated into semiconsciousness, a combination of relaxed joy and quiet despair brought comforting lines from long-ago plays and books. "I am a very foolish fond old man." "But look, the morn, in russet mantle clad, Walks o'er the dew of yon high eastward hill." "What a piece of work is a man!" "Darkness is cheap, and Scrooge liked it."

All he knew were other people's lines.

CHAPTER 39

What to Do?
1984

"Could you get a loan and pay us, then work out payments with the bank?"

The IRS agent was a seriously severe woman of indeterminate age who clearly loved her job. You could see this by the look of greedy power with which she took full advantage of her victims. With the United States government behind her. Watching her Mitch could not help conjuring images of an adding machine. The bleak gray walls and penitentiary windows of the cell they sat in only underscored the impersonal and immovable nature of the transaction at hand. Mitch felt his life crowding him into a dark place. As the woman's voice resurfaced, he realized he hadn't been listening; in fact, he had been making his exit since the minute he'd arrived. But what he did hear clearly now was this: "Otherwise, the fines and interest will keep going up. Also, we can activate a lien on your house at any time."

Mitch headed for the door. "Thank you so much, you have been very helpful and kind," and went out of the Federal Building into the middle of a huge parking lot by the freeway in Westwood. He pondered his situation. He was broke. One year in New York, living on theater salaries had deepened his debt, so now with no job, he had to deal with the IRS. The tragedy of life as a stage actor in

America was that you simply could not subsist on what the theater paid.

Across from the parking lot lay a beautiful little park with shade trees and quaint walks with old-fashioned wood-and-iron benches. He sat and watched the birds being fed by an older man wearing a handsome black chesterfield overcoat. The air smelled crisp, and the winds of March were nippy, but the sun was hot. He had always loved that about California. When the sun was out, you could feel its life. He held his face up, eyes closed, until he knew the rays would burn. As he looked down, the man feeding the birds slowly rose, dusted his hands, took off his chesterfield, and walked over to where Mitch was sitting. "Would you like to buy this coat? It's in good shape. Belonged to my brother who sadly died."

"I don't think so."

When the man came closer, Mitch could guess that he was homeless. Face wrecked but eyes alert. The old man gave Mitch a penetrating look, then nodded at the Federal Building. "Don't worry, it will all work out." He paused, then walked away. Mitch wanted to say something, maybe ask him to sit, but nothing came out. He could only watch him leave. As the overcoat moved farther away, Mitch had a feeling he'd missed something. What will "work out"? He felt close to understanding something, and then whatever it might have been faded away. Anyway, Ro, his agent, was right, and so was this man. "It will all work out."

The sun's heat had a therapeutic effect on him. What was singular about the sun? Ever since he'd been a little boy, the sun had released something in him that dissolved all his loneliness, allowing him to breathe strong again. He remembered how often in the woods behind his house he sat in the sun and knew he was not alone, and then those rays were the best part of his life. When he had to go back home, the feeling would dissolve, but the sun would continue to be good and pure.

The theater had changed him, shaped his life, yet when the shadows of his deep loneliness and dread had too often prevailed, there was always drink. Well, he couldn't return to that medication now, but there was the sun. He thought of Tucson, the great desert, the quiet and serenity that would work in him when he was there. And he thought of his friend.

He went directly to his car and, before he could think twice, was heading straight out of California toward Arizona. The good friend there, a Native American, was a wise man who both calmed and challenged him. They had met on a film set in Tucson when out of the blue the man had started talking about the history of the great saguaro cactus and how man, if he had certain knowledge, might live like this ancient cactus which can thrive in the desert because it knows the way to stay alive. "When most living things in that climate die, this giant is king." His soon-to-be friend continued, "The man who is wise enough to know how to be in the world and not of it is as the saguaro. A man without knowledge of the life in his personal desert—the city—the fool will destroy himself.

Mitch remembered how he felt hearing this biblical paraphrase coming from a "primitive" Indian—this man who had left his reservation early to attend the one Indian university, Carlyle, and who now made money doing Westerns. He had shown Mitch a hidden place where the Sonora Desert meets the Santa Maria Mountains and from whose promontory the view stretches for miles. And that was the beginning, that first tour of the Arizona desert when Mitch learned of the stillness and quiet that could put things right, a stillness that could transform him and cast light on another way of being.

He stopped in Yuma to have a bite and sat there moving his eggs around the plate in the nondescript diner, which was like so many others in the West. Driving on through the night, he stopped several times to survey the canopy of stars in the velvet black sky. As he reached Gila Bend, some eighty miles from Tucson, the sky slowly turned from a deep indigo to a dusty blue to a light rose, then became increasingly lighter, so that just as he arrived at the outskirts of the city, the sun burst up out of the desert, shimmering red and terrible. He stopped and stepped out to feel faint heat on his face. He also knew what the giver of life could do by noon: kill everything that was not covered. Only the great saguaro could stand against that blast oven and not bow.

He drove straight through Tucson toward the Santa Maria Mountains until he found the dirt road that led to his friend, whose Indian name, though he answered to William, was Sacred Horse. As Mitch pulled up to the small shack surrounded by a split-rail fence, William came out and waited by the gate. Mitch had forgotten the magnetism that burst forth from this old man. William had never said how old he was, but several of his friends told Mitch he was nearing a hundred!

"Look"—William pointed off toward a stand of saguaro cactus—"they're building a nest." Mitch saw two small birds hovering over a hole near the top of the cactus. "The saguaro is a city, and it's their time to build their home and raise a family." He stood watching for a long while as the male flew down to the ground to bring a bit of straw back to the waiting female, who would weave the find into the nest. At last, he took Mitch's hand and looked into his face. "You are troubled. Come in."

Inside the house, opposite the door was a small table of dark shining wood with a bowl and a flame licking above the rim. Below the window was a rustic table and several chairs. On the other wall was a cot and a lamp. The whole room had the feeling of a sanctuary. Mitch was instantly bathed in a wave of peace and calm.

"Drink this."

"What is it?"

"Drink it."

He drank it down. Slightly bitter, with no effect he could detect.

"We need to sweat. A short walk earns us something to eat. Come." Mitch had looked at the temperature gauge in his car: a hundred six degrees.

William gave him a hat with a canvas flap down the back and told him to roll down his shirtsleeves. Then he strode out toward the foothills of the Santa Maria Mountains. Mitch followed, not a little alarmed. After half an hour or so, William said, "That's enough. We can sit here." He pointed to a small grove of Palo Verde trees. Mitch was uncomfortable, almost sick from the heat, but under the trees, the heat dissipated a bit, and the shade was welcome. William sat on his haunches, so Mitch followed suit. After five or so minutes, he started to feel the tension in his thighs, and after five more minutes, he stood.

William opened his eyes. He had not moved and was completely relaxed. "Sit against the tree. Yes, it's good you're here. You must stay." They sat for another half hour, during which Mitch dozed. When he opened his eyes, William was looking down at him. "Let's go." The heat of the walk back was so intense that after ten minutes, William pulled out an old leather-bound water container. "Two sips."

Back at the house, Mitch fell into the chair by the table. "You don't have to kill me the first hour I'm here."

"Run some cold water on your wrists. I'll fix something for us to eat. Then you must tell me the story." The cold water helped, and they sat down to melon and corn pudding.

"Well?"

"What do you mean, a story?"

"Just that."

"No hints or help?"

"What would I know, it's your story."

The melon had the most seductive taste as if he had never tasted melon before. "Well, what's on my mind is my stepson. He's angry and can't or won't get off the drugs."

"Not his story, yours."

"Damn, I want—I need to talk about my suffering and his mother's suffering at the hands of this boy."

"You don't suffer. You have no idea what suffering is because you have never allowed yourself to suffer. Suffering is not caused by anything outside you. Not by any person or any act. Suffering is caused when you become aware you have no connection with your life and the Great Father."

Mitch felt something pierce his heart. He remembered the AA Big Book. "Made a decision to turn your will and your life over to God, as you understand him." Never in his nineteen years of sobriety in AA had he surrendered to anything, much less to a concept of God.

After a short time, William spoke in a gentle voice, as if to a child, "Everything happens in the only way it can."

"That can't be true. Man must be able to change, improve himself."

"Man cannot change."

"No? Then what's the use of going on?"

"Living as he does, there is no reason."

"There must be a way to change. Is it because he won't try?"

"He doesn't know what to try. You can move under a higher law, and then something in you can change."

"I don't understand."

"Finish your melon." Despite the puzzling nature of their exchange, Mitch could feel himself relaxing and edging into something like peace. The calm flowing out of William permeated the room.

"You want things to be different, then you must learn to be influenced by simpler action. Actions that belong to you that you pay no attention to. You need to learn the natural way of being. No one, you included, knows anything about how to search for the truth of how to live their lives." Then he stopped and sat so still, his eyes closed, that Mitch thought he had gone to sleep. They stayed this way for some time.

Finally, William's eyes came open, and he was staring directly at Mitch. "Well, are you going to tell me a story?"

"I don't see the point."

"There is no point."

After Mitch spent an hour on all the things he could remember about what he was doing and how he was having trouble handling the mess, William said, "You have told me nothing. In all your boring story, you never once told me who you are or how your inner life motivated any of these external events you describe. You float without an aim."

Mitch started to interrupt.

"Don't speak! If I didn't know different, I would say you are totally unaware of the value of knowing anything about yourself. Since you do know at least some aspects of the real life in you, I would have to say, then, that you don't know what is valuable. You have no real values. In my tradition, you would be sent into the

306

wilderness for many months alone with nothing but a knife. If you returned, you and everyone would know who you are. You don't realize your life is at stake, and since you don't and since going to the wilderness is not possible, it will be much harder for you. First, we will sit with the hot stones in the lodge and sweat. You are welcome to stay with me for as long as you wish. Then you must go back to your life and learn from it."

Mitch stayed for three weeks and helped William build a new room in his small house. He resented William putting him to work doing manual labor, but once he started and was connected to his body, he remembered the great joy of working hard, sweating, and using his skill at building. Every evening they would walk out into the desert, and William sometimes talked of the way the world worked and the immensity of the vision and the connectedness of everything. Mostly, though, he was silent and they just walked. The morning Mitch left, William told him, "Your life has all the answers to who you are and your peace and happiness. When you know who you are, then you can be useful."

Mitch didn't want to leave but knew he must. As he drove out on the dirt road, his mind was clear and life seemed possible. When he hit the seventy-five-mile-an-hour traffic of the superhighway, however, his mind loaded up with the flotsam of living in the world and its endless demands. The IRS and Pax Americana. The debt, the fighting for a life that he had never learned to master. The mad scramble of LA and the pressures of modern life pushed into him even before he'd left Arizona. He watched the flood and laughed. So much for higher strivings, deep thoughts, and mastering the world.

Then he remembered: learn from life who you are.

CHAPTER 40

Tim's First Play
1984

FROM HIS PORCH, he could see the long yard full of stones, dug up and neatly piled ready to become a noble fence and several empty wheelbarrows. The barn stood at the end of the yard and, on both sides, the corral. Then woods, and beyond the so-called mountain, just small hills but tall for Agoura, and finally the ocean that you could see from atop them.

Mitch was enjoying building a stonewall, finding the right-size stone to fit in like a puzzle piece to shape the wall. Ever since his time in the desert with the old man, he'd experienced a serene sense of usefulness in working this tiny ranch. Some ancient urge to be part of the land and using his hands and body made him whole. This belonging to a place must have always been there, but somehow forgotten until William had reminded him that "all you need to know who you are is right there, in your life."

The house, which he had rebuilt, was rustic and rambled at right angles to itself. The fine porch stretched the length of the house. Porches, he had always loved porches, starting with the first one, the best thing about his father's house. And how good it was to be home! He was going to sit and work and sit and work and in the evenings do nothing. He looked out to the hills across the road, breathing in the air was sweet and the slight breeze. Living here was a familiar embrace that came from deep in his being. He did not understand fully just how the visit with William had influenced him, but he did sense something was different. Life, much simpler now, had lost that constant frantic movement, and he faced problems in a slightly different way. Nothing external had changed all that much, but at the same time, somehow, nothing was quite the same. Existence was no longer so overwhelming. Mitch had made three TV films in a row with ease, now he felt tired to the bone but safe, protected on his land, in his house.

"Don't you want to go and see Tim? When was the last time you saw him? Can't we get going?" Lynda sat with him on the porch, up from Tucson, in order to visit Tim at school. She was distant and didn't seem to want anything to do with Mitch aside from using him as a driver up to the mountains. That suited him fine. He did not want to push things.

The phone rang. He went into the house and let the door slam. "Yes, hello… Tell me and cut the suspense… Holy cow, that's great. What kind of money?… Way to go, Ro! That'll help."

Lynda sat on the porch, feeling she had been slapped, shouted in the door, "Never mind, I'll see you later. I'll take the car."

Mitch called out the window. "Wait, I'm coming, don't leave—I said let's go see him!"

"Well, come on."

As he pulled the car out the drive, he said, "I got a job."

"Wonderful."

"Jesus."

"Sorry."

"Is it in town?"

"Yes. With, Mel Gibson."

"Who's that?"

"Never mind."

The ride up to the school in the mountains above Los Angeles was silent and tense. When they drove down the endless winding road to the small valley the school occupied, there was no one to be seen. The road had taken them through a dense forest of pine and finally opened up to a large gate that led onto a gravel road. The gate opened down a long drive where they could see the main building, a huge wooden structure. Mitch felt no desire to get out and find Tim. Lynda waited. Tim came out the front door and walked down to the car. Lynda went to meet him, and Mitch wondered what he could do to quiet the rumble in his middle. She ran to the driver's side. "What luck—Tim's going to be doing a play tonight. What's the name, Tim?"

"*The Night Thoreau Spent in Jail.* You don't have to stay, it's a simple play."

Mitch looked at the boy. He had changed. His face was clear, and he had an air of confidence Mitch had never seen before. "Of course, we'll come. Have to see what you're up to. When did you get into acting? I had no idea."

"Mr. Pierce asked me to read, and one thing led to another, so I'm playing Henry David Thoreau."

At dinner in the big hall with all the students, Mitch tried to hide in the crowd, but every other boy and some of the teachers singled him out. "Monte Walsh was tremendous, maybe one of the best Westerns ever made." The headmaster—or as the boys called him, the Warden—kept going on about it.

Tim, who was at the special table for guests because of his parents, spoke up, "I think several others ought to be considered."

Mitch felt close to the boy. "Tim's right, *Red River, High Noon, Ox-Bow Incident*...but I enjoyed making it." After dinner, they all walked out into the lovely evening.

"You want to see my room? We have a little time before I have to get ready for the show."

Following Tim to the dorm, Mitch wondered about the quality of the play he was going to see. This school was one of several in the country to offer a combination of high school curriculum, group therapy, and hard labor working the ranch and livestock, all while getting the students off their addictions. Though Mitch could sense it had been working for Tim, now far more composed, he had no way of knowing what kind of performance might be in store.

The room was small and jammed full of Tim's life, books and writing paper covering the surface of the desk, a small bed along one wall with a baseball bat and one golf club standing in the corner, more books on the bed, and an easy chair of faded blue corduroy with a footstool, hot plate, and a teapot on a table in the other corner. Everything reminded Mitch of a monk's cell, but then this school was a kind of a monastery. Mitch went to the window and looked out toward the barn and corrals.

"I've been working on a paper on the American Revolution, a kind of you-are-there piece."

"I would love to read it." His mother took his hand.

"You would?"

"Sure, we both would."

Tim looked at Mitch. "I'll send you a copy when it's finished. You too, Mom."

The play itself was tiresome, but Tim was present and authentic and showed real talent. He was actually good, and at one point sitting in chairs to represent a rowboat, his pantomime was so clear and simple and his hand movements so accurate, you could see the boat itself and the dipping of the oars. Mitch was so thrilled he wanted to shout out loud. Could this, finally, be a basis for some kind of comradeship between them? "O'erstep not the modesty of nature."

At the curtain, Mitch applauded and stamped his feet. Afterward, standing back while everyone crowded around the boy, he remembered his own first flush of belonging to something greater than himself, and then the praise—oh, yes, the praise. After telling him how good he was, Mitch pulled the boy aside and took his hand. "What you did in that rowboat was pure acting, I'm proud of you."

CHAPTER 41

Pure Hollywood
1984

TRYING TO BREATHE was the actor's biggest problem: white dust all over the stunt car, on his clothes, in his hair, up his nose. In the upside-down special-effects car the space was cramped. Jagged edges of metal just above his head would not allow him to move. The hand grenade was exactly an inch out of his reach.

The director's voice sounded as though it were coming from the next county: "All right, Mitch, we're going to roll the camera. Try to get the grenade."

"I can't move. How do you expect me to do that?"

"You're not supposed to be able to get it. That's why you die."

Then he heard the camera start and realized by the film clicking that this was being shot without sound. So as he made the vain attempt to reach for the grenade, followed it with a long line of curses, and segued into *who would fardels bear, / To grunt and sweat under a weary life, / But that the dread of something after death—*

He hit his head on the metal dashboard. "Damn!"

"The undiscover'd country from whose bourn / No traveller returns, puzzles the will / And makes us rather bear those ills we have—"

"God damn it—"

"Than fly to others that we know not of?"

He heard laughing. Then Dick the director said, "Jesus, that was great. He's good. I should have recorded the dialogue." Mitch shouted through the dust and metal, "Are you going to shoot this all night? Get me out of here!"

As he extracted himself with help from the upside-down getaway car, he realized the heat was just as intense outside the wreck as in. This kind of gaseous putrid LA heat was so different from the pure blazing bath of the sweat lodge in Arizona where he had purged with William. That had been a healing heat of pure-white steam, penetrating and nearly unbearable, but also a miracle leading to his feeling light and in touch with his body and soul.

Now back in Los Angeles, money, money, and more money was a problem. Nevertheless, his life had become simpler since his talk with his Native American friend, and as long as he could remember to just do what he was doing and not worry about how he was doing, his life could stay simple. He had revalued what was important. Now he even listened in AA meetings.

The director had cast him in this movie, *Lethal Weapon*, at their first meeting, after hearing Mitch read. "I'll have Business Affairs call your agent. Can you come to my house tonight? I'm having a little party to kick off the film."

Mitch considered how much he hated Hollywood parties. "I'll be there."

The director lived at the top of a winding road in the Hollywood Hills. As Mitch drove through the gate and approached the opulent house and gardens, he felt a twinge of envy as he considered how fulfilling it was to belong to the upper crust of the film community, instead of where he was, on the fringe. Inside the gate, many would-be actors parked cars. There were levels of fringe. "It is the green-eyed monster which doth mock the meat it feeds on..." By now, Mitch thought, he should be well over this envy, but these yearnings pained him now and then. Most of the time, he could deal with them, except when rubbing shoulders with the elite, as he was doing tonight.

He walked into a lush garden between a pool and the house, whose beautiful French doors opened to the soft night, revealing dark, sumptuous rooms all around the first floor. In these rooms, handsome men and luscious young women clustered in small groups. The noise was subdued, and the talk appeared to be "very important" until you came closer and heard "The Jaguar XJ is vastly superior to any BMW ever made" spilling out of an eager young man, or "I wouldn't use anyone else. His hands are absolute magic…" gushing from one of the young women.

He didn't know anyone there. He was introduced to Mel Gibson, the star, and had a nice chat with Danny Glover, the other star. A bit later, a nervous-looking young man came up to Mitch, told him his name, and said he had written the *Lethal Weapon* script. He had "sent it to someone at Warner's" and here he was.

"Your part, General McAllister, is the great character of this piece," the young man confided, shaking with nerves. Mitch was sure he had said the same to Mel and Danny about their roles.

"Let me get you a drink," Mitch offered to calm him down.

"I've only been here four days. I'm from Illinois. Mr. Director is nice, but he keeps fixing things in the script, making it 'better,' he says. I guess it's better, and, uh, which version did you get?"

"I don't know." At the bar Mitch ordered the kid a whiskey, fearing for the young man in this world of sharks, where "Let's make it better" means "Let me write it." He suddenly felt old. This kid, full of hope and wanting to be part of this world of film—it made no sense, but then, of course, it did. Mitch hated suffering these fits of cynicism. Why couldn't he just celebrate this good job and count his lucky stars? "You wrote a nice script," Mitch tried to assure him, "and I'm sure it will do well." Mitch looked into the young open face. The boy smiled, and they both relaxed a bit.

He wandered from room to room feeling very much on the edge of the small groups of beautiful people and so walked out and waited in the garden for his car. The stunning view of the sparkling lights of Los Angeles and Hollywood was something straight out of F. Scott Fitzgerald. From this pinnacle, everything seemed possible. Suddenly he loved Fitzgerald and that boy who had written this film and all the yearnings of all the boys who had come West to make a mark. At that moment, in this lavish night garden against the buzz of the party and the faint tinkle of crystal, Mitch understood the young writer. He recalled himself at that age and understood the wave of desire that had engulfed him all those years ago when he walked through the doors of the Carriage House Players Theater in Louisville on a day in 1953.

On the drive home, he stopped at a coffee shop on Santa Monica Boulevard. The hour was still early, and his mellow mood deepened at the prospect of pecan pie and coffee as he realized he was actually jacked up about starting work on this film. The pie came, then suddenly he was thumped on the back. He turned to see a flashy older man and a nice-looking young woman wearing too much makeup. "Jesus, how the hell are you, Mitch? It's Howard. Remember me? Howard Hanson!" He turned to the woman. "Mitch and I were in *Thunder Road* together a thousand years ago."

"Howard, yes, good to see you." Howard was one of a long line of actors in Hollywood who are committed to the illusion of being in the motion picture business. He was Mitch's age, but his face had an unnaturally orange-brown hue from self-tanning products, and his hair was dyed sandy blond. A dark trench-coat hung over his shoulders, and there were lots of gold chain around his neck. Mitch dived into his pie, hoping Howard would take the hint.

"What're you up to, Mitch? I hear about you all the time. Honey, this guy and Mitchum could really put it away. Did we have some times, right, Mitch? Big Mitch and Little Mitch—great line, right, Mitch?" And he launched into several lies about himself and Mitch in some barfight or other. Miss Heavy Makeup, standing there, was not amused or impressed and probably wondered what she was doing with a couple of Hollywood deadbeats in a cheap coffee shop. Mitch declined the invitation to repair to the Rain Check Room, finished his pie, and beat a quick retreat.

Driving home, he felt like he was in a Raymond Chandler novel. "He stuck to me like a cheap suit," he said out loud, liked the way he sounded, and repeated the deadly line with a Bogart sneer. He was feeling "blue" for this dyed-hair would-be actor and the legions like him in this town. His mood was, now, a twist on what he had felt earlier, and he wondered about the many fine actors he had known over the years, now lost. Where were they? *"These our actors, / As I foretold you, were all spirits and / Are melted into air, into thin air..."*

For the moment, he was back in New York. "Bourne back ceaselessly into the past." Mitch was quoting Fitzgerald and himself. On the drive home, an idea was beginning to dawn on him. The film and television business was changing. The studios had wised up and were done throwing money away on actors. Cutting back. He had made a lot of money in the last twenty years but now was finding that harder to do. Getting older, competing with ex-movie stars caught in this same spiral. That was the way things were now, so there was no use ranting or quoting. He was worried because he hadn't saved any money. Period.

When he looked at his mail at home, there was yet another notice from the IRS stating that he owed more back taxes and to make a date to "reconcile." Dear me. He went to the fridge, reached for the milk, picked up a jar that used to hold peanut butter which he now used for a drinking glass, and went to his bed.

His eye fell on the complete Shakespeare on the table by the bed. His mother came to him: "He was for all time, all time, all time." He looked at the jar of milk. "Drink your milk Mitchie." He took a sip, put the jar down, fell back, and went to sleep.

CHAPTER 42

Reunion
1985

MITCH TURNED ONTO Highway 38 from Interstate 10 and headed north toward the long climb up the San Bernardino Mountains. He hadn't planned to pick up Tim from the school, but when he talked to him on the phone the day before to congratulate him on graduating, he realized he was the one who'd sent him there, and so he should be the one to bring him home. Something he had to complete. Gliding through San Bernardino, before the descent, he looked for a place to eat. Sitting in a coffee shop waiting for his eggs, he considered that it had been more than a year since he'd seen the boy. True, he had been working, but that only justified one lame excuse after another—there was always a movie, a location, or maybe no excuse at all. He pushed his chair back with a grinding sound on the floor.

"Here's your eggs. More coffee?"

"Yes, thank you."

The waitress glanced at Mitch with that don't-I-know-you look, but before she could say anything, Mitch asked, "Do you have kids?"

"You're an actor. I seen you in something."

Mitch waved yes with a nod.

"Sure, got two no-good boys. I never see them. What can you do? I remember it was that Western with Clint Eastwood. You have any children?"

"I've got one boy, a good boy."

"That's nice. Holler if you need anything."

Why had he said that? His father would say in Mitch's presence to almost anyone, "He's a good boy. Mitchell is a good boy." His father would call him Mitchell. Even now, if someone called him Mitchell, a faint shadow would dart across his mind. A sip of coffee, and for the first time in a long while, he would have accepted a shot of Irish to liven up the day. He dropped the cup. Jesus Christ! The rest of his eggs and bacon went down in one burst of violent energy. Mitch said goodbye to the waitress and headed out the door.

The full sight of the huge San Bernardino Mountains spread out before him, and the peak of Arrowhead shining white in the sun summoned vague pictures of ski trips with Tim laughing, calling, "Beat you to the bottom!" So many wasted years. Mitch shuddered, opened the car, turned the ignition key, and sat for some time with the motor running. How long had his father been dead? Thirty years? He slowly pulled the car out and headed up the winding road, the huge forest on one side and the grand vista on the other.

He had to stop at a wide turn in the road. He got out to take in the endless view of the San Bernardino Valley all the way to the San Jacinto Mountains beyond. He sat on the retaining wall watching two red-tailed squirrels race up one tree, leap to another, and catapult down to the ground. He heard the chatter of a bird high up in the spruce behind him, then the distant straining grind of a truck motor coming up the grade. Finally, he watched two hawks circling off to the south. He was clear, alert, ready to face the boy.

Farther up the mountain, far out on the parapet, Tim stood leaning over the railing of the wooden deck that reached out over the cliff. It was so clear today, no smog or haze, that he could see the San Jacinto Mountains in the distance across the vast San Bernardino Valley. He had over the years come to love this far point on the deck and would sit here for hours. The space came to be known by some of the boys as Tim's roost.

He was nervous about Mitch coming to get him today. Mitch Ryan, the actor, who was supposed to be his father and who was, in reality, a visiting stranger, the man who talked on the other end of the phone like they were friends. When Tim heard Mitch's voice, his mouth went dry and he unconsciously backed away from the wall where the telephone hung. Now, standing on the deck at the edge of the world, he remembered holding the phone while the rush of words came from this man he didn't know. Suddenly movement caught his eye, and he became aware of two hawks diving toward the cliff then circling far out over the scarred side of the mountain.

He walked over to the dorm and climbed the stairs to his room. Looking around—at the small desk, the bed with the squeak that never got fixed, the snapshots of classmates, the achievement awards—the tears started to come. He choked them back and sat down on the bed. He could hardly believe he was done with Cedar School. Four years. It seemed as if he had been here forever. He'd made many friends and, as he wrote in his final paper, "I learned a lot." He had forgiven Mitch and his mother soon after they had put him here, realizing they had done what they thought best and even that maybe they were right, but the scars were buried deep and shaped who he was and who he would become.

Out the window, he could see the top of the barn and the roof he had shingled. He remembered each boy who had been on that crew and the pride that he still felt. He jumped up and shook his head, then picked up his bags and started out. In the hall, he ran into Bill Holland, who was head of the kitchen and the first person to befriend him. Stopping in the long dark hall with the hundreds of pictures all along the wall, the man and the boy regarded each other. There was nothing to say. Bill took one of his bags, and the two of them walked slowly down the hall. They stopped in front of a picture of the kitchen gang. Tim was right in the middle with his arm around Bill.

"Just remember the big black bear lesson, and you'll be fine. You can always be a cook or wash dishes. You're good at washing dishes." He smiled. "You would make a fine cook." The bear lesson referred to the time Tim foolishly climbed a tree as a bear was heading toward him on one of their hikes. Bill had used this episode to illustrate the great proverb: "When you don't know what to do, do nothing." Walking down the deck, trying to suppress his fear about his reentry into the world, he caught sight of Mitch at his car. He watched this man, a stranger who looked vaguely like someone he knew, someone from his past. Wondering what to do, he felt like running back to his room or off in the woods.

He heard the voice of Mr. Blake, the director, behind him, "There's your father. You have all your gear?" Mr. Blake had been a member of the hippy generation and still wore the bell-bottoms and long flowing locks.

"Yes." Tim still watched the man at the car below.

"I said pretty much everything last night at dinner. I'm proud of you, Tim. You grew up and learned a lot here. You'll do fine, just give it a chance, and remember your mother and Mitch. They love you, and they need your help and support. That is important."

Tim watched him walk into the office, remembering that first day with him when Tim was so hurt and angry. "Yes, of course, Mr. Blake." Then he turned and threw the duffel bag down the stairs.

He glanced over at Bill. They both looked down to Mitch, still standing by the car. Bill gave Tim a hug. "Call me. I'll see you down the line," and he walked away, back down the deck. Tim watched the slow saunter, so familiar, until Bill disappeared through the back door. Then Tim turned to the man who acted the part of his father.

Mitch's palms had been sweating on the steering wheel as he glided to a stop in front of the school. Getting out of the car, he saw Tim throw a large duffel bag down the side stair of the rustic main building. A man hugged Tim and walked away. Then Tim came down the stairs and strode over to the car. They stood for a moment like two gunfighters. Mitch held out his arms and moved to Tim. The embrace was stiff, and Tim broke it. "Hi, Dad. Thanks for driving all the way up here to get me."

Mitch frowned. Tim always used "Dad" with a bite.

"I wanted to. I wouldn't miss driving you back to Agoura." He opened the trunk. "I was at the place for just a few hours last night. Hasn't changed. Oh, and there's a new tack room that Beth designed. She's turned into a beautiful young woman."

"I know. She told me all about the tack room. She came up last weekend."

Mitch knew that the young woman had come to visit Tim every month for the last four years but he said nothing. Tim picked up his stuff, and Mitch moved to help.

"I'll get it." Tim grabbed for the duffel bag.

Mitch looked down at the old leather bag, picked it up, "I may be getting on, but I can still tote a bag or two."

"I didn't mean that."

"No harm, no foul. God, you still have this old bag. It came over with my grandfather from Ireland."

"Yes, I've heard that story."

Mitch threw the bag into the trunk and then wished he hadn't. The anger was contagious.

They drove down through the woods to the highway. "I didn't think to ask—do you want to drive?"

"I'll just take in the scenery."

"Did you drive that big old truck at the school?"

"Yes, into Running Springs to get hay and feed."

"Well, enjoy the ride. We can stop and get a bite if you want."

"It's okay, Dad, I'm fine."

Mitch watched the school disappear in the rearview mirror as they slowly pulled away. "I guess you'll miss this place."

"That's the barn, Dad. Those are haystacks, and that's a training ring where we train horses. I spent four years here, a big chunk of my life. Of course I'll miss it."

There was a long silence as they started down the mountain. Mitch felt trapped after Tim's outburst, but he decided to let it go and search for the one thing they might have in common—the theater. Before he could get started, Tim said, "Sorry, Mitch. Didn't mean to be sarcastic."

"Forget it. Did you do another play after that one I saw? I remember how terrific you were. Did you keep at it?"

Tim was looking out his window. "We did *Julius Caesar*. Shakespeare is hard."

"Who did you play?'

"I forget." Then, after a pause, he said, "Mark Antony."

"What a part. I had a great time playing that one." He was filled with stories but stopped himself. "How'd you find it?"

"Hard."

"Would you do some lines for me? I'd very much like to hear how it went for you."

"Oh God."

"I'll do some too. Come on, it'll be fun. *Friends, Romans, countrymen—*"

"No way."

They were down the mountain now and heading toward San Bernardino. They eased onto the 10 and headed west to Los Angeles. From his window, Tim watched the huge windmills, which resembled giant prehistoric animals. Mitch couldn't tell where Tim was. Was anything different? He felt the heat of the desert after the mountains and turned on the air.

Suddenly Tim said, *"Lend me your ears; I come to bury Caesar, not to praise him..."*

"Go on, that was great."

Tim paused, took a deep breath. *"The evil that men do lives after them; The good is oft interred with their bones; so let it be with Caesar. The noble Brutus Hath told you Caesar was ambitious: If it were so, it was a grievous fault..."* He stopped. "I can't remember more. Dad, you're going ninety miles an hour."

"Jesus." Mitch slowed.

Finally, Tim said with a laugh, *"If you have tears, prepare to shed them now..."*

They shared the joke. "You got it, great." Mitch thought he saw a sly smile on Tim's face. They both were calm the rest of the way.

Tim turned down the air then said in a quiet voice, "Mr. Jones, the drama and English teacher, made even the more difficult moments great. He helped everyone relax and have fun doing Shakespeare, which is not all that easy. Shakespeare wrote thirty-seven plays. Did you know that?"

Mitch smiled. "No. That many?"

As they neared home, they passed the Rock Store, just off the side of the road before the turn onto the long drive leading to the ranch. Tim said, "I can't believe Vern is still sitting there. That's wild." The owner had been a daily fixture on the porch of the small store for years.

"Some things never change." Mitch was grateful Tim remembered. He made the turn onto the decomposed granite drive. Tim's face split into a grin at the sight of Murphy loping toward them from the barn. Mitch opened the trunk then stood watching as Tim wrestled with the old dog. At that moment, terrible singing burst forth from the house:

"He was a wild colonial boy, Tim Ryan was his name He was born and raised in Ireland, in a place called Castlemaine."

Melvin and Beth came off the porch holding a banner that read, "Welcome home, Tim Ryan." and carrying party hats and leis.

"He was his father's only son, his mother's pride and joy… But we love him most, our wild Agoura boy. Yes, we love him *most*."

They made quite a pair, Melvin short and stumpy and Beth tall and solidly built, with her wide warm smile. Beth had a deeply tanned face, too much sun and wind, but it made no difference. She had a glow and a sexiness that made anyone sit up. Beth and Tim had grown up together, and she was Tim's best friend. She lived with her grandparents up the road from Mitch's ranch and had taught Tim everything about horses and ranching. She and Tim had become Heathcliff and Cathy in Mitch's mind. And though Melvin was forty now, his mental age was still that of a guileless boy. Tim had a great fondness for him, and Tim was Melvin's hero.

In blue jeans and a white work shirt, Beth moved to Tim and gave him a big hug, kissing him on the lips. Melvin waited patiently for his turn, then nearly knocked Tim over with a bear hug, saying over and over, "You're home, you're home, you're home." Then he ran a distance away, laughing. Next, he ran to Mitch, gave him a lei, sped away, turned, and announced, "And that lei is for you because you have also been away, Mr. Ryan." Then he ran a distance again and turned, waiting. As always, Melvin would come up to you, say his piece, and then turn and dash off ten feet or so.

They carried the luggage inside. Beth served iced tea and then uncovered a chocolate cake. They all talked at once. Melvin kept hugging Tim and moving around him. Mitch noticed how Tim kept looking at Beth and how she did not stray far from his side. She had become a lovely woman of twenty-five, and though Tim was younger by six years, they seemed to have grown even closer.

"Before we have the cake, there's a play. Come." They all shifted back out to the porch. "We have a surprise for you. A little show." Beth brought a bench to the top of the steps. "First, Melvin will give us a poem." Melvin froze. Beth put her hand on his shoulder and gently said, "Oh, yes, Melvin wrote this."

"It's not very good," Melvin ran up close to Tim's face, "not very good at all." Then he ran off a bit, turned, and announced, "But I wrote it because I love you and I'm glad you're home."

Melvin slowly took his place in front of them and began reciting in a weak voice not at all like his own. Tim came up and gave him a hug. "It's just us, Melvin. I want you to talk as loud as you can."

Melvin, loving the attention, began again, this time his voice booming one long, indecipherable, but passionately felt sentence:

> Alone in all his glory stood the knight.
> Always alone s-stumbling, wondering,
> Knight moving toward the l-light,
> Foolish knight to think that light was made of
> nothing…

Here Melvin launched into a little dance and sped things up. Mitch sneaked a look at Tim. He was relieved at how comfortably the boy was settling back into this life. He felt a pang of guilt for having been so worried.

Now Melvin really sped on.

> The inside f-flow of blood that starts in the heart
> And ends the same,
> The heart alone,
> The beginning and the end,
> Alone in all his g-glory stood the knight.

There was a long pause. Finally, Melvin took an abrupt bow, and they all applauded.

Tim jumped up and ran over to pump Melvin's hand. "That was a great present, Melvin. What a beautiful poem. Mitch, maybe you could get him a job. I had no idea you could read a line like that."

"He's been working on it for weeks." Beth moved to Tim's side and slipped her arm around his waist.

Melvin was so happy he danced up and down the yard. "Did you like it? Did you like it, my friend Tim?"

Suddenly Beth tensed and backed away from Tim. Melvin stopped dancing and looked up the lane toward the road. Mitch turned to see a tall young man walking slowly, indolently down past the first corral. He stopped to pat the horse that came to him. Mitch recognized something in the way the man leaned on the fence and then turned his face to the sun. Ritchie! He felt his throat tighten. Slowly Ritchie sauntered into the yard and up to the corner of the porch. As he approached, Mitch sensed a doom stronger than death as he watched the two boys touch fists.

"Hey, Tim, long time between drinks." Ritchie was smiling, but his mouth was small and mean, and there was a menace in the way he stood.

"Hey, Ritchie, you got tall—we both did."

Melvin could control himself no longer. "Go away, no one wants you here, you are not wanted, tell him to go, Tim." And he scooted around to hide behind Tim.

Mitch stepped forward. "Ritchie, he's right, you're not welcome here, so you had better leave." Tim looked at his father. The shudder that moved into him brought back the disgust at the dominating way this man had of intruding into his life. Ritchie and Tim had been great friends at school. Was it to start all over again?

"I'm going, Mr. Ryan." Ritchie moved closer to Tim and smiled. "Good to see you, man. Give me a call, we can kick around old times."

Tim shook his hand. "You look good, man."

"Take care, old scout. Ritchie turned and left.

They watched him stroll up the lane. At the end of it, he turned and waved.

Only someone who knows the slow horror of death by addiction could feel what traversed through Mitch's veins. "That one may smile, and smile, and be a villain…" He looked at Tim. He watched him smile, take Beth by the hand, and start for the house.

"Don't be afraid, Dad, I'm not going to get loaded, at least not today. Let's have some cake."

CHAPTER 43

Trouble
1987

MITCH PICKED UP the telephone. "Yes?"

"Tim left me. I thought you should know." It was Beth.

"Can you hold for a moment?" Mitch turned to the tall man who sat facing his desk, a man he had known for many years. They had started together as actors and had been partners launching a theater that had had some success. He was wearing a gray suit and a shabby, dirty shirt that made Mitch want to cover him with a blanket.

At this moment, he needed William Finch to leave. As Mitch had recently failed as a producer of a couple of independent films and subsequently gone bankrupt, so everything now smacked of mediocrity, of failure. This movie studio where he had leased an office reminded him at every turn of his languishing career. The dead script on his desk, the new one in William's hand, and the partially filled boxes around the room—all testaments to the impermanence of his life. And now Tim had disappeared.

This old friend sitting in front of him, the reminder of failure, wanted a favor. And from Mitch, no less, who surveyed those boxes that held his career in freeze-frame—a poster of *Moon for the Misbegotten*, a photo of Mitch and Lee Marvin—thinking how foolish it was to hang on to shadows of the past. He was leaving this office on the lot. He couldn't afford the rent. In fact, if he didn't get a job soon, he would have to leave his house. Now the height of absurdity was William wanting help to sell his screenplay.

"William, would you excuse me? It's about Tim. You remember my boy Tim."

"Sure." The tall, gray-faced man didn't move.

"Beth?"

"I'm here." She sounded weak.

"Are you all right? What happened? Where are you?" He scooted around the gray-faced man, immobile in his chair, and retreated to the window.

"I'm at the police station in Johnson City, Tennessee, and I don't know what happened. We stopped to eat, and he started to drink with some local men. I'm sick of the whole mess. I should never have come on this trip."

"Beth, go to the airport and come home." Mitch stepped around the boxes and returned to his desk. He had to be off the lot by the first. "William, this is personal." Then into the phone: "Do you have money?"

"Yes, I do." She spoke with shaky hesitation, and Mitch felt she was close to losing control.

"Beth, try to stay calm. You know what he's like. Wait a minute." He turned. "William, please!"

"I'll wait outside."

"I'll be a while. Call me tomorrow."

"No, I'll wait." He left.

Then to Beth: "Where's the car?"

"Gone, I doubt the police will find it." Her strained voice came across in short bulletlike bursts.

"The police will find the car, and they will find him."

"The police aren't very helpful." She paused. "These local guys probably stole the car. They were scary-looking men. I saw them in the bar. I couldn't stand to watch, so I headed back to the motel and went to bed."

Mitch waited, slapping his hand lightly on the desk, picked up the lease for this office, started to look through it, then put it down. "Beth, come home, there's nothing you can do. I've tried everything for years." He picked up the lease again and made a note to call his lawyer.

"We checked into a motel across the road from the bar." The words rattled out of her. "He'd been drinking for hours. Christ, what a mess. Your son's crazy when he drinks—helpless—and for some reason, he assumes everyone likes him. The ass." Mitch had heard the entire scenario hundreds of times. The lease was in his hand: three thousand dollars a month. He put it down and carried the phone to the window again. Beth continued. "So these boys took him to a juke joint, they called it, and left me alone. God, Mr. Ryan, he's such a bastard."

"Beth, stop. Stop talking and listen to me. Go right now to the airport and come home." Out the window, the rare rainy day in California reflected the depression that had descended into him, the hovering clouds adding to his gloom. "He will have to look after himself, and you do the same."

"Hold on, Mr. Ryan." Mitch heard muffled voices. He opened the sliding door and gulped in the fresh air, thinking he must leave this whole damn thing alone. "They located him, he's in a hospital, and they're going to take me there now. I'll call you when I get to the place."

Mitch returned the phone to his desk and walked slowly back out the sliding door to the covered balcony and watched the rain as the fine mist floated in under the eaves. The dampness rested on him. At that moment, he didn't give a damn if he ever saw Tim again.

He thought of his friend William waiting. He caught himself in the mirror on the way to let William back in, studied his face. Getting old. What he had for so long perceived in his deeply lined face as determination he plainly saw now as just stubbornness. He'd not had a drink for twenty-two years. He considered the life that was stored in those boxes. A failure in everything he tried, and his stepson a source of grief. His back tightened. He put his hands on his knees, rested for a moment, then went to the door. "Come in, William."

William was sweating. He came straight to the chair in front of the desk and sat back down. The nagging specter of his son in some hospital distracted Mitch from what William was saying. "It would be great to work together again… There's always something magic about a project when you're involved… I think it's your energy that's infectious…"

Mitch went back to the window and the rain, then turned and came right up to the strained man and said as gently as possible, "William, I am in no shape to help anyone. I'd love to be able to do something, but I'm in the crapper. I have to move off the lot, and I have no money and no job. No one would listen to me if I brought them *Gone with the Wind*."

"My play is what is needed now," William pronounced as a prophet. "It speaks to the young of today—the listlessness and unfocused children who are everywhere. Your touch, your magic touch, will bring this play to life if you will just get behind the project."

Mitch felt sickened by this fawning flattery. He thought of Tim and almost laughed at the irony of William's statement. "William, did you just hear what I said? I can't help myself right now, and also, my mind is a million miles away."

William stood up. "Putting me on the shelf, is that what you're doing? Well, I'll be goddamned!"

"William, you're not listening. My boy is in trouble."

"All these years, and you're giving me the bum's rush. I need this to be sold, and you can help if you will."

"God damn it, William, please leave."

The phone rang. "Beth?"

"He's all right, hurt but okay. He's in a hospital in Abingdon, Virginia. The people from the theater found him before the police. They've been decent about everything. Tim's pulling his usual 'I'm not worth it' act, and of course, they're buying it. The police want to talk to him, and I guess they will. I have a plane out of Knoxville at five."

"What happened? Does Tim know?" Mitch watched William sit. "Wait a minute, Beth—William, for God's sake, leave and call me later."

"I'll wait outside."

"Jesus Christ! William?" He was gone.

"Mr. Ryan? Are you there?"

"Sorry, I'm here. Where was he hurt?"

"All cuts and bruises on the face, broken ribs, and his hand's in a cast. A farmer found him and somehow got him to the hospital. They must have dumped him by the side of the road. They hurt him bad, but he's okay." Mitch heard her voice fade away to a breath.

"Beth, you sure you have everything you need?" She started to cry. "I wish there was something we could do."

"Don't cry, dear, and take care of yourself. Give me the number of the hospital and call me when you get back." He took the number, hung up, and looked at his hands. They were getting soft since he'd stopped working his horses. He locked the door, stood for a moment, then unlocked it.

William stuck his head in. "Mitch?"

"William, forget it! I can't right now, and you have got to stop pushing."

His friend stood in the door, stared at Mitch, finally looked down, then left. Mitch felt nothing he said would be helpful because at that moment, he couldn't help himself.

He went to the balcony. Down below, William slowly walked past Soundstage 21, not caring about the rain on his bare head. Mitch was reminded of the time he had run, in the drenching rain, to the top of a large hill. He had jumped a tall wooden fence and run the whole length of what had once been a cornfield. He ran as fast as he could all the way to the other side, climbed on the fence, and sat in the pouring rain. Virginia, years ago before he'd quit drinking. Now he turned, walked to his desk, and sat down. He picked up the silver letter opener his father had given him, feeling the weight in his hand. He looked at the phone, then the number Beth had given him in Virginia.

No peace, no joy, nothing. He needed to run in the rain again. He clutched the knife by the handle. "To be, or not to be, that is the question." He laughed out loud. "Wrong play."

CHAPTER 44

Winter People
1990

MITCH WAS ENJOYING the sound of the rain as he waited for his pie. Simple things were to his liking. Was he getting old? While it rained, the film cast sat in the Daniel Boone Motel in Banner Elk, North Carolina. The leading actor was having a hard time with the leading lady, who was not in good shape. The atmosphere of this second-rate—but first-class for Banner Elk—motel made him think they were passengers on a ship of fools, all these mismatched people with nothing to do but sit. The aimlessness of it all struck Mitch as tragicomic. He watched the cast of characters stand up and sit down, then stand up again and run to another room and do the same. With the interior sets still not built, the production had been brought to a halt by the rain. The entire cast and crew were jammed together on this island. All they could do was wait till the sets were finished or until it stopped raining. Or until they all died.

When he had arrived in North Carolina for *Winter People*, they had shot much less than the studio wanted in beautiful fall weather. Then the rains came, and the cast was not happy. The screenplay needed work. "Time is a-wasting," the AD would say every day. What else could happen?

"Never rains like this," the waitress announced as she brought his pie and coffee. "This is the rainy season, but never, ever like this.

You're from Hollywood." She laughed. "Never rains in Hollywood, and I've seen you in a million things. I know you'll get me a picture, but no hurry, I think you guys'll be here quite a while." They were her captive audience, and she couldn't have been happier. Beaming, she said, "Anything I can do for you, anything at all, just let me know." As she marched off, a queen in her realm, the leading lady came into view.

Leading Lady was restless, charging in and out of the bar with a drink. As Mitch sat eating his pie, watching her heading toward him, he had a deep urge to run.

Ro Diamond, his agent, had told him the story of *Winter People* over the phone. "They want you to read."

"Oh, Christ. Sure, that's okay."

"The story's set in the vast mysterious mountain forests of western North Carolina. It's a cross between *King Lear* and *Romeo*. And then there's your part."

"Wait! Don't get dramatic. Just send me the script and let me figure it out."

"I'm just so happy about the writing. It's like Shakespeare. You will love it." Well, it wasn't even close to Shakespeare, but the writing was rich enough, and it read well.

Leading Lady sat down and put her face in her hands. "I so admire you, Mitch, spending all that time doing plays, doing the great, great plays."

She was drunker than he thought, and why not, she was an Irishwoman. She looked like his mother with her big open face, high cheekbones, full lips, and dark red hair. She also had his mother's temper.

"Have you done many plays?"

"Several." She hesitated, then, "No, not many." His neck stiffened, and he thought about leaving again. He knew she wanted something. "Let's go in the bar. I want a drink. Come on." It was an order. He didn't move. "Come on, damn it, you don't drink, I know, but at least you can sit with me. Everyone else in this fucking movie hates me. Come." In the bar, she ordered a double vodka and crushed her cigarette into the ashtray. He tried to signal for his check.

She beat him to the punch. "Have you noticed the way this asshole director is treating me?" She didn't wait for an answer. "I can't work." The waitress brought the drink. "Bring me another."

"You want another one."

"What did I just say?"

"Sure, sorry."

"Also, the check." Mitch started to stand.

"Forget the check, sit down." He hesitated. "Oh, come on, stay with me a while, please." He sat. "Kurt is always polite, but I feel the resentment underneath." She took a long pull on the drink and lighted another cigarette.

Her state was getting to him, but he kept looking at her breasts and the hollow at the side of her neck, wondering, a suicidal thought, what it would be like to take her to bed. She was in bad shape, and he knew what she needed to do. But she was not ready to hear anything from him. He could say, "Cut the shit, quit drinking, and get some help," but he didn't.

Suddenly silence. He looked up. "Are you hearing anything I'm saying? I have nice breasts, don't I?"

He felt heat at the back of his neck. "Well, young woman, would you like to hear about my problems? When you get tired of yours, we could start in on mine." She laughed. She was beautiful when she laughed. "Look"—he felt close to her—"I hear you, I just don't know what to say. I would like to help, but...what?"

"Let's go to my room and see where we are."

"No, I don't think that would be a good idea."

"You think I want to fuck. Nothing is further from my mind."

"Well, it's not far from mine."

"Do you think I'm attractive?"

"Yes."

She blushed. The second drink came. She finished the first and started the next one. She stood and picked it up. "Come, I won't bite."

In her room, she sat on the bed, and he stood at the window, watching the rain driven sideways by the wind. "Tell me about how you started. Did you do plays at first? I know you did. I know you

FALL OF A SPARROW

did Iago." She rolled over on her back and kicked off her very expensive shoes. "Come and sit. First, bring that Shakespeare with you." She pointed at the coffee table. "Let's read some *Much Ado About Nothing*. I'll be Beatrice and you, Benedick." She leaped up and came right to his face. *"O that I were a man for his sake! or that I had any friend would be a man for my sake! But manhood is melted into courtesies, valour into compliment, and men are only turned into tongues, and trim ones too: he is now as valiant as Hercules that only tells a lie and swears it..."*

"Tarry, good Beatrice. By this hand, I love thee."

She smiled and moved back, then started to cry. *"I had rather hear my dog bark at a crow than a man swear he loves me."*

"That's good. Maybe sometime we could do a play."

"Oh! You're a pain in the ass." She hit him hard on the arm. He felt like a plaything. He turned and went to the door. Still crying, she sank down on the floor. He watched her act for a moment, then realized it wasn't an act, or if it was, at least it was a good act. He knelt down by her. She held out her hand. It was warm. "Would you read that big scene with me that we have coming up?" It was an act. Suddenly that was clear. She wanted to direct the scene to make sure he was not going to pull any surprises.

He stood up. "You don't need to read that scene. Down in your gut, you know what it's about, and you will nail it cold. Besides, you're drunk. What use would it be?"

"You're mad at me."

"I'm not mad. 'When the wind is southerly, I know a hawk from a handsaw.' This whole thing is your imagination. If you're worried about me, I'm with you and will be with you all through the rest of the shoot. That scene will take a whole day, and I'll take care of Ted so you can do your job. Just keep your attention on what you need to do."

"See, I knew you loved me." She stood up with difficulty, put her arms around his neck, and kissed him. "I lied!" She kissed him again. "It wasn't the furthest thing from my mind."

"See you in the morning." He left and went back downstairs, stood out in the shelter of the porch, and watched the relentless rain.

God, why do we drunks make life so difficult. Me, this actress, my son?
He hadn't seen Tim for almost two years. A great commiseration
welled up in him: this woman was terrified, and he too was always
battling some kind of fear, and fear stops life; he could see that. He
breathed in deeply, held out his hand for the rain to splash over it,
then brought the cold water to his face. For a moment, he was free.
Standing in this cheap motel in the wilds of North Carolina with all
the wind and the rain, a sense of calm settled into him. In a moment,
he saw that the inner turmoil that followed him everywhere was
nothing but an imagined world that had no substance, no reality.

As he stood in his reverie, he watched a large Greyhound bus
stop and a familiar figure jump down and run in the deluge from the
road up to the porch. It was Tim Ryan.

The boy landed on the porch with an air of determination and
stood grinning at Mitch. "Fancy meeting you here, Mr. Ryan. Do
you think I can get a job on this opus? Oh damn, I'm sorry, Mitch.
Don't mean to be flip. It's nice to see you." And then he was silent
and stood looking at the rain.

That Mitch was surprised was an understatement. He was torn
between genuine affection and a sense of dread at what his son was
doing here. The boy wasn't loaded and was wearing nice jeans and a
blazer. He looked like a young college student. He put his hand on
Tim's shoulder, and for a moment, he wanted to give him a hug. But
Tim turned toward the front door. "Come on, Mitch. Let's get in out
of the rain."

Inside, Mitch felt the air leave him and the warmth he had felt
leave too. They headed into the coffee shop. "What are you doing
in this part of the world? I thought you were still at the theater in
Virginia."

"No, Porterfield got me a nice job in Maine at a winter stock
theater. I hitchhiked to Arizona. And Mom gave me some money, so
I got a bus here. Now I need the bus fare to Maine. I wrote to Beth to
send some money. I tried to make it up with her, but it doesn't look
good." This all erupted in a burst of energy.

Mitch smelled a rat but said nothing, hoping it was just his
suspicious nature when it came to this boy. He seemed changed, and

at least he wasn't angry. But he wanted something, and Mitch felt maybe he would give him bus fare to get to Maine. All this came through him in the quick moment as they sat in a booth. Before anything could connect between them, the predatory waitress appeared, the blowsy hillbilly who was tickled to have a movie company in her command. "What's up, boys, what'll it be? You're new—you an actor?"

"Yes, I am," Tim said with a sly smile.

Mitch remembered when he first started how strange it was to say, "I'm an actor," and felt a closeness at that moment to Tim, who was unaware of it.

They ordered and were into their meal when the AD came running in. "Stopped raining, flood's over! Look out the window—sky's clearing and the sun is about to appear. It's a miracle! We're going to shoot a scene with you, Mitch."

"When?"

"Right now."

It was grand to get to work. They spent the rest of the afternoon shooting him on his horse, riding up to his manor house with his sons. It was dark when they got back. He had agreed with the makeup man to get out of his full-length beard back at the motel. Sitting in the makeup room chair next to the bar, he heard loud laughing and thought he recognized Tim's voice.

When he looked in, he saw Tim leaning, drunk on the bar, talking a mile a minute with his arm around a girl. The leading actress, stoned, was dancing behind him with a fat cowboy.

Still in his beard, he was pulled toward the bar. Tim saw him first. "Hey, Grandpa, look at that beard! Come and have a drink—oh, that's right, you don't drink. Smart, smart move, we all should quit."

The actress stopped dancing. She realized what was happening and took Mitch by the arm. "He can join us anyway. He's good at sitting and holding up his end."

Mitch tried to speak, but nothing came out. Tim stood. "Come on, Dad, relax, we're just having a little fun." He moved away from the bar and right toward Mitch, who backed away. The actress moved to get between them. "Dad, it's no big deal, don't worry, relax."

Mitch slapped him. The actress let out a muffled cry. Tim staggered back, looked at him in agony, then ran out of the bar. No one said a word. Mitch turned and walked back to the makeup room. To the chagrin of the makeup man, he tore off the beard and ripped it to shreds. He stalked to his room.

In the morning, Tim was gone. No one had seen him leave or knew how he had escaped from that lonely, isolated mountain village. It had started to rain again as Mitch stood on the porch and wondered if he would ever see Tim again.

CHAPTER 45

Cry Help
1992

MITCH LAY ON his back scanning the "brave o'er hanging firmament" that let a gentle breeze cool the hot sun on his tanned face. The outboard motor was off, and the boat floated in a lazy circle. He seldom caught anything but his fishing pole, held loosely in his hand, dangled off the side of the boat. It seemed lately he would allow himself to do nothing and surprisingly not feel guilty, thinking he must do something, get busy at life. He looked across the lake to the pines where they came down almost to the shoreline. Behind them near the top of the ridge stood the remains of ragged ancient volcanoes, second in the mountain hierarchy, giving way to the giant Sierra Nevada range, white and shining in the distance, looming as far as he could see.

Birds arrived and sat at the end of the boat—the sierra magpie, with the bright blue patch under each wing, and the bold black-hooded jay, who perched for minutes at a time. He recognized them. He knew them as he knew the lake and the fish in the water and the great range. In the safety of this knowing, he could wonder all over again, why had he been spared? He had quit drinking twenty-two years before, and most of the men he had drunk with were dead. He was alive, drinking in the miracle of the water shifting into different shades of green and silver as the breeze rippled over the lake. He had little money, but getting away up here to June Lake was a priceless necessity. The mountains fed him.

Something caught his eye. A woman was waving from the edge of the rustic dock. From her large straw hat, Mitch recognized her as the innkeeper of the lodge. He pulled the motor on and started back, not ready to come in yet but interpreting her energetic waving as urgent. The little boat putted along, used and loyal to him all the years he'd come here since *High Plains Drifter*. They had grown old together.

When he reached the dock and was climbing out of the boat, Mrs. Young came running up. She had what Mitch called a frontier face, burned and deeply lined. "Your son called," she handed him a slip of paper. "Said it was an emergency. Also, your agent called. She sounded angry.

Standing on the dock holding the line, he turned to the lake and the mountains—all the beauty had disappeared.

"Here, let me have that line."

"What?"

"I'll take the line."

"Oh, thank you, Mrs. Young."

"Marion, please." She blushed, taking the line to tie it off.

"Everyone in Hollywood is not angry, they just seem that way."

Mitch walked toward his cabin and stopped by two tall redwoods of the few left. What did Tim want?

Inside his small cabin, he sank into the overstuffed armchair and picked up the phone, debating, and called his agent first. The sun came flashing down from the skylight, piercing the dimness of the room, and illuminating the myriad dust particles that shined like tiny diamonds. No answer but he let it ring, remembering the hideous night in North Carolina when he had last seen Tim. Still ringing. He had felt some hope and pride when Tim had spent time at the theater in Virginia. Tim had stopped drinking and was working at acting.

No one answered at the agents. "Damn it, they call and then can't be found." He hung up. When Tim had returned to California after the Barter Theater, he had become even more than usually remote, which to Mitch meant only one thing: he was using. He couldn't deal with Tim's denial and collected rage at imagined or real injustices, and they had had a stupid fight, after which Tim had disappeared again for several years until he showed up in North Carolina. God knows where he had been. Mitch dialed the agent again. When Tim did show up in North Carolina, Mitch made the decision not to deal with him on any level until he sobered up. After a moment, he was pounding the phone on the stuffed arm of the chair when he heard Ro's voice. "Hello, who's there?"

"Ro, what's up?"

"Mitch, are you sitting down?"

"No, Ro, I'm standing looking out over a crystal lake preparing to jump in and—"

"How would you like to go to New York?"

"What?"

"Alan Pakula is directing a movie with Harrison and Brad, and I have a firm offer for you to play the chief of police, but the money's not too good. You should do it. It's in New York. I did my best. How do you like that?"

Mitch burst out laughing and dropped the phone, then grabbed it back. "That is great news, Ro. You have no idea."

Ro told him he had to be in New York with Alan Pakula, Harrison Ford, and Brad Pitt ready to shoot *The Devil's Own* in a month. "Also, Tim called. He left a number. I gave it to the lady up there. I hope he's all right."

"Thanks, Ro, and great about the offer."

They hung up. Mitch carried the phone out to the porch. Taking deep breaths and wondering what kind of trouble Tim was in, he called the number. Someone picked up, then nothing.

"Tim?"

"Dad?"

"Yes..." Tim didn't answer right away. Mitch struggled to leave a space. "What is it?"

"Dad, I'm really fucked up. I got beat up and rolled, think my hand's broken... I know it's a lot to ask but..." Mitch waited. "Dad?"

"I'm here."

"I wouldn't ask, but I think I'm done… If you could come and take me home to California… Maybe we can start over or…" Mitch waited some more, letting him talk. "I could get well or…Jesus, my face hurts too. Say something, Dad."

"Where are you?"

"Right now, I think…I don't know…I'm in a loft somewhere down below Houston Street. I can get to St. Vincent's ER. Can you meet me there?"

"Isn't there someone who can help you?"

"No, not a one. If you don't want to come…"

"I'll come. Go to St. Vincent's and get help. Tell them I'll be there tomorrow morning."

"Thanks." Tim's voice sounded small and far away.

"Go to St. Vincent's, I'll see you in the morning." He put the phone down and paced to the edge of the porch to look out over the silver-blue lake. "Fuck this."

He headed toward the dock to go back to his fishing but only got past the shade of the two redwoods guarding the path to the lake before he stopped in the sun and stood like a deer hearing death in the woods. He was alive in every part, like the trees. What had he done for this boy? What had he done to this boy? Was there a reason why he never made the right effort when life included Tim? Was their estrangement because of some organic clash between the man and boy? Or some flaw in Mitch's character: a missing something that sparked the anger and thwarted any tenderness or love or even civility that he would show to any human?

He walked back through the shade into the house and dialed. "Ro, would you make a reservation on the red-eye to New York, any airline, for tonight?"

"You don't have to be there for a month."

"I know. Don't ask."

Mitch took the red-eye to New York. In the cab driving to Manhattan on the Van Wyck to the Grand Central Parkway and on the long approach of the Triborough Bridge, high above Queens and over Randall's Island, the skyline of the city pulled out of him, like speeded-up film, all the long-forgotten past—all the plays, the bars, the women, the love, the despair, the laughter—everything he had lived through there. But this time, there was no thrill.

Heading to the hospital, he sat staring out the smudged taxi window at the featureless streets of the city. Down to the Lower West Side in the early morning, he watched the dregs of humanity waking up, gathering up their cardboard beds, and facing just one more day.

He walked into St. Vincent's, went up to the information desk, and checked the clock: 7:30 p.m. "Is there a Tim Ryan in a bed?"

A large black lady in a print dress consulted her computer. "Nothing on the books."

"Where's the ER?"

A harried younger doctor bearing a look of "This is not what I had in mind" answered, "You related?"

"Yes."

He started back to a black man moaning on a gurney, then turned and returned to the stricken Mitch. "We cleaned him up, but I turned around, and he was gone. Looked in bad shape. A lot of pain."

"Do you know what time he was here?"

The doctor was in front of the moaning man who was holding his arm. "Hold on, help is on the way, try to lie still." To Mitch, he said, "Sir, check at the night desk and see what time they logged him in."

Tim was not ready to quit, after all. Mitch looked around at the bare white walls and chrome chairs and started for the exit, trying to push away his endless rage and disgust, when the police entered half-carrying a man with blood all over his neck, screaming in pitiful, blind fury. The officers dropped him on a bench. "Shut up." The black man continued to moan on his gurney in the corner. Mitch could only stand and watch, trapped in this waste and pain that had at one time been so much a part of his life. Now having been suckered into believing Tim again, he felt like a fool.

More forcefully than he realized, he turned on the night nurse. "Do you have a time—?" She looked up. Her face told all. Mitch leaned his hands on the desk. "Oh, I'm sorry, forgive me. Do you have a checkout time on Tim Ryan?"

She rummaged through the log. "They clocked him in at 4:00 a.m. He was here I'd say two or three hours. I was pretty busy, so I didn't see him leave."

Mitch looked at his watch: nearly 8:00 p.m. Where would he have gone? To search out a drink at the nearest bar.

He walked out onto Seventh, looked both ways, and turned down toward the Village. The bars were already opening. Lying in front of the first bar was a derelict. As Mitch got closer, he recognized a filthy motionless Tim Ryan, wearing an old cord coat, stained shirt, and pants. His face was sallow, and one hand was bandaged. Mitch wasn't shocked. This was a drunk's logic—to leave a place and go to the closest bar.

"Hello, Mr. Ryan, how'd you find me?"

"How's your hand?"

"My hand hurts. I was in a blackout."

"I think we should go back to the hospital and let them tend to your hand."

"I'm going to have a drink first." He got up on one knee.

"If you want help, don't go in there."

"Just one." He leaned on the wall.

"I didn't fly across the fucking country to sit in a bar with you."

"Come on, just one." Tim pulled himself erect and shuffled into the bar.

Mitch stood for a moment, calming his rage. Like one who knows the end at the beginning, he stood staring up Seventh Avenue, unable either to leave or to go into the bar. Finally, he went in.

The Shamrock was one of a chain all over Manhattan. A large handwritten sign sat like a challenge behind the bar: "Double Shot of VAT 69—55 Cents." Bright fluorescent lights buzzed in the ceiling and made everyone look green, like the hard-boiled eggs on the counter. Several men, one indistinguishable from the other, slouched around tables at the far end of the long room. Tim ordered rum. Mitch's hand gripped the bar. "One simple thing to understand is that when you quit drinking, it means you don't drink. No matter what."

"I heard that." Tim nodded, picked up the rum, looked straight ahead, and took a sip as if Mitch wasn't there, then gagged, rum running down his chin.

"Isn't it difficult to navigate rum in the morning? I always got started with a cold beer." Tim turned and looked at Mitch for the first time, his face a white mask. "Did you know your father? You never mentioned him. You must have had one. What was he like?"

Mitch held Tim's gaze.

"What was your father like?"

"He's dead. He died almost forty years ago."

"But you must remember him. Did he drink? What work was he doing? Were you close? Did he love you?" Tim turned away and took another sip of rum.

"My father drank some. He was in the First World War. He suffered, as most men do in war, but he never talked about it. He was the opposite of me. Charles was his name. Quiet, didn't talk much. I never knew what he was thinking. He was like you. You look like him."

"Did you feel he understood you?"

Mitch turned to the front door, where a shaft of bright sunlight shot through the murky bar. He wanted to leave. He always wanted to leave. Instead, he ordered a soda water.

"Mr. Ryan, it's a simple question. Do you feel he understood you?"

"No, I don't think he did. But it wasn't his fault."

"Whose fault was it, then? Yours?"

Mitch slammed his fist on the bar. Tim didn't flinch. "No one is to blame. He was who he was, and he did what he did, just like you. He was a man with problems he couldn't understand."

"Bullshit."

"'Bullshit.' What does that mean, 'bullshit'?" Tim seemed to draw down into himself and get smaller. "God, Tim, can't we talk? We have never been friends, and are we always going to have this same problem? We can't go on blaming and finding fault. *No one is to blame!*" Several of the men looked up in mild protest. Mitch walked to the end of the bar, stood for a moment, then turned and came back. "You said you wanted to stop drinking. Unless we can talk, there is no way out."

"Another, please."

"Tim, don't drink anymore."

"Just one more."

"You said you wanted to quit. If you're going to drink, I'm leaving.

"Leave."

"I'm going to the hospital. You have to take care of your hand. Come with me."

"Go. I'll be right there."

Mitch turned and leaned back against the bar. In front of him were two old men sitting at a table and staring at the drinks in front of them.

"Did you love your father?"

Mitch had no voice.

"Did he love you?"

Mitch stood there for a long time before he left.

He walked out of the bar and down the street. He knew Tim would leave. The day had clouded over, and a light rain started to fall. He stepped into a doorway. Why hadn't he stayed and brought Tim to the hospital? Why had he left him? In the rain, he hurried back to the bar.

"He was out right after you." Mitch went out into the rain looking, with no hope, in both directions. He waited a while, the gentle rain on his cheek, then hailed a cab. The mist looked like a million tiny black slashes on the neon screen across the street at the corner of Seventh Avenue and Fourteenth.

"Where to?"

"JFK."

"Where you headed?"

"Los Angeles."

"Great country out there."

"Yes, it never rains in California."

CHAPTER 46

Three Movies for Minimum and the IRS
1992

WHEN MITCH LEFT the audition and headed for the Warner Bros. gate, the heat of the valley smacked him in the face. Everything around him seemed to fade into everything else, as if the sun had thrown a haze on the trees, buildings, even the people, and washed all color away. Walking to the studio parking lot, he was aware of a woman heading toward him as his inner monologue babbled on and on. After all these years, at sixty-two, to end up with no money and the IRS threatening to take most of what there was of his paycheck. He had heard nothing from Tim, and as the years slid by, the boy had receded, brought back to mind only now and then by some fragmented association. Tim's mother would call and ask if Mitch had seen him. The picture on his mantle of the boy with Lynda might as well have been invisible.

As the woman moving toward him came into focus, Mitch had a feeling he knew her. He stopped and waited for her to pass. She was several feet away, staring back at him, and he knew he was right—but from what part of his life did she come? He'd known so many people. Where had they all gone?

"Mitchell, is that you? Of course it is, what an amazing thing, running into you!" He remembered her from the Actors Studio in

New York years before. Sandra Seacat. They had done a unique and wonderful summer production of *Uncle Vanya*."

"Sandra, I might say the same thing about you." That long-ago summer, they were all performing in plays in New York, and several of them had decided to do some work on Chekhov during the day.

He took her arm. "Let's get a coffee and catch up."

"Sure. What are you doing at Warner Bros.?" Mitch was flooded with memories of that *Uncle Vanya*. They had worked every day at the Studio, which was closed in the summer, so they had the famous space all to themselves. "I'm with Jessica, but I'm going to see about a job here." They entered the café in the Executive Office Building. "She's doing a movie with Tommy Lee Jones. *Blue Sky*." He remembered Sandra was Jessica Lange's coach.

The dining room at Warner Bros. was very plush and a grade or two above the actors' cafeteria. They sat. The waiter came. "Two coffees and some apple pie. Jessica won't mind if you do a movie for yourself?"

"I am an actress first."

"Yes, you are."

"Is there anything in Jessica's film for me?" He wanted to take his question. "Remember that great summer?" He took her hand.

"Would I ever forget it?"

"Who's directing?" The coffee came. The waiter said to him, "Were you in the Hemingway play?"

"Yes, I was."

"You were excellent. I remember seeing it when I was still in school." Mitch thanked him, and he left.

"I'm going to need his job pretty soon." Mitch smiled and looked into Sandra's wide-open face. They were still holding hands.

She looked at him in a peculiar way. "No, I don't think so, a lot of generals and Atomic Energy people—no good parts. How can you be broke?"

"Do you want the long version, including a rundown of my weaknesses, or the short version, where I blame the 'industry'?"

She laughed. "Tony Richardson is directing. He loves your 'weaknesses,' and the industry is a mess. You did *Antony and Cleopatra* with Tony. I'm sure he'd be glad to see you. He's at MGM."

As he left Warner Bros., Mitch was flooded with memories of those deep days, workshopping *Vanya*. The things that could be done when the time was given, and the knowledge was there! All of them, the whole cast, showed up every day and sometimes worked ten or more hours. The choices each actor made became so original that they had astonished each other.

MGM had been sold, and Sony had bought the legendary lot. Nothing had physically changed, though, and the large gate was still there, sans the MGM sign. Most of the huge soundstages were empty or being used for TV. The dressing rooms remained the same, the names still on the doors—Tracy, Gable. He had worked here twenty years ago. His sadness was tinged with panic as he considered the fast-fading past.

Tony gave him a warm handshake and asked how he was. His face was gaunt, and he was bent over. Mitch knew he had AIDS and wondered if he had strength enough to take the strain of filming.

"I am in need of a job." Mitch felt like Willy Loman.

"Well, dear boy, there is not a thing worthy of your interest in this epic."

"I'm not particular, anything will do." He could feel the sweat in his armpits. The gaunt man who was dying looked at Mitch and understood in a moment. "Ah, there is a part, the head of the Atomic Energy Commission. He has several scenes in the beginning and near the end. There's not much money. Wait, I'll get you a picture deal. How's that?"

"That would be generous, thank you."

"Think nothing of it, dear boy, it will be an asset having you there. We are shooting in Texas and Alabama."

A picture deal is a minimum for the run of the film. As he walked slowly out of the lot to his car, he recollected that a picture deal amounted to forty-five thousand dollars. Counting his money, he bumped into an actor he knew who was running toward the gate. "Mitch, hey, *Lethal Weapon* was on last night. Great picture!"

"Thanks."

"Been to see Richardson?"

"No." Why did he say that? Mitch asked himself. Why did he say no? What was he afraid of?

"Well, wish me luck," the actor said and dashed past the gate. Mitch watched him and realized that he had just taken the man's part. The actor was his age, didn't work much, and played bank presidents and salesmen—and Atomic Energy commissioners.

Mitch flew to Alabama. He had always wondered about Alabama and the racist clichés that the state seemed to embody. They would be shooting at a decommissioned air force base near the holy city of Selma.

"Hello, Mr. Ryan. Welcome to the St. James Hotel," said a beautiful black man in the most friendly and open way."

"Thank you. So this is where Dr. King started it all."

"Yes, it is." He took Mitch's bag.

No one from the production was around, and the desk clerk told him there was no reservation for a "Mitchell Ryan."

"If you get in touch with the film company, I'm sure they will fix that." Mitch stood there, not knowing what to think. The obvious explanation was that they had forgotten all about him, but he shrugged and walked outside.

The little city of Selma rolled back from the lazy Alabama River. The doorman had told him to look at the plaque at the base of the Edmund Pettus Bridge. He walked down to the levee and saw the large stone pillars holding up the bridge. Hidden behind one pillar in a dense overgrowth of foliage, he found a small plaque: "Here, on March 7, 1965, Martin Luther King Started the Historic March to Montgomery."

He walked from there up the main street and into the town. After a block or two of Woolworths and the like, he saw substantial old houses with large front yards. Within a short three blocks, he came to a park, across from which was clearly "black town." There was no sign; he could tell just by the worn but well-tended houses and shabby front yards.

There was no visible problem anywhere in Selma. Now it was simply a small Southern town with a large black section and a much smaller white section, and they did not meet. Peaceful is what he would call this town. But walking through the tired bleak neighborhood, he was shocked at his total ignorance of the life of blacks in the South. The deeper he walked, the more run-down the places became. Some of the houses were jerry-rigged; others were literally falling apart. All the streets needed repair. The children played noisily like all kids, but their mothers looked tired, and the men were not to be seen.

He retreated in quick order. The way the blacks lived unnerved him and tapped into feelings that sent him back, brought up too many things that had been buried for too long—things that could be forgotten only if he drank, but now, without drink would burst through, harshly and bitterly and inconveniently, to make his life unbearable. His visit to his Indian friend had redirected much of his thinking, but his being had yet to catch up sufficiently. He was still permeated by all the habits of his long-indulged life. He recalled the old bum in the woods of his childhood, stripped of life and living in a fantasy, or the men in Stanley's and all the bars where he had lingered, or his son Tim, that boy who was such a heartbreaking wreck. The endless waste. Walking fast, back through the comfortable white neighborhood, he told himself he frankly didn't give a damn. He directed his focus to where he was going to sleep that night.

Back at the hotel, a sweet young girl introduced herself as the AD. "I'm so sorry, Mr. Ryan, about the mistake. You are billeted at the Budget Inn." She looked embarrassed. "It's really very nice. I'll take you there, but first, would you like to go to the office and get your per diem?" The office was in the Holiday Inn and consisted of a large suite of rooms, one for the payroll and another where someone was auditioning actors. There was a sign: "Blue Sky Readings. Older Men Needed for Army Personnel and Government Types, Also Extras." He drew his money, sat down in the lobby, and wondered how he would get through the next ten weeks.

He didn't work for several days. When he did, it was only a large party scene at the army base. All the military brass and high-rank-ing civilians, including members of the Atomic Energy Commission, were in the scene to celebrate the great progress of the AEC. It was one of those scenes that couple the principals talking to the extras. He had no lines, but at a certain moment in the scene, some general pointed out to Tommy Lee that Mitch was the head of the Atomic Energy Commission. When Tommy Lee saw Mitch, he came over and introduced himself. *Electra Glide in Blue* should have knocked you to the moon. They handled the selling of that film in the most stupid way. It's a great picture, and you were great in it. Let's have dinner tonight. You're staying at the St. James? They have pretty good food." Then he was called to work.

That first day Mitch was called at 6:00 a.m., and around 3:00 p.m., Jessica arrived on the set and came right over to him and said hello. "I'm glad you're here. Sandra said she ran into you. God, I'll never forget that *Uncle Vanya*. Can you beat that Sandra girl who got a job in a movie? The nerve." She laughed.

Then she, too, went to work, and he tried to cope with his feeling of displacement by reading the sports page for the third time.

He didn't have dinner with Tommy Lee. He watched TV on his Budget bed. The IRS put a lien on his house.

CHAPTER 47

Phone
1993

WHEN AN ACTOR is humbled and brought to a place where his whole life has become worthless, some men wake up to the fact that they are not just actors. They are not what they do, but what they are. Now this brings up a question that has never occurred to them, what are they? "Who am I?" And such questions lead to a state of perpetual agitation and many sleepless nights, or these men make the smart choice and run to escape in any form. There are many ways of escaping, from the ultimate, death, all the way down to hiring on as assistant floor director of a soap opera. Mitch somehow did nothing. He sat and read, found great joy in the classics, went for long walks near his little ranch in Agoura, and God forbid started to write his memoir. He kept it in the back of his mind to go and live in New York with the surety that the theater would welcome him back with open arms. He had worked his way through the sad and torturous eight weeks of this last movie and was thankful to Tony Richardson for the small but helpful money it paid. He had heard nothing from his agent, and it seemed, he joked, "I'm retired!"

He still lived at the ranch in Agoura and on this night, sitting on the porch watching the golden sun set through the grandfather oaks, he pondered a divided thought "whether 'tis nobler" to linger here peacefully till death which must someday come, or to go to an AA meeting… The phone sounded like the lonely knell of vespers in the slow evening. He thought of not answering, but only for a moment; the habit of rushing to get the call for success was too ingrained.

"Collect call from Tim Ryan. Will you accept?"

"Hi, Dad, what's up?"

Thousands of distant impressions flooded his mind. What came out first was even to his thinking inadequate. "Tim! Where are you?"

"I'm in Hawaii, trying to make some money. I told you I was going."

"I don't remember that. It's been a year since we heard from you." There was a long faint familiar sigh. Then a pause. "Tim?"

"I'm here."

"What I mean is, son, I wondered if things were turning out to be what you wanted."

"So, Dad, what I wanted was to make some money, to get my head straight."

"And how is that going?" Another pause.

"Dad, I think you were supposed to say, 'Tim, how are you? How great of you to call.'" Mitch heard the phone rustle and the noise of a bar. He's loaded. He remembered their last face-to-face meeting in New York when he had flown from LA to help Tim, and the boy had run away.

"Tim, I want nothing more than to help you, but you make it difficult. This part is something you need to handle on your own. I can always help you if you decide to quit drinking and using and continue with acting. You can come back, get straight, and begin to study again."

"That's a very pretty speech and rings a bell. Well, I may and I may not."

Mitch's first instinct was to hang up, but he stopped. "I would like to see you sometime. So would your mother."

"Why is it always up to me to say 'I'm sorry'?"

"I think we all have to say 'I'm sorry.' But it's hard, Tim, you have to admit, for us to talk when you are like this. Have you been using?" No answer. "You can't phone two or three times a year and expect much. I have told you a thousand times if you want to get clean and sober, I'll be there. It's up to you." He heard a loud thud. Like a dropped phone. And a Tom Waits's song on a speaker. He must be in a bar.

"Hey, Dad, what's with the lecture? I just called to say hello. To see how you were doing. Hawaii is a great place. You've been here. Maybe you could take a little time and come over."

"Tim, you've been drinking and probably more. I know, Tim. I've been there."

More noise, a smash of some kind. "Yes, again, you are right and right and right. You have been everywhere. Done everything. It's amazing your grasp of the plain facts of life. I don't suppose you could send me a few bucks? Dope is a little more expensive in the islands, which is odd, don't you think? I mean, I would have thought it would be cheaper…" There was static on the line, then some shuffling noises, then a muttered "Goddamn," then, "I'm sorry, Dad."

"Tim…" The boy said nothing. Mitch pictured the boy, the bar, and the wall phone and was sick with pity, horror, and helplessness. He could see the cheap joint, smell the whiskey and cigarettes, and feel the horror.

"Jesus." A loud sob. "Too hard. Just too hard. Wanted to say hello is all."

"Yes, it's hard. But we care, Tim, your mother and I. All you have to do is stop, son."

"Fuck, fuck, fuck, fuck, fuck, I want to talk to my father, and all I get is…Nothing."

"Tim, Tim, I just want—" Coin return, and the connection ends.

At the desk, Mitch slumped, put the phone down, and run his hands over his face. He wanted to rip it off, tear it to shreds. Abused. Why does Mitch feel abused? Couldn't it be possible to feel more for the boy in grave trouble? What kind of man was he? A hopeless father. No human sympathy, kindness, caring. Why else would the boy call? *He called asking for help, stupid!* Not words. *And all he felt was, I'm abused. All I feel is me—my problems—my feelings!*

He was suddenly very tired and headed to the bedroom. It seemed like Mitch had been up for a week. Before he lay down, he

revised his outburst to, "Well it's not all my fault, it takes two people pulling together to have any kind of relationship. God, my head
is killing me. Well, I won't think about that today." He laughed.
"Tomorrow, Scarlet, is time enough."

It was 4:00 a.m. Mitch lay for hours before he could sleep. Tim's
words, "You are right and right again," kept ringing in his head. A
telescope moved back through their life, and he watched the festering
like some disease. Of course, he was right, and he had never found a
cure or a remedy, never listened to the boy. He was convinced he was
right in his advice. Right and right and right. A shallow sleep finally
helped him forget.

Then, sounding like the blare of a fire engine, the telephone
rang once, twice, three times. He opened his eyes, looked at his
watch, five in the morning, no, no—could it be his son again? Tim's
angry words from last night had broken something in him. "Yes,
again, you are right and right and right. You have been everywhere,
done everything. It's amazing, your grasp of the plain facts of life."
Mitch sat up. Dawn came through the window. He rolled over and
stood up. The answering machine came on. "Hello, Mr. Ryan, this is
the Honolulu police." Halfway out of bed, he stopped to look toward
the office, where the call was being recorded. Police were calling.
Through the bedroom door, into the hall, and at the office door, he
heard the policeman again. "Mr. Ryan, are you there?"

Mitch sat in the desk chair and picked up. "Yes, I'm here."

"Mr. Mitchell Ryan?"

"Yes?"

"Do you have a son named Tim?"

"Yes? What is it?"

"He's had an accident, and he's in critical condition."

Critical, what is critical? A current of dread went up his back.
The stillness all around his office was oddly loud. Mitchell carried
the phone to the window.

"Mr. Ryan?"

"Yes, yes. Where is he?"

"Honolulu General." Mitch heard the policeman's voice, but
the man seemed to be speaking to a large class of rookie cops. "It was

a motorcycle accident. No one else was involved." At the window, he watched a family of small birds at the birdbath, ducking their heads to drink. "He has severe head trauma, and they're going to operate this moment. Oh yes, you need to know: he had a .20 blood alcohol content." Mitch watched the birds fly away when a large grackle dropped into the water. "Also, he wasn't wearing a helmet. I advise you to come as soon as possible."

Mitch took the number of the hospital, thanked the officer, and hung up. The desk seemed miles away. Miles to go before I rest, he put down the phone. Then he opened the top drawer, then another, and found a photo of Tim. An ironic smile and wild blond hair dominated his Irish face, but if you looked closely, the eyes radiated a depth of sadness. Mitch picked up the picture and carried a snapshot out through the French doors and into the backyard. He walked slowly to the middle of the yard and stood holding the picture. He slowly raised his head toward the sky as the gray light of early dawn filtered through the trees and slowly changed to gold. Two doves sat close to each other on a low limb of one of the linden trees. In the soft light of early morning on one of those exquisite Southern California winter days, he fell into one of the teak deck chairs. He shook his head and started to cry. The endless years.

CHAPTER 48

Hawaii
1993

THE LANDING GEAR lowering jarred him as they approached Honolulu. Mitch looked down out of the airplane window into the shining ocean traced with the white ridges of surf pulsing endlessly toward the shore. What was your father like? Did he love you? Tim's questions haunted him. Did your father love you? Did the boy want love? Mitch had none to give.

Once the plane landed, the soft, warm air had no salutary effect on him. Usually, he loved coming here, but today he hurried through the crowd of pasty tourists arriving and sunburned ones leaving and caught a bus to the car rental. He dreaded seeing his son in a coma. He didn't even know how he felt except that he was angry and nagged by a dull headache. There was no pity, no softness, and no tenderness.

He entered the ICU behind a serious horse-faced doctor. "We did all we could with the operation, but his condition is grave. He's in a coma, hasn't moved since we brought him down from surgery. I'll have the x-rays shortly…suppose you know he had a very high blood alcohol content."

"I was told."

"The trauma was caused when the skull hit the concrete bunker. The operation helped relieve the pressure on what was left of the brain. The hemorrhaging drove the brain almost to the other side of the skull and is pushing down on the stem…May I be frank?"

"Go ahead."

"We are going to operate again, in several days, to relieve the pressure because we can't stop the internal bleeding, but I don't see much hope. I'm sorry. He likely won't have any brain function. We may be able to save his life, but he will be helpless. You should try to prepare the women."

"His mother's here?"

"And his wife. They just left to eat something."

Nothing in Mitch moved. He was alone in a vast emptiness. He saw the glare of the lights jutting out in long rows across the ceiling from wall to wall. He could detect in the doctor's face the lines of care like scars. How many dead and mutilated young men had he seen? He didn't hear the doctor until he spoke again.

"What?"

"I must get to work." The doctor turned.

"Yes, thank you. Is there any coffee?"

"Yes, at the end of the corridor, turn left. A machine."

Mitch started down the hall then looked back at the ICU. His hands, cold as death, rubbed together as he stood at the doorway. Cube-shaped areas were sectioned from the others by white curtains suspended from tracks in the ceiling. He stood at the threshold, the pressure of the years weighing on his chest, then he fled down the hall and found the coffee. The machine kept rejecting his bill. In a strange stupor, he watched the dollar go in and slide out, go in and slide out. Finally, it worked, and he spilled the hot liquid, burning his hand, then threw the cup and the coffee into the trash and moved back down the hall like a maimed animal to where the doctor had pointed.

Dead. Tim was dead. He pulled the curtain aside and moved forward. The back of the bed was raised, and Tim was sitting up. Mitch sat down on a chair by the door. He raised his head to look at the boy. On both sides of the bed were all kinds of machines, some with tubes running to Tim's arm and others to his mouth. Behind his head on the wall was a painting of a field of cows.

Mitch stood and walked up to the bed and looked straight into Tim's face. Except for the large bandage around the top and one side of his head, you would think he was asleep. It seemed he would open his eyes at any moment and come out with one of his quips. The face had a calm, unhurried look, thoughtful and ready to be engaged. Mitch's hands trembled, and he swallowed hard. He backed to a table in the corner and let out a sound that was something between an unintelligible curse and a moan. He wanted to smash the peaceful, beautiful face to make him understand what he had done, what had been doing for years. The thoughts began running like hot water through his mind, and his body jerked and convulsed with every silent question. *Why are you here? Did this happen outside some sleazy bar? What are you doing with a motorcycle? Who gave it to you? What did you say to me on the phone earlier? Were you afraid? Did you do this because you hate me? Does this have anything to do with me? Did you think of your mother, your daughter?* Thoughts convulsed in a fury of energy. Then he was exhausted, and the dry tears burned his eyes. *He won't die*, Mitch told himself. *He looks too peaceful.* All he heard was the rasp of the ventilator. *Oh God, he will die.* He remembered Tim standing at that bar in New York. He saw the torn coat. The feeling of helplessness paralyzed him. What he said on the phone the other night, was it true? This was a reality he couldn't live with. He turned to leave. Tim's mother was at the door with Beth.

"Oh God," Beth said.

Mitch walked out. In the hall he slumped on a bench. He remembered his father in the coffin.

He strode to the elevator, hit the main-floor button, then saw the stairs and charged down the three flights and out to the sparkling Hawaii day. There was an assault of light. Red and brown bodies streaked by—backs, legs, breasts—then cabs and cars with no tops. He knew what he needed to do: find out how this happened. How Tim had got hold of a motorbike. Beth had given him the address where Tim worked, a mall near the beach on Hotel Row.

Hitting the street, he was propelled toward his car. The need to find out anything seemed somehow related to his car and filled his mind, crowding out the pain and guilt. Someone Tim worked with could surely tell him about the boy.

He drove around in that fog that comes over you when you don't know what you're looking for, trying to remember something you forgot. He was filled with a powerful pull to find out what might relieve this gut ache. Suddenly it dawned on him that Hotel Row must mean all those hotels along Waikiki Beach. He parked the car. People were everywhere.

He pushed his way through the throng and moved past several hotels, huge gaudy imitations of the grand past, the Royal British Arms, the Belvedere. Like a back lot, the whole line of self-conscious buildings looked like scenery, a façade, a movie set. Through the gaps between hotels, the ocean was a mere backdrop, a scrim. Then near a large roundabout formed by three streets meeting, he saw off to the left a mall. Moving down the large half-enclosed complex, he came to an opening with a view of the ocean through a garden and stood there for a moment, wondering what Tim would have thought of this view. Suddenly it wasn't a movie backdrop but beauty and color, the sea, an indescribable blue of many different shades, traces of the islands in the distance. Did Tim see the beauty or a Hollywood back-drop? Next to this opening was a kiosk with a man holding a kitch-en-related implement and, beside him, a lovely young girl. A small crowd was gathered in front.

After the man finished his spiel, Mitch asked, "Do you know if Tim Ryan is working today?" The man looked Mitch over and walked to the back of the kiosk. "No, he doesn't work here; he was useless and a hopeless drunk. I fired him."

"Do you happen to know where he lives?"

"No, and I don't care. I hope never to see the bum again."

Mitch felt his throat constrict. Resisting his welling of anger, he turned to leave. Anne, the assistant who had been listening, said, "I know where he lives."

They were sitting in a coffee shop. "Are you his father?"

Every part of Mitch suddenly wanted to bolt, but after a moment, he said, "Yes, I am."

"I need to tell you how I feel about Tim, which is the opposite of Mr. Donner, the boss. Tim is a sweet, caring man."

Mitch sank down in himself, his head bent over toward the table. Tim was no more. "Are you all right?" He slowly raised his head and looked at her. She was blond and shy but had a presence. For a young woman, he guessed twenty-two, her body was composed, not moving all the time like most young people's. "I'm fine, just tired."

"Your son, when he worked here, had a hard way about him but was always kind to me. Everyone liked him. He did drink too much, but he was very good at selling."

Mitch felt his back against the booth seat and his hands on the table—anything that would signal that he was really here in this place. He called the waitress. "Just coffee."

"May I be honest with you?"

"I hope so."

"I only knew him for a month, but I could see right away that he was very unhappy. The only time he seemed free and content with himself was when he would do Shakespeare, and he would recite that at the drop of a hat. When he was selling or in the bar, he would give a show for everyone. They all clapped and thought it was great. So did I. You could see he loved Shakespeare and was a good actor with a beautiful voice."

Mitch turned away from her and moved up to the counter. "Could you hurry with the coffee? We're a little late." Taking deep breaths, he came back to the table.

"Shakespeare, he must have learned that from you. He told me you had done a lot of Shakespeare. Tim talked of you from time to time. 'My father the actor, I guess he loved acting he did it his whole life,' and then he would say, 'I don't care about acting, it's all in the past.' But I didn't believe him. A day before yesterday, when he got fired, we were together and he confessed that he loved acting and was planning to go back to it someday soon. I was trying to get him to apologize to the boss, and if he did, I was sure he would get his job back."

So he was fired. Mitch wanted to ask for the address to Tim's place, but he couldn't pull away from this child. Should he tell her that Tim was going to die, only being kept alive with tubes? What good would it do?

She went on, not noticing what was happening to Mitch. "I have to tell you that later that same night, he came to my apartment to make a phone call. I let him use the phone, and in a short time, he was sobbing and I heard him say, 'I'm sorry, Mother.' He couldn't stop sobbing, so I held him and he let me…and he cried for a time and then left. He was so sad."

A piercing stab went down Mitch's body. The thought of Tim's mother getting a call from Tim brought all the endless phone calls back through all the years and his call that same night seemed to unfold in an inner need for forgiveness, for rest, for an end to all this uselessness. He wanted to forgive everyone but himself. It was not true that no one was to blame. Mitch was to blame. It was Mitch who was responsible. Tim had called him last night, and Mitch had been distant. What had he said? What had Tim said? He heard her voice and was pulled back to the young girl.

"It's good you're here. I think he needs you. I know he will love to see you. Just a woman's intuition, but I'm sure he admires you. Maybe you can help him get his job back. If you talk to Mr. Donner, it would help."

His voice croaked when he pulled out a small notepad and pen, "Would you write down Tim's address, please." He stood and put some money on the table. "Be right back." In the toilet he sat on the pot, his mind exploding with contradictions. Should he tell this woman about Tim? Did he owe it to her? She'll find out sooner or later. Christ, what was the right thing to do?

When he came back to the booth, she was standing. "Please, please let me come with you."

He could see she was very concerned and cared about Tim. "Listen, child, I need to be alone if you don't mind."

"Oh! I need to come with you. I'm so worried about him. Please, I need to come."

Mitch watched her and was surprised at how open she was about her affection. Did she suspect he was hurt? Did she think maybe he was hurt bad, maybe dead? Could he tell her? "Very well, come."

As they walked toward his car, she said, "You know, I'm an actress, and Tim told me to go to Los Angeles, but I don't know... what do you think?" This was all so absurd. He pulled back down inside himself, feeling like the little boy he used to be. Bringing her was a mistake.

They drove in silence. He was aware of her not moving. "At the next light, turn left. Get the first parking place you can find." There was no place until he made a few turns and parked. It's up around the corner. They walked several blocks.

"This is it," she said almost gleefully. He looked at the somewhat elegant but trashed apartment building. Over the door chiseled in the concert wall, he read, "Captain Cook Arms." He saw the flashing neon next door, "The Night Owl." At the door to Tim's apartment, up a deeply worn-out art deco staircase, Mitch knocked for some reason then tried the knob. Then door was open. They both stood in the doorway.

"Tim, are you here?" Anne's voice was timid.

The first thing Mitch saw was a bottle on the table by the sink. The small room was gloomy and dark and smelled of alcohol. The light came through the one window. Clothes were strewn on the bed. He followed more clothes lying on the floor and over to the door of the bathroom, and there it was, slouched on its side: the familiar leather bag, the bag that had been his, given to him by his father and brought from Ireland by his grandfather. He knelt down and put his hand on the old cracked leather side and gripped the shredded handles.

She watched him. "Well, he'll have to come back here for his things."

Mitch picked up the bag and slammed it against the wall, did it again, then dropped the bag, looked at Anne, and strode to the corner between the bathroom and window. Anne turned around in a little circle, sensing something should be done.

Mitch leaned his head on the wall. Through the haze, an image of his father pushed past the horror of his maimed son. A simple forgiveness was in him. To his surprise, he started to weep. Anne moved to him and touched his back. He reached around without looking at her and took her hand. There they stood, holding hands, a sad, jaded actor and a sweet, innocent child, with a lost boy between them.

After a moment, Mitch turned to her. "You are very dear and most kind, but could you leave me here to wait for Tim? It would be a help if you could remember any friends he had or maybe places he went to a lot."

"Well, I don't know about any friends, but he did talk about a place out on Route One. He took me there once. It was very nice… he loved it. Overlooking the ocean. I was in a little village called Makalmo. I could go with you after I get off work."

"Thank you, but I think I really need to be alone."

"Yes, I understand. But promise me you'll come to the mall with him or come and let me know what's happening.

"I will."

She left and he was alone, more alone than he had ever been. Should he look for more information about the boy? Why? There were so many questions, but what could he find? He started to the door. *Let me drive out to this Makalmo just to see where he had been.* He stopped and looked at the old leather bag, picked it up, and rubbed the soft worn leather, over 130 years old, then laid it gently back down on the bed and walked out and down to the street.

There was the Night Owl on the corner next to the Captain Cook Arms. *Sure would like a drink*, he was revolted to find himself thinking. Tim must have had a few at this hole. He went in. A perfect island bar, everything was dingy and falling apart. Along the walls were faded photos of early Hawaii native surfers. At the bar, he ordered a ginger ale. Four or five tough-looking islanders were drinking beer at the end of the bar. There would be bursts of laughter and a cross between English and Hawaii slang. He envied them there seeming freedom, with not a care. Remembering that lie froze in his brain. How had it come to this? His life had brought him to this moment. Sitting in a bar grieving for his son. The news that Tim had called his mother and the knowledge that Tim had called Mitch, the same night, brought about a tragic shock and a feeling that was vibrating all the way back to his drinking days. How had he escaped? Or had he escaped? Was he going to be haunted forever?

"Bartender, could you help me? I'm looking for a boy. He lived in the apartment house next door.""

He was a very large Hawaiian. "I get a lot of people in here. White or islander?"

"White. He is a tall blond kid and good-looking."

"Yeah, there is a kid comes in here, you a cop."

"No."

"Was always loaded, spouted Shakespeare all the time, a real deadbeat. Hung around with the whores a lot. They thought he was funny and gave him a free dip now and then, they told me. He was mostly with Hanna. I think that was her name."

"Do you know where I could find her?"

"No idea, they all work up and down Wentworth Street, one block south."

As he finished his ginger ale, he watched the bartender filling the draft beer mugs for the boys at the end of the bar. The beer spout handles marked Bud and Schlitz and Michelob brought a picture of his father cursing the "Goddamn job" he had for years selling bar junk to stupid bar owners. A whole series of images of his father followed, everything jumped out at him, the coasters, the sign's showing beautiful women holding a cold bottle of beer, the napkins, the mugs. He put both hands on the bar and his head dropped. What a life.

He went down to Wentworth Street, a honky-tonk bar neighborhood, and at first, he didn't see anything that looked like what he wanted. Then as he walked along, he caught a smile from a young Hawaiian girl with obvious intentions. Next he came upon several women all standing together. He walked up, and they all turned before he spoke. He looked at the strangely alike faces, a hard, bitter essence, coming through the rouge. "I'm looking for Hanna."

"I'm looking for Hanna!" One of the hags spat out.

"What do you want her for?" They all laughed.

"I just want to talk to her."

"Well, she is not here now. How about me? You can talk to me." She made a stab at looking alluring. Mitch sat on his irritation.

"What if I was a cop?"

They all smiled, and the woman who spoke first stepped forward. "I'm Hanna. You're not a cop. I know them all. What the hell do you want?"

"I'm sorry, I'm looking for my son. The bartender said that you knew him."

"Come to take the little brat home, ain't that a kick in the ass."

"It would be helpful if you could tell me you know him. The bartender at the Night Owl down the street said you knew him."

"How would I know? I'm a busy lady." She walked him away. "I do quite well, you see. So what's in it for me? I can't waste time chewing the fat with you when I could be making things happen."

"I'll pay you for your time. He was tall and blond, good-looking, and he like poetry; Shakespeare."

"Oh yeah, I know him, sad-eyed Shakespeare. What a drunk and loved the stuff. Couple a' nights ago, he was with me, came back later on a suicide bike. He couldn't walk, much less ride a bike. Yeah, took some shit and rode off into the night."

"When was that, two nights ago, you say?"

"Yeah."

"Did he make a phone call?"

"No."

"He said where he might be headed?"

"Well, after he cried a little and I gave him a shot, he announced, 'This is my last evening of drink and dope. I'm going to start a new life.'"

"Anything else?"

"No. I told him to call a cab, but it didn't do no good."

"Thank you…Thank you. Is fifty bucks enough?" He dug out his wallet.

She moved closer. "For another dollar, we could go upstairs."

He laughed. Out of this strange exchange in the dead of night, a lovely smile broke out on her face, and she laughed with him and almost looked pretty.

"Thank you." He gave her the fifty. "Some other time." He walked away toward his car.

"Take care, I hope you find your boy."

"New life. Start a new life."

Tim. oh, Tim—Tim is dead.

He walked to where he thought his car would be and realized he had forgotten where he parked and even forgotten what kind of car he had rented. In a daze, he walked up past the Night Owl, past the Captain Cook Alms. Did he really mean it? Start a new life. How many times had he, Mitch, said the very same thing only to have it thrown back in his face? He walked on to another street, not knowing where the hell he was. Doubling back to the apartment building, he sat on the front stoop. The night was hot and muggy, and his shirt was sticking to his back.

He rested on those steps for an eternity and at last roused himself and went in search of his borrowed car that he remembers now was a Chevrolet. After a short time, he found himself standing in front of a blue Chevy.

As he drove away and headed for the highway to find the village of Makalmo, his whole being entered an almost deathlike calm: out the window, the sad, degraded neighborhoods of Honolulu and all their grotesque beauty were in contrast to the lush many shaded colors of the original island whose hills rose high in back with the sea endless in front.

Out of the city and then shooting into a long tunnel and out into the night full of stars. To a bluff over the sea, then dip down to a little settlement. He saw, as he approached the town that sided up to a black lagoon, a small sign: "Makalmo." On his right, jutting out into the bay, was a large rambling restaurant the Blue Inn.

He looked around inside and walked out to the balcony. The ocean was endless black, and the brightness of the moon gave it a patina of silver. He sat at the bar. "Jesus, if I drink another soft drink, I may die." He hadn't eaten all day. He went to a booth. Down the wall were palm leaves arranged in an artistic pile with angry carved faces in the middle. Island gods. When the waitress brought the food, he asked her about Tim, a young man on a motorcycle, would have been two days ago, late, maybe two or three.

"How late are you open?"

"We close at three. Cheryl works the last shift she might know, should be here any moment."

"Hello, I'm Cheryl." She was middle-aged and middle plump. "You were asking about a boy? More coffee?" He had been sitting with cold coffee and not a bite eaten.

"Yes, I was. He might have been here two nights ago."

"That would be Tuesday. I think you're talking about someone who was here, a young man about thirty and good-looking? Seemed to have been in a fight, had blood on his face. Been drinking and I asked him if he thought he had had enough. I remember he laughed and switched from whiskey to beer."

"That could be him. Do you know if he was on a motorbike?"

"Sure was, I told him to be very careful when he left, then he started spouting poetry. He was very sweet."

"Do you remember anything else? Did he use the phone?"

"I'm not sure, but ask Mike behind the bar, he may know. The boy took his beer outside and ordered another one. When I took it out, he was sitting at the water's edge, and the tide was running at him. He didn't seem to mind, had to call him twice. Then he yelled thanks. In a little while, I told him it was last call. He came through the bar to the parking lot. I followed him and told him again to be careful. He seemed to be very disturbed. He hailed some more poetry and then drove away. I've got to get to work. I hope he is all right. Is he missing?

"Yes."

"I'm sure he's all right. If I think of anything else, I'll tell you. You related?"

"Yes, we are." He sat and thought of a lonely boy sitting by the ocean and remembered another lonely boy years ago.

He went to the bar. "Cheryl thinks that a boy was here two nights ago. Do you remember if he made a phone call?"

"I think the kid asked where the phone was. I didn't see if he used it.

He must have called me from here. "Where is it?"

As he came in front of the phone, he read, "Call Jane 203 466 8721. Anyone, you, can call me Jane?" In front of the phone with notes and numbers down both sides and the sickening green paint on the walls reflecting his insides. He collapsed in an old wicker chair and shivered and watched the roaches heading down the hall. Strange bugs with long antennas reaching out in front. He had never watched roaches. Now he couldn't stop. The parade marched on like they were pilgrims searching for the redeemer. After some time, he raised his head and saw a number written in lipstick. Mostly the numbers were written with a pen, but this one was painted in lipstick.

"You've got to call, be good to yourself." Why would anyone write their name? Sure, lonely people in bars, a whole world. With the door open to the toilet, the smell filled the hall. He leaned on the wall. It's late, too late. He shut his eyes—life, the Dodgers, clams, swimming in the ocean, eating ice cream, Malibu jail, June lake, New York bar, eternal Shakespeare. His mind was racing down the rabbit hole, searching. He opened his eyes and saw the dingy hall that led to the bar. Beautiful. He admired the craftsmanship of the framing and the way the light dances down the wall.

He walked out to the balcony, then down through a shabby, neglected rose garden, across a path, past a stonewall to the sand, then down to the gentle lapping tide. Here at the edge of the world, his mind could not rest. What had he learned about Tim in his travels through the familiar underbelly of the drunkard's world?

He remembered when he was a lonely drunk, wandering from bar to bar looking for some spark of life beyond the moment-to-moment horror of his wretched life and finding for a brief time a stranger who could be taken for a comrade. A well-dressed man, say, drunk at the bar who would allow you to tell the tragic story of your failure in school, a doctor you say you wanted…and the sad death of your mother. There is always in these funeral caves, men like yourself to listen to your lies and tell their own the glorious fantasies of a made-up life, anything to relieve the horror of the moment. And always a girl—oh yes, a lovely sweet girl who will hold you and sympathize with you and listen to you. Most importantly, she must listen, and she must realize that you are worth something, and someday people will see you for what you are. Then you can't resist the daredevil stunts the showing off, climbing to the top of the bridge and walking across the railing with the bay far below. Or getting the shit kicked out of you for telling a loudmouthed marine twice your size to shut up, just to show off. Then you will duck into the toilet, and in the mirror, a flash of blood in your mouth, and the wretchedness of your stupid life will draw from you a vow to end all this tomorrow and start anew. You leave the bar and leap on your symbol of your manhood, your motorbike and at reckless speed defy all the laws of sane driving.

Mitch's thoughts evaporated, and he could do nothing but stand by the ocean see nothing at all. The heavy cloud of mixed pity and loss worked as a vale, and all that was before him was gone—he was blind. It was sickening to begin to realize how alike they were, these two men who never knew each other. Then like a fade up in a film, the moon slowly became a long streak of silver across the water. His eyes followed the moonbeam from the edge all the way to the moon. He hesitated a moment and then steps forward. The water was soft and hardly moving. He went in further and stood up to his knees. The sky was immense, and the water under him was laced with silver. He raised his arms and floated right up to the moon.

"There's a special providence in the fall of a sparrow…"

CHAPTER 49

Back to the Past to the Future
1994

"THAT'S NICE BOURBON." The man in the window seat was speaking. "You don't drink?"

"Not in the morning." Mitch looked at the wrecked face next to him, remembered those mornings, and turned away.

Flying to New York now, five months after the hospital in Hawaii and watching the boy die, there was no shiver of excitement about returning to the city, and he had a vague premonition that something—maybe everything—was not right. Along with a new sense of exhilarating freedom from the endless strife was the deep shadow of helplessness. Free was what he was now. Starting a new life. Still the feeling of helplessness that had consumed him since Tim's death was connected to the inescapable guilt that he had never really taken responsibility for the boy. Yet the thing about helplessness was just that—no one could help another person unless he wanted help. Mitch recognized that, but still he was haunted. He could have done more. He should have done more. The boy had been difficult from the beginning, and Mitch had backed off, always trying to run the show, telling Tim what he should do, but never really helping him. He hadn't loved him. Mitch made an involuntary jerk.

"Hey, you okay?

Maybe I should have a drink. "No, I'm fine."

In the cab he viewed with detachment the skyline and the structure of the Triborough Bridge, with its long uncovered rampart leading to the huge steel structure looming high against the city—ah, *Winterset*—then down the East Side to the hotel.

He was thrown right into work, and after getting his wardrobe and being given a totally different scene than the one he had studied, he was driven to the police precinct on East Sixty-Eighth Street, where they were to shoot most of his scenes for *The Devil's Own*. In the dressing trailer, he was told that the two stars were at odds, "Too boring," and after all these years, he knew better than to get sucked into the gossip. He did the new scene with Harrison Ford and finished early. They were scheduled to do another one, but after they read the pages, the producers decided a rewrite was in order. That was when Mitch realized they had not much of a screenplay. There was a good story, but no script. Ah, the big-budget movies! So after lunch, he was released for the day.

He walked over toward the West Side, into the park. The wind cut down across the mall, revealing a panorama of grays and browns and faded greens. An unnerving vibration took him back, years back, and yet at the same time was completely unknown, as if seen for the first time. He spotted the Plaza Hotel and walked toward that monument of memory. In the lobby, he headed for the Palm Court, where he sat and ordered a coffee and roll. The waitress recognized him from something. "I never forget a face, but I'm bad on names." She leaned in, too close.

"Mitchell Ryan."

"You're in the movies in California, right? How do you like New York? You've been here before?"

"Yes, I have." As if he had said no, she added, "Well, look around. It's a great city, you'll love it." Then she was gone.

He remembered the first time he had come to this hotel and suddenly felt old, but the clearness of that day so long ago was sharp and immediate. The 1950s and the thrill of the city and the glory of this great hotel were like nothing he had ever seen. New York, New York would never be that exciting again.

The waitress brought him back. "More coffee?"

"Yes, please."

New York was intoxicating in those days, as if set up just for him. How he had gorged on all the magic and power of Broadway and the theater, how he had lusted for the actor's life…and the drinking life. What insanity. Was Stanley's even there anymore? No matter. The name meant nothing now.

He could have continued his reverie at the Plaza all day but was pulled to the theater district. He felt a strange anxiety walking down toward Broadway. At Fifty-Seventh and Sixth all was different. At Seventh Avenue, there was no Russian Tea Room, where he used to meet Archer, or when any of his crowd had money. Carnegie Hall looked totally unfamiliar without the tearoom next door. What was this? Was he changed that much?

He walked over to Broadway and then down past the Winter Garden. He stopped in front of the Cort Theater, where he had done *Medea*. He remembered Zoe and her producer husband, who had died not long ago. He had dear thoughts of Judith Anderson and those wonderful walks to her hotel after the play. Her voice: "Oh, Medea, the dark black bloody hell is brought down upon your head." He looked down Forty-Seventh Street to the Ethel Barrymore Theater, where he had done *Wait Until Dark*, and thought of Lee Remick, who had died so young. He stopped and ordered orange juice at one of the dozens of stands dotting Times Square and sat on a bench in the middle of the square. A booth was serving long lines of people waiting to get half-price tickets to a Broadway show. The kiosk took up the small piece of real estate, and Times Square was not the same. The square looked like someone had given the place a bath. The statue of George M. Cohan stood where it had always been, with a disgusted look on its face.

He strolled over to Forty-Fifth Street, stopped at the Booth Theater, built by Edwin Booth himself, where the great actor had played his famous Hamlet. He laughed to remember the Hamlet young Mitch Ryan had done in Louisville a lifetime ago. Suddenly he shivered. A stranger. Removed. *"There's a special providence in the fall of a sparrow. If it be now, 'tis not to come; if it be not to come, it will be now; If it be not now, yet it will come: the readiness is all…"*

The great power of Shakespeare and the old Booth Theater touched him deeply. The truth and power of storytelling. It's not too late. He moved to the Helen Hayes, remembering Fredric March and Jason Robards in *Long Day's Journey into Night*. He felt closer than he had ever been to James O'Neill and his deep lament: "What the hell was it I wanted to buy, I wonder, that was worth—" Then he walked past the Music Box, where he had seen *Picnic*, and thought of all the people who had been part of his theater life—Ted, James, Irene, Salome, so many more. *"These our actors, / As I foretold you, were all spirits and / Are melted into air, into thin air: / And…like this insubstantial pageant faded, / Leave not a rack behind. / We are such stuff / As dreams are made on, and our little life / Is rounded with a sleep.* He could have wept, standing there on Forty-Fifth Street, with the crowds moving past him, carrying dreams in the back of their minds, dreams as vivid as his, only his were right out front.

By the time he reached Joe Allen's bar, he was overtaken by the realization that he was no longer any part of this New York theater life, which was now being played out by new actors and actresses. The vision he had harbored all these years, the one that had called to him from California, was gone. The Broadway of the great playwrights—Williams, Miller, Inge, Albee, O'Neill—had been replaced by names he didn't know.

It was a hard blow. He quickly ordered a nice lunch and greeted one or two old friends he was surprised to see in this hangout, ghosts from another life. The first thing he said when he saw Joe the owner was, "It's not like the old days."

"There have been many old days since you left, Mitch."

The gloom continued into the next day, escalating into a grotesque mockery. He went to the Actors Studio with a glad heart but then sat stunned watching an actor he had once known work on a scene from *Krapp's Last Tape*, the very scene that same actor had been working on thirty-five years before when Mitch had left for California. Walking away, he realized that he had been harboring the notion for all these years that he could come back and go right into a Broadway production, no question, and everything would be as before.

His breathing restored itself as he gained distance from the Studio. The city made itself known. Back uptown on Broadway, he looked east and could see across to Rockefeller Center and up and down Times Square. He walked farther up to Central Park and reentered the great green quiet of that sanctuary in the middle of Manhattan. He took a deep breath, and New York came alive. No matter the changes, the city would always be a great place to land with your dreams, just as he had done years ago. Mitch didn't know the full truth then, but that moment of release had gently pushed him past a threshold and squarely into the real world. Nevermore would he need to believe the fantasies of what life should be. He would learn to embrace what was.

Now flying west again, he became aware of how different he was on this trip back from when he had flown east for this film two weeks earlier. Had the time been only two weeks? He realized he was flying home. After landing in Los Angeles, he searched for an hour until he found his car in long-term parking. He sat in the dark car and felt the warmth of familiarity, then drove home.

There was a message from Ro. "It's Friday. I hope you got home safe. There's a new sold sitcom, *Dharma and Greg*. They want you to read for them at Fox on Monday at ten in the morning. I know how you feel about sitcom and TV in general but go. Don't be stupid. I love you."

He called Ro. "I would be overjoyed to read for a sitcom, and I'll get it."

So he read, and he was fine.

Ro phoned later, beside herself with excitement, to tell him he was being called back to read for the executives at Fox. This time he would be reading with Susan Sullivan, who was auditioning for his wife. He knew Susan. They had done a short series together several years before, and she was a good friend.

Sitting with Susan in the outer office, waiting to audition, she said to him, "Read this with me one more time. I think there's something else we can find in this relationship."

Out of what he thought was the dead past came his response: "Why? We don't want to leave the performance in the hall, do we?"

"Are you going to come up with the same shit you pulled on the last show we did? Are you an actor or not?"

"Is this acting?"

"You're hopeless. Why are you here, whining like a temperamental artistic asshole? You have so much to be thankful for. Most actors never come close to the work you've done. So wake up! Shut up with all this crap. Stop acting like a three-year-old."

He was mortified and ashamed. She was right. What was he doing? "I'm sorry. I guess it's time to move on to four, or maybe even five."

She smiled. "Come on, let's read it over, you big idiot." He looked at her face and saw not just an actress or even an old pal or colleague but a real person who actually cared about him. It was something he had never realized or known: that people cared about him, wished him well, accepted him for what he was, and not all the flash upfront. They were called in to read at that moment. All went well, well enough so that next they would read for the network, ABC. And that went well also.

He thought she was "winging it," so he ad-libbed, at which Susan came back with something, and then they got into an argument in character, to the amusement of the ABC execs. They finished and were applauded. Susan left the office in a fit of laughter.

"We had different scripts."

"That's what it was—well, you handled it great. You are something, Susan."

"You did okay yourself." She kissed him.

As they were leaving, Chuck Lorre, the writer and producer, came out wondering what had happened. When they told him, he said, "Well, it was better than what was written. You never dropped out of character once."

As Susan and Mitch walked out to their cars, she did a little dance step down the steps into the parking lot. "Wouldn't it be great to get this? It's already sold for two years, you know." They had stopped by Susan's silver Mercedes, which sat there in deep contrast to his ten-year-old Honda parked alongside. He felt compelled to produce some smart crack but stopped himself. "Well?" Susan gave him a sharp look.

"Yes, it would be a great job." She turned to him, took a deep breath, and gave him a huge hug.

"Also, get a new car. It's embarrassing watching you drive a ten-year-old Honda with two smashed fenders."

He watched her drive away, then slowly turned to consider his Honda. She was right. He was embarrassed to bring this junker onto the lot. Suddenly he started laughing, threw off his sport coat, kissed his steering wheel, and said out loud, "I love this car. It's gone two hundred thousand miles. It's my friend!" He drove off the lot, quoting for courage, "a poor player that struts and frets his hour upon the stage And then is heard no more." I won't get this show anyway.

The next morning, he was driving out to Malibu to see a friend when the call came from Ro. "You got the part. You will never have to worry about money for the rest of your life," she announced, almost jumping through the phone. He thanked her, said he would meet her later for dinner to celebrate, and pulled over near Topanga to sit on a sand dune overlooking the beach and the Pacific Ocean.

"You will never have to worry about money for the rest of your life." This was pronounced a little like a jail sentence. He laughed. Never had the ocean looked more beautiful. He laughed some more. Wind and the whitecaps flashed in the sun. He watched a young family playing in the sand, a father and mother and two boys. Suddenly the laughing stopped. Ever since he could remember, darkness had always been a part of him, a black soul entering into him and sucking him down. When he drank, the terror was released, and the search for a furious truth came pouring out of him—but only on the stage. This cleansed him and kept him alive until the drinking nearly killed him. Then by some miracle, he finally quit, and now that search was over.

The wind and the crashing waves embraced him, and he remembered his father telling him of his grandfather coming from Ireland, waiting at the harbor for the broken-down ship to take him to America. What had he felt? Did his grandfather want a new life? Did he, like Mitch, wonder what was to become of him? Strange to be having these feelings at sixty-two, but there it was: What is to become of me?

The old leather bag he had found in Tim's apartment was there in the trunk of his car, all one hundred fifty years of wear and tear. He went back, brought out the bag, and sat down with it on the sand dune. How did this valise connect the men so important to him—Edward, his grandfather; Charles, his father; and Tim, his boy—these men somehow bound together yet forever strangers? Are we the same—the same fears, the same hurts, the same need?

But they were dead, and he still had a chance to live. It was years since he had gone from one great part to the next, but life had merely…shifted. Why couldn't he accept this? He was an actor, plain and simple: "an abstract and brief chronicle of the time." He had always done his job. By now, he'd spent more time in Hollywood than in New York and had done more films than plays. Susan was right. He had been lucky, blessed even, to have had a chance to do the work he'd done. True, his life on the stage was gone, "melted into thin air," and would never come back, the way of things and something to be faced. Whether he was in a play or film or soap opera or now a sitcom, he would just do the best he knew how. He was an actor, and an actor acts.

As he watched the family playing in the white sand and looked out to the brilliant green sea and up to the sky, he glowed with contentment that, somehow, he was able also to accommodate the melancholy that would always be part of him. A seagull glided by on the wind right in front of him, and he heard the voice of his first teacher, Doug Ramey, across the years: "The only thing that counts is the work. A process, and nothing matters but the doing."

ABOUT THE AUTHOR

THE BOOK IS called *Fall of the Sparrow*, creative nonfiction, 110,000 words. The manuscript is finished by Mitchell Ryan.

He is an actor, artist, and writer. He had a career on stage and screen, including the classic roles in *Hamlet* and as Iago in James Earl Jones's *Othello*, Leontes, Petruchio, and others in fifteen of Shakespeare's thirty-six plays. He was Jason in *Medea*, Agamemnon in *Iphigenia* with Irene Papas, Tyrone in *Long Day's Journey into Night*, Jamie in *Moon for the Misbegotten*, and the Ape in *The Hairy Ape*. He was in a broad range of roles across such feature films as *Monte Walsh*, *The Friends of Eddie Coyle*, *Magnum Force*, *Lethal Weapon*, *Liar-Liar*, and hundreds of television appearances in every genre, in addition to starring roles in two hit series, 107 episodes as Burke Devlin in the cult and occult *Dark Shadows* and 119 episodes as Edward Montgomery in *Dharma & Greg*.

This book deals with his battle with alcoholism and winning, his long powerful career, and his tragic relationship with his son.

This book is his story about how he became sober, his career as a serious actor, and his son, Tim, who, wretched, ended his life without ever really having one.

This is not a typical actor's autobiography. "And then I made this film." "And then I did that play." It is the story of an actor.

But more than all, this is the story of a man becoming. He was lucky enough to survive his mistakes.

You might say, the book's as good as his credits. Credits, yes. He is happy to tell you he has worked on the stage with the likes of Irene Papas, Judith Anderson, Collen Dewhurst, Lee Remick, Salome

Gens, Christopher Plummer, and many others. And he has worked in films with George C. Scott, Lee Marvin, Robert Mitchum, Jack Palance, and John Cusack. The book tells the story also of working with these men and the story of some of the fifty or so films he has made.

CPSIA information can be obtained
at www.ICGtesting.com
Printed in the USA
BVHW031818260821
615346BV00007B/110/J

9 781662